MORE PRAISE

"*Mad Dog Justice*, a tale of f.
es, is pure Mark Rubinstein. It's smart, it's sophisticated, and it's scary as hell. . . . It won't be long before Rubinstein will take his rightful place among Flynn, Lehane, and Harris as one of the best psychological thriller writers out there."
  —Scott Pratt, bestselling author of the Joe Dillard series

"The action flies off the page from the very beginning of this high-voltage thriller, and a palpable feeling of panic is often claustro-phobic. 'Mad Dog' Roddy Dolan—former boxer and tough guy, now a physician and respectable family man—calls into question what once were fixed points on your moral compass. It's impos-sible not to be drawn into his world."
  —Elissa Durwood Grodin, author of *Physics Can Be Fatal* and
    Death by Hitchcock

"Mark Rubinstein has written another riveting psychological drama. From the shots fired in the first pages to the final haunt-ing and shocking ending, *Mad Dog Justice* will draw you into its characters' world—and never let you go."
  —E. J. Simon, author of *Death Never Sleeps*

"*Mad Dog Justice* thrums with relentless intensity and suspense. Rubinstein has created a palpable cast of characters who stay with you long after you finish the book."
  —Jessica Speart, author of *A Killing Season* and *Restless Waters*

"*Mad Dog Justice* is a thrilling adventure along that ever-widening chasm between innocence and immorality. Rubinstein's dynamic characters are both likable and despicable as they grapple with noble values in a complex society that threatens their survival."
  —Helen M. Farrell, MD, forensic psychiatrist and writer,
    Harvard Medical School, and author of the *Frontpage*
    Forensics blog (for *Psychology Today*)

"From the opening sentence to the last word, *Mad Dog Justice* had me riveted. You don't have to have experienced *Mad Dog House* to love this novel."
>—Christopher David Petersen, author of *Tear in Time* and *Tomb of Atlantis*

"*Mad Dog Justice* has tremendous literary quality. Rubinstein weaves words and thoughts as a Flemish artist lovingly would craft the world-famous Chantilly lace. That sort of wordsmithing injects a conceptual photograph into the reader's brain. Is it because the author is a psychiatrist who understands the manipulation of the brain, or is it that the psychiatrist has pupated inside the chrysalis into a literary genius?"
>—Dan Santos, CMSFS (R), author of *Insurrection: Appalachian Command* and the forthcoming *Insurrection: The Rockies*

"Mr. Rubinstein does it again! Not only is *Mad Dog Justice* a book that demands to be read from cover to cover in one sitting, but long after you finish it, you'll still be thinking about it. Simply brilliant!"
>—Dianne Harman, author of *Blue Coyote Motel*, *Coyote in Provence*, *Tea Party Teddy*, and *Tea Party Teddy's Legacy*

"If you are an adrenaline junkie, you will love this book! If you like Robert Ludlum, Eric Van Lustbader, and Barry Eisler—you will love this book. . . . From the opening chapter to the last, *Mad Dog Justice* takes the reader on a roller-coaster ride with Dan and Roddy as they deal with the aftermath of their actions in the first installment of the series. This work, though, reads quite well on its own. High-octane thrilling and un-put-down-able!"
>—Nancy Gazo, Mystery Writers of America member and reviewer

"Mark Rubinstein's mastery lies in his incredible attention to details. His stories are intractably woven, quick paced, and never short on suspense!"
>—Tina Schwartz, Assistive Technology Specialist

"*Mad Dog Justice* . . . takes you on a gripping psychological ride that will keep you on the edge of your seat. . . . Rubinstein's literary mélange is at its usual complex and multidimensional best—but even more so."
> —Judith Marks-White, author of *Seducing Harry* and *Bachelor Degree*

"*Mad Dog Justice* is an authentic thriller. It races at the speed of light, propelled by mysterious killer stalkers, unnerving details, and fascinating relationship issues between friends and spouses; Rubinstein keeps you guessing, on several levels, until the last word."
> —Dorothy Hayes, author of *Murder at the P&Z* and writer for WomenofMystery.net and CriminalElement.com

"Mark Rubinstein's taut thriller explores the aftermath of a crime and the unraveling of two friends in a gripping tale of morality and mortality."
> —Elizabeth Joseph, Ferguson Library, Stamford, Connecticut

"Oh, what a tangled web we weave! As protagonists Roddy and Danny become ensnarled in a web of lies and intrigue, author Rubinstein leads us through the intricacy of emotional, physical, and psychological consequences of their actions in a page-turning thriller. I kept thinking: Shakespeare meets CSI."
> —Lynn Allison, author and medical reporter, American Media Inc.

"*Mad Dog Justice* is as intriguing and addictive as the previous novels of fascinating man and brilliant storyteller Mark Rubinstein. All I can say is, keep on writing, Mark, and we'll keep on reading!"
> —Cindy Armor, Reading Specialist and Educator, Connecticut Public Schools

"The characters' paranoia and the incredible suspense jump off the page!"
　　—Karen Vaughan, author of *Dead Comic Standing* and
　　　Daytona Dead

"*Mad Dog Justice* is a compelling story of old friends faced with the consequences of their actions. Mark Rubinstein knows these guys. His detailed descriptions and unexpected plot maneuvers work beautifully. Treat yourself to some fun with this one."
　　—Rose Buzzutto, RN

"Rubinstein's dialog draws the reader into the story inextricably so that he is living the story along with the characters. A wonderful, fast, frenzied read. Not for the faint of heart."
　　—Harvey Morgan, Certified Manufacturing Engineer,
　　　International Brotherhood of Transport Workers

"From the first page you are on a roller coaster full of intrigue, betrayal, and mixed emotions. It was great to see 'old friends' from *Mad Dog House* continue their journey. I look forward to more."
　　—Cathy Werner, local volunteer, avid reader, and high school
　　　mentor, Leander, Texas

"There are those who say that *The Godfather: Part II* is better than *The Godfather*. *Mad Dog Justice* expands on *Mad Dog House* as you snake your way into the brilliance of the abyss. Prepare to be on pins and needles. Mark Rubinstein does it again. You don't want to go down that rabbit hole but you must. His characters are a part of you and you have to know what happens to them."
　　—Terri Altergott, PBC

"*Mad Dog Justice* is a very engrossing thriller. The suspense will keep you up and turning the pages. I loved the wild ride right to the end. This is a must-read!"
　　—Barbara Wells

Mad Dog Justice

Other Books by Mark Rubinstein

Fiction

Love Gone Mad (Thunder Lake Press)
Mad Dog House (Thunder Lake Press)
The Foot Soldier, a novella (Thunder Lake Press)

Nonfiction

The First Encounter: The Beginnings in Psychotherapy
with Dr. William Console and Dr. Richard C. Simons (Jason Aronson)

The Complete Book of Cosmetic Surgery
with Dr. Dennis P. Cirillo (Simon & Schuster)

New Choices: The Latest Options in Treating Breast Cancer
with Dr. Dennis P. Cirillo (Dodd Mead)

Heartplan: A Complete Program for Total Fitness of Heart & Mind
with Dr. David L. Copen (McGraw-Hill)

*The Growing Years: The New York Hospital–Cornell Medical Center
Guide to Your Child's Emotional Development* (Atheneum)

Mad Dog Justice

A Novel

MARK RUBINSTEIN

Thunder Lake Press

Thunder Lake Press
25602 Alicia Parkway, #512
Laguna Hills, CA 92653
www.thunderlakepress.com

Publisher's Note: This is a work of fiction. It is a product of the author's imagination. Any resemblance to people, living or dead, is purely coincidental. Occasionally, real places or institutions are used novelistically for atmosphere and are employed in a fictional manner. There is no connection between the characters or events in this novel to any real-life people, places, organizations, or companies of any kind.

Ordering Information

Quantity sales. Special discounts are available on quantity purchases by corporations, associations, and others. For details, contact the "Special Sales Department" at the address above.

Orders by US trade bookstores and wholesalers. Please contact BCH: (800) 431-1579 or visit www.bookch.com for details.

Author photo: Gerriann Geller

978-0-9856286-0-8

Printed in the United States of America

Publisher's Cataloging-in-Publication
    Rubinstein, Mark, 1942-
        Mad dog justice : a novel / Mark Rubinstein. -- First
    edition.
        pages cm
        ISBN 978-0-9856268-0-8 (pbk)
        ISBN 978-0-9856268-1-5 (e-book)

        1. Detective and mystery stories. 2. Suspense
    fiction.   I. Title.
    PS3618.U3M34 2014   813'.6
    QBI14-600102

First Edition
18 17 16 15 14   10 9 8 7 6 5 4 3 2 1

For Linda

Justice is a certain rectitude of mind whereby a man does what he ought to do in circumstances confronting him.

—*St. Thomas Aquinas*

Chapter 1

Danny Burns sits at his desk and rubs his forehead. His temples throb. Violently. It's another headache, and this one's going to be a bone crusher. It feels like a bench vise clamping down on Danny's head. Doc Gordon says it must be from tension because he can't find a thing wrong.

Tension, worry—that's all life's been since he and Roddy killed Grange and Kenny ten months ago.

It's nearly eight o'clock on this frigid night in late February. The office is so quiet, Danny hears hissing in his ears. There's an occasional whooshing of tires as cars pass by on McLean Avenue, two stories below. The windowpane rattles in a gust of wind. Danny reminds himself to talk to the landlord about installing thermal pane replacements. *Yeah, don't hold your breath,* he thinks. *Donavan will never get it done. He's too busy flipping properties all over Yonkers.*

The April 15 tax deadline is getting closer, and Dan's got an avalanche of work. Most clients don't use the worksheets he sends them. They mail in a jumble of jottings along with heaps of crinkled documents. He spends more time sorting through junk than entering data into the computer. It might be wise to hire another assistant for the next two months.

Danny knows he hasn't been focused on his work. God Almighty, he used to zero in on things like a laser beam. *Detail*

Dan is what Angela called him, but for the last ten months he's lucky if he remembers to slip into his pants each morning. And Angela's been on top of him, *big-time*.

"You're not listening to a word I say. You're in another world," she yells as he retraces his steps, looking for his wallet or cell phone. "Danny, something's happened to you in the last few months."

A nerve-jangling blast of sound interrupts his thoughts, and he lurches for the telephone. "Daniel Burns," he says, trying to sound professional.

"Danny, when are you coming home?"

"Angie, honey, I have a ton of work."

"Daniel . . ."

She uses his formal name only when she's really pissed. She picked it up from Ma years ago. But nowadays, she uses it way too often. It's annoying, but why start an argument? The headache will escalate into a jackhammer pounding mercilessly on his brain.

"Danny, you used to rush home for dinner. Now you're a ghost."

Ghost. An icy shiver crawls down his spine. Ghost was Grange's moniker, and Danny's reminded of that night in the woods with Roddy, Grange, and Kenny. He'd give a million bucks to forget it all.

"Angie, I've been working on some deals for John Harris and Mike Sobin. You know Mike. He's a very picky guy and flies off the—"

"Oh, c'mon, Danny. You've had tougher clients than Mike and never stayed at the office this late. What's going on?"

"We're getting closer to tax time, and I'm—"

"That's nonsense. It's been almost a year since I had the real Danny . . . *my* Danny. Since you and Roddy got rid of the restaurant, you've been jumpy and remote."

"Remote?"

"Yes, Danny, *remote*. And Tracy says it's the same with Roddy. And she wonders why you two see so little of each other these days. I was thinking about that, too. What's going on?"

Danny wants to protest, but Angela's right. She reads him like an open book. He closes his eyes and sighs. How can he tell her he and Roddy worry every day, wondering if the guillotine will drop? Will it be the Jersey mob or the Russian Brotherhood or Grange's shadowy associates coming for them? And how can he tell Angela about that night near the swampy pond—with lanterns, peeping frogs, and crickets—the night of terror when they killed two men? The night that changed their lives forever.

Jesus, this is torture. We'll never escape the monster we created when we went into business with Kenny Egan, a real slime ball who's rotting in the soil an hour away from where we live in Tuckahoe.

He's about to say something when he hears a sound—something near the outer door. Is it the floor creaking? Is someone walking across the reception room floor?

Still holding the receiver, Dan peers at the partly opened door to his office. Angela's still talking, and her words pour from the receiver in an eddy of noise tumbling into his right ear. Dan has no real thoughts at the moment—there's just a primal awareness of danger.

He hears the creak once again, but it's masked by a gust of wind against the windowpane.

The hairs on Dan's wrist stand up as voltage sears through him.

"Wait, honey," he says, craning his neck. He pushes his reading glasses down his nose, looks across the room, sees nothing, and says, "Angie, I'll be home soon—"

It's there. A blurred movement, very fast.

Danny pushes his chair back, squints, and tries focusing on the door, when at the same time, he hears a muffled sound, like a cork being pulled from a wine bottle. Danny's right hand and the telephone receiver explode in a shocking blast. Blinding pain ignites in his hand, and shards of plastic slash his ear and face. Something sears the back of his scalp.

Danny is thrust back in his chair. His body tightens and goes into a spasm as another cork pops. Something slams into his chest as he and the chair tumble back.

The overhead lights swirl, and Danny realizes he's on the floor. The ceiling moves, and he hears furniture scraping; he knows he's leaking away. He can't breathe. A sucking sound comes from his chest. His mouth goes dry, and a coppery taste forms on his tongue. The room pinwheels like he's in a whirlpool's vortex. Everything is bleached, and his insides shudder. His mind is jumbled, going crazily from one thought to another. It all comes down to this truth:

Jesus, sweet Jesus. I deserve this.

Chapter 2

Dr. Roddy Dolan sits in a chair in the surgical waiting area. His arms are crossed with his hands tucked into his armpits. It's hard to believe Danny's been shot. It's been hours, and there's still no update on his condition. A thrumming sensation rampages through Roddy, as though a tuning fork vibrates in his chest. Is this payback?

"How could something like this happen?" Angela asks, pacing back and forth. Her dark eyes are red-rimmed, and her usually olive complexion is chalky white.

Roddy's wife, Tracy, holds Angela's hand as she walks with her. "Do you think it was a burglary?" she asks, looking at Roddy.

He shrugs and shakes his head. "How would I know?"

Roddy's scalp tingles and then goes numb. His mind races, but one thought pierces him like an ice pick to his forehead: *John M. Grange and Associates. What we did that night in the woods . . . We're being hunted.*

"If he hadn't been on the phone with me," Angela says with a shudder, "I don't . . . I can't even think about it."

"What did you hear?" Roddy asks.

"Just—just Danny told me to wait, like he heard or saw something. And there was a popping sound, and then I heard a loud cracking. I think it was the telephone, like it blew up. Then there was static and humming, and I knew something terrible happened." Tears form wet ribbons down her face. "Oh, Roddy, he'll be okay, won't he?"

"I wish I could say, Angie. We have to wait for the surgeon." Roddy's voice sounds small and distant in his ears. He feels disconnected from himself. This is the situation his patients are forced to deal with, but tonight it's his turn.

Dr. Jeffrey Ketchman is a burly man in his midfifties with rugged features and wavy brown hair. He wears surgical greens and white rubber clogs. He introduces himself and sits down in the lounge. "Let me assure you, things are going well."

"Thank you, Doctor," Angela says, wiping her eyes. "This is Dr. Dolan, a surgeon at Lawrence Hospital and our dear friend." Ketchman and Roddy shake hands.

"Please tell us the situation," Roddy says.

"Mr. Burns was shot by a small-caliber bullet. It punctured a lung, which is still collapsed. But we're taking care of that, Mrs. Burns," Ketchman says, turning to Angela. "He's very lucky. The bullet missed the aorta, went through the lung, and out his back. Nothing else vital was hit. He doesn't even have a broken rib, only soft-tissue injury. He lost a great deal of blood and was in shock by the time the EMTs got there. He's being transfused."

Angela stifles a sob. Tracy slips an arm around her.

"We know he has asthma, and we don't want to compromise the other lung. To keep pain and stress at a minimum, we have him on a morphine drip, so he's sedated. He's also on antibiotics, and there's a chest tube implanted to help the lung drain and reinflate. It's standard procedure with this kind of wound. We equalize the air pressure so the injured lung can get back to normal."

Roddy nods. He knows this scenario very well.

"One bullet went through his hand, straight through the metacarpal bones," Ketchman says, demonstrating on the back of his hand. "It shattered the telephone receiver, and he has a few minor facial cuts. The phone deflected the bullet, so he got away with some lacerations and a minor scalp wound at the back of his head."

"But he'll be all right?" Tracy asks in a shaky voice.

"Yes. If not for the asthma, we'd have no real worries. We'll keep him sedated and give him time to heal. Nature will take its course."

"Can we see him now?" Angela asks.

"Of course, but only one visitor at a time in the ICU. He's sedated and may not make much sense."

Roddy approaches Danny's bedside and pulls the flimsy curtain aside. The place is like every ICU Roddy's ever seen, especially at Lawrence Hospital: IVs drip, monitors beep, and the patients look like death warmed over.

Tubes snake everywhere. Dan's being transfused, hydrated, and medicated. He's on his back and his eyes are closed. His mop of red hair spreads onto the pillow like a halo. A flash image forms in Roddy's head—dozens of years telescope in that moment: Roddy was sixteen and leaving a training session with Doc Schechter at Herbie's Gym. His Golden Gloves bout was a week away.

On the corner of Emmons Avenue and Sheepshead Bay Road, Roddy saw Danny lying helplessly on the sidewalk. Two members of the Coyle Street Krauts—eighteen-year-old guys—were kicking him mercilessly. Danny—his blood brother since they were nine years old—was out of it, as the thugs' shoes slammed into him again and again.

Roddy went mad dog berserk, which is how he got the moniker "Mad Dog." He spun one hood around and sank a stone-handed punch into his gut. The guy doubled over; Roddy hurled him onto the fender of a parked car. He slid down to the curb.

Roddy lunged at the other one before he could launch another kick at Danny. The guy was a big-boned Germanic-looking kid—huge but flabby.

"I'll kick your Mickey Finn ass," the guy snarled. Rearing back, he telegraphed a punch.

Roddy ducked and the guy's club-like paw flew over him. His own fist shot up in a pile-driving uppercut. The kid's jaw snapped up and he wobbled backward. Roddy landed a lightning-fast series of chopping blows. They were hard, thumping shots, and it all seemed like a dream. The crowd that gathered roared, but Roddy heard nothing, neither the street throng nor the police car's siren.

A huge pair of arms circled him. He was thrown to the ground by two burly cops. Face down, he felt handcuffs snap on his wrists. "You're under arrest for assault," an officer growled, pulling him to his feet. Craning his neck, Roddy saw the two Germans hobbling away.

"No! No!" cried Rosario, the butcher, running out of his store. His bloodstained apron covered his rotund belly. "Those two attacked this boy," Rosario yelled, pointing at the retreating Germans. Danny lay there. Blood dripped from his mouth, forming a coagulating puddle on the sidewalk.

"You okay, son?" one cop asked, kneeling next to Dan.

Danny's eyes rolled up into his head.

Now Roddy peers closely at Dan and sees that same face he saw on the pavement years ago. He can hardly believe his childhood blood brother lies in an ICU bed at St. Joe's after being shot. *Are we being hunted because of what we did to Grange and Kenny and what happened at McLaughlin's Steakhouse?* The ICU seems to darken as Roddy's vision dims.

Roddy sits at the edge of the bed, leans down, and whispers, "How you doing, kemosabe?"

Danny mumbles, "Dunno nothin."

Dan smells of antiseptic—of betadine and bandages. Spittle sits at the corners of his mouth. Roddy wipes it away with his finger. He places his palm on Danny's forehead. No fever. Good . . . no infection. Danny will make it.

Danny's eyelids flutter. His lips part. His breath smells like acetone.

"Dan, listen to me. Don't say anything. Nod your head if you can hear me."

Dan's head moves slightly, but Roddy wonders if Dan truly understands anything. Is he so metabolically shocked he'll utter some garbled nonsense amounting to a confession? Will he spill everything in a drug-induced haze?

Roddy looks up. The morphine is dripping at a slow rate, just enough to keep Dan in a stupor. Reminds Roddy of the night with Grange, when they hauled the fat bastard upstate to Snapper Pond. Dan's in a twilight state—but not as deep as the one Grange was in. Dan's eyelids flutter again; they remind Roddy of a hummingbird's wings.

"Dan, you're in St. Joe's. You were shot, but you're gonna be okay. You understand?"

A grunt comes from deep in Dan's throat.

"Dan, it's Roddy. You hear what I'm sayin'?"

There's another grunt.

"Don't say a word to anyone. You'll be out of here soon. Then we'll talk. You understand?"

A brief moan comes from Dan's throat.

"Not a word."

Roddy puts his ear to Dan's chest. His heart beats steadily, strongly. Only a few squeaks and bubbles come from his one working lung. There won't be an asthmatic attack so long as Dan's sedated.

"Say nothing, kemosabe."

Danny snorts.

Roddy's eyes water and his vision blurs. His throat constricts. He bends down and caresses Danny's mop of hair. Sorrow fills him as he looks at Danny's face, one he's looked at since before he has memories—back to the beginnings of their lives. He plants a kiss on Danny's forehead.

"Be well, my brother. Be well."

Danny grunts and his eyelids flutter. "Roddy," he rasps.

"Yeah, Dan. It's me."

"We had to do it. We had no choice."

"I know, Dan, but don't say—"

"Had to do what?" says a voice from behind.

An electric charge bolts through Roddy; he whirls around and stands by Dan's bedside. His heart throttles in his chest.

A tall man with dark hair and bushy eyebrows stands at the bedside curtain. He wears a gray sports jacket, a black tie, and black trousers. A wool overcoat is draped over his arm. The fragrance of cologne fills the curtained-off area.

"I'm Detective Harvey Morgan of the Yonkers PD," he says. Morgan's eyes narrow. A V-shaped crease forms on his forehead. "What is it you *had* to do?"

"I—I don't know what he's talking about, Detective. He's completely out of it."

Jesus, a goddamned detective. And his antennae are way up.

"What do you think he meant?" Morgan's head cants slightly.

"I have no idea." Roddy's hands feel weak.

"None at all?" Morgan's eyes dart from Roddy to Dan and then back to Roddy.

"No."

Danny snores loudly.

Roddy shoots a quick look at Dan. "I don't think he's in any shape to talk, Detective."

Morgan nods his head toward the lounge. "Can I speak with you for a moment?"

"Sure, Detective," Roddy says. His heart begins decelerating.

In a small lounge down the hallway, Morgan tosses his overcoat on a couch and takes a seat in a nearby chair. He crosses one long leg over the other. He motions to another chair. Roddy sits, wondering if he can keep his hands from trembling. Morgan's cologne is less penetrating now, but Roddy still smells it.

"I understand from your wife that you and Mr. Burns go back a long way."

"Since childhood."

Morgan has deeply recessed, dark eyes. They glitter in the room's lamplight. "Any idea why this happened?" he asks.

Roddy shakes his head. He wonders what Morgan thinks about Danny saying, "*We had to do it. We had no choice.*" Churning begins deep in Roddy's guts. His skin feels like it's crawling. "You think it was a robbery?" Roddy asks, trying to deflect the detective.

"It's possible, Doc. We'll know more soon. Forensics is crawling all over Mr. Burns's office. They may have some answers for us."

Roddy holds Morgan's stare as the detective's eyes bore into his own.

Morgan sets an elbow on the chair's armrest and rests his chin in his palm. "Lemme ask you, Doc. Mr. Burns have any enemies?"

Roddy shakes his head, wondering if he's coming across too earnestly, like he's seen in a million cop shows on TV.

"Anyone who'd wanna hurt him?" Morgan squints and his lips purse.

"No." Roddy shakes his head.

Morgan nods. "He's an accountant, right?"

"Yes."

"Any unhappy clients? Anyone who's in trouble with the IRS? Someone who might have a vendetta against him?"

Vendetta . . . a strange and telling word.

"No, nothing at all." Roddy's blood is humming.

"Your wives say you guys are best friends, right?"

"Yes."

"He'd tell you if something like that was going on, right?"

"I'm sure he would."

"What about his personal life?"

"What do you mean?"

"Maybe a girlfriend, something he wouldn't tell his wife. Something that could have, let's say . . . *repercussions*? You know— a jealous husband or a woman he might've jilted." Morgan's eyebrows dance. His lips press into a thin line. He looks like he's stifling a smirk.

"*Danny*? Never."

"You're sure?"

"He's not that kinda guy, Detective."

This guy sees the seamy side of life. He can smell bullshit a mile away.

Roddy's heart begins bludgeoning his chest.

Morgan's dark eyes look questioningly at Roddy. Now his lips curl into a full smirk. Roddy holds Morgan's stare and waits. He feigns calmness, but his blood feels like it's simmering.

"Any idea what Mr. Burns meant in there, Doc?"

"About what?"

"'We had to do it. We had no choice.' What'd he mean?"

Roddy closes his eyes and shakes his head.

When he opens them, he sees Morgan's eyebrows arch toward his hairline.

Roddy feels his heart throbbing in his neck. "Look, Detective, the guy's all drugged up. He doesn't know what he's saying."

"Tell you what, Doc. Here's my card," Morgan says, handing Roddy a business card. "Call me if you think of anything, okay?"

"Sure."

"You have a card?"

Roddy reaches into his pocket, removes his wallet, and extracts one. He hands it to Morgan, hoping the detective can't tell his fingers are trembling.

Morgan glances at it and says, "General surgery, huh?" He slips it into his pocket. "I may call you when the ballistic report is in. Meanwhile, think about what I asked you."

"No problem."

He watches Morgan stand and leave the lounge. Roddy feels blood drain from his head and his heart quivers like jelly.

Chapter 3

Roddy steps out of the elevator into the lobby at Lawrence Hospital. The place is a maelstrom of visitors, doctors, nurses, and aides. It's six thirty in the evening, nearly twenty-four hours since Danny was shot.

Roddy suddenly realizes he missed the fourth-floor skyway leading directly to the garage level where he always parks. He's been in a fog—a haze of preoccupation—since what happened last night. It almost feels like a dream state. Now he'll have to either get back in the elevator and take it to the fourth floor or walk the garage ramp all the way up to level four.

At least the surgeries he did today went well. When he's in the OR, he feels he's in another dimension, one where the patient's abdominal cavity takes him away from thoughts about Danny, Grange, Kenny—and what happened ten months earlier.

Instead of taking the elevator upstairs, he decides to walk up to level four of the garage. He walks down a corridor, presses a wall button, and an automatic door swings open. He walks quickly along the corridor, aware of its Plexiglas siding. A cold wind gusts against the windows. Roddy buttons his overcoat, anticipating the garage's frigid air. The facade of the multitiered garage, with its dull interior lighting, is visible through the Plexiglas.

He presses another wall button; the next door swings open. He's at level one of the garage. The damp air smells of exhaust fumes. He'll hike up the ramp to level four. It'll get his blood moving after a long day standing in the OR.

Standing is a helluva lot better than lying in bed—the way Danny is right now. There's no way on earth Roddy believes what happened to Dan last night was a random robbery. For the hundredth time, Roddy wonders if the shooters were Grange's mob associates or some goons from Jersey or Brooklyn—ones to whom Kenny owed a ton of money. More likely it's Grange's people . . . and there could be a vendetta against him and Danny, to use Morgan's word. Vendetta: from Latin and Italian—*vindicta*, meaning vengeance.

The garage is fairly empty at this hour—only night staff and visitors have parked their cars here. Roddy trudges up the oil-stained ramp. The garage smells of cement, tire rubber, and motor oil. The place is cold. Caged bulbs on the concrete ceiling cast dull, yellowish light throughout. Shadows are everywhere. Looking out the structure's apertures, Roddy sees the hospital lights and the village of Bronxville.

He hears something behind him, jingling keys or metal clicking. Maybe a car door opening; it's strange because he didn't notice anyone getting into a car as he passed. He turns and looks back, aware his heart has accelerated. Scanning the ramp, he sees rows of parked cars and painted yellow lines on the cement floor. Nothing else. He stands stock-still for a moment, and listens. He hears nothing. Once again, his eyes sweep over the cars, painted lines, and pillars. He sees no one.

He turns and resumes walking up the ramp. At level two, Roddy hits his stride. He can't wait to get home and have dinner with Tracy. Tom will be sulking in his room—probably listening to his iPod—while Sandy will be doing her homework. What a great kid she is. But Tom? The kid's constantly sullen, and Roddy smells trouble coming down the pike.

Don't be so quick to judge, Roddy Dolan. You were far worse at his age—street fighting, stealing, gambling, and running ciga-rettes up from the Carolinas—penny-ante bullshit and some not-so-minor crap. You nearly landed in prison at seventeen because of that screwed-up appliance store burglary. And what are you now? You're nothing but a murderer when push comes to shove.

Roddy's in a rhythm now, tramping up the ramp toward level four. He forces himself to think about the appendectomy he did this evening to avoid thinking of Snapper Pond and the .45 he used on Kenny and Grange. Memories of that night nag at him, though he shunts them aside as best he can.

Until last night when Danny got shot, the rawness of it all seemed to be fading. He's been sleeping better these last few months, awakening only once a night, not to piss, but to cogitate about that night. Is it possible things might have been different? Maybe he could have handled Grange differently, not put the fat bastard in the ground. Before last night, he would wake up and lie in bed, staring at the ceiling. But his heart no longer pumped like a piston that had broken through its crank case. His body no longer pulsed as he waited for sleep to return. Gone were the night sweats or chills, and he no longer heard his heart drubbing like a bass drum through the pillow. He hadn't dreamed about a grave or a loaded pistol for at least the last month, maybe two. And images of Snapper Pond no longer invaded his thoughts at random times during the day.

Tincture of time seemed to be working, until last night. Even though there's more distance from what happened, Roddy knows he feels less alive than before the horror of Snapper Pond. It's as though some part of him has shriveled. He feels things less in-tensely; he's less emotional—even less loving—with Tracy. He no longer feels that rush of desire mixed with intimacy. The flavor, the spice of being alive seems to have faded.

Yes, murder can make you feel like a beast, killing to survive. *Will I get beyond this? Do I need help? Should I see a shrink? If I do, I can't talk about Grange and Kenny. It's a life of secrets. Will the old Roddy ever return? And just who was the "old Roddy"? Was he a caring, loving professional with a great wife and kids, or just a street thug from a tough neighborhood in Brooklyn, a murderer masquerading as a decent man living a quiet life in the burbs?*

Can you kill two men and simply go on with your life as though nothing happened? His fear of being arrested or of mob goons retaliating had begun fading to a distant shadow. Had he *really* thought the McLaughlin's fiasco was just a minor bump in the road, an unpleasant interlude that would fade away?

But Danny getting shot changes everything.

If I'm killed, what happens to Tracy and the kids? Jesus, don't let that be the end of all this. Am I praying now? It's just a small jump to where I'll turn to religion, like Danny does. Roddy recalls that insane, dreamlike drive down the Taconic from Snapper Pond after he'd shot and killed Grange and Kenny. There was that mind-numbing moment when Dan asked him that question. *"Roddy, you believe in God?"*

Halfway up the ramp leading to level four, the smell of exhaust fumes grows stronger. It mixes with the biting cold of damp winter air and swirls into Roddy's nostrils. He tastes the noxious mix on his tongue. The pungent odor reminds him of driving the Sequoia that night. There was the smell of gunpowder, the reek of Grange's empty bowels, the moist soil, and the fungal stench of the pond.

He rounds a concrete pillar. About to trudge the last forty yards to his parked Rogue, Roddy sees the source of the fumes. His heart crawls up to his throat. A jolting sensation pulses through him. A black Lincoln Navigator is parked with its engine running. Its nose faces the cinder-block wall. Its rear bumper faces his car. Roddy's body freezes as he stands next to the pillar, motionless, eyes locked on the Navigator. The blackened window on the driver's side is lowered halfway. A man wearing a dark coat and a black beret sits behind the wheel, smoking a cigarette.

The Navigator's lift gate is open. Another man, wearing a waist-length, black leather jacket, stands behind the gate with one foot perched on the rear bumper. His back is to Roddy as he talks into a cell phone. He can't make out the man's words, but he's talking in some Eastern European language. There's urgency in his voice. A chill overtakes Roddy as he stands hidden by the concrete pillar.

This could be it: an ambush. Roddy doesn't recognize them as hospital employees. And they're not getting out of the vehicle to head to the hospital to visit someone. They're parked in a mob-mobile, a Navigator with blackened windows, waiting, with the engine idling, near Roddy's car. What could they possibly be doing other than waiting for *him*? The guy at the rear could pull a weapon from the cargo bay—it would take only a second—while the other guy's ready to pull out, burn rubber, and make tracks.

Roddy thinks the guy at the rear of the Navigator switches to English, but he can't make out the words in the cavernous expanse of the garage. The man's back is toward him. His voice is muffled. Roddy strains to hear. The guy behind the wheel doesn't look Italian, doesn't look like he's from Brooklyn or Northern Jersey. Looks like a thug from some depressed Eastern European shithole, a place where they traffic in women, drugs, and guns. And the guy speaking on the phone . . . it sounds like Russian or some Slavic language. Or is Roddy jumping to panic-riddled conclusions, latching on to virtually anything after what happened to Danny?

Roddy's knees feel like rubber. He's suddenly aware his breathing is rapid and shallow. He moves back very, very slowly. On watery legs, he turns and treads slowly down the ramp, heading back to level three. His heart beats an insane tattoo in his chest.

On the downhill ramp of level three, Roddy glances to his right through the angled space between concrete support pillars.

There's the undercarriage of the Navigator. At the far side, he sees the guy standing behind it from his right knee down. The man's left foot is still propped on the Navigator's rear bumper.

Crouching, Roddy slinks to level three. At the elevator, he presses the "Down" button.

Waiting, he hears the sudden hum from inside the shaft. The elevator is slow; it seems to take forever to get to level three. Maybe he should make a quick retreat on foot and get back to the lobby. Just then, the elevator doors slide open. He steps in and presses "Lobby." The doors close. The fluorescent-lit compartment descends. Despite the garage's chilled air, Roddy is soaked in sweat. His armpits are drenched and his shirt sticks to his back.

He's deposited on the ground floor and walks quickly down the corridor to the hospital lobby. The place is busy as nurses, aides, doctors, and porters traverse the expanse. A few visitors stop at the reception desk asking for directions.

Roddy heads for the Emergency Department as thoughts of Russian mobsters blitz through his mind. It's a rush of images from McLaughlin's: barrel-chested goons with thick, heavily tattooed necks and Slavic accents, sipping vodka, chomping prime steaks as Kenny Egan rushed from table to table, whispering God-knows-what into their ears. There were also the mafia types from Brooklyn and Jersey. The whole mobbed-up, gangster-loaded scene had made him want to puke when he, Tracy, Danny, and Angela had gone there for dinner. And being in business with Kenny meant, ultimately, he and Danny were in bed with the mob. And now this: either Russian honchos or mafia mobsters invading their lives.

John M. Grange and Associates was what the bastard's card had said.

And just who are Grange's associates?

Maybe it's best to notify hospital security, tell them a couple of creepy-looking guys are hanging around the garage. Is he jumping to conclusions? They could just be two guys waiting for a visitor to come back from a ward. Why go into a panic?

In a nearby corridor, Roddy grabs the cell phone from his coat pocket. His thoughts jumble. He's not sure if he wants to call the hospital operator and ask for security or if he'll call Tracy and have her come to pick him up. His hand shakes violently. The phone nearly slips from his grasp. He clutches it tightly and realizes he can't really dial any number.

Right there, with the phone in his hand, the device trills its marimba sound. It's Tracy, the readout says.

Tracy . . . home . . . the kids. Is it all over now? Is the life I've been leading about to disappear?

Fumbling with the phone, he nearly drops it. He finally presses the button. "Honey, I'm at the hospital. What's up?"

"Oh, Roddy. I just called because . . . I don't know . . . I'm nervous."

"About what?"

Christ, my voice is warbling. And I feel like I'm gonna puke.

"I can't stop thinking about Danny. Will he be okay?"

"Absolutely, honey. I called Ketchman today. He said Danny's doing fine . . . better than he expected. He's awake and alert." He wonders if Tracy hears how shaky he sounds. His voice—the great betrayer—sounds an octave higher in his ears.

"Roddy, you sound upset."

"Of course I am. After what happened to Danny, how could I not be?"

"You're sure he'll be all right?"

"Ketchman says he'll be out of the hospital in a few days."

"And you?"

"It's just that . . . I don't know, Trace. I've had a long day and I feel lousy. On top of that, my car won't start. Can you pick me up? I'll be at the ER entrance."

"I'll be right over." She pauses and then sighs deeply into the phone. "Roddy, you sound . . . I don't know. Are you sure nothing's wrong?"

"I'm just stressed out, honey, like you. But everything's gonna be fine. Don't worry."

Jesus. I'm such a lying bastard.

Chapter 4

Stepping out of the elevator at level four, Roddy thinks about last night's incident, right here in the hospital garage. Were those guys at the Navigator waiting for him? Can't be sure, but he'll move cautiously, see if anyone's lurking. If he sees a single soul, he'll turn back. It would be better to park somewhere on the street from now on, or maybe use that privately owned parking lot two blocks away.

It's just after eight thirty, and while plenty of cars are still parked here, there are no people in the garage. It's the middle of the three-to-eleven-p.m. shift, and visiting hours are over. So far, so good—nobody seems to be around. And there's no smell of fumes, just the odor of damp cement.

Were those guys last night just killing time? *Killing* could be the right word. Is he just seizing on some coincidence and interpreting it as something ominous? Since Danny got shot, Roddy's cued into everything, anywhere—big or small. When Tracy drove him to the hospital this morning, he kept looking through the passenger's side-view mirror to see if they were being tailed. Each time he spotted a dark SUV behind them—any model, no matter how far back—his heart nearly jumped out of his chest.

Up ahead, he spots Walt McKay, the surgical team's anesthesiologist. Walt was in a rush to get home after they finished the last surgery—an emergency appendectomy on a ten-year-old kid.

He said it was his daughter Alice's eighth birthday, and he didn't want to keep the family waiting. When the patient was out of the OR and in recovery, Walt tossed his coat over his surgical greens and beat it out of the hospital. He made it to the elevator about thirty seconds before Roddy, so Roddy took the next one down to level four. Walt's wearing his surgical clogs, just as Roddy does when leaving the hospital after a long day. Walt joked that when he gets home wearing his scrubs and clogs, he'll say he thought it was a costume party.

Roddy's eyes swerve left and right; he peers into each car parked on level four as he walks toward the Rogue. He's hungry as a bear, having eaten nothing since breakfast. Tracy will be waiting for him, and they'll have a simple dinner together.

His eyes sweep up and down the ramp, and he reaches into his overcoat pocket for the car keys.

Walt's about thirty feet from his Honda, which is parked next to Roddy's car. He reaches into his overcoat pocket and extracts a set of keys. He presses the unlock mechanism and the Honda chirps, as its lights flash on.

Roddy hears a car engine's rumble behind him. He can tell from the approaching sound that the vehicle is moving slowly. He feels the hairs on the back of his neck stand on end. If the car comes abreast of him, he can duck into a space between parked vehicles.

And then what?

Jesus, I'm getting paranoid.

The vehicle pulls alongside Roddy. From the corner of his eye, he sees it's an old-model Chevy sedan—an Impala at least ten years old.

Roddy feels every nerve in his body firing. He's in neural overload—totally juiced and ready to bolt between the cars to his right.

But the Chevy passes him, moving forward slowly. Roddy

doesn't have a good view of the driver or passenger, but from behind, they look like a couple of casual guys simply cruising around, looking for a parking spot in a still-crowded hospital garage.

As the Chevy slowly nears Walt, it angles slightly to the left and closer to him. Walt glances back, raises his right arm, and jiggles his keys, a signal he's vacating the spot—a common courtesy. The Chevy slows and its blinkers start flashing. The driver will take Walt's space.

Strange though—despite slowing, the Chevy keeps moving forward. Roddy sees a space only three cars beyond Walt's. The guy's going to maneuver the Chevy into that space.

Walt's only a few feet from his Honda. Roddy has stopped in his tracks; he's standing motionless on the ramp, watching Walt approach his car. The Chevy pulls alongside just as Walt turns to open the driver-side door. The other vehicle partly obscures Walt, but at that moment, Roddy hears a muffled pop—or maybe it's a soft *pfft*, echoing in the concrete expanse.

Walt's knees buckle. He crumples to the cement floor between cars.

The Chevy peels rubber and races toward the exit ramp. It fishtails and turns sharply as its tires squeal. A second later, it's gone. A pall of grayish fumes fills the air. Roddy hears the Chevy's tires shrieking on level three and the sound diminishes as it descends.

Roddy lunges forward and runs to Walt. The anesthesiologist lies face down on the cement floor. His dark blue overcoat is spread over the pavement. Protruding from beneath the coat, Walt's legs—clad in green scrub pants—are splayed.

A sharp pang shoots through Roddy as though electricity courses through his skin. He kneels beside Walt and sees a blood-rimmed hole in the back of his skull. It's no bigger than the tip of Roddy's pinky finger. Walt's blondish brown hair is matted with blood seeping around the hole. There's no sign of an exit wound. A bullet has lodged deep in his brain. Walt's face is milky white, has gone slack, lost its muscle tone.

Roddy grasps Walt's wrist and feels for a radial pulse. None. His fingertips shoot to Walt's neck, but there's no carotid pulse either.

Roddy feels chilled to his core. *That bullet was meant for me.*

It's unbelievable. Walt McKay's dead.

Only minutes ago, they were joking in the surgical suite's locker area. But his life is gone and Walt's now a corpse. How can that be? He's known Walt for eight years; they've worked together through hundreds of surgeries, shared plenty of cafeteria lunches, gone out together with their wives, and played four-wall squash a few times. Walt McKay—always ready with a joke to relieve OR tension. Walt—a guy who'd give you the shirt off his back, a married man with three kids. Jesus, how can this be?

Roddy's hands tremble as he reaches into his coat pocket, and in a hazy fog, grabs his cell phone. He's not even thinking as he dials 911. He's not sure his tongue will form the words he'll need to talk to the police.

With Walt McKay lying in a limp heap and Roddy kneeling over him, it all coalesces and hits him like a sledgehammer: my life is over.

Chapter 5

Roddy slumps into a leather chair in the doctors' lounge. His mind reels from the bleak reality of what's happened.

Walt McKay is dead, a guy I worked with for eight years, a great guy, a family man who never spoke an unkind word about anyone. He died from a bullet meant for me. And what happens now? What about Tracy and the kids? And Danny, Angela, and their kids. Are any of us safe?

He closes his eyes and tries to erase the image of Walt lying on the concrete. The sound of those squealing tires reverberates in Roddy's ears. He knows Walt's rush to get home was the reason he was mistaken for Roddy. He got to the garage less than a minute ahead of Roddy.

It should have been me, not poor Walt.

Roddy glances up at the wall clock: ten thirty. He called Tracy and told her what happened.

"Oh my God. How terrible," she cried. "And so soon after what happened to Danny. What's going on?"

Roddy hears a commotion in the hallway. Bronxville detectives are still questioning people: nurses, doctors, Walt's colleagues and friends. Roddy was questioned by two different detectives for more than an hour. One detective said the hospital would be in lockdown for at least another hour. Roddy feels exhausted; he must have answered a hundred questions, and there will be more tomorrow from the hospital administration. And, no doubt, from more detectives. Roddy wonders if Walt's death could have been prevented if he'd told someone, anyone—hospital security, the Bronxville PD—he'd seen some unsavory-looking characters loitering in the garage on level four. Right there, near his car. Exactly where Walt was killed.

Suddenly, Roddy's thoughts drift back to that night in McLaughlin's back office, when Grange showed up and demanded money. With the juice running, Kenny's debt had blossomed to half a million dollars.

He hears Grange's basso voice rumble. *"Yeah, keep noddin', Mr. Fuckin' Tough Guy. 'Cause you got plenty of dough. Even your wife works, like you need the money."*

When Danny protested, saying neither he nor Roddy borrowed money from Grange, the loan shark laughed. He turned to Roddy and said, *"Everyone pays the doctor . . . and the undertaker. You ain't cryin' poverty, are you?"*

After Roddy shook his head, Grange looked right into his eyes and said, *"Don't cry poverty to me, Mr. Fuckin' MD, with your house in Bronxville, right on a golf course. Whose pretty little wife with the blond ponytail works at Sarah Lawrence. Shit, if all librarians looked like her, I'da spent more time with the books. Don't tell me you can't rustle up the money."*

"Hey, Doc, you look terrible . . . like you just lost your best friend."

Voltage shoots through Roddy, and he nearly jumps at the sound. And there's that cologne again; the fragrance crawls up Roddy's nostrils.

"Pretty jumpy, aren't you, Doc?" says Detective Morgan. He stands there, looming above Roddy. The guy must be a solid six four, wide at the shoulders and maybe two hundred twenty pounds.

"What're *you* doing here?" Roddy asks. His nerves thrum like taut wires strung through his body.

"I'm on assignment."

"But this is Bronxville. It's not your jurisdiction."

Roddy's toes curl inside his OR clogs.

"Yeah, Doc," Morgan says, unbuttoning his overcoat as he sits in a chair facing Roddy. "Bronxville's a village. Its police department doesn't have the resources to handle a full-blown murder investigation like what happened to the doctor in the garage. So they called the state police, which usually happens in a case like this. And the state has the BCI—"

"BCI?"

"The Bureau of Criminal Investigation. It's the detective branch of the NYSP. It has a thousand investigators who look into serious felonies. They assist local law enforcement agencies with major crimes."

"But why're *you* here?"

"Actually, Doc, I'm not here because of what happened tonight, even though I heard it happened right in front of you. Is that right?"

Roddy nods.

Is he gonna question me about Walt McKay?

"And, of course, the hospital's in lockdown."

It occurs to Roddy if whoever killed Walt was really gunning for him, he's got to get to them before the cops do. Because if the cops draw a bead on who did it and start asking questions, the trail could lead right back to him and Danny and what went down at Snapper Pond.

"I'm lucky, Doc," says Morgan. "I just took a chance to see if you'd still be here. I have a few questions I'd like to get cleared up, but it looks like I surprised you, huh?" Morgan's lips spread into a smirk. A goddamned smirk, like he knows something Roddy doesn't. Morgan's fingers begin tapping on the arm of the chair.

"Surprised me? Not really, Detective. I'm just upset about

what happened."

"Understood, Doc. You knew the vic?"

"I worked with him."

Morgan shakes his head. He leans back in his chair, waits a beat, and says, "Hey, Doc, I looked you up—Google and all that good stuff. You're a top-notch guy . . . rated one of the best surgeons in *New York* magazine. You have high marks on Rate MDs and some other online sites. And you should see the raves about you on Angie's List. I'd never get those kinds of ratings in my line of work, if you know what I mean." Morgan chortles.

"And I read about your military background . . . Fort Bragg and the 82nd Airborne. A hard-ass bunch of soldiers. Every bit as tough as the Navy SEALS. I was in the First Cavalry Division out of Fort Hood, Texas. Ever hear of them?"

Roddy nods.

Jesus, this guy's Googled the hell outta me.

Roddy knows the proverbial other shoe's about to drop. Morgan's not here to trade war stories. He's here to follow up on Danny getting shot. And the guy's suspicious about something. He's just going through the buttering-up stage right now.

"We had some paratroopers from the 82nd attached temporarily to our unit," Morgan continues, lacing his fingers behind his head. "They got into barroom brawls in every shit-pile watering hole from Austin to Waco. I guess when a guy jumps out of airplanes, there's nothin' can scare him, right, Doc? Of course, mine was before your time in the army. I'm fifty-two years old, and you were in the service when you were seventeen, right? Became an Army Ranger, too. I heard 70 percent of guys who go in for Ranger training don't make it—they're booted out on their asses 'cause they don't have the mental or physical stamina for it. Right, Doc?"

Danny was shot two nights ago and Walt McKay was killed tonight, and this guy's talking about twenty-five years ago—Fort

Bragg and Ranger school?

"You've been through some pretty rough shit in your lifetime, huh, Doc?"

Why's Morgan going through this buddy-buddy bullshit? It's a warm-up session for what's coming. After all, this guy came to Lawrence Hospital tonight just looking for me. Morgan's antennae are way up there, but about what, exactly?

"So what brings you here, Detective?"

"Tell you the truth, Doc, I have a few questions about the Burns situation. I'm sure you're upset about tonight's shooting, but I'd like to get back to two nights ago, if you don't mind."

Roddy senses the detective has more than *a few questions*. Morgan's smirk makes Roddy feel the guy knows he's on a track to *something*, that he knows a whole lot more than he's telling. Roddy wonders if maybe he's becoming a touch paranoid. But then there's Walt McKay.

No, this isn't paranoia. It's not his imagination. Roddy's world is collapsing.

"Questions about what, Detective?"

Morgan leans forward, rests his elbows on his knees. "You were in the OR when Burns got shot, right?"

"Yes."

"Can anyone verify you were here?"

"Of course—my surgical team."

"And you went to St. Joseph's, right?"

"Yes."

"What time did you get there?"

"Could've been eight thirty, maybe a bit later. I don't recall exactly."

Roddy knows Morgan's trying to rattle him with this line of questioning. He can tell Morgan's no slouch—he's probably been working the Yonkers streets for twenty-five years and seen enough cases to recognize certain patterns. Just like Roddy knows the surgical signs and symptoms of a hot gallbladder or a fiery appendix. Time and experience are great teachers.

"Lemme ask you something, Detective," Roddy hears himself say through a dense field of static.

Morgan peers questioningly at him. Those bushy eyebrows arch upward.

"Am I a *suspect* in Danny's shooting?" Roddy forces a grin but feels his pulse racing.

Morgan laughs softly, and shakes his head. "No, Doc, you're not a suspect," he says with a forced smile. "I'm just confused about the timeline and I'm tryin' to get it straight."

Roddy's insides hum. He maintains steady eye contact with Morgan. The guy never seems to blink; he just stares at Roddy with those dark, penetrating eyes.

Roddy's gut gurgles. His shoulders tense, and he's certain he'll develop a cramp in his trapezius muscles. He crosses one leg over the other and feels his pulse pounding in the area behind his knee. The radiator hisses, and Roddy thinks the lounge is like a steam bath in Brighton Beach. Jesus, what made him think of the Brighton Beach baths? It's the home of the Russians.

"I wanna speak with you," Morgan says, "because we got the preliminary ballistics report on the Burns shooting. There was some question whether it might've been a robbery gone bad. But the report leads us to think in another direction."

Roddy tries to keep his legs from going into a spasm, especially his hamstring muscles.

"The two slugs were from a .22-caliber pistol."

Roddy nods but says nothing. Less can be more . . . sometimes. And besides, who cares about the caliber of the bullets? Except for shooting Grange and Kenny, he's had nothing to do with guns in twenty-five years.

But Roddy's stomach clenches.

"The shots were fired from the doorway, a distance of about

fifteen feet," Morgan says. "It was easy to determine the distance and angle of the shots once we recovered the slugs."

Roddy nods. He has the feeling Morgan's dangling a rod. And Roddy's the fish.

"And from what Burns said he heard—that little popping sound—it seems pretty clear the perp's .22 had a silencer. That's consistent with it being a hit, not some random robbery that went bad."

Roddy feels his pulse in his wrists.

"Wouldn't a silencer leave marks on the bullets you retrieved?"

"That's what most people think, Doc, especially people famil-iar with guns from twenty or more years ago."

Bastard knows I had sniper training from looking me up online. He knows much more than he's letting on. I'm walking a high wire with this guy. Gotta be careful.

"But in the last few years, technology's improved," Morgan continues, leaning forward with his elbows on his thighs. "You see, twenty years ago, a weapon using a silencer—either a rifle or a pistol—would've left markings on the slug. There'd be an altered striation pattern on the bullet head. But most silencers today are made with metal baffles that don't touch the bullet as it passes through, so they don't change the slug's appearance. The only way there'd be markings would be if the silencer was misaligned; then the bullet would brush against the baffles on its way through the suppressor. Back in the old days, silencers were made with mesh or wipes that contacted the bullet as it went through, so they left telltale markings. But not anymore."

Roddy hears another smirk in Morgan's voice, though it hasn't yet gone to his lips.

"The point being, Detective?"

"The point being, Doc, it looks like someone was on a mission to take out your friend Burns. Someone with a silencer on a .22. It was very likely a hit, not some amateur who panicked during a half-assed B and E."

Roddy's chest tightens, as though damp clay surrounds his heart. He swallows hard. "How can you be so sure it wasn't a botched burglary?" he asks, aware his voice sounds like it's bleating and knowing Morgan's 100 percent right after what happened to Walt.

"It's pretty clear, Doc." That half smirk forms again on Morgan's lips. "It looks like a head shot got blocked by the telephone receiver. The slug was deflected, and Burns got a minor wound instead of a brain buster. And that other shot? It was a pop right in the middle of his chest, near the heart. Those two shots along with the silencer put this thing in the ballpark of a professional."

"It could've been a burglary; after all, they took stuff." Roddy knows he won't be able to misdirect Morgan.

"It's all bullshit stuff, Doc. They took his wallet and a Dell laptop, an Inspiron 15z—including the flash drive. Yeah, they took some computerized files. Maybe they wanted them, but I don't think so. So, they rummaged around, knocked some things over, rifled through some files to make it look like a burglary. But you know what?"

Roddy waits, says nothing.

"They didn't take Burns's Rolex. It's worth thousands. Thieves always go for the jewelry. So, believe me, Doc, it was no burglary. And besides, who'd wanna break into an accountant's office at night? It's not a rich target like a high-class home with jewelry, art, and other valuables. Unless they wanted some financial files, it was a hit, pure and simple."

Roddy wonders if his eyes are bulging because they feel like they'll burst from pressure building in his head. Heat creeps into his face. A droplet of sweat slides from his underarm down his side. Soon he'll be marinating in his own sweat.

There's no doubt about it; this is the worst-case scenario: Danny's been targeted; Walt's been shot right near my car; and a hound dog of a Yonkers detective is sniffing around like he smells red meat. It's a nightmare come true.

Roddy knows he's next in line.

He wishes his heart would downshift to a slower pace.

"There're a couple of questions I'd like to ask you, Doc," Morgan says, crossing one leg over the other, leaning back in the chair. "I spoke to Burns, and Mrs. Burns, too. And I did some online research." Morgan pauses and peers at Roddy. The detective squints, as though he's digging for some line of questioning Roddy won't expect, something to throw him off balance, something to rattle him.

"Tell me about the restaurant business . . . about McLaughlin's." Morgan's face looks neutral, expressionless.

An electric pang shoots through Roddy. It's an open-ended question. It opens the door for Roddy to say anything—some tidbit that could lead to a squall of other questions.

"What's that got to do with Danny getting shot?"

"There could be a connection," Morgan says, half closing one eye.

"What kind of connection?"

"I dunno. But I get to ask the questions, here, Doc. Tell me about McLaughlin's."

"It's way off topic, Detective."

"Indulge me, Doc. How'd you get involved?"

Involved? I don't like that word. He's angling for something. And it could be because he's talked with Danny. Dan's been awake and fully alert for an entire day now. No doubt Morgan's spent some time with him and asked plenty of questions. What the fuck did he say that has Morgan sniffing up this tree?

Chapter 6

"I don't know where to begin, Detective."

"Begin at the beginning." Morgan stretches his long frame and again laces his fingers behind his head, leaning back in his chair.

Jesus, he's got all the time in the world. He's gonna pump me as much as he can.

Roddy gives Morgan the CliffsNotes version of how they got into the restaurant business. Avoiding too many details, he describes how he and Danny became Kenny's silent partners in McLaughlin's. And he tells Morgan how after Kenny disappeared, the previous owner, McLaughlin Jr.—who they hadn't paid off fully—repossessed the place.

As he's describing it all, Roddy sees the restaurant in his mind: the tables, the masculine décor, the clamoring crowds, the open grill pit with two chefs, people bellied up to the bar three deep, and Kenny charging from table to table like a madman, hyped up and maxed out on drugs.

Morgan sits with his head tilted. His eyes look like they're nearly closed with lids at half-mast.

And even as he's talking, Roddy thinks, *Kenny Egan? Getting into bed with that weasel? Why am I telling this detective about that fiasco? It's the old story—let a guy talk on, and he'll vomit the whole enchilada. Give him enough rope and he ends up twisting in the wind.*

Roddy knows he'd hoped Morgan would be more interested in Danny than in McLaughlin's. That maybe he'd want to dig a little deeper into Dan's personal and professional life than when they met two nights ago at St. Joe's.

"So lemme get this straight, Doc," Morgan says, again leaning forward. He shakes his head and blinks a few times.

Roddy thinks Morgan isn't trying to mask his skepticism.

"This guy, Kenny Egan, formerly known as Kenny McGuirk, comes to your office one night, two Septembers ago. You haven't seen him in nearly thirty years. He's a guy who used to gamble, whose moniker was 'Snake Eyes,' who's been livin' in a bettor's paradise—Vegas—where he's managed some restaurants. He pops in out of the blue and tells you about a restaurant proposition in Manhattan, this place McLaughlin's. Right?"

Roddy nods as something cold snakes through his chest. Morgan's done plenty of digging into the case in a mere two days. He knows almost as much as Roddy about McLaughlin's and how the whole mess got started.

How much did Danny tell this guy?

"And this Kenny Egan character wanted you to invest as a silent partner in a restaurant. Am I right?"

Roddy nods, wishing he could bolt up from the chair and leave the lounge.

"So, like a smart man, you send him to your accountant and best friend, Daniel Burns, who's now lyin' in the hospital recovering from bullet wounds as we speak. And Burns goes over everything. So then you and Burns go into business with Egan. Am I getting this right?"

"That's right, if you want to call it that," Roddy says, staring into Morgan's flickering eyes.

"Well, what would you call it, Doc?" Morgan once again leans back in the chair and crosses his arms.

"We were silent partners. We weren't involved on a day-to-day basis. We just put up money as investors. I was at the restaurant maybe three or four times . . . for dinner. I had nothing to do with running the place."

"Okay. So you each put a hundred K into the business and Egan puts in three hundred, right?"

"Right."

"What was Burns's role in this setup?"

"Same as mine, a silent partner. And the restaurant's accountant."

"So Burns looked into everything and okayed the deal?"

"Yes. He thought it made financial sense after he looked at the numbers."

"Okay, Doc," Morgan says, pursing his lips. "So you're in business and things're lookin' good for a while. But then the place starts losing money. You know why?"

Jesus, did Danny spill everything to this guy?

"It turns out it was poorly managed."

"By whom?"

"By Ken Egan. He said there was a lot of stealing going on. Employees were lifting all kinds of stuff—alcoholic beverages, steaks, you name it. It was a thief's paradise. Kenny said it happens in every restaurant."

"So let's assume that's true, Doc. You and Burns decide to get out, right?"

"Yes."

Morgan exhales and nods his head. He rubs his chin with his forefinger and thumb. "So you meet with Egan and tell him you're both pulling out, right?"

"Right."

"How'd he take that?" Morgan's bushy eyebrows dance upward, droop down, and then rise again.

"He was upset, but the place was hemorrhaging money."

"So what happened?"

"I don't know what you mean." Roddy feels a cramp begin in the arch of his right foot. Soon he'll feel a wrenching spasm, and he'll have to rip off his clog and begin rubbing the foot.

"Oh, c'mon, Doc. Sure you do. What happened to Egan?"

"I don't know. He disappeared."

"Just like *that*? He disappears into thin *air*?"

"I don't know."

"And you guys close the restaurant and the previous owner, McLaughlin, exercises his lien, and that's it?"

"What can I say? I don't know."

"How does a guy just disappear? Huh?"

"Detective, I have no idea." Roddy's hands curl in his lap as an image of that last night in McLaughlin's back office floods his mind: that fat bastard Grange slugging down the Klonopin-laced scotch, the Glenfiddich—*that good shit*, as Grange called it—and then passing out like a bloated sack of shit; the three of them, he, Kenny, and Danny hauling that lard-assed bastard out the restaurant's back door to the Sequoia; and the insane drive upstate on the Taconic to that shitpit, Snapper Pond.

"When was the last time you saw Egan?"

"The last night I was at the restaurant . . . that April. Danny and I met him in the back office and decided to end the operation. Kenny had a headache, so we drove him home."

"Where was that?"

"We dropped him off at a pharmacy near his apartment."

"And that's the last you saw of him?"

"That's right."

"What'd you do after you dropped Egan off on 9th Avenue?"

How does he know where we dropped Kenny off? What the hell did Danny tell this guy?

"Just give me a timeline of what you did afterward, Doc."

"I'd driven into the city for the meeting, and Danny took

the train in from Tuckahoe. So we drove in my car to Dan's office in Yonkers to talk about the tax picture after we got out of McLaughlin's. It would be a loss on my return."

Jesus, this guy's got me talking about the night we killed Kenny and Grange. He's zeroed right in on things. I'm sticking with the story, just the way Dan and I planned that night in the parking lot of the Tuckahoe station. Is Danny sticking with the story?

"Then what?"

"I drove Dan to the Tuckahoe train station, where his car was parked; then I went home."

"What time was that?"

"It was late. Probably close to midnight."

"Can anyone verify all this? That you were in Yonkers and then Tuckahoe before you went home?"

Don't let it look rehearsed. Don't overplay it.

"Actually, I'll never forget that night. There was an incident at the train station. As I was dropping Danny off, a bunch of police cars pulled up and stopped us. They even frisked us. There'd been some muggings and stolen cars at the station late at night, and they checked us out. I'm sure it's in the Tuckahoe police records."

Morgan pulls a small pad and pen from his jacket and jots something down.

An image of the six Tuckahoe cops with their guns drawn flashes through Roddy's mind. Yes, they were the best thing that could have happened—the stop was iron-clad proof he and Danny were in Tuckahoe that night. Roddy even recalls two of their names—Smythe and Caldwell—etched on their name tags as police lights swirled in the parking lot. He recalls the smell of fumes from the squad cars, the galvanic current streaming through his skin as he wondered if the cops would command him to open the Sequoia's rear hatch. There were the pink cones of light from the sodium vapor lights, the residue of soil from Snapper Pond on his boots, and the smell of parking lot asphalt. His heart slammed furiously in his chest. Amid these thoughts, Roddy looks up and sees Morgan's still writing. How long has it been since the detective's last question?

"Let's get back to Ken Egan," Morgan says, looking up from the pad.

"As a matter of fact, after Kenny went missing, we reported it to the NYPD."

I should've told him this right off the bat. Jesus, I'm rattled. Gotta calm down.

Roddy takes a deep breath; he knows he's talking too much—and way too fast. The words are spilling from his mouth—a verbal deluge. He's talking like a guy with plenty to hide.

"The Missing Persons Squad, right?"

So, he already knows about it.

"Exactly. Danny and I went down there and spoke with someone."

"Uh huh. Your friend Burns told me everything."

I can't believe Danny would spill everything to this guy.

"He told me you spoke to a Captain Greene."

"That's right."

Roddy's thoughts race frantically as he recalls everything about that night and what happened afterward.

Morgan shifts his eyes back to the pad. He writes something down. His eyelids look heavy, almost sleepy. "Let's get back to Egan," he says, looking up at Roddy. "How much did he ante up as his share to buy the place?"

"Three hundred thousand," Roddy says as his throat begins clogging with phlegm.

"What I mean, Doc, is how much of his *own* money did he put up?" Morgan's eyelids rest at half-mast, like he's bored with the line of crap he's being handed.

"I don't follow."

"You know if he borrowed any money to buy the place?"

"I don't know. I'm not a financial guy. I was just a backer. Danny did all the paperwork."

"And Burns never looked into how Egan got all that dough?"

"As far as I know, it was Kenny's . . . from working in Vegas." Roddy's heart slams heavily against his ribs.

"Did you know Egan was gambling?"

"Not when we went into business. Captain Greene said they went to his apartment and looked at his computer. He'd been to lots of gambling sites."

"Yeah, that's what Burns said. And Captain Greene confirmed it." Morgan pauses; his head bobs forward and his eyes narrow, as though he's thinking carefully about what he'll say next. "And lemme tell you somethin' else, Doc; Captain Greene's unit did more research into Egan than you know. Just before you and Burns entered into this deal with Egan, there was a sudden infusion of two hundred fifty K into his bank account."

Morgan pauses and taps his pen on the little pad.

"What do you make of that, Doc?"

Roddy sighs and shakes his head.

"It was wired to Egan's bank from a privately numbered account in the Cayman Islands. Meaning it was inaccessible to anyone but the account holder."

Roddy feels his own eyebrows arch.

Don't pretend you didn't know this. Don't overdo the drama. Keep it real.

"By any chance, do you know who Egan's benefactor was in this little deal?"

"I never knew the money wasn't his. And I never examined his bank account. I only know Danny did a credit check on Kenny, and it was good. And Kenny gave him a certified check. That's it."

"But the Cayman Islands, Doc. What does that bring to mind?" Morgan leans forward.

"An offshore account . . . a tax haven."

"How 'bout laundered money, Doc?" Morgan's lips twist slightly.

"Could be."

"Doc, you ever hear of the Fontana brothers?"

"Captain Greene mentioned them." Roddy's skin feels like it's curdling.

"They're a Jersey mob into plenty of heavy-duty shit."

"That's what Captain Greene said."

"Prostitution, gambling, garbage hauling, construction . . . you name it."

"Greene said that, too."

"How about the Russian Bratva?"

"Captain Greene said something about messages from them on Kenny's voice mail, if I recall."

"Absolutely correct, Doc. So, any idea where Egan's dough came from?"

"Danny and I didn't borrow a nickel from anyone."

"So you're safe? Is that what you're thinking?" Morgan's head tilts back. "You're absolutely clean in this mess?"

"Detective, I'm a surgeon. Danny's an accountant. We backed a restaurant as silent partners. Happens every day of the week. I had nothing to do with the place. I didn't like the deal at first, but Danny's my financial adviser, so I went for the ride. It was an investment . . . and it turned out to be a bad one. But I don't have a clue about all this."

"So your friend, accountant, and partner didn't demand to know from Egan where his dough came from? It was just there, so Burns took the deal. Is that it? A sophisticated guy like Burns—a CPA and a certified financial planner—gets snookered so easily? Is that what you're sayin'?"

"Hey, it's out of my league, Detective."

How dumb can I play it? Danny should've looked more carefully

*into Kenny's financing. What a fucked-up situation it's all turned
out to be.*

"You know, Doc, I'm a little suspicious of this whole thing. I
mean of Burns. He shoulda known better . . . a lot better. It looks
like he didn't do a thorough investigation of Egan's finances,
right, Doc?"

"I thought he did," Roddy rasps.

"I'd think a sharp guy like Burns would smell something rotten right off the bat, wouldn't you, Doc?"

*If this guy's right, Danny didn't do his due diligence on Kenny.
Danny believes in numbers—they always tell the story. Yet he didn't
look into where Kenny's money came from—especially a snake like
Kenny. Did Danny know more than he let on? And there's no de-
nying, he's been very distant these last ten months. We don't get
together anymore. Is he hiding something from me? Is it possible . . .
even one hundredth of one tenth of 1 percent possible that Danny
was tied up in some way with Kenny and Grange? No. It can't be.
It's impossible. Jesus, am I really getting paranoid?*

"And right now, Doc, your best friend and former partner's
in the hospital after taking two slugs. And you know nothing? I
mean . . . about the restaurant. And you have no idea of Egan's
whereabouts, where Egan got his dough, who was backing him,
or who wanted to put a couple of bullets in Danny Burns?"

Roddy shifts in the chair.

"And another thing, Doc. That poor guy in the garage took
a bullet a few hours ago, and he was parked right next to your
car. Funny coincidence, isn't it? Tell me, Doc. Am I getting this
right?"

"I guess so." Roddy swallows hard.

"Hey, Doc, the Bratva's way beyond Brighton Beach now.
They're not just in Brooklyn. They're everywhere."

"I wouldn't know about that." Roddy feels a railroad train
rumble through his chest.

"Oh, they've hit their stride these last few years. They're into loan-sharking, prostitution, sex trafficking, credit card fraud, money laundering—plenty of bad shit. And they're ruthless. They make the Italians look like candy-asses. They'll stop at nothing to settle a score. They'll even go after your family."

Roddy feels as though his skin is shredding.

The lounge goes silent. Roddy waits, looking at Morgan, who stares directly at him with those unblinking eyes.

"Anything else, Detective?"

"Yeah, Doc."

Morgan goes silent, just waiting.

"So what is it?"

"What're you gonna do? Hire a bodyguard?"

Morgan leans forward. That semismirk returns to his lips. His gaze turns hard.

"That's what I should do? Hire *protection*?"

"It'd be a lot easier to tell me what you know. Because you and your accountant friend could be in a world of trouble. Believe me, Doc. More than you can imagine."

"There's nothing more I can say." Roddy keeps his hands clasped in his lap. He's clenching his fists so tightly, his fingers are almost cramping.

"You sure about that?"

"And where would I go for protection anyway, assuming I needed it?"

"If it involves organized crime, there's always the FBI because the Yonkers and Bronxville police can't protect you from the mob." Morgan shakes his head. "Hey, remember that scene from *Jaws*, Doc, where that sheriff, the Roy Scheider guy, looks behind the boat and sees that shark burst outta the water and bite down on the chum? Remember what he says?" Morgan pauses and then says, "We're gonna need a bigger boat."

Roddy waits, saying nothing.

"Well, you're gonna need one, too. Bigger than anything we can provide."

Roddy stands and hears cracking from his knees.

"We had nothing to do with any mob."

"Have it your way, Doc." Morgan leans back in the chair and tilts his head.

Roddy moves toward the door.

"Oh, Doc?"

Roddy turns back and exhales. "Yeah?"

"Whaddaya think Burns meant when he said, 'We had to do it. We had no choice'?"

"I have no idea."

"Really?"

"Really."

"You change your mind, you know where to find me, Doc."

"I haven't got any idea about any of this," Roddy says, shaking his head.

"Take care, Doc."

Roddy knows he has to talk with Danny so they're on the same page with Morgan. Because this Yonkers dick is talking to them separately—playing them off each other, because he smells rotten fish in this whole thing. He's digging and pushing deeper and deeper, sniffing everywhere.

But now, with Danny shot and Walt McKay dead, everything's changed. There's no way Roddy sees his life the way he did only a few days ago—before it all came churning back like that shark Morgan talked about . . . the one from *Jaws*.

It's here, and it's now, and that shark's gonna chomp and maul its way through everything.

And everything that's been good—for him, Tracy and the kids, and for Danny and Angela, too—is gonna be gone.

His life as he's known it all these years, it's over. It's dead and gone.

Chapter 7

Roddy pulls the Rogue into the attached garage of their Tudor-style home in Bronxville. He sits behind the wheel listening to the engine tick, realizing he has no clear recollection of driving home from the hospital. He's been in a complete fog—cogitating endlessly about what happened tonight.

Morgan's words echo in his ears: *"There's always the FBI."*

And there was that wiseass crack: *"We're gonna need a bigger boat."*

Roddy knows he has to do something, but *what*?

His thoughts swirl in endless loops . . . Danny . . . Tracy, Angela, and all their kids . . . Walt McKay, poor guy, and his family . . . Morgan's prying . . . Grange and Kenny eating dirt upstate . . . the Russians . . . the Fontana brothers . . . and mob associates of Grange . . . if Grange was connected to organized crime . . . Jesus, what a snake pit he and Danny have stumbled into.

Roddy doesn't know how long he's been sitting in the car, but a glance at the dashboard clock tells him it's eleven thirty. It seems like only minutes ago he was with Morgan in the doctors' lounge. He gets out of the Rogue and enters the house through the door to the kitchen. Tracy gets up from the breakfast room table and rushes into his arms. She's wearing a nightgown and bathrobe.

"Oh, Roddy, this is awful. Walt McKay? I can't believe it," she whispers in a shaky voice. She rests her head against his chest. He wonders if she hears his heart drubbing like a jackhammer.

"I know, honey. It's terrible."

"What happened?" she asks, pulling back and looking up at him. Her green eyes are wide with worry.

He pulls her closer to him. "The police don't know yet. It might've been a random thing, but they're not sure." The edges of the kitchen are blurred—the cabinets and sink grow fuzzy—so Roddy closes his eyes. It feels so comforting to hold Tracy close to him. He breathes in the scent of her hair.

"And Danny," she says. "This is all so incredible."

"I spoke with Ketchman today. Danny's gonna be out of the hospital in a few days."

"First Danny, now Walt. What's going on?"

"They're not related, honey." Roddy feels like cringing at his own lie.

Lying on his back, Roddy cranes his neck and peers at the night-stand clock. It's 2:11 a.m. He hasn't had a single second of sleep. He hears Tracy's steady breathing to his right. Hers is the sleep of the innocent. And Roddy . . . his is the wakefulness of the damned.

His mind has been on a nonstop rampage. It should be *him* lying on a cold metal slab in the county morgue instead of Walt McKay. And if not for the luck of the Irish, Danny would be in the Yonkers morgue or laid out in a Tuckahoe funeral home by now. Yes, they'd both be dead and their families would have to go on without them.

Roddy's pajamas and pillow are soaked. The hair at the back of his head is matted with sweat. He sits up in bed and swings his feet to the floor. He tries to swallow, but his throat is too parched and it feels like razor blades are lodged there. Roddy realizes he's sweating so much, he'll soon dehydrate. He decides to shower and let the hot water wash away some of the tension and worry consuming him. And maybe something will come to him—an idea of what to do—because sometimes ideas come to him in the shower. One thing's certain: he can't sit passively like a target duck at a Coney Island shooting arcade.

He pads into the master bathroom, closes the door, strips off his pajamas, and tosses them into the hamper. He gulps down a cup of water, feeling its coldness all the way down his gullet. Shivering, he reaches into the glass-enclosed shower, turns on the hot water, and adjusts the temperature. Soon the room is filled with steam vapor.

As Roddy stands beneath the near-scalding stream of water, his thoughts continue on a fast track to nowhere. As water sloshes over his head, he's reminded of the night he and Danny drove back from Snapper Pond. After getting home, he'd showered that night, too, knowing he'd crossed a line—he'd murdered two men, one in cold blood and the other in self-defense. Unable to sleep afterward, he'd nearly jumped out of his skin with every sound he heard—a car passing by or the normal sounds of a house at night. He knows those same sick feelings will return now.

It's ten months later, and an ominous black cloud has rolled into their lives. He can't tell Tracy a thing, and he can't be truthful with Morgan—unless he wants to be indicted for double murder. Premeditated, with malice aforethought. Along with Danny. And then they'll rot forever in some prison hellhole. It all goes back to that snake Kenny Egan, that obese loan shark Grange, and the whole McLaughlin's debacle.

And then there's Danny.

Since Snapper Pond, he's been distant. It's as though the guy's built some invisible barrier between himself and Roddy. Yeah, they'd agreed to keep low profiles, but there's something cool, even snarky in Dan's voice when they're on the telephone, which hasn't been often.

And they've seen very little of each other since it all went down. It's amazing; Roddy calls the entire scenario that night *Snapper Pond*. It's become a code phrase for everything that happened: from the McLaughlin's escapade to that night in the woods and everything since then. And he and Tracy have been together with Danny and Angela maybe two times over the last ten months and only when Tracy invited them to their home for dinner.

Jesus, they used to see each other at least twice a month. And he and Dan were on the phone every week. But it's all changed. Roddy has this strange feeling that a layer of ice has formed on the deep lake of their friendship. Something erosive has crept into their lives.

It's amazing how one mistake can mushroom into something you could never anticipate—like poison seeping into every part of your life. If only Roddy'd stuck with his instincts; he'd never have gone into business with Kenny. But Danny crunched the numbers and said it would all work out. The numbers . . . Danny's always trusted the numbers. But this time they were all bogus.

It's useless to ponder the past and what he should or shouldn't have done. There are no do-overs. That only happens when you're a kid. In this world, you live with your mistakes; you keep moving ahead to stay in front of the steamroller called life.

Soaping his arms and shoulders, Roddy thinks back to his time in the Rangers. Sergeant Dawson would have plenty to say about this situation: "*Once you know the enemy's position, you figure out a plan. You go on the offense. Don't ever play defense.*"

And Doc Schechter—his old boxing trainer—would add: "*Don't be a wild beast, Roddy. Tame the animal inside. Execute a strategy. Stick to it and then take your opponent out.*"

But you can't execute a strategy if you don't even know who the enemy is. Where does that leave him? He'll try to learn as much as he can. How can he do that? From what Morgan said about the Russians—if they're the ones after him and Danny—they'll strike their families. Roddy shudders at the thought of something happening to Tracy and the kids. He and Danny will have to get their wives and kids out of Bronxville and Tuckahoe pronto.

A vision of Walt McKay intrudes as Roddy shampoos his hair. Walt lying there like a dead animal—limp and lifeless—on the damp, cold garage floor. Roddy knows it's his fault Walt's dead. Jesus, his wife's a widow, and his kids are fatherless. Roddy can't bear the thought of going to the funeral. Even trying to picture Walt's family crying over the coffin sends Roddy into a dreary tailspin. And seeing hundreds of hospital colleagues at the requiem Mass would be absolutely intolerable; a swell of nausea rises from his guts.

But before he even thinks of any funeral, he must take care of certain things.

He's got to get to St. Joseph's and talk with Danny. They've gotta make sure they're on the same page for this bloodhound Morgan. Otherwise, it'll be all over. They'll end up rotting away at Attica, Sing Sing, or some other upstate shithole.

For the rest of their worthless lives.

Chapter 8

Danny's been transferred to the medical floor, where he's been assigned a single-bed room. When Roddy arrives, he finds Dan sitting in a bedside easy chair, wearing a hospital johnny coat covered by a matching hospital-issue robe. Gone are the IVs and tubes protruding from everywhere. His color is back to normal.

"You look great," Roddy says, bending down toward him. Dan stretches his arms out. It's comforting to feel Dan near him. They embrace and clap each other's back with Dan sitting in the chair. "How do you feel?"

"I gotta get outta this place. I can't stand being here."

"Jesus, Dan. It's only three nights ago you were at death's door. Don't rush it."

"I feel good to go." He leans toward Roddy and whispers, "Frankly, kemosabe, I don't feel safe here."

Roddy nods. "Look, Dan, I know you've been through a lot, but I gotta bring you up to speed with what's happened."

"I hope you have some good news."

"Afraid not." Roddy sits on the edge of the bed, leans toward Danny, and tells him—in a very low voice—about Walt McKay. He relates every detail of what happened and tells him about the interview with Morgan. "Actually, the guy was interrogating me—and he was focused on the restaurant and Kenny. He suspects we're hiding something."

"You're sure the bullet was meant for you?" Dan half whispers, with widened eyes. His pupils look dilated, and a sheen forms on his forehead.

"Not a shred of doubt, Danny. We're *both* in someone's crosshairs. That's the bottom line, plain and simple."

"Now I really wanna get the fuck outta here." Dan's eyes flit about the room. He rubs his mop of red hair. "Doc says I'll get outta here in a few days. The only trouble I'll have is with this." He lifts up his casted right hand and grimaces.

"Dan, if it's some mob—especially the Russians—Tracy, Angela, and the kids aren't safe. We gotta get them the hell away."

"Oh, shit. What the fuck am I gonna tell Angela?" Dan's lower lip quivers as the sheen on his forehead glistens brightly in the light slanting in through the window.

"The same thing I'll tell Tracy."

"Yeah . . . what's that gonna be?"

"Let's lay it out together, right now, so we're on the same page. But before we do that, I have to ask you, what the fuck've you been telling this dick, Morgan?"

"He's been all over me like shit on a pig."

"So what'd you tell him? We gotta get this straight."

"I told him the basics."

"Meaning what?"

"Like we agreed the night it all went down. I told him about Kenny and his three hundred K and the restaurant and our getting out."

"Did you tell him we know Kenny got two fifty from someone else?"

"No. I made out like he put in the whole three hundred."

"Morgan knows about Kenny only putting in fifty. He knows the other two fifty came from an unknown source, from the Cayman Islands. He told me it's part of the record from Missing

Persons in New York."

"So that's where he learned it, Roddy—not from me. It's obvious NYPD did a lot more investigating than we knew about when we went to see that guy Greene at Missing Persons."

"What about Kenny going missing? Why'd you even mention that?"

"I *had* to. I couldn't cover that up. Remember, it's on the record with the NYPD."

"Okay, Dan. Tell me every word you told Morgan."

"No problem. But you know, Roddy, that bastard Morgan's never gonna talk to us together," Dan mutters. "He'll question us separately, just to look for contradictions. And he'll play us off each other, too."

"That's what they do," Roddy says. "And he'll do it because he's smart. He's got a good bullshit meter; and right now, the needle's jumpin' sky-high on the thing. Nothing I said passed the smell test. So, take your time and tell me everything the two of you talked about."

Over the next half hour, Danny recounts the three separate conversations he had with Morgan, since he's been fully awake and alert.

"Jesus, Dan. You told him too much."

"Only what was necessary."

"You went into way too much detail, but that's the way you are. Especially when you're nervous. *Detail Dan*, like Angela always says."

Roddy regrets saying the words the second they pass his lips.

"Ah, come off it," Danny rasps loudly. His eyes glare and then bore into Roddy.

"Danny, keep it *down*."

Sweat droplets form on Danny's forehead.

"If these detectives sense you're covering up or hiding any shit," Danny says, "it just opens up more doors for them to knock on and push through. So I told him as much as I could to look cooperative without saying anything that'd make him think we had anything to do with Kenny disappearing."

"Yeah, Dan, but there's a way you can be vague but not say *too* much. Why give away the whole goddamned ranch? Listen, I gotta be honest with you. When Morgan threw that shit at me about Kenny's two hundred fifty K coming from the Cayman Islands, he thought he was onto something big. And you know what?"

Danny waits, wide-eyed, with his head nodding slightly.

"I gotta say this, because it's true."

"Say what?"

"We shouldn't have to be dealin' with this crap now. You fucked up. You should've looked more carefully into where Kenny's money came from," Roddy says, the words slipping out. He hadn't meant to be so forceful, so blunt. He feels himself recoiling at the vehemence of his voice and his choice of words: *You fucked up*. Not fair and not the way to go.

"What the fuck're you saying, Roddy?" Dan's head shakes from side to side.

Roddy wants to hesitate and think through his next words, but they pour from his lips. "If you really wanna know, Dan, you should've been more careful. We wouldn't be in this deep shit— you in the hospital, Walt McKay dead, and we've got targets on our backs. For Christ's sake, even our families gotta be hidden."

"What're you fuckin' doing—laying blame?" Danny growls as his eyes widen. His brows arch, and Roddy sees the whites of Dan's eyes above his irises. "What're you saying? You're putting this shit on *my* shoulders? You have some fuckin' nerve, Roddy. You're my best friend, always have been, and now I gotta hear talk like this? Holy shit. I never thought I'd hear crap like this coming outta your mouth. What the fuck? Jesus, I'm so disappointed I don't know what to say. I can't even put it into words."

"C'mon, Danny, you gotta be realistic."

"As a matter of fact, Mr. Tough Guy, Doctor fucking Mad Dog Dolan, biggest badass in Sheepshead Bay, Brooklyn, New York, US of-Fucking-A, lemme put it to you this way as long as we're tossin' shit on the table. And I've thought about this plenty since it happened."

Danny swallows, shifts in his chair, and winces. He's pouring sweat; it drips down from his hairline. He tries to wipe some of it away with his palm.

"I wonder why the fuck I was stupid enough to let you strong-arm me into hauling that fat fuck Grange upstate. It was *your* goddamned idea, not mine," Dan snarls. His eyes bulge and look ruthlessly bloodshot. "And you didn't have the decency to tell me about it beforehand—"

"Because you'd have panicked if I had, Danny."

"*Bullshit.* You didn't trust me—your best fucking friend, your goddamned blood brother from the very beginning, from before either one of us can even fucking remember. You didn't trust me worth a damn. You just hinted at what you wanted to do while we sat in McLaughlin's back office waiting for Kenny and Grange to show up. And I was a schmuck—a fucking panty-waist because I just went along with you, with committing murder. I should've told you to fuck off as soon as I realized what was going down."

Danny's sweat-drenched face glistens in the morning light.

"Bullshit, *yourself*, kemosabe," Roddy hisses. "You knew what was going down as soon as we got on the West Side Highway. Even before then. As soon as Grange passed out from the Mickey Finn. Don't bullshit me. You fucking knew, Danny. And you didn't say *squat*."

"You're right, Roddy. And you know what? You know the *fuck* what? I shoulda told you to stop the goddamned car and turn around. I shoulda told you to head right the fuck back to Manhattan. But I didn't, because I'm a schmuck. Just a total schmuck. And if that didn't work, I shoulda told you to stop the car and let me the fuck out. I'da walked home . . . all the way back to Tuckahoe."

Danny sucks in a breath and then lets it out slowly.

"But I *didn't*. I just sat back like a goddamned wuss. I let you call all the shots, and now we're here, up to our lips in shit," Danny snarls and then coughs raucously. Mucous is building up in his chest. Roddy hears it rattling around; Danny could launch into a full-blown asthmatic attack. His neck veins bulge; his eyes close and his breath begins sounding like a punctured bellows. His face turns purple and looks congested. Looks like he's about to burst a blood vessel.

"So what're we now? Just what the fuck're we?" Danny gurgles through the phlegm. "Two assholes blaming each other for what happened. Let's face it; we're just a couple of murderers who left two corpses in the woods. And now whadda we have? A pack of goons're after us. And the cops're sniffin' around like we stink as bad as that shithole in the woods where we dumped those bastards. Jesus Christ, I'm such a fucking asshole." He shakes his head, moves his bulk in the chair, and winces again.

"So what was the alternative, Danny? Just pay up? Let that fat extortionist take us for five hundred K?"

"We wouldn't be here right now if we had."

"Danny, lemme ask you something."

"What?"

Roddy catches himself. If he asks Dan about a possible connection to Grange—if he even hints he's had thoughts that maybe Dan was in on Kenny's scheme—their friendship is down the drain. Gone. Forever. A momentary wave of guilt washes over him for even thinking it. Danny involved in the scheme with Grange and Kenny? It doesn't make a particle of sense; Kenny would've ratted Danny out the second Roddy held the .45 to his head at Snapper Pond.

I'm going back and forth and doubting everything. Am I going paranoid?

"So what the fuck you wanna ask me, Roddy?" Dan's eyes are wide. His face is flushed, still purple.

"You think Grange would've stopped at five hundred? You *really* think he wouldn't up the ante to a *million* or even more? He had a surgeon and an accountant on his fish line. Two Westchester candy-asses like us. You think he wouldn't've hooked on to us like a leech and bled us drier than a communion wafer, two Irish schnooks from Brooklyn? What's with you? What? Were you born yesterday? C'mon, Danny, you're a money guy. You know the world. It's a fuckin' cesspool—especially greedy pricks like Grange. The guy never saw a penny he didn't want in his own pocket. Not one fucking penny," Roddy whispers. "We did what we *had* to do and *now* we're in deep shit and we gotta do something."

"Yeah? Like what?" Danny whispers back through a mucous plug in his chest. "What're we gonna do, *tough* guy? Kill more people? And who the *fuck* are we gonna kill? What're we? Back in Brooklyn? Huh? Back in that shithole by Sheepshead Bay? You wanna know something, Roddy? I'm looking at you right now, right here today, and you know what? You look just like you did back then—like a goddamned mad dog. If I didn't know any better, I'd think we slipped back in some fuckin' time machine."

Danny snorts and exhales loudly. His nose starts running; clear liquid dribbles down from both nostrils.

"We gotta do something?" Danny says. "Like what? What the fuck're we gonna do? Huh? Who goes down *this* time? The Russian mafia? The fucking Italians? The Fontana brothers? Maybe John Gotti . . . oh, I forgot. He's already dead. How 'bout Vladimir fuckin' Putin? Huh? Maybe we can get to him. Why not the KGB? Or how 'bout the CIA? Jesus, let's face it. We're toast."

Roddy feels every blood vessel in his body overheating. A

momentary thought glimmers in his brain about Danny and the distance that's grown between them, how he gets the feeling Dan's been avoiding him. Jesus, it's so goddamned tempting to call him on it—to unload and let Danny know how he feels. But before he says anything, another thought comes to him: talking about their relationship right now is a useless diversion. It's a road trip to no place good. It's potentially more destructive than anything it might possibly reveal. And it'll solve nothing.

Roddy inhales deeply and lets the swirl of thoughts slow down. He feels the muscle tension begin dissipating in a system cooldown.

Keep your cool. Don't get sidetracked into accusatory cul-de-sacs that'll do nothing but flame resentment. Neither of you needs that right now. You need to be on the same page and figure this out.

"All I know, Danny, is this: soon as you're out of the hospital, you gotta get lost. Me, too. And we gotta convince Angie and Tracy to take the kids and leave."

"How're we gonna do that?"

"Let's dope it out."

"Yeah . . . for how long do we *vacate*?"

"Until we solve this thing," Roddy says, aware his heart rate is decelerating.

They fall quiet for a moment. Dan inhales deeply and seems to catch his breath. Roddy listens for squeaks or mucous coming from Dan's chest but hears nothing. The room seems very still.

"What're we gonna solve, Roddy?"

"We gotta learn who's coming after us and why."

"What about our practices?"

"You have people working for you. I have my partner. He'll cover for me."

"So what do we tell the girls?"

"C'mon, Dan, we're smart guys. We can figure something out."

"Yeah, like we figured out how to handle Grange and Kenny?"

A half hour later, Roddy sits in his car outside St. Joseph's Hospital. Workers are streaming into the place for the morning shift. It's nearly eight a.m. It's a work-a-day world. And he's not going to be part of it much longer. No, he's going to *vacate*.

The key is in the ignition, but Roddy doesn't turn it. He closes his eyes, and the strangest thing happens: it feels like he's back in the Sequoia—that huge, forest-green SUV with its rear storage area packed with shovels, a pick, his toolbox, plastic wrap, and that old army .45. Danny's sitting in the front passenger seat, to his right. They're on the West Side Highway heading north through Manhattan. Grange is in the backseat snoring like a boiler factory; Kenny's back there with him, wearing his maître d' tuxedo.

They'd hauled the loan shark's fat ass out to West 46th Street, where the Sequoia was parked. Roddy's thoughts fast-forward. In a moment, it feels like they're on the Taconic with its dark tree line on either side of the deserted parkway. Kenny's going through his insane, drug-fueled rant, punching the sleeping Grange, rifling through his pockets, grabbing his wallet, dumping it in the plastic bag Danny's holding open as he leans over the front seat. Kenny's screaming he wants to keep the shylock's Rolex, but Roddy tells him to drop it in the bag. Then Kenny's taking off Grange's belt and shoes, and tossing them out the window into the vegetation along the highway, only a few miles from Snapper Pond.

Yes, Danny knew exactly what they were going to do; Kenny certainly did. There's no doubt about it: from the moment Grange passed out after drinking the spiked scotch, it was clear they were gonna put him in the ground. Danny's just getting off on some self-serving bullshit—he's convinced himself he had no idea what was going down until it was too late.

But maybe Danny's right: maybe it was possible for them to have paid Grange off before the vig got too high. Maybe, just maybe, the bastard would've gone away, just disappeared like the ghost he claimed to be. Maybe things would be different now if Roddy hadn't been so quick to go mad dog and veer in a lethal direction. *If* . . . the biggest little word in the English language. You can change the entire course of world history by using the word *if*.

Don't kid yourself. Half a million would never've been enough for that loan shark. He'd've come back for more . . . and more after that.

Besides, it doesn't matter now. It's over and done. Now they have to come up with some plan of action. But what? What can they do except run and hide?

Roddy snaps himself back to the present. He presses the "Contacts" icon on his cell. He hits the number and hears the ringing at the other end. Roddy knows from their years together that his partner always answers his cell phone on the first tone.

"Yeah, Roddy, where are you?" says Ivan Snyder. "The guys in the OR are waiting for you."

"Ivan, you have a few minutes?"

"Yeah, sure. I'm between surgeries. But where *are* you?"

"Listen, Ivan. I have to leave town for a while. Have David do my surgeries today and for the duration. He's very good. I have complete confidence in him."

"For the *duration*? Whaddaya talkin' about?"

"Something personal. I have to leave."

"Now? We're busy as hell. I'm swamped. We have wall-to-wall patients. Our schedule is insane, and—"

"I know, Ivan, but I've got no choice."

"When will you be back?"

Roddy now realizes how tentative his life has become. He can't even answer the simple question about when he'll return. His throat closes off as he looks through the windshield at the hospital workers entering St. Joseph's.

"I don't know. I have to call hospital administration and tell them I'm taking a leave."

"A leave? You don't know when you'll be *back*? Hey, Roddy, we're running a busy practice here. I can't keep it going myself. I need to know when you'll be back."

"I wish I could give you a definite on that, Ivan, but I can't."

"Listen, we're already handing surgeries off to the Isler brothers. With you gone, our income's gonna plummet and I'll be overloaded. Sylvia and I are looking at some huge expenses these days. My kid's about to start college and . . . oh, forget that. I can't afford to cut back right now. What the hell's going on?"

"We'll straighten it all out when I get back."

"When you get *back*? And you don't even know when that is? What's going on?" There's a long pause. Roddy hears Ivan exhale loudly. "Listen, Roddy. I've been thinking for a while we have to take on a junior partner, and now this shit you're dumping in my lap . . ."

"Who do you like?"

"You already mentioned David. I know he's good."

"Sounds fine, Ivan. Do what you think is best." Roddy's foot taps a rapid tattoo on the Rogue's floorboard. He grips the steering wheel with one hand and pushes. He feels it bend forward.

There's silence on the other end. Roddy can almost hear Ivan's mental gears whirring.

"Roddy," Ivan says, his voice pitching higher, "I hate to sound so bottom line, but I can't afford this kind of thing. You're not gonna be around and you can't tell me how long you'll be away, and you force me to take on another surgeon now."

"Just lay it on the line, Ivan."

"I need some sort of accommodation from you."

"Whatever you want, partner," Roddy says, wanting to shut down Ivan's whining. Roddy feels brittle, as though he could explode with rage for what's happening to his life. "Feel free to cut my share. Or if you want, cut me out completely while I'm gone. Talk to David and get the papers signed. Get ahold of that lawyer we used back when we partnered up. Make some temporary arrangement, and I'll add my signature when I get back."

"When you get *back*? This is crazy."

"You have my complete authorization to make any arrangement you feel is best. When I get back, we'll work it all out."

"Roddy, what the hell's going on?"

"I can't tell you right now, Ivan, but do what you have to do."

"Roddy . . ."

"Just do it, Ivan. I'll be in touch when I get back."

Chapter 9

By nine fifteen in the morning, Roddy's back home. Tracy's left for the library at Sarah Lawrence and the kids are in school.

He walks around the empty house—through the living room with its stone fireplace, sofas, easy chair, and knickknacks. He enters the den with its microfiber-covered sofa, scattered newspapers and medical journals, chestnut beams, stucco walls, and mullioned casement windows. He plods through the kitchen, dining room, and then upstairs, where he peers into Sandy's and Tom's bedrooms.

Entering the master bedroom, he looks at the bed he and Tracy share. It looks so comforting, and it's filled with Tracy's warmth each morning as he lies next to her. God, how he loves this place. A pang of sadness assaults him as he realizes he'll be leaving very soon. Tracy and the kids will have to get to a safe place—maybe stay at her sister's house in Nutley. He wonders how on earth he'll convince her to do it without telling her the reason. But first he'll take care of a few things, which means among others, talking with the hospital administrator—Dr. Eve Barton—about a leave of absence. There, too, he'll be forced to fabricate some sort of story. Secrets and lies are what his life boils down to—again, after all these years.

Twenty minutes later, he's made the arrangements with the hospital, saying he'd be away for two weeks due to illness in the family. But will two weeks be enough time?

Roddy sinks down onto the living room sofa. He can't just sit around and wait for something to happen, as though he's a duck in a shooting gallery. He whips out his cell, scrolls through his contacts, and presses a speed dial number.

"Carmel Medical Associates," says the receptionist.

"Dr. Masconi, please."

"Who may I ask is calling?"

"Dr. Dolan, Rodney Dolan."

"Hold on, Doctor."

He waits, hearing Shakira singing "Hips Don't Lie." His foot starts that quick tapping, but it's not in time to the music. His insides hum. It's that tuning fork feeling, one he learned long ago is an internal signal of danger.

"Rodney," says a robust voice.

"Vincenzo . . ."

They always called each other by their formal names—jokingly—ever since meeting the first day of medical school, over a cadaver in the gross anatomy lab. Since then, they've kept loosely in touch. Maybe twice a year they get together with their wives at a restaurant somewhere in Westchester—halfway between Vinzy's place in the Bronx and Bronxville.

"How ya doin'?" Vinzy asks.

"Good, Vinzy. You?"

"Could always be better."

"Still taking care of the old Italians holding out on Arthur Avenue?"

"Yeah, but Medicare's cutting back. The patients are mostly Hispanic now . . . along with Eastern Europeans."

Roddy's reminded of what Morgan said about the Russians. *They're everywhere now.*

"What's up that has you calling this early on a workday?"

"I need a favor, Vinzy."

"Shoot," he hears Vinzy say and imagines him sitting at his desk with his stethoscope slung around his neck.

"Funny you should put it that way."

"Meaning?"

"Vinzy, I need a piece."

"Every doc should have one in the office, Roddy. I'm running a clinic and we're a prime target—you know, addicts and all that."

"You still have some connections in the community? Some of the old-timers? Friends of yours?"

Roddy knows Vinzy—with his checkered background and his uncles having been mob guys in the Italian section of the Bronx—won't ask questions. Prying isn't his style.

"A few. The old ones are dying off, but I know some people. When do you need it?"

"Today. That possible?"

"Hold on for a second, Roddy." Vinzy's voice grows faint as he turns from the phone and says, "Yeah, Marie. Get that blood work done stat." Then he's back. "Roddy, you know Arthur Avenue, don't you?"

"Yeah. Tracy and I shop there once in a while."

"Okay, on Arthur Avenue, one block north of my clinic, there's a cheese store. Actually, it's only a couple of doors down from Teitel Brothers. You know that place?"

"Of course."

"It's called Mario's Laticini. Old man Mario died a few years back, so now it's owned by a guy named Charlie. When you get there, ask for Charlie. He's usually in the back making mozzarella, and he can take care of you. I'll give him a call first and let him know you're coming. He's always there, so it won't be a problem. Probably set you back a bundle, in cash."

"Thanks, Vinzy. One other thing . . ."

"Yeah?"

"Can you find something out for me?"

"I can try."

"There's a guy named Grange . . . John M. Grange. A loan shark. A huge guy . . . must weigh three hundred pounds. Calls himself Ghost, if that's any help. Can you ask around? Anything you find out could be helpful."

"Lemme ask around. John Grange . . ."

There's a brief pause. "I'll make some calls and find out what I can. If you don't hear back from me in the next half hour, you're good to go with Charlie. But info on this guy Grange might take a while."

"Thanks, Vinzy. I owe you."

"I hope you're not gambling, Roddy."

"Na. It's for a friend. Not me."

"Yeah. I'll get back to you about this Grange guy if I learn anything."

Roddy leaves the municipal parking lot on Arthur Avenue. He scans the street, seeing a row of four-story brick-faced and clapboard buildings, each with a storefront on the ground floor. The street is the last vestige of a once-thriving Italian community in the Bronx. He heads north along the west side of Arthur Avenue, passing a meat market, a nail salon, a storefront dental office, and a row of Italian food specialty shops. He comes to a store with a green awning, Mario's Laticini.

Entering the store, Roddy is surprised: he's not assaulted by the pungent odor of aged cheeses. He realizes the place makes and sells fresh cheeses only—mozzarella, smoked mozzarella, ricotta, and ricotta salata, which he recalls eating at Danny's house. Angela's a great Italian cook.

A stout, middle-aged woman wearing a white apron smiles from behind the counter.

"Is Charlie here?" he asks.

"He's in the back, just finishing up," she says in heavily accented English, nodding her head at a set of doors. "Go straight back through there."

Roddy walks through swinging doors and finds himself in a good-sized kitchen. A short, rotund man in his midfifties stares at him. He has a closely cropped horseshoe-shaped fringe of hair on his scalp and a nose ending in a bulbous tip. His face is round and fleshy with huge hound-like dewlaps. Puffy, reddish-brown bags hang beneath his eyes. Reminds Roddy of the actor who played Clemenza in *The Godfather*. An apron covers his generous belly, beneath which he wears a white T-shirt that exposes thick arms and hairy forearms. His hands are in plastic gloves for kneading cheese. He rips the gloves off. On a nearby countertop are a few dozen freshly made balls of mozzarella sitting in water. "Can I help you?" he asks with a thick accent.

"I'm Roddy Dolan . . . and I'm told you're Charlie."

"Ah yes," Charlie says with a nod of his huge head. "Dr. Vincenzo said you'd be here. Just gimme a minute while you stay right here." Waddling, he carries a tray of smoked mozzarella to the front of the store. He returns a few moments later. "Dr. Vincenzo told me what you want. You come with me."

Charlie leads him through a door from the kitchen to a small rear office. He locks the door behind them. A solid-looking steel safe sits in one corner. Charlie bends down, turns the dial a few times, and opens the safe's door. Out comes a cloth-covered tray, which Charlie sets on an old wooden desk.

"You need this for whadda you call it . . . protection?"

"Exactly."

"You gotta choice," Charlie says, lifting the cloth.

Four handguns lie on the tray. Eyeing them, Roddy spots one that looks perfect. "May I?" he asks, pointing to the piece on the end.

"Yes, please. You take a look."

It's a snub-nosed revolver—a stainless-steel, matte-finished Taurus with a pebbled, black rubber grip—a .357 magnum that can also fire .38 slugs. Roddy likes the feel of it in his hand; its heft is perfect. The weapon balances in his palm, and there's plenty of room for his index finger to slip onto the trigger. It's a model 617SS2, a midweight piece that holds seven rounds—unusual for a revolver. It holds one extra shot—you never know what you'll need in a firefight, and that single shot can make a world of difference in a tight situation. It can be fired using either double or single action. He flips the cylinder open and sees it's empty—no bullets. He spins the cylinder; it has precision mobility. Good construction. He tests the cylinder-release lever. Sweet. And then the trigger action—smooth; not too much pressure needed to squeeze off a shot, so the pistol won't wiggle or move when the trigger is squeezed.

"Looks good. How much?"

"She's good at nine hundred."

"And bullets?"

"One box for you. She's a no cost."

"It's a deal." Roddy reaches into his pocket, takes out his wallet, and extracts nine one-hundred-dollar bills. He hands the wad over to Charlie.

Charlie opens the top desk drawer. "You wanna .38s or the magnums?"

"Magnums."

"She's all yours," he says, handing Roddy a heavy cardboard box. It's filled with Remington steel-jacketed hollow-point .357 magnum rounds. There are fifty in the container.

Just one slug will stop a man dead in his tracks.

"If you wanna know, she's clean."

Roddy nods.

"She's got no . . . how you say? She got no record."

Back home, Roddy decides to leave the revolver in the car. Tracy or the kids will never find it there. It's too risky to hide it anywhere in the house. Sitting on the living room sofa, he goes over what he and Danny discussed: getting Tracy, Angela, and the kids out of Bronxville and Tuckahoe. It'll be dicey, but there's no choice. He and Danny will be walking the fine line between tidbits of fact and a hastily fabricated pack of lies.

His cell rings. He checks the readout.

"Yeah, Vinzy."

"You got that equipment?"

"Got it. And thanks."

"I have some information for you."

Roddy's heart shoots into overdrive.

"Guy's an old-timer . . . a made man, if you know what I mean. He's associated with the Brunetti family on Staten Island. Real name's Gargano . . . John Gargano. He's pulled back on most of the action over the last few years, and he's not much of an active earner anymore, at least according to my uncle. I was told he has a habit of disappearing for months at a time. That's why he's nicknamed Ghost. Among other things, he was always heavy into loan-sharking."

Not a surprise. It fits with what happened ten months ago at McLaughlin's.

"Hasn't been around for a while, but that's not unusual for this guy. Rumor is he may've gone into WITSEC."

"The Witness Protection Program?"

"Yeah, but my uncle doubts it. Truth is, with these old-timers, you never know. Some go to Italy to live out their years. Others go to Boca or Vegas, Costa Rica or the Caymans."

"Any real chance he went to Witness Protection?"

"Not according to my uncle. That's always a floating rumor when a guy doesn't show his face for a long time. My uncle said there're some people who think he might've been clipped."

Roddy feels his pulse ramp to NASCAR speed. If any of the Brunetti associates knew Grange was meeting them at the restaurant the night he disappeared, it could explain why Danny got shot and why they're gunning for him, too. The mob never lets a made man's death go unanswered.

"Any word about that?"

"About what?"

"Whether he was clipped."

"No. My uncle couldn't say anything more. Just that the guy's friends are looking into things. They're . . . how should I say it? Asking around."

Chapter 10

It feels strange driving around Bronxville and Yonkers with a loaded revolver in the Rogue's storage console. The ride from home to St. Joe's was nightmarish. He glanced in the rearview mirror every few moments, thinking he saw a dark Lincoln Navigator behind him. His skin prickled and he lifted the lid of the console, just to be safe. When the SUV pulled alongside him at a traffic light, it was a Cadillac Escalade driven by a woman with two kids and a dog in the back.

It's now four in the afternoon. Roddy walks along the corridor to Dan's room at St. Joseph's.

"Hey, Doc," a familiar voice calls.

He turns and sees Morgan.

"Glad to see you're here," Morgan says. "Saves me a trip to Lawrence Hospital."

"What do you want to talk about?" Roddy stifles the urge to shake his head and sound exasperated. No matter how casual he wants to appear, he can't stop blinking his eyes. And he feels the blood drain from his face.

"I have news for you, but let's talk in private," Morgan says, heading toward a lounge area.

They enter a room furnished with functional-looking chairs. A wall-mounted flat-screen television is muted. A lone patient in pajamas sits next to an IV pole on wheels. "Do you think we can talk in private?" Morgan asks the guy and flashes his badge.

The man nods, gets up, and wheels his pole out of the lounge.

"So what's this news?" Roddy asks, trying to appear unruffled.

Just take it easy, like you were taught in the Rangers. Interrogation techniques can vary slightly, but they're all basically the same everywhere. Just stay cool and look calm.

"The ballistics report just came in." Morgan waits a couple of beats, obviously gauging Roddy's reaction. Roddy feels his face tighten, but he tries to stay loose and maintain steady eye contact. An electrically wired feeling ramps through his body. He feels an urge to stand, to do anything besides sit and wait for Morgan to drop a bomb on him.

"Turns out, Doc, the slugs that killed Dr. McKay were fired from the same pistol used to shoot your friend, Daniel Burns."

It feels like a sledgehammer slams into his chest. The room looks bleached, and Roddy feels light-headed. If he stands now, the lounge will spin. He could keel over in a dead faint.

"It's something to think about, isn't it, Doc?" Morgan's eyebrows form bushy arches above his eyes.

Roddy shakes his head. He feels like he's choking and tries to catch his breath. His thoughts race wildly, and he's certain he's marinating in sweat. He catches a whiff of Morgan's cologne and feels a twinge of nausea.

"What can you tell me in light of this development?"

Roddy's mind launches into a hyperkinetic storm. *Who's coming after us? Is it Grange's people? Or the Russians? Where can we go? What do we do next? Danny's still in the hospital, and I haven't even told Tracy we have to leave Bronxville.* Morgan's words barely seep through a field of static, like a vague ribbon of sound.

"Huh," Roddy hears himself say.

"I asked you, what else do you know about your friend getting shot?"

"I don't really . . . I don't . . ." Roddy's tongue feels thick, and he struggles to get words out.

"Doc, are you hearing a word I'm saying? Maybe you're a little rattled right now, huh?"

"I . . . I don't know what to tell you, Detective," Roddy says through a wad of phlegm. He knows he's barely hearing Morgan.

"Doc?"

"Yeah?"

"You listening to me?"

"I'm listening."

But he's flipping through his mental file cabinet, trying to process a cascade of jumbled thoughts, one on top of another, each intruding on the other in lightning succession.

"So you're sure you don't know a *thing* about the attempt on Mr. Burns or the hit on Dr. McKay?"

Roddy can barely maintain eye contact, but he doesn't look away or even blink. That would be what the cops call a tell.

Roddy says nothing. *Yes, the less said the better right now. Just take it in, look casual, as though it's no big deal.*

"You wanna know what else we learned about the McKay shooting?"

"What?"

"You know the garage has CCTV cameras all over, right?"

"I assume so."

Jesus, is there a video of me turning away after seeing those guys waiting at the Navigator the night before Walt was shot?

"And these days it's all on a chip. You just punch in the date, and up comes that day's video. Then you just enter the time and up it comes."

Roddy nods. His pulse thuds heavily in his neck.

"So, the video record shows exactly what happened."

Nodding his head, Roddy stares straight into Morgan's eyes.

"It shows McKay approaching his car as a 2003 Chevy Impala moves up behind him. He apparently hears the vehicle, glances back for a second, and waves his keys in the air, thinking the guy wants his spot. Two men are sitting in the front and one is in the back, on the driver's side. Turns out the car was stolen, so the plates don't tell us a thing—and as it pulls up alongside McKay, the left rear window slides down and a hand holding a pistol pokes out. The thing has a sound suppressor fixed at the end. A shot's fired and McKay goes down like a sack of potatoes."

Nausea rises from Roddy's stomach as an image of Walt lying on the concrete floor comes back to him—the overcoat spread on the concrete, Walt lying on his belly, face to one side, the small hole in his head. The blood, the exhaust fumes, cold air, the squealing tires from the level below . . . it's all a sickening flash in Roddy's head.

"Using the video record, we tracked the car coming into the garage," Morgan says. "It came in through the south entrance soon after McKay entered the garage. It's clear he was being followed. Maybe *stalked* is the right word. They probably had someone in the hospital watching and most likely communicated by cell phone. After McKay goes down, the car takes off like a bat outta hell. There's no clear view of the occupants, but they appear to be three white men. There's not much else to go on. It was a hit, pure and simple."

Roddy tries not to grimace; he wants his face to be like a mask. To move a single muscle would be a tell—a sign the detective has zapped a raw nerve. He peers at Morgan as hissing begins in his ears.

"But you know what, Doc? There's something else that's interesting."

Morgan waits.

"Tell me," Roddy says as his mouth goes dry.

"You must've noticed it. After all, you discovered the body. McKay was wearing green surgical scrubs, just like *you* were. And clogs, too . . . like you wore after getting out of the OR."

Morgan peers deeply into Roddy's eyes. "But the really interesting thing, Doc, is that McKay kinda looks like you. I don't mean his features, but his build. You two could've come outta the same mold. What're you, Doc, about six two?"

"Six one," Roddy says, feeling he'll cringe in a moment.

"And you weigh in at a good two hundred pounds, maybe a bit more, right?"

"Two ten."

"That's just about what McKay weighed before he took one to the brain. So from a distance, and certainly from behind, it looks like they took him for you. Nearly the same height and weight, an athletic-looking guy, with light brown, blondish hair. A fairly close match, don't you think? And it makes even more sense since you both were leaving the hospital at the same time. Whadda you think, Doc?"

Roddy's thoughts whirl in a dozen directions, and he struggles to stay on track with Morgan.

"Look, Detective . . . I don't . . . I mean . . ."

"And there's something else. McKay's car was parked right next to yours—a gray Nissan Rogue, correct?"

Roddy nods as bile threatens to crawl up his gullet, where it'll burn the back of his throat. He tries to swallow, but there's no saliva.

"So, since they're clearly related, is there anything you can tell me now about the Burns or McKay shootings?"

"Detective, I don't know what you want me to say."

"Listen, Doc, you gotta be worried that what happened to Burns is gonna happen to you. The guys who killed McKay were gunning for you, right?"

"I have . . ." He shakes his head. "I have no idea, Detective."

Gurgling comes from Roddy's guts. They're in full-blown rebellion, squirming and rolling over on themselves. He shifts in the chair, trying to smother the sounds.

"Let's stop playing games, Doc. You telling me you don't know a thing about what happened to Burns or McKay? McKay, a guy who's the same height and weight as you? A guy dressed in scrubs like you, who walks outta the hospital half a minute before you? A guy who works with you and whose car is parked right next to yours? And he's shot by the same gun used to shoot *your best friend*? Is *that* what you're tellin' me?"

"Detective, I have no idea."

"Don't bullshit me, Dolan."

"I don't get it. Why're you questioning me like I'm some kind of suspect?"

"Because you're a material witness."

"What did I witness?"

"You aren't a lawyer, that's for sure, Doc. A material witness is simply a person who has information about a criminal matter."

"I don't have any information."

A zinc-like taste forms on Roddy's tongue. His mouth fills with thick paste.

"I don't believe you."

Roddy sighs.

"You know a helluva lot more than you're lettin' on, Doc."

Something ignites inside Roddy. He feels an insane urge to get in Morgan's face, to stand up and shoot a quick fist into his gut. And then launch a powerhouse uppercut to his jaw. *Shit. I'm thinking like I'm seventeen again, back in Brooklyn—before the army, when I turned my life around. Everything's circling the drain. I'm headed back to the tar pits of my past. Jesus, I even have a gun now.*

Roddy shoots up from the chair. "I have things to do, Detective. So, if you don't have any more questions, I'm leaving."

"One more, Doc."

"What's that?"

"Don't you feel bad for Dr. McKay and his family? Poor guy's dead; his wife's a widow, and his kids are fatherless. Don't you feel a goddamned thing for these people?"

"Don't try pulling a guilt trip on me. Of course I feel awful about it. Walt and I worked together, and I liked him. I feel terribly for his family . . . more than you can know." Roddy's face feels hot, flushed. "But nothing's gonna bring Walt McKay back, and I can't tell you anything that'd help with the case."

"Well, Doc, one last question," Morgan says, standing. He moves a step closer to Roddy. The detective's eyes are intense, unblinking. They're only a few inches apart. Roddy holds his stare, though it feels like the mad dog wants to burst out of him.

"Yeah?"

"What're you gonna do when they come for you? And what're you gonna do when they come for your wife and kids?"

Chapter 11

The kids are upstairs in their rooms. Dinner was over a while ago, and the dishwasher is going through its last cycle. Sitting with Tracy in the den, Roddy feels his throat closing off, but he knows he must start explaining some things now. He'll be serving up a medley of half-truths and distortions, and all the while, he has a revolver in the console of his car.

"Trace, we need to talk about something."

She looks up from the American Library Association newsletter. Her green eyes glitter in the glow of the gas-lit fireplace. Her honey-blond hair is pulled back in the ponytail he's adored since the first moment he saw her. Her eyebrows arch as she leans forward. "About what, Roddy?"

"About what happened to Danny," he says, as tension builds in his legs. He feels like he wants to move them, but he doesn't want to look as nervous as he feels.

Her lips part as though she's about to say something, but she remains silent.

"Danny's getting shot may have something to do with McLaughlin's."

Her breath sucks inward in a near gasp. Her eyes widen and she stares at him. "Roddy, what are you saying?"

"It may be related to what happened with Kenny."

"Kenny? Kenny Egan? Isn't he in Las Vegas?"

"We don't know where he is, Tracy."

She blinks repeatedly. "But . . . but you told me after the restaurant closed, Kenny went back to Vegas." Her eyes look wider than he's ever seen them. Her fingers begin trembling.

"The truth is, we assumed he did, but I don't . . . we don't really know." It feels as though gauze covers his tongue, and his throat closes.

"I don't understand. What does Kenny have to do with Danny being shot?"

"I'm not sure it does, but I can't take a chance."

"Take a chance? What are you *talking* about?" Tracy's hand goes to her chin. The newsletter drops to the floor.

"Listen, Trace, I didn't tell you everything."

Her chest heaves and her eyes narrow into slits. "Okay, Roddy, what happened?"

"You know the restaurant was losing money."

"Yes. Kenny was mismanaging it."

"And we got out. We—"

"I know all this, Roddy." Her foot begins tapping on the carpet.

"Well, there's more to it than I told you."

"There's *more*? Okay, Roddy, tell me." She leans forward and stares intently.

"The truth is, after the restaurant closed, Kenny disappeared."

"*Disappeared*?" Tracy's head shakes imperceptibly from side to side. Her eyes grow wide.

"Yes. He vanished."

She blinks a few times. Her lips form a severe line. Her face reddens. "Why did you tell me he'd gone to Vegas?" There's more blinking; her mouth drops open.

"Because I had no idea where he was, and I couldn't imagine where else he'd go."

She stares at him and then looks off to the side as though she's focused on some distant object. She turns her head and exhales.

"People don't just disappear, Roddy. These days, anyone's traceable. He *can't* be unreachable."

"Honey, believe me, Kenny vanished."

Her eyes look hard and steely, and her chest heaves. She lets out a breath and says, "Okay, Roddy, so why are you telling me this *now*?"

"Tracy, you remember last April, that night when I went into the city to meet with Kenny and Danny, when we decided to end the partnership?"

"And . . ."

His thoughts stream recklessly as he searches for words; he tries sorting them into some linear progression.

"And *what*, Roddy?"

"We discussed ending the partnership. Kenny was upset, but he understood why we were pulling out. Afterward, he had a headache. So we drove him back to his apartment, but he wanted to stop at a pharmacy. Dan and I headed to Yonkers . . . to his office to talk about the tax implications of the whole thing. You remember that night, don't you? I left you a note telling you not to wait up for me."

"Yes, I recall," she murmurs.

"Well, the next day, Kenny didn't show up for work."

"Uh-huh."

"And he never showed up again."

Tracy squints. "What do you mean, 'He never showed up again'?"

"No one ever heard from him again. And you know that McLaughlin exercised his lien and foreclosed on the restaurant."

"I know all this. But why didn't you tell me about Kenny's disappearing?" She leans forward and tilts her head.

"Well . . ."

"And what does this have to do with Danny getting shot a few nights ago?"

Roddy feels an inner trembling. He hopes Tracy doesn't notice how jumpy he feels or how high-pitched his voice sounds.

"Okay, Trace," he says, wondering how he'll get through this minefield of half-truths and evasions. "Danny called Kenny, and so did Omar, the maître d', probably a dozen times, but we never heard back. Eventually, we notified the New York City police."

"And," she says with her lower lip protruding.

"They got into his apartment and discovered some things."

"What things?"

"It was disturbing."

"C'mon, Roddy, just *tell* me." Tracy's lips now form a thin line. She crosses her arms in front of her chest.

"Apparently, Kenny was doing drugs. But more important, there were messages on his voice mail from guys who the police say were involved in mob activities."

Roddy sees her intake of breath, and Tracy's face blanches. She leans forward on the sofa and her hands clasp around her knees. Her knuckles look white.

"Mob activities?"

"Yes, gambling."

"How do you know all this?"

"Danny and I went to the head of the Missing Persons Squad in Manhattan."

"You went to the New York police and I'm first hearing about this *now*?" She shakes her head. And blinks rapidly.

"Because I didn't want to—"

"How does this involve Danny getting *shot*?"

"I don't know for sure, but Kenny must've owed the wrong people money because the messages on his voice mail weren't friendly."

"Roddy?" Tracy's hand shoots to her mouth.

"Captain Greene told us gamblers like Kenny can get into trouble. He wondered if Kenny might have been killed."

Tracy gasps.

"And now it's possible the mob might be after Danny and me."

Tracy's irises look lost in a sea of white. She leans back on the couch, as though she's repelled and wants to distance herself from Roddy.

"*Why*? Why would they come after you?"

"I don't know. But since we were Kenny's partners . . ."

Tracy's hands begin shaking. "You waited until *now* to tell me this?"

"I didn't want to worry you."

"And now? *Now* I can worry?"

"No, but—"

She crosses one leg over the other and leans forward. She clutches herself with her arms crossing her chest. "But *what*, Roddy? What's going on?" Her posture stiffens, as though she might leap from the sofa.

"I don't know exactly, maybe. Listen, honey, the only thing I care about is you and the kids."

"Meaning what, Roddy?"

"Meaning . . . I'm not sure you should stay here anymore."

"*What*?" She shoots to her feet. She crosses her arms and paces a short distance away. She whirls and faces him. Her mouth drops open.

He gets up, moves to her, and takes her hand. "I think maybe you and the kids should stay at your sister's house in Nutley. Just for a little while."

God, I sound so tentative . . . so unnerved.

She yanks her hand out of his and moves away. "Roddy," she says as her eyes bore into him. "You're telling me Danny may have been shot by people who're after both of you . . . people who may've *killed* Kenny? You're telling me you learned about Kenny disappearing almost a *year* ago, and you said nothing to *me*? And now . . . now you're saying that maybe the kids and I could be in *danger*? Because of what? Some people from some mob? Are you *serious*? And you're first telling me all this *now* . . . after Danny's been shot?"

"Trace, I didn't want to—"

"You didn't want to *what*, Roddy?" Her face reddens. "You didn't want to tell your wife that we could all be killed because of Kenny Egan . . . who's now *dead* because he owed money to some mob?"

"We don't know for sure that Kenny's dead."

Her mouth hangs open. "You don't know for *sure*? But you *think* he's dead? How . . . how could you *do* this?"

"I didn't want you to worry . . . to be involved."

"How could I not be involved? I'm your *wife!*" Her face is frozen in an expression of disbelief. "Have you told me everything, Roddy?"

"Yes," he says, nearly cringing at his lie.

"Absolutely *everything*?"

"Yes, honey, I have." He can barely tolerate his own voice.

Tracy resumes pacing. She brushes back a lock of hair from her forehead. "This is unbelievable, completely beyond anything I could have imagined. I don't know what . . . I just can't . . . Who have I been married to all these years? Just who *are* you?" She stops pacing and turns back to him.

"Trace . . ." He reaches for her.

"No, Roddy . . . *no*." She steps back, trembling. Her eyes are wet, and her eyeliner looks smudged. "Do you trust me?"

"Of course I do."

"Do you? Do you *really* trust me?"

"Trace, I trust you and love you, more than—"

"Roddy, do you trust *anyone*?"

"Please, Tracy, let's be sensible."

"How could you not tell me all this?" Tears drip down her face.

He reaches for her again, but she backs away.

"Honey, I figured—"

"What did you figure, Roddy? Just what were you thinking?"

He stands there, nearly paralytic, feeling his life shredding apart. And he's weaving a web of lies and deception. His mouth opens, but there are no words; there's nothing he can say.

"Roddy," she says, crossing her arms in front of her and shaking her head from side to side, "what am I to you?" She peers into his eyes.

"Honey, you're my wife, and I love you more—"

"Okay, so you love me. But do you *trust* me?"

"Of course I do."

"*Of course you do*? But you tell me nothing. There are men out there . . . men with guns. Danny—your best friend since you were maybe two years old—is in the hospital after he's been shot. You've known about this Kenny Egan thing for almost a year and you kept it a *secret* from me?"

Roddy's legs feel as though they're going watery. He moves to the sofa and plops down.

"You've put our *children* in danger. Now you're telling us we have to leave this house, our home, and you're afraid for your life and our lives? And you told me *nothing* until now?"

"Tracy, I didn't—"

She moves toward him with her eyes flashing. Her arms are still crossed and she's trembling. "Look, Roddy, I know you had a miserable childhood. I understand all about your mother and father and how your mother's lousy boyfriend, Horst, beat you. I know all about the old neighborhood and how tough it was. I get it. But there are limits.

"We've been married for fifteen years; we have two kids. We built what I *thought* was a good life—a solid marriage, a lovely home and family life. But it's . . . it's very clear that you don't trust me. You don't *really* trust me . . . your own wife. I don't know if you can trust *anyone*."

She turns and begins pacing again with her arms still crossed in front of her, as though she's clutching herself to keep her insides from falling out. "You just can't believe that someone can love you and care for you and be on your side no matter what, can you?" She stands stock-still for a moment and then shakes her head as tears stream in narrow runnels down her cheeks. "You just don't really trust me."

"Tracy, that's not true. I—"

"Roddy, trust is the foundation of a marriage. My God, after all we've been through together, struggling to make ends meet, working and living together, having children, making a good life and . . . and . . . it boils down to *this*?"

It's probably an hour later. Roddy finds himself in the den, then the living room, and at some point, goes upstairs. He hears Sandy crying and knows Tracy's told the kids they're leaving for Nutley first thing in the morning to live with Aunt Colleen and their cousins. He knows he's talked with the kids, but it all seems blurred and remote—lost in a haze of dread and regret. Drawers open and shut as Tracy prepares for their departure.

Roddy's now in the kitchen while Tracy is back in the den; he hears her on the telephone. She's talking with her sister, Colleen. "I can't worry about school right now," she says. "Maybe I'll register them in Nutley. We'll be at your place by nine."

She makes a few more calls: her supervisor at the library, one of her coworkers, a neighbor—the mail will be picked up so it doesn't collect in the box—a couple more, one after another.

Roddy nearly collapses on the living room couch. Everything in their lives is crumbling. Tracy's still on the telephone. He hears her from the den.

"It's hard to believe, Angie. And they didn't say a word about it."

There's a pause.

"I've noticed it, too."

"Yes . . . there's been a change in their relationship."

"I think we've only gotten together twice since then. And I don't hear Roddy talk about Danny anymore."

More silence as Tracy listens.

"Where in Riverdale, your brother's place? I'll be at Colleen's."

There's no doubt about it: Danny's grown distant since it all went down. Is it that Danny's afraid he might say the wrong thing if they're all together—that he'll let something slip, especially after a few glasses of wine? Or is Danny avoiding him because he's ashamed he didn't look into Kenny's finances carefully enough?

Or is it something less benign?

Roddy again wonders if Danny knew something about Kenny's shady dealings. But it's ridiculous to think Danny was involved with Grange—or Gargano, that missing mobster.

But when it comes to people and money and greed, you never know. When money is at stake, plenty of people lose their sanity. They no longer act rationally.

You just can't know what drives people to do what they do in this world.

Chapter 12

Roddy watches Tracy and the kids walk toward her Honda. He stands on the front lawn as Tracy opens the trunk, sets their suitcases inside, and lowers the lid. She wouldn't even let Roddy carry them out to the car. And she hasn't made eye contact with Roddy this morning. Sandy turns suddenly and dashes toward Roddy. He spreads his arms, swallowing hard to get rid of the lump forming in his throat.

"I don't want to live in New Jersey," Sandy blubbers, throwing her arms around his waist.

"It's only for a few days, sweetie," Roddy says, kneeling down. He looks at Tracy, who stares at him. Her eyes have a cold, intense look.

"But I have school and my friends."

"Mom will call school when you get to Nutley," he says. "She'll take care of everything. And you'll be back here very soon. I promise."

Tracy walks toward them and takes Sandy's hand. "C'mon, we have to go," she says, glancing at Roddy. Her look says it all: *I'll never forgive you for this.*

Tom gets in the backseat, looking sullen. He says nothing.

Roddy stands on the lawn, watching Tracy's car pull away. He tries sorting out his feelings but cannot. He only knows his world is darkening.

An hour later, Roddy is in a Stop & Shop and purchases two disposable cell phones. The irony of it all isn't lost on him: it's the same supermarket where he bought a disposable cell to call Grange when he set up the meeting at McLaughlin's. The night they killed him and Kenny. The night that led to this moment.

Driving to St. Joseph's Hospital, he takes the Cross County Parkway and gets off at exit 3; he gets onto Yonkers Avenue. He drives to Nepperhan Avenue and heads west toward South Broadway. He drives with one eye on the road and the other in the rearview mirror.

Roddy switches lanes. A few moments later, he spots a black Navigator changing lanes. It's now three cars behind. It looks exactly like the vehicle parked in the garage the night he saw the men waiting there. A flash image of Walt McKay comes to Roddy. His hands tighten on the steering wheel and begin cramping. He loosens his grip.

Roddy cruises into the right lane and peers into the mirror. The Navigator stays in the middle lane—keeping a safe distance. It's still three cars behind. He suddenly realizes the streets are filled with dark-colored SUVs—Navigators, Escalades, Pathfinders, and Land Cruisers—all looking similar. Could he be seizing on any vehicle that looks like the one he saw in the garage? Is he being followed, or is he just too wired and suspicious?

He stops at a traffic light and glances in the rearview mirror. The low winter sun glares off the Navigator's windshield, and he can't make out the occupants. He peers into the driver's side mirror but can't get a better look. Still no view of the vehicle's interior. The Navigator stays three cars behind him.

The light changes; he pulls ahead and makes a left onto South Broadway, heading toward the hospital. He could swerve and make a sudden turn without signaling and then take a circuitous route—try losing the Navigator—but Roddy decides he won't play cat and mouse. It's not the way to go. He won't let himself act like prey. In the Rangers, the emphasis was on stealth and offense—to combine them whenever possible. It's far better to be the hunter than the hunted. Yes, be a predator. He won't be another Walt McKay and let them come up behind him for a kill.

Roddy moves the Rogue to the middle lane. He glances in the mirror again. The Navigator shifts to the right lane. It hangs back, leaving a good distance between them. Roddy slows down, just to see if the Navigator pulls alongside him. It hangs back.

No other vehicle is in front of the Navigator. Roddy's certain it will pull alongside him—on his right side—at the next red light. That's when a shot will be fired, just as it happened with Walt McKay. Roddy presses the lever for the passenger's side window; it lowers. He raises the console cover and lets it stand upright between the front seats.

Approaching a red light, Roddy slows, reaches into the console, and lifts the revolver. He doesn't recall it being so heavy. He places it on the passenger's seat as his Rogue rolls slowly to the red light, where he stops.

The Navigator slows as it approaches on his right side. Roddy glances in his rearview mirror: the SUV is virtually crawling up on his right. Roddy is certain something will happen when it's alongside him—a window will slide down and a pistol will protrude.

Roddy grips the revolver's rubber handle and waits for the vehicle to pull up next to him. He turns his head slightly to the right but avoids a full turn of his neck. He raises the pistol and waits.

The front end of the Navigator is at his right rear. It moves forward—so slowly it seems to be barely moving. Roddy's heart rate accelerates. The Navigator's hood is adjacent to the Rogue's passenger door.

Roddy's got the pistol ready. He cocks the hammer. It clicks and locks into position.

The Navigator inches forward. Roddy raises the pistol—it

floats upward, easily and steadily. He holds it against the passenger seat back so the men in the Navigator won't see it. His entire body stiffens. The pistol is level and unwavering in his hand. His finger is curled around the trigger.

The Navigator rolls so slowly, it's agonizing.

Roddy waits, ignoring the flogging beat of his heart. The Navigator doesn't have darkened windows. He'll be able to spot whoever's inside. The vehicle rolls forward and aligns itself with the Rogue.

The driver's window is lowered. The guy behind the wheel is about thirty years old with dark, closely cropped hair, a few days' growth of beard, and rough-hewn features. He could be Italian, Russian, Albanian, virtually any ethnicity. Roddy won't hesitate; he'll pump round after round into the Navigator—shooting the driver and whoever's in the rear seat.

Roddy draws a bead on the driver's left ear. His eyes flit to the rear of the Navigator. No passengers. The driver's alone. He turns his head slowly toward Roddy. Without blinking or flinching, he stares coldly at Roddy. The revolver points at his face but seems to make no impression on him; the man's look is steely, and his dark eyes show no fear.

Roddy holds the revolver on him. He has a bead on the spot between the man's eyes. The guy's hands are on the Navigator's steering wheel; he stares directly into Roddy's eyes.

The guy's eyes shift to the gun pointing at his face. Very slowly, he raises his right hand from the steering wheel. It rotates in Roddy's direction. With his thumb and forefinger, the man makes the sign of a gun and points it directly at Roddy. He holds his hand steadily in position; he never wavers; he doesn't blink, just stares at Roddy. He makes a clicking sound with his tongue, as though he's firing a weapon. A moment later, he turns back, sets his right hand on the steering wheel, and looks straight ahead.

When the light changes, the guy hits the gas pedal. The Navigator peels away and makes a sharp turn from the right-turn-only lane. Roddy tries to follow him, but a parade of cars in the right lane prevents him from moving into that lane and turning. By the time the last car turns into the street, it's too late. The Navigator is far ahead with at least ten cars separating them.

Horns blare behind him. Roddy steps on the gas, and the Rogue leaps forward. Roddy clutches the steering wheel tightly. He suddenly feels weak, depleted.

It's the drained feeling after an adrenaline surge.

A block farther on South Broadway, he sets the pistol inside the console. At that moment, Roddy realizes he can't drive the Rogue anymore. They know his car from the garage and a skilled bomb maker would need only a few minutes to install an explosive device and detonator.

Walking toward Danny's room, Roddy half expects Morgan to pop out of a doorway, but there's no sign of the detective.

The door to Dan's room is closed, so he knocks.

"Come in," he hears Dan call.

Entering the room, Roddy sees Dan in bed with the head of the bed raised at a forty-five-degree angle. A man stands at the bedside. Roddy thinks it's probably another detective. But as he approaches and gets a closer look, Roddy knows instantly the guy's a civilian. He's probably in his midfifties and is wearing a charcoal-colored, herringbone chesterfield coat draped over a dark blue suit that looks custom made. Truly top-shelf threads. Between the suit and coat, Roddy estimates the guy sports at least $5,000 of cloth on his back.

"Roddy Dolan, this is John Harris," Dan says. "I've mentioned you to each other and you finally get to meet."

Roddy extends his hand. Harris's is cold, and his handshake is a fraction removed from dead flounder-limp.

"Dr. Dolan," Harris says. "Dan talked about you when you fellows were partners in the restaurant. He said you might be interested in some real estate investments in Westchester County."

Roddy does his best to smile and says, "I don't think so." Based on Harris's threads and patrician look, Roddy has the distinct feeling Harris views him—and Danny, too—as working-class stiffs, their professions notwithstanding.

Another investment? No way.

Harris turns to Danny and says, "So don't worry about a thing, Dan. The Aruba deal's on hold. We won't be moving ahead on it, so don't even think about it right now." Harris glances at his watch. "I've got something to attend to, so, Dan, just get better and get out of here."

"I'll probably be discharged tomorrow or the next day."

"And we'll get together and talk about some other properties," Harris adds.

"Sure."

"And enjoy the truffles," he says, pointing to a box on the bedside table. Harris looks toward the door, but then turns to Roddy. "Ever taste these?" he asks. "They're Teuscher . . . the best truffles in the world. You can't get them just anywhere, you know."

"Really?"

"Not at all. I order them from their 5th Avenue store at Rockefeller Center."

Roddy nods and tries to keep from shooting Danny a caustic smile.

"They're sublime, especially with a Château Margaux . . . or any fine Bordeaux, for that matter. Or with a Côte de Beaune like a Puligny-Montrachet. They're heavenly."

Roddy thinks, *A fucking wine snob.*

"Well, I've got to be going," Harris says, again eyeing his wristwatch. "I have the jet waiting at Westchester Airport. Have to look at some houses in Palm Beach, but I'll be back in a few days. Give me a call, Dan, when you feel ready to get back to work on those Westchester properties. And don't worry. That Aruba deal's not working out, so I'm dropping it."

He turns to Roddy. "Nice meeting you, Dr. Dolan. You might want to think about putting a few dollars into a property I'm developing in Ardsley . . . an assisted-living facility. You know, the baby boomers are getting old and these facilities are the wave of the future."

Roddy nods, doing his best not to roll his eyeballs upward.

Harris glances again at Dan and heads for the door.

Roddy watches as he leaves the room and walks down the corridor. When Roddy turns back, he sees Dan has his eyes closed. His head shakes back and forth.

"I know. I know. Don't say it," Danny mutters as he shakes his head.

"Say what?"

"What a blowhard he is."

"I didn't say a word."

"Yeah, yeah, I know what you're thinking."

"That's because you're thinking the same thing," Roddy says with a grin. "The guy's pretty full of himself, and he's a braggart."

Danny shrugs. "He's an okay guy."

"You're damning him with faint praise, Dan." Roddy pulls over a chair and sits down.

"Look, he came here to visit and brought me something . . . *personally*," Dan says, waving at the box of truffles. "Everyone else just sent flowers or cards, but the guy made a trip to fucking Yonkers."

"That's stepping down in the world for him."

Dan chortles and nods.

"He's the real estate big shot you took to the restaurant when it was still alive, right?"

"Yeah," Dan says. "I had lunch with him a few times, and now I do some work for him. He means well and, actually, I've gotten used to him."

"So how're you feeling?"

"Better. A *lot* better. Ketchman says I could be getting outta here tomorrow."

"Know where you're going?"

"I'll know by tonight. I'll keep you posted. How 'bout you?"

"I'm not sure yet. When I find a place, I'll call you." Roddy reaches into his pocket and hands Dan a prepaid cell. "Use this to call me. My number's taped to the back."

"Tracy and the kids leave yet?"

"Yeah, this morning," Roddy says as a lump forms in his throat. "How about Angie and the kids?"

Danny sighs. "They're in Riverdale. Jesus, I can't believe it's come to this."

"It's a fucked-up situation, Dan."

Danny tosses his bedcovers aside, gets up with a wince, and pads over to a nearby chair.

"Look, Dan, I want to apologize for saying what I did about looking into Kenny's finances. I was out of line."

"Forget it. I owe you an apology for the shit I threw at you."

"I wasn't thinking right, Dan. I'm sorry."

"Forget it. It's water under the bridge."

"Okay. Enough said. Apologies accepted all around, right?"

"Right, kemosabe."

"So we gotta figure a way out of this thing."

"Figure what? Just what the fuck are we gonna figure? Some bastards are after us, and we don't even know who they are. And we—"

"Excuse me, gentlemen," a voice says.

Roddy looks up and sees Morgan—all six foot four of him in the doorway.

"Did I interrupt anything important?" Morgan says, stepping into the room.

Roddy's insides jump. His mouth goes dry.

"I see you guys are in conference," Morgan says, entering the room. "A little powwow, huh?"

"What's up, Detective?" Danny says. His voice is even. Roddy doesn't detect any warbling—the vocal betrayer—one of Dan's giveaways.

"I was just going," Roddy says, standing.

"So soon, Doc? Why not stay a while and we can have a three-way chat?" He smiles enigmatically, and then turns to Danny. "You're looking a lot better than the last time I saw you."

"Yeah. Only the hand hurts."

Morgan nods and sits in the chair Roddy vacated. "Yeah, a busted-up hand's gonna take time. How long you gotta wear that cast?"

"At least six weeks."

Roddy can barely keep from moving in place. His right foot begins tapping soundlessly on the linoleum floor.

"Hey, Doc, how 'bout a little privacy? Mr. Burns and I gotta talk."

Roddy's heart shoots into overdrive. He glances at Danny, who suddenly looks pale.

"We could both answer any questions," Roddy says.

"I don't think so, Doc. There're a few things I wanna clear up with Mr. Burns. Maybe you and I can talk another time, huh?" Morgan says with a smile in his voice.

Danny stays in the chair as Morgan perches on the edge of the bed.

"I always come across you two guys in a huddle," Morgan says.

Danny gets up, moves to the window, and looks out at the

Hudson River.

"So lemme ask you something, Mr. Burns."

"Yeah?" Danny turns and faces Morgan. He feels a film of sweat forming over his cheeks and forehead.

"I met three times with your friend, Dr. Dolan."

Roddy only mentioned talking with Morgan twice. This guy's toying with us.

"It was very revealing."

"Oh yeah? How so?"

"He told me where Egan's two hundred fifty K came from."

Morgan's eyebrows arch and then drop down. The crease between them deepens.

"Yeah, Roddy told me about the Cayman Islands thing, Detective. He said he heard it from *you*."

"Oh, so you guys talk with each other, huh?"

"Of course we do. You know that. Stop yanking my chain."

"Sure. Why not? After all, you're good friends, huh?" Morgan breaks into a Cheshire cat smile and then shakes his head.

"Yeah, we've known each other all our lives."

"So what else you know about getting shot, Mr. Burns?"

"I don't know what you mean, Detective."

"Sure you do." Morgan's voice is steely. Any hint of a smirk is gone; he gives Danny a hard look.

"Look, Detective. I was shot by some thug and I have no idea why. And you're telling me I know something I don't. Why don't you just tell me what you're looking for and I'll do my best to help you?"

A high-pitched squeak comes from deep in Dan's chest—the first sign of an asthmatic attack. At that moment, Danny feels an insistent itch at the end of his nose. It's tantalizing, but he resists scratching, afraid Morgan could see it as a sign of fraying nerves.

"So lemme get this straight, Mr. Burns," Morgan says, standing to his full height. "You had no idea that two hundred fifty of the three hundred K Egan put up for the restaurant came by wire from the Cayman Islands? You telling me *that*?"

"Yes, I am." Danny says, aware his voice sounds raspy. Phlegm collects on his vocal cords. He covers his mouth with his palm, coughs, and clears his throat. He swallows the stuff, knowing this could be the start of a deluge of mucous.

"So the bottom line is you didn't do your due diligence when you looked into Egan's financing."

Son of a bitch, talking to me about due diligence. He's got some goddamned nerve.

"I did what was appropriate, Detective."

"And what was that?" Morgan moves closer to Danny. The guy looms over him.

Danny's casted hand begins throbbing as a swell of anger rises within him. This cop is questioning his business acumen—his ability to determine the net worth of a business or to calculate if it's a good investment.

"Well, I looked at Kenny's bank statement, and it was exactly as he represented—more than three hundred K sitting there in pure, cold cash—he had liquidity."

Morgan says nothing. His eyebrows rise, and that smirk is perched on his lips.

"I checked with two of the three credit rating companies— Experian and Equifax, and Kenny had a very good score. And to top that off, Detective, I made an inquiry with the bankruptcy court in Nevada to find out if he'd ever gone belly-up. And the answer was *no*."

"And that was it?"

Wiseass . . . thinks by challenging me he can push me into losing my temper.

"No. For your information, Detective, that wasn't *all* I did. Just so you know, I went to the restaurant and looked it over very carefully. I retained a guy who's a business broker and advises about these kinds of transactions. He specializes in restaurant takeovers and buyouts and assesses whether or not an asking price is reasonable."

"Yeah? Who's that?"

"Martin West . . . guy in White Plains."

Morgan nods and looks like he's ready to say something, but Danny goes on. "And I spoke with the restaurant owner. We haggled over the price. I got him down considerably and extended the buyout terms to a five-year period at a reasonable interest rate. I forced him to become another silent partner because by waiting five years for the final payment, he had a financial stake in the place doing well. And what's more, I made sure he could put a lien only on the restaurant's assets, not our personal ones, if for some reason we couldn't cover the monthly nut and had to fold."

Morgan's hand goes up, as though he's heard enough, but Danny keeps going.

"I examined the lease, which had ten years left on it, so we wouldn't face a rent hike anytime soon. I looked at their books for the previous five years, analyzed their cash flow, and did a full accounting and financial analysis. So, Detective, I certainly *did* do my due diligence."

"But you didn't look into Egan's finances enough to see where he got the two hundred fifty from, did you?"

"I did what I could. I called people in Vegas. I think you call them *references*, Detective. Kenny had a fine track record as the manager of some top-notch restaurants—the Prime Steakhouse at Bellagio, for one, and a few others, too. I was told Kenny was a whiz with the clientele . . . made everyone feel at home. And to tell you the God's honest truth, I thought his account balance and credit ratings were all I needed since he intended to pay his share with a certified check. You know what that is, don't you, *Detective*?"

Morgan keeps silent, but those thick eyebrows are still sky-high.

"That seemed thorough enough for me." Dan coughs again and brings up a wad of phlegm. He swallows it.

"So tell me something, Mr. Burns. After you and Dolan decided to pull out of the restaurant, Egan just disappeared from the face of the earth, right?"

"I don't know what to tell you."

Morgan nods, crosses his arms in front of his chest, and waits.

"Lemme ask *you* something for a change," Danny says. "Why're you asking me all this crap? Why can't you just find the bastard who shot me?"

"Oh, we'll do our best."

"And what the hell does my getting shot have to do with Kenny Egan's finances a year and a half ago?"

"Oh, you don't think Egan's finances and activities are important?"

"I'll tell you what's important—that I get the hell out of this hospital and get on with my life. That I get back to the office and my clients." As those words pass his lips, Dan virtually feels a thump in his chest and hears *pfft* or *pop*, the sound just as the bullet penetrated him. It's a momentary flash that sends a chill through his spine.

"Speaking of your office, you going back there at night?"

"Not a chance. Not until you solve this case. Or if the landlord puts in better security."

"You know what, Mr. Burns? I have the feeling you and the good doctor hold the keys to this case. You telling me I'm wrong?"

"You're dead wrong, Detective."

"You know *you* could be *dead wrong*, Mr. Burns, if you aren't more forthcoming." Morgan's tongue protrudes into his cheek. He nods his head and squints.

"I don't like your implication, Detective."

"You're a poor liar, Mr. Burns."

"I think it's time for you to leave, Detective. And please, I'm asking you very politely. Stop harassing me before you and the Yonkers PD hear from my attorney."

"Don't threaten me, Mr. Burns."

"We're done here," Dan says, heading for the bathroom. "Be sure to close the door on your way out."

Morgan stands and glowers at Danny. "Mr. Burns, I *do* believe you and your doctor friend are in a world of trouble. More than you'll ever be able to handle. Believe me, the shit's gonna hit the fan. Big-time."

Chapter 13

Roddy sets the plastic fork onto the coffee table beside a container of chicken salad. He finishes off the cooled-down coffee and puts down the Styrofoam cup.

He sits in the darkened living room. He doesn't even want to open the refrigerator because the little interior light could be a clear signal someone's home. The house is dead quiet; he hears the basement furnace kick in followed by the water pump. It's eight in the evening. Roddy wonders why he didn't get out of Bronxville after visiting Danny this morning. Especially after seeing that steely-eyed bastard in the Navigator. He knows he's reluctant to leave everything behind. The lovely Tudor house is the last vestige of the wonderful life he's been living.

Jesus. Is this the way you feel when your life's falling apart and coming to an end?

So here he is gobbling takeout crap from the deli counter at Stop & Shop. Alone and in the dark, literally—there's not a single light on in the house—knowing he'll take off early in the morning, and he hasn't the foggiest idea where he'll be sleeping tomorrow night.

The mahogany grandfather clock chimed only a few minutes ago—right on the hour. It's a mournful sound, especially on a cold February night amid the eeriness of being alone in the dark—like when he was a kid and that bastard Horst would lock him in a closet. He hasn't thought of that in years. But now recollections of Brooklyn and his younger years intrude at random moments of the day or night.

Ordinarily, on a night like this, the house would feel warm and cozy, and he'd have a sense of family cohesion, of being loved. Tracy would be reading a library journal or novel, or maybe she'd be watching television. The kids would be in their rooms. The fireplace would cast its flickering glow through the den, and he'd be sitting next to Tracy, feeling the warmth of her body next to his. The aroma of a home-cooked meal would linger in the air, and it would all signify home—and the life he's adored.

But not tonight and maybe never again. His teeth begin chattering, as though he's freezing. Gooseflesh covers his arms even though the thermostat's set for seventy-five degrees. It's an inner coldness coming from his core.

For at least the thousandth time over the past few days, Roddy recalls the chain of events leading to where he and Danny find themselves tonight: Kenny's proposition about the silent partner thing, the steak-chomping goons and gangsters who chowed down at McLaughlin's amid the feckless uptown crowd of star fuckers and gawkers, and then learning Kenny owed Grange tons of money. The juice was running, and by the time Grange showed up, they were nearly half a million into the hole.

The hole . . .

Roddy wishes he could obliterate the memory of Snapper Pond and the grave. With lanterns and the shovels thwacking into the soft, swampy soil near the pond. Digging a hole for Grange. And for Kenny, too. The thought of the grave sends a hot streak of dread through Roddy. He'd fired four shots but recovered only three shells—couldn't find the fourth one—lying near or deep inside the grave. He rummaged around by lamplight, feeling for it, but no such luck. It was gone. He still worries someone could find it. What a sick scenario it was—from the back room at McLaughlin's to dropping Danny off at the Tuckahoe train station.

He became a mad dog that night, for the first and only time in years—in decades. And he's paid the price because he hasn't been the same since. Yes, Tracy's right. It's painful to admit, but he brims with mistrust. It runs like a deep current in his being, and maybe it will never leave him. Since Snapper Pond, he's changed, or as his shrink friend Dick Simons would say, he's regressed—gone back to an earlier time in his own being, one that made sense back in Brooklyn, among the street toughs, phone booth bookies, barroom thugs, pool hall gamblers, cardsharps, crooks, dead enders, and lowlife wannabes. He needed to survive back then, to keep his head above the oil-slicked waters of Sheepshead Bay and its sleazy denizens.

And now the beast rules once again.

Roddy feels he's a night creature lurking in the shadows of life around him. Jesus, he feels like a lone wolf in a dark lair . . . or like a mad dog.

He feels adrenaline-jacked and jumpy, like he has to keep moving. He gets up, paces for a few moments, and looks out the front window onto Clubway. It's deserted, as it usually is at night. It's a quiet, dark street at the edge of the Siwanoy Country Club, just off the fairway of the ninth hole, in lovely Bronxville, a peaceful bedroom community.

Roddy heads for the kitchen. In the dark, he opens the refrigerator only a few inches and grabs a bottle of Bud. He closes the door quickly and twists the top. Then he raises the bottle to his lips and swigs the brew. He chugs it down and feels the cold, tangy bite at the back of his throat. Swallow after swallow—until the bottle is drained. A fuzzy semiwarmth invades him as the alcohol seeps into his brain.

He's painfully aware of the silence in the house. Roddy knows he can't bear sleeping in the bed he and Tracy have shared for years. Much too painful a reminder of what's changed in his life. He'll just crumple onto the living room couch and wait for sleep to come.

He wonders if this deep loneliness is how you feel when you know you're dying. Is this how it is when everything you know or have ever known is over, gone forever? Is this the sensation you have before you slip into nothingness?

He suddenly recalls Danny's question the night they drove south on the Taconic from Snapper Pond.

"Roddy? Lemme ask you something."

"Ask."

"You believe in God?"

For a while, Roddy drove in silence. He thought about the stream of his life—the flow of past and present—as the Taconic's tree line streaked by in the night, while the Sequoia's tires drubbed on the asphalt highway.

Finally, he answered, *"Dan, for you there's a God."*

Yes, Danny has a good soul, and he shouldn't be punished this way. He was never a Brooklyn hard-ass like the other guys who hung around Leo's or the pool hall or the Nostrand Lanes Bowling Alley. Danny was the only one from the old crowd who went directly to college, not the army or driving a truck, or prison, or working as a low-level errand boy for some bookie or mob underboss in Mill Basin. Danny was a straight arrow whose sights were set on a decent, hardworking life.

A straight arrow, and yet Roddy finds himself mistrusting Danny, his best friend going so far back he can't remember when they met. Aside from Dan's mother, he was the only good person in Roddy's childhood. And here he is, wondering if Danny was part of Grange and Kenny's shakedown conspiracy. *How loathsome can you get, Roddy?* A tide of self-hatred washes over him as he pictures Dan lying in that hospital bed the night he was nearly killed.

Oh, how ugly I am with my suspicions, my mistrust, and my readiness to see the worst in everyone but myself.

Roddy tosses the empty bottle into the kitchen trash bin, opens the refrigerator a few inches, and grabs another. He takes a swig and heads back to the living room. As he plops onto the sofa, his thoughts return to Tracy and the kids. As much as he's loved this house, it's nothing more than stone, wood, and stucco—merely building materials, a construction of parts, nothing more. Without the people he loves, it's meaningless—it's nothing.

Roddy gulps another mouthful of beer and moves to the living room window. Peering through a slit in the drapery, he sees the road. There are no streetlights, and he hasn't turned on the porch light. The night is so dark, the air looks purple.

Across Clubway is the edge of the fairway. Looking into the night—maybe a hundred feet to the right of the house—Roddy sees the outline of something. He squints and peers through the darkness.

It's there: a Lincoln Navigator parked on the far shoulder. Like the one he saw this morning in Yonkers.

A gust of wind kicks up and Roddy sees it: a wisp of exhaust curls out of the vehicle's tailpipes.

The Navigator is idling with its headlights turned off.

Roddy's heart jumps in an electric swell.

Separating the venetian blinds, he looks carefully. He can't see the driver in the murky interior; it's likely the windows are darkened. There's no ambient light. There's no way to tell who—or how many men—might be waiting in the Navigator.

With his heartbeat thudding in his throat, Roddy wonders when the vehicle's doors will open and a bunch of guys will get out. He knows they'll be packing heat—Glocks, Rugers, maybe Tec-9s. Lethal shit, loaded with lead, designed to kill. His handgun would be no match for such firepower.

They must know he's home alone.

What does he do?

Back in the Rangers, you learned ambush tactics: you searched for a place to hide where the enemy's options were limited, like a narrow passageway through a ravine—a choke point where you could pick them off one by one. It had to be a place from which they couldn't make a group assault.

But he's in his own house. He doesn't want to hide in a closet or in the upstairs bathroom. They'd blast holes in the wooden door and he'd go down in a fusillade of lead. There's no basement crawl space in the house, but on the ceiling of the upstairs linen closet, there's a hinged hatch leading to the attic. He could get up there, take his cell phone with him, and call 911 while he lies amid the updraft of stifling attic heat and scattered mouse droppings. But he'd be trapped in a confined space. It would be only a matter of time before they'd find him and blast him through the ceiling.

He'd be dead meat with his blood dripping down through holes in the ceiling.

Roddy could lie prone on the carpet at the top of the stairs. He would be barely visible from below. The only way they could come at him would be in single file up the stairs. He'd expend only one bullet per man—enough for seven of them.

But they could machine gun the place or firebomb the house, or toss a grenade, and it would be all over.

Looking at the Navigator, Roddy sees the lit end of a cigarette arc through the inside of the SUV. The tip glows brightly as the driver sucks on the butt. The orange light barely illuminates part of a face—the portion around the mouth and beneath the nose. The glow dims and dips downward.

Whoever's in the Navigator is waiting. Why? What are they going to do?

But why wait for them to come to him? You don't wait for the enemy to execute their plan. You take the fight to them—quickly and with extreme prejudice.

Roddy sets the bottle of beer down and goes to the Parsons table behind the sofa. He picks up his handgun. It feels hefty with seven rounds in the cylinder. It could be his great equalizer. But he can't approach the SUV directly. He'll have to use stealth—ambush whoever's inside the thing. What's the best way to come at them? How can he get to their vehicle without them knowing he's coming? How does he turn it into something like a black ops operation under cover of darkness?

At the coat closet, he grabs his ski jacket and slips into it. His muscles feel coiled, ready. It's an adrenaline dump directly into his bloodstream. Yes, he's primed and getting ready to go primal. The ski jacket is perfect: it's deep blue, virtually made for a nighttime foray. He's wearing jeans, which are dark enough. He reaches onto the closet shelf, pats around, and comes across it: a black wool ski mask. He slips it over his head and adjusts it. Then he feels for his leather gloves, finds them, and puts them on.

His skin feels like it's wired, as though an electric current runs just beneath it.

He slips the pistol into the ski jacket's pocket and zips it. He heads into the kitchen and opens the door leading into the garage. He's immersed in darkness next to the Rogue. It occurs to Roddy that even approaching from behind, he could forfeit the element of surprise if the Navigator's doors are locked. He'd tug on the handle and nothing would happen. The men inside would whip out their guns and start firing. He'd be dead in a second or two.

He moves toward the worktable. Leaning against the pegboard is a tool he bought last year: a minisledgehammer with a forged-steel head weighing three pounds. It has a twelve-inch handle. He feels around the tabletop, and in a moment, the tool is in his gloved hand. He tucks the sledgehammer into his belt and opens the garage's side door. He steps into the backyard. The air is still and cold.

Roddy moves to the rear of the backyard and slips through a small opening in the hedge separating his house from the Hartmans'.

He's in their backyard.

Light from the Hartman house casts dull luminescence over their backyard. He moves quietly across their property, estimating that by now he's parallel to the Navigator idling on the street.

He hoists himself over a six-foot-high cedar fence separating the Hartman property from the Williams house, drops down on the other side, and makes his way to the far end of Scott and Terry Williams's property. If he sneaks along the far side of their house, he'll come out on Clubway, a good fifty feet behind the SUV. The only possible hitch could be if the Williams house has motion-activated spotlights.

Crouching, he moves steadily, hugging the outer wall of the Williams house, staying as close to it as possible, hoping it lessens the chance a motion-activated light will switch on. He controls his breathing, letting air in and out through his nose. He stops and crouches where the house faces Clubway. He peers through the darkness across the street. His estimation was correct: he's well behind the rear of the SUV. But he must traverse the Williamses' front lawn and make his way across Clubway—unseen.

A large clump of rhododendron sits in front of the Williams home. He crosses the lawn and crouches behind the foliage. He estimates the distance across Clubway to be about forty feet. After crossing the road, he'll be on the same side as the SUV. But the area in front of the Williams house is dimly lit by diffuse illumination from the house. And the porch light—basically, decorative—is on. He'll have to risk crossing Clubway. Unless the driver looks in his rearview mirror, the chance of being seen is minimal.

He moves quickly across the street and crouches on the grass shoulder. He waits, listening to his breath snort loudly in his ears.

The ski mask feels hot and itchy on his cheeks. He can't just walk up to the SUV from behind. He drops to the ground and begins crawling toward the vehicle—alligator style, an army crawl. The minisledgehammer drags along the grass. The pistol is well secured inside the zippered pocket.

He moves forward, on his belly, hugging the grass—knees bending and then straightening, forearms pulling him along. He closes the distance between himself and the Navigator. About ten feet behind the vehicle, he smells its exhaust—penetrating and pungent. The closer he gets, the less likelihood there is of being seen so long as he stays low to the ground. At the rear of the SUV, he stops, reaches for the hammer, and slips it from his belt. He unzips his pocket so the pistol is quickly accessible. Inching forward, he moves along the right side of the Navigator.

It's best to come at them from the right side, away from and behind the driver. It's unlikely the Navigator has reinforced windows; it's probably an ordinary commercial vehicle.

The hammer is in his right hand; the pistol is in his left. The leather gloves are thin; he has a fine feel for the trigger. He inches his way past the right rear tire, pulls his legs up, and goes into a crouch. He gathers his breath. In a swift movement, he shoots to his feet and swings the hammer. The right rear window shatters in an explosive blast.

"Don't move," he shouts, leaning through the opening. The sledgehammer lies on the grass; the pistol goes to his right hand. Roddy scans the interior. The rear bench seat is empty. The driver is alone.

"Please," the man cries, staring wide-eyed at Roddy.

The pistol points at his head.

"Show me your fuckin' hands," Roddy growls in a deep rasp.

The driver's hands shoot up.

"Unlock the doors."

"The button's down here at my left," the driver says in a shaky voice.

"Unlock 'em."

Four door locks clunk up.

Roddy rips the passenger-side door open and leans in. The car's interior lights go on.

"Please, mister. I'm only a driver. Eagle Car Service . . . I'm waiting for a pickup."

Poor bastard's just a driver. I've head-fucked him. But now I gotta keep up the act because he'll run to the cops the minute he gets outta here.

"Please. I'll give you my money. Just don't hurt me."

"Your wallet."

Fumbling in his coat, the guy produces a wallet.

"Drop it on the seat."

The driver sets his wallet on the passenger's seat. He gasps and inhales. Then his head bobs up and down as he lets out a series of guttural sobs.

Roddy rummages through the guy's wallet. The license and ID card come out. The man's name is David Singleton. He works for Eagle Car Service.

He's gonna call the cops as soon as I'm gone. Gotta make it look like a robbery.

Roddy pulls out a wad of bills. "This *it*? This all you got?"

"Yes. Please don't hurt me," the driver blubbers. Tears stream down his face.

"You wanna die?"

"No . . . please . . ."

"Get the fuck outta here, or you're a dead man."

He tosses the wallet on the seat and slams the Navigator's door shut.

The Navigator peels away, speeds down the street, makes a left turn, and disappears.

Roddy picks up the hammer and slips the pistol into his

pocket. He makes his way to the back of the Williams house, over the fence, across the Hartman backyard, through the hedges, and back to the garage.

Inside the house, he slips the pistol inside a breakfront drawer. He suddenly remembers the Hartmans mentioned a few weeks ago they were going to Florida until mid-March. Poor fucking driver—got the shit scared out of him. No doubt he'll call the cops. If they come knocking on doors, Roddy won't know a thing. He's been sleeping for the last few hours after a long day at the hospital. And the driver will never recognize his voice.

Roddy's not certain he'd recognize his own voice. He's not the same man he was a few days ago.

The beast he thought he'd buried has returned.

Chapter 14

When the telephone rings, Colleen answers it. "Tracy, it's for you. It's Angela."

"Hi, Angie," Tracy says. "How's Danny?" Tracy gazes about Colleen's kitchen—sees the electric stove and thinks of her Garland gas range at the house back in Bronxville.

"He'll be out of the hospital tomorrow. How's Nutley?"

"What can I say, Angie? It's really hard on the kids. How's everything in Riverdale?"

"The kids can't believe this. And I'm scared to death after what happened to Danny—and the incident with Roddy at the hospital."

"*Roddy*? What happened?" Tracy's body stiffens. A charged pang shoots through her.

"Danny said there were men waiting in the garage for Roddy—near his car—the night after Danny got shot," Angela says in a quaking voice. "Some mob types . . ."

Tracy fumbles with the telephone, nearly dropping it. She grabs the kitchen counter and, weak-kneed, slumps onto a stool.

"Angie, forgive me. I have to go."

Tracy slips the phone back on the receiver, barely aware of Angela's voice trailing off as she hangs up.

She sits at the kitchen counter holding her head in her hands.

Her eyes are wet and her throat tightens.

"What's wrong?" Colleen asks, sitting on the adjacent stool.

Tracy looks at her sister—her red hair is turning prematurely gray; her blue eyes and sharply etched features loom in front of her. "I can't believe it. Roddy's still hiding things from me."

"What do you mean?" Colleen murmurs, stroking her sister's hair.

"There were men waiting in the hospital garage for him the night after his best friend, Danny, was shot. And the following night, our friend Walt was killed right next to our car. And Roddy never said a word to me about men waiting for him."

Colleen gasps and slips her arm around her sister's shoulders.

Tracy shudders at the thought of Roddy seeing men in the garage . . . and then poor Walt McKay. "Colleen, how on earth do I deal with this? After all these years, I learn Roddy's lying to me, covering up what's going on in his life."

"I understand, sweetie."

Tracy peers at Colleen. Her sister's eyes are cast downward, as though she's lost in thoughts of her divorce from Gene two years earlier.

"Colleen, Roddy's been living a lie for nearly a year. And now I have to rip our lives apart, take the kids out of school, and go into hiding?" Tears gush from Tracy's eyes. She shakes her head. "And I just learned from Angie that he's *still* lying to me."

"It must be very hard. I understand," Colleen says, shaking her head.

"You don't really know Roddy's background."

"I know his father died in prison."

"Yes, he was stabbed to death because a drug deal went bad. He was there for armed robbery. And Roddy's mother was a drug-addicted prostitute."

"My *God*," Colleen says, as her hand goes to her mouth.

"It wasn't until she met this man—Horst—that she stopped selling herself."

Colleen shakes her head again. "It's a life we can't even begin to imagine, Tracy."

"She stole money, food stamps, forged documents, and was drunk all the time. Horst abused her and tortured Roddy."

"*Tortured* him?"

"He'd beat him with his fists or a strap. When Roddy was little, Horst would lock him in a closet for hours at a time. When I first met Roddy, he hated dark places. It was a long time before I could get him to go to a movie. When Horst was drunk, he'd burn Roddy with cigarettes. And his mother would laugh, if she was sober enough to know anything.

"When he could, Roddy would stay at Danny Burns's place. Roddy still talks about Danny's mother and about a boxing trainer, a man named Doc Schechter. And some sergeant from the army, a Sergeant Dawson. These people helped turn his life around."

"My God, it was *that* bad?"

"Yes. Finally, when he was a teenager, he beat Horst half to death, and that was the last he saw of him. Roddy's mother wasted away from alcohol and died. By then, Roddy was in medical school."

"But, Tracy, look how far he's come," Colleen says, crossing her arms on her chest. "Try thinking of it that way."

"I just wonder how much he's really changed. As a teenager, he was part of a gang. They would go into German bars with wooden blackjacks and they'd break skulls. He and his ethnic friends—the three I's: Ireland, Italy, and Israel. And he nearly went to prison at seventeen for grand larceny. I don't know, Colleen. How much is there he still hasn't told me?"

"Listen, Tracy. He was a tough kid from a poor neighborhood. You knew all about his past. It's not news to you." Colleen gets up and refills her coffee mug. "Tracy, he went into the army and turned his life around: summa cum laude from college, medical school with honors, and he's on the faculty at Columbia. You have to focus on the man he is *now*. Why look at his past, one you've always known about?"

Tracy leans her elbows on the counter. "You know, there are no family pictures of Roddy as a kid. The only ones are from school . . . class photos. Can you imagine that? You live in a house for seventeen years and there's not a single picture of you or your parents. And in those class pictures, he looks like such an unhappy kid.

"He's always called Danny's mother, Peggy, the angel of his life. When Roddy was arrested, she got his teachers to write letters to the judge saying how smart Roddy was. That's why he was sent to the army and not prison." Tracy gets up and goes to the sink. She fills a glass with water and sips some to soothe her dry throat.

"Look at what he overcame, Tracy. He made a good life for himself and for you and the kids."

"I don't know, Colleen. I'm wondering if I've been kidding myself all these years. I mean, look at Roddy's background. How on earth could he go through a horrible childhood like that and not be terribly scarred? Completely ruined for life? I'd like to think he changed—that he really overcame all those things and became someone who could love and trust and live a good life. But I don't know if that's possible. How can a man survive that and turn out to be capable of really loving and trusting someone?" Tracy looks at her sister.

Colleen's eyes are wide and her head is shaking from side to side. "Tracy, I think you need some time to—"

"*Time?* I've been married to a man for fifteen years, and after all that time, I now realize I don't really know him. Maybe he's like his father and mother were. God, I hate to say it, but maybe he's just a bad seed." A trenchant wave of sadness washes over Tracy as she thinks of Roddy's childhood. She recalls the times he talked about the *tar pits* of Brooklyn—the horror of his childhood—and how he couldn't believe he'd escaped from it all.

"Maybe so, Tracy. I can tell you when I married Gene, I never thought he'd be the two-timing philandering sort. He seemed like a straight arrow. And look at me now, divorced and dating. Trying to sort out my life."

"That might be how Roddy and I end up . . . divorced."

"It's not the end of the world, Tracy."

Tracy closes her eyes and nods her head. "I don't know what to think."

"You don't have to make any decisions right now," Colleen says. "But I'll tell you this. There's life after marriage. Nutley's a lovely town. We have good schools here, and there's an active social life for single parents. Right now, just take it one step at a time."

"You know how I feel, Colleen? Like the past is back in spades. Or maybe it never left. Maybe Roddy's always been like he was on those Brooklyn streets all those years ago, and I never wanted to see it. And now everything's just coming apart at the seams."

Chapter 15

Roddy gets out of the taxi at the intersection of Palmer Avenue and Parkway Road. He wears a brown leather jacket and dark gray cargo pants, and he carries a canvas satchel with items he'll need. His inside jacket pocket holds the loaded pistol.

Entering Chase Bank, he sees Ginny Clyne, the white-haired branch manager, sitting at her desk. She waves to him, and he nods at her. He recalls his last contact with Ginny: he'd returned the fifteen thousand in hundred-dollar bills he'd brought to McLaughlin's that night as a down payment. It was used to lure Grange into thinking they'd pay him half a million dollars in extortion money.

The juice is running.

That was the beginning of this nightmare. But not really, because Roddy realizes it all began one evening a year and a half ago, when Kenny Egan came to the office and proposed he and Danny become silent partners in McLaughlin's.

Ginny greets him in her usual warm way and asks a teller to escort him to the safe deposit area. Roddy feels furtive in the privacy of the cramped booth, as though he's doing something illegal. Maybe it's because he's carrying a piece. Or does he feel this way because of what he did to that poor driver last night?

He opens the metal box. It's all there: their marriage license, their birth and baptismal certificates, the necklace and brooch

Tracy's mother gave her years ago, his army discharge papers, and some old silver coins Tracy's father gave the kids. There's the emerald ring Roddy gave Tracy on their tenth wedding anniversary—she wears it only on special occasions—and the deed to the house. Seeing objects that mark milestones in their lives, Roddy is flooded by a wave of sadness. He swallows hard—again and again—trying to get rid of the lump in his throat.

He inhales deeply, extracts an envelope, and begins counting hundred-dollar bills. He's again reminded of that night in McLaughlin's back office when he and Dan handed Grange thirty thousand—an opening gambit to convince him they'd pay the loan shark the money he wanted within a few days. Then Grange demanded his self-congratulatory drink, Glenfiddich scotch—*that good shit*, as he'd called it. The Klonopin-laced drink Roddy had prepared sank Grange into a twilight sleep.

And then: Snapper Pond.

But Roddy can't waste time mulling over a past that can't be undone. He must move on, get away from Bronxville—leave his home and the hospital. And above all, keep Tracy and the kids safe. And somehow, he must learn why he and Danny are in someone's crosshairs. He can't sit back and wait for something to happen. Sergeant Dawson's words resound in his head:

Always be the hunter, not the hunted. Never let yourself be prey.

He pulls out a medium-sized envelope, slips in fifty bills, and returns the rest to the larger envelope inside the box. Five thousand in cash should be enough. He's got two credit cards and won't hesitate to use them; after all, he's not being tracked by law enforcement and there's no need to worry about leaving an electronic trail. On second thought, those guys in the garage could have been from Little Odessa, Brooklyn. The Russian Bratva is big into credit card fraud and has long tentacles into the world of plastic. He'll use credit cards only if necessary.

Leaving the bank, he waves to Ginny, wondering if he'll ever see Bronxville or Tracy and the kids again.

Roddy walks onto Parkway Road and heads for the Bronxville Metro North train station. He's primed for anything. Escape and evade is a mantra from his Ranger training; it will dictate his next moves. Roddy scans the street as he walks. He swivels his head from side to side, hearing his neck bones crack as he does. He recalls the keys to survival Sergeant Dawson pounded relentlessly into the platoon: "*Use all your senses. Be primed for what you see, hear, and smell. Live by your wits. Vanquish fear and panic. A Ranger does what he must; he eats snakes, bugs, and tree bark to survive. Remember, you're never out of tactics for staying alive.*"

Roddy knows a good soldier stays aware of his surroundings no matter what the situation. There can never be a lapse of attention. A break in concentration can mean death. Danger heightens the senses—primes a man for full use of his capacities. And Roddy's in the bull's-eye of a kill zone. You must act, no hesitation—not for a millisecond. You harness your instincts and use them in the service of survival. And you show no mercy.

It's all connected—his Ranger training from thirty years ago and the here and now on Parkway Road in the lovely village of Bronxville. Past and present are simply pages in the same ugly book.

Roddy glances over his shoulder. He thinks he sees someone duck into an alley between two stores. It was a momentary blur; he's uncertain who or what it was. He stands still and waits. No one emerges from the alley. A few cars and SUVs pass by. Roddy's reminded of that thuggish-looking guy in the Navigator. Most SUVs in this town are driven by women going about their daily tasks. He scans everything as though he's on scout patrol in the Georgia forests. For a moment, he actually feels he's back in time—nearly thirty years ago—with Bravo Company, on a forced, full-gear trek through Fort Benning's swamp-filled woodlands.

He looks back down Parkway and sees a man in a dark leather

jacket ambling along the far side of the street. Is that the guy who ducked into the alley? The man walks casually on a cold winter day. Roddy's hand slips into his pocket; he grips the pistol. He turns and continues walking toward the station. He feels the air on his neck and his skin feels tender. He knows this feeling: it's a sense of exposure, of vulnerability and the possibility of death coming from an unseen place. He sees and hears everything: tires whooshing past him on the street, car horns, a truck's exhaust in the wintry air. He even hears the click mechanism as a streetlight changes from red to green. He glances back: the guy is window-shopping in a sporting goods store on the far side of the street.

A group of teenagers approaches on his side of the road. They carry book bags; they are wearing baggy pants and baseball caps. They're a harmless bunch, lost in the hormone-driven tangle of adolescent angst. Yet he scans them carefully. As they near him, two teens eye him curiously. He looks directly at them and they avert their eyes.

Roddy keeps walking and hears cars approach from behind. He listens for the sound of one slowing as it nears him. He won't be a victim like Walt McKay. He can't banish the image of Walt—dead on the concrete floor.

Roddy recalls the maxim from paratrooper training: there are two kinds of soldiers—the quick and the dead. He's ready to act: he'll duck for cover or spin quickly and shoot at the nearest threat. Casting a look back, he no longer sees the guy in the leather coat. Maybe he entered the store.

Roddy bristles with wariness as he nears the train station. He recalls the same feeling from years ago—as you came to Coyle Street, enemy territory, where the Germans lived. If you couldn't run like a jackrabbit, you'd be beaten to a pulp.

At the platform ticket machine, he slips a bill into the slot and presses the touch screen for a one-way ticket to Grand Central and a ten-trip MetroCard for the New York City subway. The tickets drop into the slot.

The station clock reads 4:15 in the afternoon. He'll catch the 4:20, and according to the schedule, he'll get to Grand Central at 4:48, just as rush hour begins peaking. Perfect timing: he'll blend into the crowd—just one more soul among thousands of commuters scurrying like ants through the gigantic terminal. They'll all be heading home. But he no longer has a place to go at the end of the day. A deep sense of alienation—of complete isolation— seeps through him. He feels it in his bones.

Glancing about, he sees only a handful of people on the southbound platform waiting for the train to the city. No one's waiting on the opposite side of the tracks because the northbound train just departed.

The city-bound train roars into the station at 4:20. Right on time. A sucking wind rush accompanies the train as Roddy positions himself to board the last car. When he enters the train, the interior feels overheated. It smells like old clothes mixed with a uriniferous odor from the restroom. He takes a seat on the right side, at the rear of the car. It's safest since no one can approach him from behind. And he'll have a good view of anyone boarding his car.

A scattering of people occupy the car, mostly black and Hispanic women—housekeepers and nannies for the upper-middle-class types living in the tony burbs north of Mount Vernon and the Bronx.

Leaving the station, the train picks up speed, heading toward the city. Roddy feels bone-tired and wants to settle back in the seat, close his eyes, and drift off. But he can't allow himself to nap.

About two minutes out of the Bronxville station, the car's front door opens. A tall man wearing a waist-length, black leather jacket and faded jeans enters from the car ahead. Is he the guy he spotted on Parkway Avenue, the window-shopper? Roddy isn't certain; he was too far away to get a good look at him. The man has a Bluetooth device over his left ear and carries a folded newspaper under one arm. He lets the front door close and peers about the car. The guy has a hollowed-out, Slavic-looking face. He's rugged-looking and steep-jawed. And he needs a shave. Could be Russian, Ukrainian, or Albanian, or maybe from some other Eastern European country—but for sure, he wasn't born in America. He reminds Roddy of Wladimir Klitschko, the boxer, but not as tall. His eyes are lifeless. His light brown hair is shorn in a military cut.

Roddy eyes him, looking for telltale tattoos—hallmarks of the Russian Brotherhood. None are visible on his hands, face, or neck. That doesn't mean his torso and back aren't covered with a swarm of Brotherhood *abzuka* markings—a history of the guy's trek through the Russian prison system. Nor is there a hint of a bulge beneath his jacket. But that doesn't mean a thing—Roddy doesn't look like he's carrying, either. The guy sits one row in front of Roddy, across the aisle on the left side of the car. He moves to a window seat, opens a copy of the *Daily News,* and begins reading.

Roddy eyes the man out of the corner of his eye. He decides there's a more surreptitious way to do it. It's nearly dark outside on this somber winter afternoon, and in the fluorescent-lit car, Roddy gazes into the window to his right. In the reflection of the car's interior, he gets a clear bead on the man. Thumbing through the newspaper, the guy looks relaxed—maybe overly so—but Roddy can't tell if there's anything to set off an internal alarm.

The conductor enters the car through the front door, the one used by the Slavic-looking guy moments earlier. He begins collecting tickets. Roddy watches as Slavic Guy hands over his ticket. The conductor punches it and slips it into his pocket. That means Slavic Guy doesn't have a round-trip ticket, a ten-tripper, or a monthly. It's a one-time, one-way ride, the same as Roddy's. The needle on Roddy's internal danger gauge hovers near the red zone. His muscles begin to quiver. He reaches into his pocket and grips the revolver's handle.

Watching Slavic Guy through the reflection, Roddy tries to discern if the man is actually reading the newspaper. He stays on the same page for what seems a very long time. Roddy even wonders if the guy can read English but tells himself not to jump to conclusions on flimsy evidence.

At Mount Vernon West, a book-bag-carrying group of black teenagers enters the car. The noise level escalates as they horse around, laugh, and yell amid the train's clacking and roaring. Slavic Guy doesn't look up; he's now thumbing through the newspaper. Roddy wonders if his indifference to the tumult is feigned. Is he just using the paper as a prop? It's impossible to tell.

At the next stop—Woodlawn—most of the cleaning women and nannies get off.

At the Botanical Gardens station, a bunch of young girls wearing Campbell plaid pleated skirts with navy blue blazers and overcoats board the train. Must be a parochial school nearby. Roddy keeps eyeing Slavic Guy, trying to determine if he does anything even remotely suspicious. He's now looking at the sports section. Considering the length of time he's had the paper open to the same page, he must have trouble reading English, or maybe he's not reading at all.

At the Fordham station, a group of college kids boards the train. The car is now crowded with people; many are standing in the aisle. The noise escalates to a stentorian level. Roddy can still see Slavic Guy through occasional gaps in the crowd filling the aisle.

The train crosses the bridge over the Harlem River and rumbles along a trestle toward the Harlem–125th Street station. It passes four-story tenement houses crouched alongside the elevated tracks. A crowd of kids congregates at the doors. Roddy stands, grabs his canvas bag, and moves toward the front of the car to the first set of doors. If anyone's watching, it looks as though he'll get off at 125th Street. He edges toward the door but doesn't look back to where Slavic Guy sits. As the train pulls to a stop, the kids wait for the doors to open. Their yelling and laughter are at an ear-splitting level. When the doors slide apart, the group clamors en masse onto the platform. Roddy slips out with them, glances about, and darts into the car in front of the one he exited.

The next-to-last car is nearly empty. Roddy huddles into the last seat on the right side. Looking out the window, he scans the platform, looking for Slavic Guy. There's no sign of him. The train remains stationary as the pack of kids makes its way noisily to the exit stairwells.

Roddy waits for the train to leave the station and make the last lap to Grand Central Terminal, ten minutes away.

Chapter 16

The train lurches and starts moving.

Roddy's heart thunders as he wonders if Slavic Guy is following him. He looks out the window at tenement buildings and housing projects. The train picks up speed and hurtles toward Grand Central Terminal. At 97th Street, the tracks dip and the train barrels into the tunnel beneath Park Avenue. The whooshing and clacking intensify within the tunnel's confines. About thirty seconds into the tunnel, the overhead lights flicker and the train goes dark. When the lights come back on, Roddy hears the rear door behind him slide open.

Slavic Guy moves slowly into the car, walks down the aisle, and sits on the left side of the car, three rows in front of Roddy. He no longer carries the newspaper.

Roddy's skin prickles as gooseflesh crawls over his arms and neck. It feels like a wire hums in his chest. Its thrumming radiates down his arms to his fingertips. Objects look sharply etched in the car's fluorescence as the train speeds through the darkened tunnel.

He's sitting between me and the nearest door, so when I leave the train, he'll be right behind me. The bastard's following me. He's gonna get close and put a bullet in my head.

Roddy can almost *feel* his pupils dilate. Adrenaline pumps through him, leeching into every part of his body. He slips his hand inside his jacket pocket; the heft of the revolver feels reassuring. He gets up from his seat and moves down the aisle toward the front of the car. People look up at him as he passes. At the front of the car, he looks directly into the Plexiglas window. In the reflection, he sees Slavic Guy sitting impassively, peering into the tunnel's blackness to his left. Roddy's certain the guy's doing just what Roddy did—using the window's reflection as a mirror—to watch Roddy.

With his body jangling, Roddy slides the door open and stands in the cramped compartment between cars. Dank air rushes by as the train moves through the acrid, fume-filled maze leading to the terminal. Red and white lights flash eerily on the tunnel walls.

Opening the rear door of the car in front of him, Roddy moves forward, walking quickly up the aisle. This car is more crowded than the last two. It makes sense since most people prefer being toward the front of the train. They'll be able to get quickly to the main concourse. Threading his way through the thickening crowd, Roddy gets to the first door of the car. He resists the temptation to glance back; he just keeps moving forward.

He passes through two more cars, heading toward the front end of the train. He looks back through the Plexiglas window of the door at the head of each car. The crowd makes it difficult to get a clear view, but at one point, he spots Slavic Guy wending his way forward, half a train car behind him.

With his heart pounding, Roddy pushes through the crowded aisle as the train nears Grand Central Terminal. In the first car, he slips through the thick pack of people and gets to the forward set of doors. Looking through the door's window, he strains to see the platform. His feet feel like they're in motion, as though he's running while standing still. Peering out, he can see the train isn't yet adjacent to the platform. He hopes he's on the side of the train where the doors will open so he can make a quick exit. If the platform is on the other side, a mass of people will stand between him and the exit. Slavic Guy will have plenty of time to move closer. And then what?

Roddy peers back but can no longer see his pursuer. But there's no doubt the guy is right there, less than twenty feet away, hidden in the mass of people. The crowd begins pressing toward the doors. Roddy's in luck; he sees the platform as the train slides adjacent to it. The doors on the side where he's standing will open, and he'll hustle off.

He can tell the train is pulling into the lower level of the terminal. Those passengers still sitting collect their belongings and begin filling the aisle. The conductor's voice announces the arrival at track 102. The train slows to a crawl. Roddy waits. He can nearly *feel* Slavic Guy edging closer through the crowd.

The train stops. The doors don't open. Roddy waits, pressed against the door. His entire body feels like it's throbbing. His feet want to move, but there's nowhere to go. People in the crowd mutter; they press closer. The doors stay closed. Roddy looks through the door's window; the platform leads to a long ramp at his left. He feels a sudden urge to pound his fist on the door.

It must be a full minute before the doors slide open. When they do, people gush from the train. Amid the horde, Roddy lunges onto the platform. He swivels left and strides quickly up the ramp toward an archway leading to the terminal's lower level.

The lower concourse is mobbed with commuters. It's nearly five o'clock; the place is a maelstrom of movement and noise. Throngs of people stream in every direction. Roddy's heart rate accelerates as he picks up speed, passing Zaro's Bakery and a shoeshine concession. He casts a glance back at the mass of humanity vomiting forth from the ramp. No sign of Slavic Guy.

Every sense is primed as Roddy keeps going. He feels that inner surge of readiness he felt back in his army days. He's pumped, galvanized, even wired. He was trained for this—to take in his surroundings in a second, to hear, smell, and feel everything around him. It's a state of total arousal. He moves past people wheeling rolling suitcases and carrying duffel bags and backpacks, briefcases, shopping bags, travel gear, and packages.

He passes the center food concession and the ramp leading to the Oyster Bar. The food court is filled with the steamy scents of pita, hummus, chipotle sauce, croissants, and baked bread. He sees and smells it all in a half second. He passes Junior's—jammed with people eating—gets to the stairway at the Vanderbilt Avenue side of the terminal, and scrambles up three flights of steps, taking two at a time, thankful he's stayed in shape.

The main concourse roars in an oceanic rumble. It's a cavernous expanse with a vaulted turquoise ceiling displaying the zodiac constellation. The space is filled with a roiling sea of people—crisscrossing tides of humanity. Long lines snake from the ticket windows; people mill about the information booth; others prattle on cell phones, text, snap pictures, and fiddle with their smart phones. A group of Asians smiles as one snaps a picture of the others in front of the famous clock above the information booth. Waves of commuters head for the train tunnels amid the roaring echo.

Roddy's eyes rove over everyone, gathering information in a primal state of readiness. He heads toward the Lexington Avenue side of the concourse. Glancing up at the east balcony, he sees a mobbed Apple outlet. He's jolted by the memory that the last time he was at this spot, he was having dinner with Tracy in a restaurant where the Apple store now stands.

National guardsmen in camouflage fatigues and black boots are everywhere. Strapped to each soldier's waist is a holstered Glock. He's reminded of the Taurus in his pocket. A quick flash of Danny in the ICU and then of Walt McKay floods him: guns, bullets, blood, death, and the mob. He passes a soldier standing with a leashed German shepherd, a black beast with tawny markings—no doubt, a bomb sniffer.

Passing the Hudson News concession, almost trotting, he strides into the Lexington Passage, a store-filled arcade with people streaming in both directions. He comes to a wide stairway leading to the Lexington Avenue subway line where the 4, 5, and 6 trains run. He scrambles down the stairs and swipes his MetroCard through the turnstile's slot.

Crossing an overhead walkway, he gets to the uptown side of the station. Glancing back, he sees nothing suspicious. It seems he's lost Slavic Guy. But there's no way to be certain amid the throbbing mass of humanity. He scampers down a stairway to the Lexington line's northbound platform. A mob of people wait for the uptown trains—the express on the middle track and the local on the side track. A vented duct blows heat over the platform. It emits an oily odor. Squeezing through the crowd, Roddy hunches down to make himself a little shorter; he tries to blend in. He looks about: no sign of Slavic Guy. Roddy waits, knowing he'll jump on whichever train arrives first: local or express.

Standing at the platform's edge, he hears a sound from deep within the tunnel: an express train is approaching. He cranes his neck and peers into the tunnel where a nimbus of light appears on the darkened wall. He feels a distant rumble and a slight shuddering of the platform. The crowd senses the approaching train and presses closer to the platform's edge.

Roddy spots a heavily built man with dark facial stubble. Squinting, Roddy sees the edge of a blue-black tattoo on the man's neck above the collar of a black anorak—no doubt, part of the Russian mob's body markings. A shock-like surge ramps through Roddy. The guy is tough-looking: wide faced, grizzled, with deep-set, dark eyes. He's steep-jawed and has prominent cheekbones. He stands only a few feet away. A Bluetooth device angles over his right ear. His eyes roam over the crowd, bypassing Roddy. Does he know Roddy's seen him? Is he trying to blend in and appear benign?

Jesus, there's more than one. And they're in telephone contact. Or am I going crazy?

Roddy peers into the tunnel and sees the train's light approaching rapidly. Suddenly, he realizes he's in danger at the platform's edge.

With the train rocketing toward him, he could be pushed onto the tracks. It's so easy to do in a thick crowd. The guy could then melt away.

Roddy pivots and moves back from the edge.

The subway throttles into the station with a gust of air, a roar, and a faint odor of ozone. It screeches to a halt. A loudspeaker announces its arrival. A horde of passengers pours from the train onto the platform. They thread through the waiting crowd, and the platform is a chaotic mass of people. When the clot of humanity has exited, those waiting press forward into the car. Roddy is swept along with them. People push and press; everyone is compacted into the car's confines.

The doors slide shut and then snap open. The train is so packed, the doors can't close. People press together more forcefully. Roddy squirms deeper into the car, stepping on someone's toes. He spots Bluetooth Guy near the door, so he threads his way deeper into the throng.

The doors close again, open, and close once more. A voice over the PA system says, "Step into the train and watch the closing doors."

Roddy tries pushing through the crush of people—maybe he can get to the other side of the car—but it's impossible. The people are packed shoulder to shoulder and chest to back. There's barely room to breathe. Roddy writhes his way deeper into the mass. A man next to him mutters, "Jesus, guy. Take it easy."

It's impossible to change position or move away.

Roddy's in the middle of the car. And Bluetooth Guy is right behind him, amid the crush, getting nearer—only a few feet away—unseen, angling closer. Roddy can't even reach into his pocket for the pistol. A solid wall of humanity prevents him from moving an inch. The hairs on his neck bristle as the subway roars through the tunnel's darkness.

It nears 59th Street and slows. As the brakes engage, the train comes to a squealing halt. Passengers begin pushing, shoving, squeezing out of the car, disgorging onto the platform. A horde of people wait outside, ready to stampede into the train once it partially empties. Roddy is swept toward the door by the departing mass. He elbows his way out and finds himself on the platform.

He races to a nearby escalator. People are packed two abreast on the moving stairway. It rises slowly. A frantic glance back tells him Bluetooth Guy is at the bottom of the escalator. He's shoving people aside, moving upward, his eyes staying on his quarry. Roddy turns and pushes past people, taking two steps at a time. Slipping around them, he moves like liquid up the escalator and makes his way toward the top, where the local train runs.

He glances back and sees a commotion on the escalator. It's Bluetooth Guy pushing his way toward him. Rising slowly on the moving stairway, Roddy can now see a train disgorging passengers on the upper platform. It's a local, heading toward the Bronx. If he can shove his way past this last group of people, he'll be on the platform and can slip into the train before the doors close. Bluetooth Guy will be left behind amid the crowd.

He's blocked from jumping ahead on the escalator—too many people jammed in close together. *Jesus, this is taking forever.* The escalator continues its slow rise. Roddy's heart stampedes as he reaches the top and bolts toward the train—just as the doors slide shut. The train stands still. Roddy slams his palm against the door, hoping the conductor will open the doors. The train doesn't move. Roddy pounds his fist on the door.

He turns and looks back.

Bluetooth Guy is coming. Fast.

The train begins moving. Picks up speed.

Roddy whirls around. Realizing he's at the metro-level entrance to Bloomingdale's, he races into the store. Rotating his neck, he glances in every direction. No sign of his pursuer. Roddy's in the men's casual-wear department. Brushing past rows of jeans, sports jackets, slacks, belts, and gloves, he smells leather and fabric. He keeps moving, scampering past racks of clothing and displays. His breath whines in his ears.

Scanning the store, he sees a stairway. He scrambles up the stairs and comes to the store's main floor. He looks back, no longer seeing Bluetooth Guy. But the man could have ducked behind a display or might be moving along a parallel aisle among the store's myriad racks and shelves.

As he passes through the cosmetics department, a floral fragrance assails him. His eyes sweep the area. In the reflection of a mirrored pillar, Roddy sees a man wearing a black anorak. It's a momentary flash—maybe half a second or less—and Roddy can't be sure it's Bluetooth Guy.

Another glimpse—in the periphery of his vision—as the figure moves behind a display. Roddy's insides jolt. Looks like it was Bluetooth Guy.

Roddy strides toward the 3rd Avenue exit, passes shoppers and browsers, moves past an in-store bakery and glances back. No sign of Bluetooth Guy.

He exits the store onto 3rd Avenue. The frigid night air hits him like an arctic blast amid the rumble of busses, a northbound stream of headlights, the rush of taxis, and the hissing of a truck's air brakes. WALK and DON'T WALK signs blink amid a maelstrom of noise and people streaming through the winter air, breath vapor rising in the lighted street.

Roddy sees an older woman opening a taxi door. She's exiting the cab. A young, fashionably dressed woman holding two shopping bags waits for the older one to get out of the taxi. Roddy watches. The older woman's foot hits the pavement.

At that second, Roddy lunges ahead and cuts in front of the young woman at the curb. "Sorry," he calls, and jumps into the taxi. He plops into the back bench seat—behind the driver—and tries to close the door. The young woman grabs the outside handle and tugs the door open. "Hey," she shrieks. "What are you *doing*?" and uses her body weight to hold the door open. Roddy clamps his hand on the inside handle and pulls. The door slams shut.

The vinyl seat is cracked, concave, and still warm. He sinks into the depression left by countless asses. The cab is overheated and smells of the older woman's perfume.

"Head north on 3rd," Roddy shouts to the driver, a Middle Eastern–looking man with a closely cropped beard.

The woman pounds frantically on the taxi door. Her voice penetrates the window; her face contorts in rage. The taxi lurches ahead; her voice fades away amid the street noise as the vehicle moves uptown.

"Where to?" asks the driver.

"I'll let you know. Just go."

Roddy's heart pumps like a piston. He slumps down in the seat, opens his canvas bag, and removes a black baseball cap. He pulls it low over his eyes. The taxi cruises into the thick stream of traffic. Amid honking horns, a siren pierces the night air. A moment later, traffic is at a standstill; the ambulance siren pops and then returns to its insistent whine. There must be an accident up ahead. The taxi stands in the middle lane of 3rd Avenue. It might as well have stalled.

Roddy straightens up and peers quickly out the taxi's rear window. The avenue is a mass of movement beneath sodium vapor lights and a sea of headlights behind him.

Bluetooth Guy is right there, maybe fifty feet away. He popped out of Bloomingdale's and stands outside the store, peering north and south along the avenue. And he's talking into his earpiece.

If he sees me, the guy could run up to the taxi, pull a gun, and pop me through the window.

Roddy's heart feels like it's leaping into his neck. He ducks down, slips his hand inside his pocket, and grasps the revolver's handle. He sees the driver sneak an uneasy peek at him through the rearview mirror.

Traffic begins to move, but it's agonizingly slow. The driver jockeys for position, changes lanes, lurches ahead, stops, and starts again. Horns honk, and the street is flooded with people—shadowy, ghostlike figures in the night. They thread their way between stopped cars on the street. A bus in front of the taxi stops suddenly. The driver slams the taxi's brakes and Roddy is hurled forward. His head nearly rams the Plexiglas barrier between the front and rear seats.

The driver changes lanes again, veers left, and lurches forward. Roddy sees the nearest street sign: East 64th Street.

"Hang a left on 65th," he says.

The taxi inches to the west side of 3rd. At the next corner, the driver turns left onto East 65th.

"At Park, make another left."

Park Avenue in the southbound direction is less jammed than 3rd, but it's still slow-going. After what seems like an eternity, they pass through the divided aerial roadway of the Helmsley Building and continue south along lower Park Avenue. Traffic thins out, but people still swarm toward subway stations at the end of the workday. He's lost Bluetooth Guy, but there could be a third man following. They're in telephone contact. Roddy thinks back to Sergeant Dawson.

Live by your wits. Improvise. Vanquish fear and panic.

Looking behind the taxi, Roddy sees an ocean of headlights. He smells exhaust fumes, even with the taxi windows closed.

"Go down to 14th Street," Roddy calls to the driver and

reaches for his wallet. "I'll get out at Union Square."

He pulls out a twenty and hands it to the driver through the opening in the Plexiglas barrier. "Keep the change," he says, jumping out of the taxi as it pulls up to the curb. He sprints to the subway entrance and rushes down the stairway leading to the downtown side of the station. He swipes his MetroCard, but it doesn't register.

Too fast. Swipe the card gently.

He swipes again; it still doesn't work.

Slow down . . . slow down . . . get it right.

He swipes the card once more—very slowly, holding his breath—and the mechanism activates. He pushes through the turnstile and races down the stairs to the platform. He has a choice: either the downtown local or the express. They run along each side of the platform.

He'll take whichever comes first.

Just as he reaches the platform, the express train roars into the station. When it squeals to a stop, the doors open and passengers pour out of each car. Just in case he's been followed, Roddy waits for a few seconds. Then he jumps into the train a moment before the doors slide shut. Amid the press of people, beneath the fluorescent lights and subway ads for hemorrhoids, moles, skin tags, and acne, he edges toward a center pole as the train hurtles downtown.

At the Bowling Green station, Roddy hears an announcement: it's the last stop in Manhattan.

Next stop: Court Street–Borough Hall. Brooklyn.

The train rushes through the tunnel beneath the East River. Picking up speed, it shudders and roars at sixty miles an hour. Red and yellow lights flash on the tunnel walls and the train rocks left and right. It's a thunderous sound with a rap-like rhythm as they streak beneath the riverbed.

It seems like Roddy left Bronxville an eternity ago. His army training has helped him stay alive—escape and evasion tactics—but he has to do more. He can't keep on running. *Gotta do more—much more.* But he can't take the fight to the enemy unless he knows who they are. He must somehow learn who's after him and then go on the offense.

The train shrieks to a stop at the Court Street–Borough Hall station. The crowd piles onto a grease-stained platform. Roddy ascends a flight of stairs; he presses the baseball cap down and keeps his head low. He pushes through a turnstile and climbs another flight of stairs.

He walks quickly past the Ionic columns of the Borough Hall building into the Brooklyn night. The air smells different: fresh and clean. A melancholic feeling of déjà vu floods him. It's so powerful, he stops in his tracks. The street appears blurred, dreamlike—as though he's in a daze. Strangely, he thinks back to his time in Brooklyn. He wonders where Jackie Kurtz is now. Is he even alive? And what's he doing? And Tommy Hart, Johnny Rinaldi, Benny Gantz, and the others. A lump forms in his throat.

Never forget who you are or where you came from.

He moves away from the colonnaded building, crosses the street, and makes his way through eddies of frigid Brooklyn air.

Chapter 17

The Marriott is an ultramodern, twenty-five-story building near the Brooklyn waterfront. It's in the MetroTech Center, a business and educational hub created as part of the revitalization of Downtown Brooklyn. Roddy recalls reading about it in the *Times*.

No one would ever think about looking for him here.

Approaching the hotel, Roddy peers across the expanse of windswept Adams Street. A newspaper page twists in the blustery wind, flies through the night air, and presses against a hedge on the median divide. Cars pour down the avenue in an endless procession of head- and taillights. Seeing the rear entrance of Brooklyn's Supreme Court building, Roddy is jolted back to the day the judge sentenced him to three years of army service instead of a juvenile detention center. It's the day Roddy's always thought of as the first day of his new and better life.

He's back where he started—in more ways than one.

Entering the hotel, he takes the escalator to the mezzanine, rising through a spacious, foliage-filled atrium with a skylight roof. At the reception desk, a pert, blond woman wearing a smartly tailored gray blazer greets him with a warm smile. Her name tag reads "Holly." She's maybe twenty-five and wears her hair pulled back in a scalp-tightening ponytail, just as Tracy does. She has porcelain-pale skin, green eyes, and Celtic features; for a moment, Roddy thinks he could be standing before a younger version of his wife. There's an intense feeling of déjà vu mixed with an awareness of his present plight. He feels a wrenching tug of regret as he thinks of Tracy and the kids staying in Nutley. It dawns on him with sledgehammer intensity that his marriage could be on the verge of ending.

"What can I do for you, sir?" Holly asks as she tilts her head and smiles.

"I'd like a room on a high floor."

"Certainly, sir," Holly says with a nod. "How long will you be staying with us?"

"Can I let you know in a few days?"

"Of course, sir," she says. Their eyes meet. Holly's irises are Caribbean green and look bottomless, just as Tracy's do. Roddy feels suddenly as though he's slipped back in time to when he and Tracy met by chance in the medical library at New York Hospital. The memory of that day usually warms him, but not tonight.

As Roddy hands Holly his credit card, he smells her skin; it's vaguely reminiscent of Tracy, but his wife's scent is unlike any other woman's he's ever known. It's not perfume, soap, or lotion. It's simply Tracy. Watching Holly slide his credit card into the slot, he notices her fingers are tapered with buffed nails. She wears clear nail polish and hardly any makeup—also reminiscent of Tracy. He's so aware of missing Tracy, he wonders if he'll be seeing her—even sensing her presence—everywhere.

The room is a spacious, L-shaped single; a king-sized bed is covered by a down comforter. There's a mahogany credenza and desk and a built-in chest of drawers in the room and a fifty-two-inch flat-panel HD television mounted on the wall. And there's the obligatory minibar stuffed with miniature bottles of top-shelf booze. A large thermal-pane window faces the Gothic towers of the Brooklyn Bridge spanning the East River. Crossing the bridge, necklaces of red and white lights slink languorously in the distance. Lower Manhattan's crenellated wall of glittering lights looms just beyond the bridge and reflects on the inky waters below. Gazing at the city's looming towers of glass and concrete fills Roddy with a sense of estrangement. Tracy and the kids are apart from him; he's back in Brooklyn—but not the Brooklyn of his youth—not Sheepshead Bay with its moored fishing boats and waterfront restaurants. He's in a distant place, far removed from where he's been for so many years. And so different from his long-ago past.

The sight of the red monolith known as One Police Plaza on the other side of the river reminds Roddy of looking out the window of Captain Greene's office the day he and Danny reported Kenny missing.

And this room: comfortable in a functional sort of way. It has a decorator's sensibility—silk flowers, a faux oil painting, and fabrics in beige, ivory, and chocolate brown, lit by the soft glow of cookie-cutter bedside lamps. The room is orderly and serviceable in a stylishly impersonal way, completely lacking the loving touches of home. The room is quiet, even tomb-like. Absent are the ordinary sounds of life to which he's accustomed. Roddy hears only the blood rushing in his ears.

He unpacks his few items of clothing and sets his cell phone on the desk. He tucks the pistol in the bedside table drawer. The sight of it sends a quick shiver down his neck and spine. It's emblematic of how drastically everything has changed. He takes out the disposable cell he bought when he picked one up for Danny.

His cell phone rings—not the disposable. Looking at the screen, he sees it's from Colleen's house in Nutley.

"Tracy?"

"You have some nerve," she says in a quivering voice.

"Tracy, what's wrong?"

"It's *Sandy*," she nearly sobs.

"What's going on?"

"I . . . I told the kids that some unsavory characters were connected with the restaurant and you didn't want them coming to our house. And Sandy . . . she . . . she began crying hysterically. She told me she was outside the house last spring when a big, fat man approached her and said he was looking for Dr. Dolan."

The day Grange came to the house and gave Sandy his business card.

"And he touched her and kissed her. He gave her a card and said he'd come *back*." Tracy barely controls her sobs. "Sandy was scared to death. And she said she told you what happened and gave you this man's card."

A sickening eddy of dread washes over Roddy as he recalls Sandy standing near her bedroom door, her eyes red-rimmed and her face pale. He recalls her knuckles twisting around each other as she said, "*You won't tell Mommy?*"

He agreed not to tell Tracy.

"*He just touched my hair.*"

And then: "*His breath stinks.*"

"*How do you know?*"

"*He kissed me.*"

He recalls the toxic brew of rage that poured through him like molten lava. He felt his brain would explode, shattering his skull into bits and pieces. He knew at that moment that he would reach back to his past—was certain the mad dog would return. He'd be forced to fight for himself and his family.

The consequences didn't matter.

That day sealed Grange's fate. And Roddy's, too.

"Roddy, are you hearing a word I'm saying?"

His twisted reverie is broken. His pulse pounds through his body.

"Yes, Tracy. I'm listening."

"And now Sandy thinks this man is coming after you. She said his name was on the card."

"Trace, I—"

"Who is this man?"

"Listen, Tracy—"

"A man comes to our *house*—a child molester—and Sandy *tells* you, and you don't tell *me*? You keep it a secret? From *me*? Sandy's *mother*?"

"Tracy, calm down."

"Who *is* this man?"

"He was the brother-in-law of a former patient. I don't even remember his name. I called him, and he wanted to know if I would do a gastric bypass so he could lose weight. I told him I didn't do that kind of surgery and never to come to our home. He apologized, and I never heard from him again." Roddy's skin feels like it's shriveling.

"This man *kissed* Sandy. He fondled her hair, and you never *told* me?"

"I didn't want to upset you. I got rid of him, and that was the end of it. He was just a fat slob with no judgment."

"But this is . . . it's insane. I can't live with your lies." She lets out a sob. Roddy feels his heart being crushed as Tracy cries into the telephone. "It's been nothing but lies. I know you're still keeping things from me."

Roddy envisions Danny, Kenny, and himself in McLaughlin's back office the night Grange first showed up. He recalls the buzzing overhead light, the kitchen clatter, and the dining crowd's choral roar bleeding through the door. And Grange's threats . . . and then the nightmare that followed. It all streaks through his mind as Tracy's voice seems to fade in his ear.

"Roddy, are you there?"

"Huh?"

"This man comes to the house and he . . . and you never told me? And now we're in New Jersey while you're . . . I don't know where you are . . . and Sandy's scared out of her mind?"

"Let me talk to her."

"Why? What could you possibly say to her that will change *anything*?"

"Please, Tracy. Let me talk to her. I just want to—"

"Roddy, we're *so* over."

The line goes dead.

Chapter 18

The Doral Arrowwood Hotel sits on 114 acres of rolling hills, meadows, and reed-filled ponds in Rye Brook, New York. It's a short ride by car service to Danny's office in Yonkers. But that's not an option right now. Danny's staying put in the hotel.

The hotel's manager is a longtime client, and Danny landed an executive suite through the guy's efforts and goodwill. On an upper floor, the suite has two well-appointed rooms with a fully equipped kitchenette. The suite's office area has the whole enchilada, including a plug-in for his laptop, high-speed Internet access, a fax machine, and a top-of-the-line scanner and copier—everything he needs to help Natalie, his office manager, run his business right from the suite. She's had the office locks replaced, and the landlord installed security cameras in the lobby, elevator, and stairwells. Dan's glad Natalie knows the ropes and is überefficient. It's simply a matter of staying in touch. No matter what the bastards who shot him took, Danny still has all his clients' records stored in Dropbox, which he can access in a matter of seconds on his new laptop.

So now he and Roddy are living like fugitives while Angela and the kids are staying in Riverdale, in her brother's cramped apartment. *God, what a jackass I was for hooking up with Kenny Egan*, Danny thinks.

Dan's thoughts swirl in a jumble. He wonders why he was so

stupid he didn't see that was coming down the track. Why had he let Roddy and himself stumble into the bind they're now in? Because of his own stupidity—that's why. Because of his wish to become more than an accountant. Because he wanted to rub shoulders with the New York glitterati. That's why he let it all happen. He and Roddy went into business; and what did it lead to?

They violated the laws of God and of man.

In a cold sweat, Danny kneels at the edge of the bed and begins praying.

Oh, my loving and merciful God . . . where are you now? Are you dead like Da, or do you hear me? Can you forgive me for what I did? And will Roddy ever forgive me for what I did to him? That was my biggest sin of all, betraying Roddy. Dear God, do you hear me when I confess everything to you?

Danny's convinced death lurks everywhere. It follows him—relentlessly—and there's no escaping what will happen. And while Danny sometimes wonders if there's truly a place called hell, he knows his life has become a hell on earth.

Apprehension seizes him. It's a sense of dread so deep, he feels it sucking the breath from his body. His heart begins thumping insanely. He gasps for breath. It's not the asthma—it's pure nerves—and the air hunger is so bad, it feels like he's being garroted.

He staggers to the bathroom, grabs his inhaler, and with shaking hands, puts it to his lips and presses the lever. He sucks inward, deeply, desperately, hoping for a breath of precious air as medicine-laced mist fills his lungs.

But his breathlessness worsens, so he grabs the orange vial of pills at the side of the sink and dumps a few Klonopin tablets into his trembling palm.

Oh God, please help me.

The pills are in his mouth, but his tongue feels like fur and the tablets stick to it. He clutches a glass, fills it with water, and gulps. He slugs more water, but isn't sure the pills are down, so he refills the glass and guzzles more. He stumbles back to the bedroom and onto the bed, lies on his back, and stares at the ceiling.

Oh, please . . . sweet Jesus . . . let me breathe.

A veil of calm descends, slowly, but he feels it taking over.

Klonopin, how ironic—the same shit Roddy used to put that bastard Grange into some half-assed state so we could dump him into the hole.

And Roddy's name is on this bottle as the prescribing doctor. Jesus, life just mocks you at every turn. Roddy's told Dan it takes at least twenty minutes before the Klonopin even begins taking effect—before he feels that warm smoothness that lightens the horror of it all. And yet, within a few seconds after gulping the pills, Dan feels his breathing slow, and his heart downshifts from its pumped-up racing. The cloud of dread begins to dissipate.

Though he's no longer kneeling at the bedside, Danny continues praying.

Oh, God in heaven, please help us get out of this hole.

And please, dear God, forgive me for what I've done to Roddy and our families.

Danny decides he must talk with Roddy. It would be such a relief, and besides, there are things he must say. He can't hold it in any longer. He grabs the disposable cell, looks at the number taped to it, and dials. Roddy picks up on the second ring.

"Roddy, where are you?"

"I'm on the move."

"I'm at the Arrowwood." Dan pauses, feeling a slight flood of relief hearing his kemosabe's voice. "How're Tracy and the kids?"

"Don't even ask. How about Angie and yours?"

"Good. Good. But I'm living like a hermit."

"Me, too."

"You learn anything?"

"Nothing else. Like I told you, he was a made man."

A twinge of dread grips Danny as he hears those words. "So

they wanna clip us?"

"Looks that way."

"How would they know we had anything to do with him?"

"He must've told someone about us," says Roddy. "We gotta figure something out."

"What're we gonna figure, huh? Tell me, for the love of Christ, what's there to figure out?" Danny's hand trembles as he holds the phone to his ear. He breaks out in a cold sweat.

God in heaven, it's all coming down on us.

"Jesus, Roddy. I can't stop thinkin' about it."

"About what?"

"Those two bastards in the ground somewhere upstate. It never goes away. It's like a bad dream, a never-ending nightmare. You know, the earth must be frozen by now. It's probably hard as stone."

"Look, Dan. You can't let it get the best of you. We did what we had to do and—"

"I can't forget the way we hauled that fat bastard outta your SUV and then dug that goddamned hole. I keep thinkin' how we couldn't get that star sapphire ring off his fat finger and how you used the cable cutter. Jesus, I almost puked when you did that. I still get nauseous when I think about it. And then—"

"Dan."

"Then rolling him into that pit. You know what, Roddy? I still hear that thud when the bastard hit bottom."

"Listen, Dan. You—"

"And then throwing the ring and finger into that swamp, and the gun, too; and then that sick son of a bitch, Kenny, jumping into the hole and cutting off Grange's ear with the shovel and holding it next to his own and laughing like a sick hyena. Jesus, Roddy, I can't get it outta my mind. You know what? I still smell that hole, the dirt, and the piss and shit. I swear, Roddy, I really do. And I sometimes see Kenny, half naked, smoking and sweating and pissing his pants because he was so scared when you put that .45 to his head."

"Dan, he deserved what he got. He—"

"And I think about how I felt and what I said. I can't forget it. It's in my head forever. It just won't quit."

Even as he speaks, Dan's thoughts swerve back to those moments.

"Tell me, you son of a bitch, who ran Angela off the road?"

"I dunno."

"Shoot him, Roddy. Shoot the motherfucker."

Danny knows something hateful and vengeful erupted from within him that night. Danny knows he'd have blasted Kenny Egan to bits that night if he'd had the chance.

And Danny wonders about his own role in the entire McLaughlin scheme. How big a part did he play in what went down from the very moment he decided to partner up with Kenny . . . and the mob? Holy shit . . . the *mob*. The word alone sends shivers through him. It's enough to shrivel his soul.

"Tell me, Roddy, how do you live with what we did that night? Huh?"

"It's been fading for me. Until you got shot, the memory was getting dimmer."

"Not for me. I can't forget those woods. That moon and the bare trees. It was so eerie, and those peeping frogs and the crickets."

"C'mon, Dan, you gotta get a handle on it."

"I can't, Roddy. I just *can't*."

"Kenny admitted what he did. He was gonna bilk us for everything. And he's the one who ran Angie off the road and nearly killed her."

"Would you've killed him if he hadn't gone for that pistol?"

"I dunno."

"Think about it. Would you've done it?"

"Hypotheticals don't do us any good, Danny."

"Maybe not, but it's playin' games with my head, Roddy. You know . . . when the kids're watching *The Walking Dead*, I can't look at that shit. It drives me up a wall. And I can't watch anything on TV with guns or shooting. I start gettin' short of breath."

"You taking the Klonopin I prescribed?"

"Yeah, but it's gonna take more than that to get my head straight."

"Listen, Dan—"

"You know, since it went down, I've been to Mass every Sunday."

"You gotta do whatever makes you feel better."

"I wish I could go to confession," Dan says, picturing the confessional with its kneeler and lattice screen. A momentary wave of warmth calms him.

"Jesus, Danny. Not *confession*. You'll blow us sky-high."

"I gotta talk to someone. I can't go on this way."

"Don't say a word to anyone, Danny. Not to Angie or a priest. Not to a living soul. If confession makes you feel better, confess *privately* to God . . . not a fucking priest. Keep it to yourself. You *hear* me?"

"Yeah, yeah. I hear you." Danny closes his eyes and inhales deeply. His breath whistles through his nose. He weighs telling Roddy what he's been thinking since he was shot. Can he do it? Can he actually say it and not worry about the inevitable blowback sure to come his way? Does he risk arousing the mad dog inside Roddy? Why not take the plunge? After all, Roddy's his friend, his blood brother, and they'll always be friends, no matter what happens.

"Roddy, I've been thinking—and hear me out on this."

"I'm listening."

"It's been on my mind for a while now, even before I got shot."

"Yeah? What is it?"

"I gotta tell you, Roddy, because it's been buildin' up like a pressure cooker and I just can't go on this way. I'd be holding out on you if I didn't tell you." Danny waits, clutching the cell phone as tightness grips his chest—it's the fucking asthma.

Roddy says nothing.

"Listen, Roddy, maybe we're best off going to Morgan and telling him what happened."

There's silence. Danny wonders if Roddy will erupt in fury. There's an intake of breath on the other end.

"What the fuck're you sayin', Danny? Go to the *police*? You gotta be kiddin'."

"No, I'm not. Why don't we tell the cops and hope for the best? Right now, we're holed up and don't even know who's coming after us or when it's gonna happen. If we go to the police—"

"*Dan*, you can't be serious. We tell Morgan a *thing*, he'll push and probe, and we go down the tubes. We're talkin' premeditated murder here. Murder in the first degree. No matter how you spin it, it's prison—Attica or Sing Sing—for the rest of our goddamned lives. And what're we gonna have left then?"

"I don't know if I can go on this way, Roddy."

"*What*? You don't know if you can go on? What're you . . . fuckin' crazy? We have no choice. *None*. We did what we had to, and now we'll do what we gotta do, Dan."

"I don't know, Roddy. We're all fucked up now, and we're going nowhere."

"Going nowhere? Whaddaya wanna do, Dan? Put us in prison? Is that it? All my life I've been thinkin', *Like father, like son*. And what do I hear my best friend sayin'? You wanna put me in Attica like my father? Is *that* it?"

"Listen, Roddy, I've always gone along with you. All my life, I've let you steamroll over me, like that night we killed Grange and Kenny."

"That's *bullshit*, Dan. Pure bullshit. I never rolled over you.

Ever."

"I let you call the shots about Grange and Kenny. And now I'm payin' the price. I'm in hell—it's a living hell. I just can't take this anymore."

"You have to, Danny. We've gotta keep going. What the fuck do you want? You think *this* is hell? Life in prison . . . *that's* hell. You can't even *imagine* what it's like. And our families'll be left with *nothing*. Not one fuckin' thing."

"Yeah? So tell me, Roddy, what do they have now? They're in hiding because we put their lives in danger. You're not at the hospital, and I can't set foot into my office. The cops are circling, and the mob's after us. So tell me: what the fuck do we have? We're stuck in this snake pit and I see no way out. It's only a matter of time before they get us."

"Unless we get to them first," says Roddy.

"Get to them *first*? Get to *who*? Who the fuck do we get to? Who the hell *are* they? And even if we find out who *they* are, what do we . . . two guys—a doctor and an accountant—do up against the *mob*? You gotta be kiddin', Roddy. And what if it's the Russians? They'll stop at nothing to get us. They'll go after our families, our wives and kids. What do you propose we do then?"

"Look, Danny, we gotta think this through and find out which mob is behind this . . . the mafia or the Bratva."

"The *mob*? The fuckin' *mob*? Just the word makes me cringe. Jesus, Roddy. What the fuck did we get into?" Danny's heart feels like it jumps in his chest.

"We gotta try to figure it out."

"Even if we dope it out, what can we do? Huh? You got an answer for me?"

"Listen, Dan. We take it one step at a time."

"One step at a time? What steps can we take, Roddy? What goddamned steps? Huh? Or are you gonna do something without me knowing anything?"

"What're you talking about, Danny?"

"You gotta promise me something."

"What?"

"You don't do anything like what happened with Grange and Kenny. You gotta promise me we talk before you do anything."

"I have no problem with that."

"We gotta be on the same page. No acting on your own."

"Agreed."

"And another thing."

"Yeah?"

"You say you wanna think this through."

"Yeah . . ."

"If you don't come up with something in a week, I'm talkin' to Morgan to see what our options are."

"Are you *nuts*? One *week*? You can't put a deadline on this. Go to the police? That's crazy, Danny."

"No, it's not. It might be the only *sane* thing to do. We're caught in a squeeze, and I see no way out."

"Dan, we can't act out of fear or worry. It's never the way to go."

"It's not just fear. There may be a way to cut a deal."

"Cut a deal? That's ridiculous. Dan, we'll end up in prison. Twenty-five to life, that's what we'll get."

"Roddy, let's face it. We're dead meat. And lemme tell you something. We're not nine years old anymore, and we're not the Hardy Boys. All I care about is my family. I gotta protect Angie and the kids, and I gotta do the right thing. If it means I go to prison, that's what I'll do. I don't give a shit."

"Don't fuck me over, Dan. Don't make me end up like my father."

"I'm not fuckin' you over, Roddy. I'm thinkin' about how we can get out of this with as little damage as possible."

"No, Dan. You're thinkin' about fuckin' over our lives.

Completely and forever. I can't let you do that."

Danny inhales and hears those bubbles in his chest.

"Whaddaya gonna do, Roddy?"

"C'mon, Dan."

"No. What're you gonna do? Silence me?"

"Don't be ridiculous."

"I'm not bein' ridiculous. I'm serious. Whaddaya gonna do, huh?"

Dan hears static on the line, nothing else. The air in the room seems dead.

"Roddy, if we're lucky, you have one week. Then I'm gonna do what I gotta do. If you don't like it, well, you do what *you* gotta do."

Chapter 19

On this gray winter morning, Roddy leaves the Marriott and heads toward the Court Street subway station.

Yesterday's phone conversation with Danny echoes in his thoughts. How did everything get so screwed up? Danny wanting to see a priest . . . confess . . . contact Morgan and blow it all wide open. A ponderous load of guilt must be weighing him down. Dan setting a one-week time limit before he goes to Morgan and tries to arrange a deal—absurd. Nothing but self-immolation.

And Dan's last words to Roddy keep reeling in his thoughts. *"I'm gonna do what I gotta do. If you don't like it, well, you do what you gotta do."*

When Roddy called Nutley last night, Tracy wouldn't talk to him, but he spoke with the kids. Sandy's voice trembled.

"Daddy, is that fat man coming back?"

She was on the verge of tears.

"No, sweetie. He's not coming back."

"I'm scared."

"There's no need to be scared, sweetie. He's never coming back," Roddy said, shuddering inwardly.

No . . . Grange is gone for good . . . and maybe my life is gone, too.

"When can we go home?"

"Soon. I promise." But he wondered how he'd make good on

such a pledge.

Speaking with Tom, Roddy detected a hint of apprehension in his son's voice. How much fear was the kid trying to mask?

Roddy's thoughts return to Tracy. He realizes how empty his world is without her, how diminished and alone he feels, and he knows he would do anything to get her back.

"Roddy, we're so over."

Crossing through Columbus Park, Roddy wonders why he's heading to the south end of Brooklyn. Is it because that's where the Russians live? Why would he want to go there? Or is it something else—returning to his past, the place where he learned to think and act like a mad dog?

Walking toward the subway station, Roddy scans the park and surrounding area. He's cautious passing any shop or building entrance, or if he sees someone loitering on a street. He's changed baseball caps and bought two more jackets. He won't wear the same one two days in a row. He hasn't shaved for days, and his face is covered with thick stubble. As an extra precaution, he wears wraparound sunglasses while on the street. And he scopes out everything. Nothing escapes his eyes.

He recalls Sergeant Dawson's words about escape and evasion behind enemy lines: *"Improvise. Blend in with the population. Wear and do nothing that makes you stand out."*

At Borough Hall, he makes his way down the stairway into the labyrinthine maze of the subway system. His eyes crawl over every man he sees—even teenagers. He's exquisitely aware of anyone who looks potentially aggressive. Or of anyone who appears overly casual. His heart jumps whenever he sees someone wearing a Bluetooth device.

Standing on the platform, he spots a man wearing a black leather car coat. The guy is short, with dark, slicked-back hair and a Roman nose—could be Italian, maybe Eastern European; he's leaning against a pillar reading the *New York Post*. Roddy eyes him from a distance of about fifty feet. A few moments later, the man tucks the paper under his arm and moves toward the end of the platform, away from Roddy. He then resumes reading the newspaper. It's unlikely he's a threat.

A moment later, Roddy notices a young black man strolling toward him. He wears baggy jeans and a navy blue hoodie. He's maybe nineteen, twenty years old. Roddy's muscles tense and his hand slips into his jacket pocket. He clutches the revolver grip. Roddy speculates what the kid might be up to. He recalls from countless movies that hit men come in all sizes, shapes, and colors. There was an episode of *The Sopranos* when Tony was nearly shot by a black kid who ran up to his SUV. It turned out to be an attempted mob hit.

The kid notices Roddy; their eyes lock. Roddy's body stiffens, but he wants to avoid a confrontation—an eyeball-to-eyeball stare down. But he can't take his eyes off the kid. As he stares directly into Roddy's eyes, the kid's gait turns into an aggressive strut—a rolling pimp walk. His chin thrusts forward; his shoulders sway from side to side. He never blinks and doesn't avert his gaze for half a second.

About ten feet away from Roddy, the kid's cell phone lets out an ear-splitting rap rhythm in the confines of the enclosed station with its tile walls. Still staring directly at Roddy, the kid grabs the cell from a side pocket of his cargo pants, stops, and says, "Yo."

The kid stands with the phone at his ear, listening. He glares at Roddy, belligerence seeping from every pore of his body. Roddy's fingers tighten around the pistol grip. The kid's features harden and his look turns baleful.

Roddy's heart quickens. Is this guy gonna start something? Is this a chance meeting, or could it be something else—an encounter that isn't so random, one that's planned? Roddy decides to play it carefully and lets his eyes wander to a point beyond the kid's shoulder and a bit off to the side. But he keeps him in his peripheral vision. He feels the kid's eyes crawling all over him. It's a testosterone-filled challenge—he's daring Roddy to make eye contact again.

Roddy realizes this isn't how a hit man would operate. The kid's not a threat. He's just an angry young punk with a hard-on for the world. Roddy's also aware that time has changed him. Gone are the days when he'd have stared the kid down or even walked up to him and given him the Robert De Niro *You lookin' at me?* line. That was the Mad Dog thing to do—answer the challenge with one of his own—and if needed, throw the first punch, a lightning-fast, power-loaded fist coming with pile-driver intensity from nowhere.

But those days are long gone, and the Mad Dog is much smarter now, less testosterone-poisoned than years ago.

Roddy turns and peers down the tracks into the tunnel. His hand remains in his pocket—on the pistol grip. He can still see the kid out of the corner of his eye. Another minute passes, and the kid ambles away—still bristling truculence.

When the R train rolls in with its brakes screeching, Roddy boards and rides it to DeKalb Avenue, where he transfers to the Q train on the Brighton Beach line. Plenty of Russians live in Brighton Beach, the largest Russian enclave anywhere outside their mother country. Slavic-looking people occupy the train, all speaking in harsh-sounding English or Russian. They're getting off at the last stop: Brighton Beach—Little Odessa by the Sea, as it's called.

At the Prospect Park station, the train leaves the tunnel and emerges onto an elevated track. It rumbles through Brooklyn, stopping at Church Avenue and Newkirk Avenue, and continues southward through the flatlands of Flatbush. At the Kings Highway stop, Roddy is overcome by a nostalgic ache as he recalls the excursions he, Danny, and Jackie Kurtz made as teenagers, visiting the stores along this commercial thoroughfare.

The train pulls into the Sheepshead Bay station—the stop before Brighton Beach. From the height of the elevated structure, Roddy looks out over the old neighborhood, wondering if he'll make some connection with the past.

Leaving the train, he waits for the station platform to clear, making sure no one is following him. His eyes scan left and right as the platform empties. After a full minute, he clambers down the stairway to Sheepshead Bay Road, and moments later, he's deep in the midst of his past. It's more than a quarter of a century since he's been here.

Sheepshead Bay Road looks familiar, but appears narrower than he remembered. Retail stores seem to crouch over the street. Ethnic restaurants are everywhere—very different ones from those of his youth. A pizzeria, gyro joint, a taco stand, and a Chinese takeout place are near the station, and the Johnny Fell Inn is no longer at the next block; in its stead looms a huge Chase Bank.

But there's no gentrification: no Starbucks or high-end boutiques or organic food shops catering to vegans.

I'm a long way from Bronxville.

Gone is Herbie's Gym, where he trained and boxed as a kid. A Citibank branch stands in its place. He takes a detour to where Leo's Luncheonette was located. It's gone. On the empty lot behind where Leo's stood—where he ripped off Cootie Weiss's ear in a fight when he was twelve—stands a six-story apartment house.

El Greco—the Greek's—is still perched on the same corner near the bay. Roddy remembers the night he, Frankie Messina, and Kenny Egan planned the appliance store burglary. It all comes back in a mercurial rush of images: the narrow alleyway, he and Frankie loading the truck, the siren's shriek and whirling police lights, the 61st Precinct's piss-stinking holding cell, the arraignment and his appearance before the judge. Then: the army—a life-changer.

Across the street is where Roddy beat the shit out of those German guys who were pummeling Danny. Rosario's butcher shop's been replaced by a Korean nail salon. How ironic it all seems: he's looking at the spot where he saved Danny, and yet Dan is now about to jeopardize everything they've worked for all their lives.

"If you don't like it, well, you do what you gotta do."

On East 19th Street, leafless sycamore tree branches sway in the wind. Roddy stands before a two-story attached house, where he lived in the basement apartment for his first seventeen years. It brings an image of his glazed-eyed, whiskey-guzzling mother and her woman-beating boyfriend, Horst. Roddy visualizes himself at fifteen, coming home from Mike's Pool Hall to find his mother bloodied and unconscious on the couch. Horst had beaten her half to death for having burned the beef stew she'd been cooking. And when Horst lunged at him with a kitchen knife, Roddy pummeled him with a series of chopping blows and kicks. After Horst was discharged from Coney Island Hospital, he never returned and was out of their lives forever.

Roddy thinks of his father in Attica. *Like father, like son*, he ruminates for the ten thousandth time in his life. He recoils at the thought of a shank slicing his father's guts. Roddy knows how fragile life is. All you are or have ever been can be gone in an instant, just as it was for Walt McKay and almost was for Danny.

And now Dan threatens him with a deadline: one week to find out who's coming after them. And then do something about it. Something *acceptable* to Danny. If not, he'll go to Morgan.

A block away, he stops in front of a gray clapboard house, where Danny and his mother lived. Peggy Burns—the angel of his life—took him in when Horst beat or tortured him. But she's dead, too. A flood of sadness overtakes him, and the street seems to darken.

It occurs to Roddy that thirty years ago, everyone knew him as the Dolan boy, the tough kid who hung with the Sheepshead Bay Boys. Now, if he dropped dead on the street, they'd have to rummage through his pockets to locate his next of kin. He's an outsider here, an alien, a complete unknown. His anonymity staggers him like a shock to the heart. He wonders what makes a life worth living. Is it love? Commitment? The giving of one's self to another? Children? Is there anything left in this life for him? Bleakness fills him and leaves him feeling hollow.

At Emmons Avenue, he crosses the footbridge over Sheepshead Bay and walks to the concrete esplanade overlooking the Atlantic Ocean. The sea is green-looking with choppy whitecaps in the grayish distance. A gloomy mist hangs over the water. Roddy smells rain coming. Steel-wool-gray clouds clump massively at the horizon. He gazes toward Coney Island in the distance, where the steel skeleton of the towering Steeplechase Parachute Jump stands.

Seeing Coney Island, Roddy's reminded of the nighttime Cyclone rides with Danny: the Parachute Jump and its dizzying descent, firing pellet guns at the target-shooting concession on Surf Avenue; and Nathan's Famous, where, on freezing winter nights, he and Danny gorged on hot dogs and fried clam bellies amid the bright carnival atmosphere of Surf Avenue.

He comes to the huge granite slab along the esplanade, where as nine-year-olds, he and Danny swore their blood brother oath, becoming Cochise and kemosabe to each other by slitting their wrists and mingling their blood.

But now he has doubts about Danny's loyalty and is even questioning Danny's involvement with Kenny in McLaughlin's. Even more alarming is Danny's readiness to run to Morgan. Danny—with that *best boy* conscience of his—is about to toss in the towel and confess everything. He's become a loose cannon and can no longer be trusted. In his way, he's nearly as dangerous as the mafia or the Bratva.

Danny—his lifelong friend and blood brother—could put them both in prison for the rest of their lives.

Beneath a somber sky, Roddy looks out over the Atlantic. The water roils and sloshes against the rocks below. Clumps of green and brown seaweed float in swirling eddies on the foaming surface. In the distance, he sees the silhouette of a freighter—ghostly looking in the misty winter dreariness. It will soon pass Breezy Point and the Rockaways, and then head east through Long Island Sound to the open reaches of the Atlantic. The air smells of brine. Roddy watches the rolling clouds move toward land. He tastes salt, thinking some sea spray has hit his face but realizes tears have snaked down his cheeks to his lips.

Roddy returned to the place of his youth to reignite the mad dog. Even though he felt that vicious surge when he thought mobsters were parked near the house, Roddy wonders if too much has changed for him to return to those days. So many years have passed and too much water has flowed beneath the bridge spanning Sheepshead Bay.

Sitting on the rock where he and Danny sat so many years ago, beneath a darkening sky, amid the horror of the present, it strikes Roddy with stunning clarity: everything in his life—from this moment on—is a complete unknown. He's no longer a kid from the streets, and Danny's not a boy either. They've gone on with their lives and have traveled their own paths. Their roads are diverging.

And now his lifelong friend may destroy everything.

Chapter 20

Danny's skin feels like it's curdling. He's going stir-crazy in this hotel. He's keeping up with business all right; he's on the phone and using the computer, scanner, and fax. Thank God Natalie's running things in Yonkers. It's mostly massaging clients' returns to lighten their tax loads. Everyone wants to finesse Uncle Sam, but that old guy gets his piece of the pie.

As if it really matters, because when Danny gets right down to it, he's not certain he'll be alive a week from now. And this confinement is hard to bear.

His only excursions have been to the hotel dining room. If he gobbles down any more food, he'll tip the scales at two thirty. Last night, he gorged on a charbroiled New York strip steak with goat cheese smashed potatoes and a salad. And then a monstrous piece of creamy cheesecake. Reminded him of McLaughlin's with its prime meats and gargantuan iceberg lettuce salads smothered with gorgonzola and bacon bits dressing—and the restaurant's array of mouthwatering desserts. Jesus, everything reminds him of the restaurant.

Just what you need, Danny Boy—cholesterol-laden crap so you'll have a heart attack and drop dead, just like Da did in the innards of that shit-ball furnace he was repairing, amid the soot, dust, and fumes. Dan's certain his genes guarantee he'll have a massive coronary—stop his ticker cold—unless another bullet does the trick first.

Maybe that's what he deserves—a slug right in the brain.

But maybe he and Roddy can get out of this hole if he contacts Morgan and really talks with the guy. Even though Roddy's dead set against going to the cops, it might be the only way to see this thing through to some reasonable end. Roddy would see it as a Judas kiss if Danny cut a deal for them with the DA. Yes, latch on to a deal, one that would keep them alive and get their families out of harm's way.

Danny tries imagining the conversation with the detective.

You see, Detective, liquor, wine, and steaks were disappearing. Kenny was screwing up—and we were taking losses. So we told Kenny we were getting out.

After he disappeared, Captain Greene said Kenny owed money to the wrong people. And maybe they're after us because we were his partners.

So these guys wanna kill you instead of collecting their money? Can't be, Mr. Burns, because money trumps everything with these guys, and dead men don't write checks.

Conversation over.

Morgan would sniff out that line of crap a mile away and *really* start interrogating him. He'd push, probe, and needle Danny. Each question would lead to a dozen more, and then who knows what he'd unearth?

Unearth?

Yeah, sure. Why not just tell Morgan to go ahead and dig up the grave at Snapper Pond? Find Grange—or whatever his real name is—and what's left of that skinny Irish bastard Kenny, too.

Jesus, why'd he partner up with Kenny Egan?

And why did he listen to Angela, who has always nagged him?

Danny, you're too conservative with money. Be a little daring. Take a chance. Become a silent partner. It won't kill you.

But that's bullshit. He shouldn't try convincing himself he was pussy-whipped into this thing—that it's somehow Angela's fault. A shudder of shame racks Danny for even thinking he could shift the blame onto her. This mess is his own doing and it's his cross to bear, not Angela's or anyone else's.

Danny broke faith with Roddy and led him down this treacherous path. Why did he shoot for the stars with that degenerate, Kenny "Snake Eyes" Egan?

Because Danny never had real confidence in himself, that's why. Because he somehow felt he was less than an equal when it came to the guys back in Sheepshead Bay. He always avoided all the bad shit that went down. Everyone called him Danny Boy because he was a pudgy-faced, redheaded, freckled kid who was smart, who gave a shit about school, who pleased the teachers, was good with numbers, belonged to the math club, and got straight As. He never sat with the cool guys in the cafeteria and was never really part of that macho Sheepshead Bay, kick-ass crowd of toughs and small-time gangbangers.

Yeah, the girls liked him because they thought he was cute— especially with his ginger-colored freckles, red hair, and boyish face. They'd sing "Danny Boy" when they passed him in the school hallways. But his only true friend was his blood brother, Roddy. If not for Roddy, those hard-boiled bastards would have bullied him mercilessly and he'd have been the never-ending butt of their cruel comments, jokes, and catcalls. He'd have been ranked-out endlessly, from daybreak until sunset every day of the week and twice on Sundays.

Along came Kenny with the McLaughlin's deal. So he got into bed with Egan and fucked over Roddy. It was a complete betrayal of his blood brother. All because as a kid, he was never daring enough, or slick enough, or worldly enough. And he wanted to prove something—that he had balls and money and could handle power and people. That he could swing a big dick—and become a player by owning a Manhattan steakhouse, right in the middle of everything. A place where the Donald Trump and John Harris types congregated, where Mike Bloomberg, Alec Baldwin, Derek Jeter, Pete Hamill, and the glitterati did their thing.

And then—worse than anything he could ever have imagined—he was involved in the murder of two men. One way or another, Danny will pay for what he did.

His disposable cell rings.

"Roddy?"

"Who else would it be?"

"Where've you been?"

"Nowhere I wanna be."

"Yeah, tell me about it," Danny says with a heavy sigh.

"Dan, I've been thinking."

"Yeah?"

"There was this gap between when you got shot and when I saw those guys in the garage."

"Yeah?"

"When these mob guys are on a vendetta, don't they usually settle the score all at once? Doesn't it all go down on the same day?"

"I wouldn't really know," Danny says.

"Doesn't that make sense? They don't leave loose ends hanging around."

"Okay. So?"

"I just wonder if they came for me—whoever they are—only because they knew you were alive."

"I don't follow."

"I'm just thinking out loud. I'm wondering if maybe you're the primary target."

Bubbles start popping in Danny's chest. His bronchioles narrow, and he feels mucous collecting in his tubes. Fucking asthma. "But who'd be gunning for me—and why?"

"I don't know. Maybe some former client in deep shit with the

IRS or some employee you fired."

"I don't know, Roddy. I can't remember anyone who left on bad terms or had a real grievance against me."

"You sure, Dan? Think. Maybe someone got screwed over by the IRS and blames you?"

"I've never had a major screwup, ever. And the only clients I've lost are those who died or moved to Florida or Arizona. And even if that was the case, why come after you, too?"

"You got a point. I'm just trying to think this out from every possible angle."

"And why *now*?" Danny says. "Why ten months after what went down upstate?"

"Well, I learned from my contact that Grange could disappear for months at a time. That's why he was called Ghost. So maybe they only just realized something happened."

There's a pause in the conversation. Static fills Danny's ear. Roddy says something, but he's drowned out by interference.

"So what do you think?"

"Roddy, I didn't hear you."

"I have an idea is what I said. How 'bout I go see Omar? You remember him?"

"Kenny's assistant maître d'. You think he might know something?"

"I have no idea, but you want me to come up with some answers, right?"

"Yeah, sure."

"You said one week, right?"

"Yes, but—"

"Omar was at the restaurant almost as much as Kenny."

"It seems like a long shot, Roddy."

"Maybe, but what else do we have? And what about that hostess Kenny hired . . . Crystal?"

At the mention of her name, Danny visualizes Crystal—tall,

her blond hair in an elaborate chignon, her hips swaying as she moved in a sexualized strut, leading diners to their table, and those bee-stung lips pouting lasciviously.

"What would she know?"

"Hey, Danny, how much do *we* know?"

"I get your point."

"You know where they live?"

"I'll check my computer. I'm sure I still have their W-2 forms in there."

"Do it. We gotta make something happen before we're dead meat."

Chapter 21

Over the years he's lived in Bronxville, Roddy's forgotten how congested a rush-hour subway car could be.

On the 4 train, Roddy stands against the middle doors of the car. In Ranger mode, he scans the crowd. The subway speeds beneath Manhattan streets, rocking and clacking, people's heads bobbing in unison as the train roars uptown. Never before have so many ordinary men looked so potentially threatening. What would a hit man look like? Roddy wonders. Most likely, a harmless-looking guy—just another face in the crowd, someone who could melt seamlessly into the subway car's clot of humanity after he'd shot or stabbed his target. Roddy stays vigilant and scans every person standing in the sardine-packed car. He gets off at 86th Street and climbs up the stairs leading to the street.

Standing at the intersection of Lexington and 86th, Roddy has no way of knowing if he was followed. He starts walking east on 86th, eyeing everyone and everything. Passing a Verizon store, he spots a guy leaning against the building; he's smoking a cigarette and watches as Roddy walks by. Roddy can feel the man's eyes on his back. He turns and glances at the guy, who averts his gaze. Roddy walks a few yards more, turns again, and notices the man is gone. He scans the street—including the other side—but there's no sign of him.

At the intersection of 3rd and 86th, Roddy sees a holdout

from decades ago—Papaya King. As kids, he and Danny bought hot dogs slathered in mustard and washed them down with the then-famous papaya fruit drink.

But those days are dead and gone.

Heading north on 2nd Avenue, Roddy notices the east side of the avenue is walled off by a chain-link fence; it's where the 2nd Avenue subway line is being carved out of granite beneath the street. Walking into a brisk wind, Roddy turns back and checks to make sure no one is following. He sees a man dart into a store halfway down the block. With his radar activated, Roddy decides to make a move.

At the intersection of 90th and 2nd, Roddy turns the corner and stops abruptly. He leans against a building's wall, waiting. If anyone's following, he'll turn the corner and virtually slam into Roddy. He slips his hand into his pocket, feels the pistol, and waits.

After five minutes, Roddy decides he's not being followed.

Approaching 92nd Street, he decides to take an extra turn around the block to make certain he's not being tailed. He circles the block slowly until he's once again at the intersection of 90th and 2nd Avenue.

Midblock on the south side of 92nd Street, he comes to a brownstone between 2nd and 1st Avenues. He climbs the outside stairs and opens the door. In the vestibule, he reads the nameplates on the intercom. Finding "Noori" next to a button for apartment 3-A, he presses it.

"Yes," says a voice on the intercom.

"Omar, it's Roddy Dolan . . . from McLaughlin's."

"Dr. *Dolan*? Please come up."

The buzzer sounds along with an electric click in the door handle. Roddy pushes it open and makes his way up a narrow stairway to the third floor.

Omar stands at the open door to his apartment. He looks no

different from when Roddy last saw him: same medium height, olive complexion, his thick black hair swept back with a severe widow's peak, and a pencil-thin moustache, but in contrast to the tuxedo Omar wore at the restaurant, he's now dressed in jeans and a sweatshirt.

They greet each other warmly and Omar invites him in. It's a typical brownstone apartment facing north on a quiet side street: a living room, kitchen with an eating area, and a bedroom. It reminds Roddy of the apartment he rented when he was at New York Hospital when he met Tracy. That place, too, faced north, and they loved the diffuse light coming in through the windows, even in winter. It was where Tracy and he first made love. His throat thickens at the thought of Tracy. He wonders where she is and what she's doing at this moment. A pang of sadness seizes him as he recalls the last words she said on the telephone.

"Roddy, we're so over."

Roddy and Omar do some catching up. Omar's been working at the Capital Grille on 42nd Street, and his wife works for Verizon on East 86th Street. His daughter is an honor student in middle school.

When Omar asks about Roddy's family, sorrow seeps through Roddy as he thinks again of Tracy, Tom, and Sandy.

My life's in the cellar. I'd gladly trade places with Omar and live his life.

"Omar, I came to see you because I'm trying to understand what happened to Kenny Egan." Roddy looks down and notices his foot tapping on the floor.

Omar's lips curl downward and his face darkens. He shakes his head. "Not a good man, if you'll forgive my saying so."

Since Omar's no longer an employee, Roddy is certain he'll speak candidly about his former boss.

"Omar, please be frank. I know Kenny did a terrible job. But I'm trying to find out why he disappeared."

The irony of all this is so striking. Here he is, asking about a dead man—one he shot and killed—as though he has no idea what happened to the guy.

"I'm not surprised he's gone," Omar says. "When I was first hired, the restaurant was running smoothly. But it soon went to the dogs." Omar shakes his head, and his tongue pokes against the inside of his cheek. "I didn't like the crowd. I don't mean the regular people and businessmen; they were fine, and I enjoyed serving them. But there was a certain element that began coming—criminals—and they worried me."

"They were just customers," Roddy says, trying to gauge Omar's response.

"Yes, but I had the feeling Kenny was doing business with them."

"What kind of business?"

Roddy's foot tapping quickens. His cheeks feel hot. Omar might know about Kenny's dealings. Maybe some answers are forthcoming.

"I don't know. They whispered back and forth . . . Kenny and those Russians . . . and the Italian mafia, too. I just had the feeling Kenny was up to something."

"Any idea what it was?"

"No. And I didn't want to know. Kenny was spending more time in the back office than in the front of the house. One time— and I wasn't snooping—I opened the office door and Kenny was playing blackjack on the computer. He was gambling, losing money, drinking too much, and using cocaine, too. His nose ran all the time. He was a different man from the one who hired me a few months earlier."

"Was there anyone Kenny seemed really close to?"

Omar shakes his head. "Kenny was *everyone's* friend, if you know what I mean."

Roddy nods his head. "Can you tell me anything more about

Kenny and those mob types?"

"I wish I could, Dr. Dolan, but that's all I know. I just had a bad feeling about the place, and it turns out I was right."

"Yes, you were, Omar. The place was a den of scorpions."

Chapter 22

Roddy stands at the corner of 3rd Avenue and 84th Street. Trucks, taxis, and cars barrel uptown on 3rd through a haze of exhaust. The cold air holds the fumes at ground level and Roddy's eyes sting. He's again reminded of living on the Upper East Side years ago when he and Tracy met.

Crystal's building, on the intersection's southwest corner, is more than twenty stories high and built in a wedding-cake style with set-back tiers beginning at the upper floors. Danny told him she lives in apartment 12-K.

The doorman, a burly, red-faced man, greets him. When he asks to see Crystal Newcomb, the doorman says, "Sorry, sir, but she moved a few months ago."

"I'm sure she left a forwarding address."

"I'm not supposed to give out that information, sir," says the doorman in a lowered voice. He glances right and left and then looks into Roddy's eyes.

"Understood," Roddy says and glances about. The lobby is empty, and no one is approaching the front door. "Maybe you can tell Ben Franklin where she's living now." He slips a $100 bill from his wallet, folds it twice, and hands it to the doorman. The guy's eyes shift left, then right; he pockets the bill and murmurs, "I redirect her packages to 301 East 79th Street. The building's called Continental Towers."

Continental Towers is a brown monolith at the intersection of East 79th and 2nd Avenue. The building is set far back from the street. The sidewalk fronting it must be fifty feet wide. A hunter-green awning projects out to the curb.

Entering through a revolving door, Roddy stands in an expansive lobby reminiscent of a hotel. The lobby ceiling is two stories high. A doorman's lectern is near the entrance. A concierge's desk is at the rear, behind which stands a man wearing a jacket and tie. At the right rear of the lobby, a door leads to an in-house dry-cleaning service. The place looks like a self-contained city, with dozens of people coming and going each minute. A continuous chorus of voices and the dinging of five elevators echo through the lobby.

He asks the doorman for Crystal Newcomb.

"Who may I say is calling?" asks the doorman, whose name-tag reads "Luis."

"Roddy Dolan, from McLaughlin's."

Some moments later, he's directed to the elevator, having been told she lives in apartment 40-A.

Stepping out of the elevator, Roddy makes his way down a football-field-length corridor. The aromas of coffee and toast fill the air. The sequence of apartments runs from 40-G to 40-A. The A-line faces the B-line apartments.

When the door opens, Crystal greets him wearing a terry-cloth bathrobe. Her blond hair cascades down the back of her neck. It's damp; she recently showered. Roddy inhales the fragrance of shampoo. Crystal's lips have that plump, trout-pout look from injected collagen or Juvéderm. It was part of her signature look at the restaurant. Roddy's reminded of the way she escorted diners to their tables at McLaughlin's—her hips swaying as she cradled leather-bound menus in her arms.

Without makeup, her face looks softer and less sexually aggressive than when she prowled the front of the house at

McLaughlin's. Roddy senses Crystal's restaurant seductiveness was an act—a theatrical production for the sake of the glitterati, gawkers, mob goons, and anyone craving a woman's sexual sizzle. She was a caricature employed to entice men amid the primal aroma of charbroiled steaks and chops. It was one of the few good moves Kenny made while running the place.

Standing at the door, Crystal smiles. Her breasts nearly burst from the terry-cloth robe, which shows the slope of her shoulders and the pale flesh of her neck. She cants her hip. "My, my, look what the cat dragged in," she murmurs.

The directness of her gaze startles Roddy. He's suddenly aware of looking seedy since he hasn't shaved in many days. "May I come in?"

"Of course, Dr. Dolan."

"It's Roddy."

"Sure, Roddy. Are you all right?" She dips her head, and her eyes narrow.

"I'm on vacation. Please forgive how I look."

She smiles. "I'm so surprised to see you," she says, opening the door widely.

Her apartment faces southwest. At the fortieth floor, Crystal has an unobstructed view over a large swath of prime Manhattan real estate. Huge picture windows line the western and southern exposures. A glass door leads to a balcony facing south, high above 79th Street. The Chrysler and Empire State Buildings are visible in the wintry distance—morning light casting a bright orange glow on their eastern facades.

"It's an incredible view," says Roddy.

"I'm renting from the owner," she says with a quick smile and leads him to a spacious dining alcove off the living room.

The place is furnished in teaks and honey-colored woods. A three-piece ensemble dominates the living room. One sofa is upholstered in buttery-looking leather, the other two in plush velvet. The couches are arranged around a pewter and glass coffee table that must have cost thousands. Colorful Persian rugs cover much of the polished red hardwood flooring. High-end artwork—either expensive reproductions or genuine works by Picasso and Klee—adorn the walls. The apartment's owner must be a knowledgeable and wealthy collector.

Floor-to-ceiling bookshelves line the den wall, which can be seen through open French doors to the right of the entrance foyer. A door at the other end of the apartment is closed. Roddy assumes it's the master bedroom. The place must be stratospherically expensive—on the Upper East Side, the Silk-Stocking District—and perched on the fortieth floor with spectacular views. Roddy wonders how Crystal can cover the nut on this apartment. He thinks of Omar's place, and it occurs to him that Crystal has options far beyond what Omar could reasonably contemplate.

"Can I get you a cup of coffee?" Crystal asks, sauntering through the living room.

"Sure, Crystal. Coffee would be fine. How've you been?"

"I'm doing well, thanks. And you?"

"Oh fine," Roddy replies, peering at an expensive reproduction of Munch's *The Scream*, set in a sandalwood frame. He recalls Tracy's art history course—the one she took at Westchester Community College—and her explaining the painting depicted unreasoned fear, the anxiety that escorts us through the maze of life.

Unreasoned fear? My fear has a damned good reason.

"How's Mr. Burns doing?" asks Crystal.

"Oh, he's fine."

"Such a nice man, Mr. Burns," Crystal says, sitting across the table from Roddy. Her body lotion is vaguely reminiscent of jasmine. It's not similar to anything Tracy's used, and yet he's suddenly reminded of the tang of Tracy's skin and the fragrance of her hair each morning as he nuzzled her among the warmth of the bed linens. God, how he misses her. There's something elemental about a woman's scent, he thinks, and when he pictures Tracy again, he grows momentarily light-headed.

Crystal shifts her position in the chair, and her breasts nearly tumble from the bathrobe. She cinches the robe more tightly and shoots Roddy a quick smile.

He wonders what made him think of coming to see her or Omar. In a deep recess of his mind, he asks himself if he'd be better off talking to one of the former busboys or bartenders to get a better take on Kenny Egan. What on earth would Crystal know about Kenny's less-than-savory activities? Would she really know any details of Kenny's romancing the goons? He'd thought Crystal was nothing more than a vacuous lure for the steakarati, but now he isn't so certain.

Roddy peers out the south window at the midtown skyline with its geometric formations and spires. From the fortieth floor, he hears nothing of the traffic roar—just a faint whooshing—a strangely hypnotic white noise far below.

Crystal pours coffee into mugs and sets them on the table. "So what brings you here, Roddy?"

"I was hoping you could tell me a little about Ken Egan. He and I went way back, and it still bothers me how he just disappeared."

The bald-faced lies we tell in this life.

Crystal shakes her head and her mouth droops. "I always wondered why you and Mr. Burns stayed friends with Kenny. Because you're the last guys on earth I'd ever imagine being his partners—an accountant and a surgeon—even if you were only silent partners. It was such a strange fit."

"How do you mean?"

Just let her talk. Let her open up a bit.

"You're both family men from the suburbs, and you're partners with *Kenny Egan*? Kenny from *Las Vegas*?" She chortles. "What's wrong with *that* picture?"

"How much did you know about Kenny?" He sips coffee, trying to appear casual, but his muscles are so tense they'll soon begin aching. And that right foot begins its incessant floor tapping.

"What did I know? Only as much as I needed to. He was a heavy drinker and a drug user, too. He once asked if I'd like to do a line of coke with him. But I declined. To be perfectly frank, Roddy, he was pure sleaze, through and through. I still don't understand how you and Mr. Burns became his partners."

It occurs to Roddy that his previous assumption about Crystal—that she was an airhead who used her sexual allure as currency and had little else to offer—was way off target. Yes, she could use her looks to her advantage, but she's perceptive and quite smart.

So, I made some asinine assumptions. I'm a typical man.

"What about the people he hung around with at the restaurant?"

"Oh, you mean those guys who looked like they'd just stepped off the set of a mob movie?"

"Yes."

"They were the real deal."

"You think they had hooks into Kenny?"

"Who knows?" she says, shrugging her shoulders. "But if I had to bet on it—another of Kenny's vices—I'd bet he was into some under-the-table deals with some of them."

"Anyone in particular?"

"At first I thought it was the Italians. They were hanging around the place. But over the months, it changed. It looked to me like the Russians took over. By the time the restaurant closed, there were Russians everywhere."

"Anyone specific you can recall?"

"It sounds like you're more interested in Kenny's associates than in Kenny."

"I'm just trying to get a sense of his life."

"Well, if you'd been there more often, you'd have seen what was going on."

"Like what?"

"It was a den of thieves. If it hadn't closed, I'd have left very soon. It was getting seedier by the day."

"So I gathered."

"But there were nice people, too . . . the repeat customers who were there pretty often. Mostly businessmen who came for lunch. There was Mr. Conklin, a big shot in Local 319, a nice man who probably cut some deals with Kenny. And there was Mr. Nolan from the Hotel and Restaurant Workers Union, a sweet man. I'll bet Kenny was greasing his palm. And there was Mr. Harris, the real estate guy, a real dear of a man. They were all good customers and nice men, not copping cheap feels or trying to get into my panties. Men make certain assumptions about a hostess in a restaurant like that—not all men, but some—like those mobsters from Brooklyn and Jersey."

"You mentioned John Harris," Roddy says, recalling Harris standing at Danny's bedside only a week earlier. An image forms in Roddy's mind—of Harris's patrician face, his high-end threads, and his name-dropping: Teuscher truffles and Puligny-Montrachet and Château Margaux. What a snob, and no doubt, a high-end foodie—a real gastronaut.

"Oh, Mr. Harris is a kind man . . . if you can get past that white-bread country-club manner of his. I met him through your friend Mr. Burns. Mr. Harris became a regular because his Manhattan office was nearby, on 57th Street. He had lunch there at least once a week."

Roddy nods, wondering if he was a bit too quick to judge the man; in medicine it's called jumping to a *concussion*. Yes, Harris was a pretentious connoisseur, but that's not a crime. Roddy realizes he sometimes lets his Brooklyn past—the flotsam and jetsam of growing up near Sheepshead Bay—taint his view of others, especially braggarts dripping lucre.

"In fact, Mr. Harris helped me change my life," Crystal says.

"How's that?"

"I'm thirty-two years old and I've been around plenty of blocks. He thought I had potential for something much more than being a restaurant hostess. Through him, I landed a job at Regency Realty on 86th and York Avenue. Right now, I'm an intern and I'm taking courses so I can pass the licensing exam. I'd like to be a real estate broker. The Manhattan market's very hot right now, and I'd like to tap into that."

"How'd he help you?"

"He made a phone call, and the next thing I knew, I was working at Regency. I'm very glad there were some legitimate businessmen at McLaughlin's because I had plenty of seedy offers—some that were quite substantial, if you know what I mean."

"I do, Crystal. But, just so I'm clear, you don't know anything else about Kenny Egan? His connections either in the restaurant or somewhere else?"

"Just that he was in way over his head. He was always doped up and trying to make a score. But he was gambling and losing lots of money. And those mobsters? Who knows what arrangements Kenny had with them? Actually, there were times I was scared to go to work because you never know what could happen with men like that."

Roddy gets up from the table knowing there's nothing more to be learned.

"Thanks, Crystal. I just thought I'd give it a shot."

"I wish I could be more helpful."

Roddy reaches into his pocket for a pen. "If you think of anything, call me." He rips a piece of paper from a pad on the table and writes the number of his prepaid cell.

Walking toward the elevator, Roddy realizes he still has no idea who's trying to kill Danny and him—or why they're targets—and he's learned nothing from talking with either Omar or Crystal. And to make matters worse, Danny won't hold out much longer. He'll break down soon and end up calling Morgan.

Roddy's hit a dead end, and if he isn't very careful, he'll be a dead man.

Chapter 23

Danny sits at the desk in his hotel room, thinking about the conversation he had with Natalie, his office manager.

"Dan, Detective Morgan called. He wants to speak with you. He wants to hear from you within the hour."

"What'd you tell him?"

"Like we agreed . . . you're not in the office. He asked where he could contact you. I told him I'm not authorized to give out that information."

That was nearly three hours ago. Danny wonders what Morgan wants. To hassle and harass him again about how he and Roddy actually know who's after them? Okay, so the whole setup with Kenny and McLaughlin's was ripe for mobsters and now some mob vendetta. He can understand Morgan's thinking. He's taking the most logical path to arrive at his conclusion.

Danny feels a tug of fear-filled temptation to blow it all wide open. In a way, it would be a relief to tell Morgan exactly what went down that night—and *why* it happened. It's so tempting to pick up the phone, dial the Yonkers police, and ask for Detective Morgan. It's so much easier to tell the truth than live a life of lies and deception. Because when you lie, you have to be true to your lie, and one untruth inevitably leads to another and then another after that. It's a never-ending series of evasions and distortions, and you've got to remember everything you said so there's no contradiction. But if you tell the truth, you don't have to remember a thing.

You just tell it like it is . . . or like it was.

Yeah, if he tells Morgan what went down, he and Roddy'll be chin deep in shit, but their families will be safe. And that's the most important thing . . . Angie and the kids. Actually, they're the *only* important thing. The rest is nothing but bullshit.

Jesus, this whole thing is torture. Danny knows he made a very bad decision about Kenny and McLaughlin's. And it was an even worse choice—and Roddy's right; it was a *choice* Danny made—to go along with Roddy and kill Kenny and Grange. He should've put his foot down and refused to be part of it.

So now it's payback time, and the big guy in the sky is calling in his chits. The way Danny's living now—holed up in a hotel room, fearing for his family's safety and for his own life, doing his best to keep away from Morgan—is its own kind of hell. Yes, he's living in hell, and when he dies, that's where he's going anyway. So what's the difference?

Live or die . . . hell is where you are.

What was it Ma used to say? "*May the grass grow long on the road to hell for want of use.*"

Danny's certain he'll tramp down that pathway to the fiery gates. It's where he is right now.

There's a purposeful knock on the door. It borders on being a solid thump. Then another two raps—very hard.

Danny's heart freezes. He stands stone-still.

A fourth thump resounds—even louder than the others. It penetrates Danny's skull.

"Who is it?" he asks as he begins trembling.

"Detective Morgan. Let me in, Mr. Burns."

Dan feels a shiver in his neck as he unlatches the safety lock and opens the door. Morgan fills the doorway. He gives Danny a hard look. "You think you can hide from the police?"

"How'd you find me?"

"Easy, but I'm not gonna give away any trade secrets."

Morgan strides into the room along with a cloud of cologne. "You get my message?"

"Message?"

"I spoke with your office manager and told her to have you call me within the hour. Can't you tell time?"

"What's so urgent? Any developments?"

A torrent of thoughts rushes through Danny's mind. *What else has Morgan learned? What new factoid or theory is he gonna come up with? Who has Morgan talked with? Has he interviewed former employees of McLaughlin's? Do I have to keep up this charade forever?*

"The only development is that my material witnesses are holding out on me and they're hiding."

"Meaning what?"

"Meaning I don't like when someone with information about a capital case disappears."

"Detective, I don't know a thing. I was—"

"Know what you're doing?"

"I don't get—"

"You're obstructing justice. I can have a judge issue a warrant for your arrest. Or I could haul you down to headquarters and have you questioned. *Extensively questioned.* Then we'll see how little you know." Morgan runs his tongue over his upper teeth. His eyebrows reach for the sky.

"Look, Detective, I've been thinking—"

"Ever been in jail, Mr. Burns?"

Danny's heart feels like it's stopped. He grows light-headed.

"I asked you a question. Ever been in jail? A holding cell?"

"No, but I'd like to tell you—"

"Because I can have a judge issue a warrant for your arrest in a heartbeat. Just say the word and it'll be done."

"I think I'll call my lawyer," Dan says, moving to the telephone. He reaches for the phone, trying to keep his hand from shaking.

"Yeah, you do that. Ask him to define obstruction of justice."

Dan turns to Morgan and says, "I've already told you everything I know." His lips tingle.

"Lemme paint the picture for you, Mr. Burns. You were shot with a .22 pistol, and a doctor at Lawrence Hospital was killed by the same gun used on you. And *another* doctor from Lawrence Hospital—a guy whose vehicle was parked next to the dead doctor's—is nowhere to be found. Know who I'm talking about?"

"I don't know where Roddy Dolan is."

"You have no idea?"

"No, I don't, Detective."

"Lemme put it to you this way, Mr. Burns. Next time you speak with your friend, tell him to contact me. Real quick or else he'll be facing charges. Obstruction of justice is a serious felony. And that's what you're both looking at. Dolan's not at the hospital. He's taken a leave of absence. He's not home, either. A neighbor's watching the house. His family's in another state and his wife doesn't know where the hell he is. The Yonkers police want to talk to him, and so does the BCI."

"What's the BCI?"

"Never mind what it is. Just tell Dolan he's wanted for questioning in a homicide . . . one Walter McKay. You tell your friend Dolan. Got it?"

"Yes, but—"

"Lemme tell you something. I'm doing you a favor by coming here. I got better things to do. And if you don't straighten up, arrest warrants will be issued real soon."

Morgan looks around the suite. "Where're your wife and kids?"

"Somewhere safe."

"Where's that?"

"I'd rather not say."

Morgan heads for the door, turns, and says, "You two better wise up, pal. Real fast. Otherwise it's gonna be jail time, and we have detectives who'll sweat it out of you. They'll get more outta you than you ever knew you had to give. Got it?"

Chapter 24

Danny's disposable trills. Nearly jumping at the sound, he picks it up. His hands are still shaking. "Roddy?"

"Who else could it be?"

"You never know. Guess who left here fifteen minutes ago . . . Morgan."

"*Jesus.* You didn't tell him anything, did you?"

"No."

"You sure?"

"Of course I'm sure." Dan peers about the room, looking at the laptop sitting on the desk and then out the window at the bare trees on this gray winter day. The room still smells vaguely of Morgan's cologne.

"What'd he want?"

"He wants to see you. He bitched that we're obstructing justice and he could have arrest warrants issued if you stay hidden. What do *you* think we should do?"

"I'm staying put."

"Morgan's closing in."

"Only if you *let* him, Dan."

"Man, I'm getting real nervous. I'm getting a very bad feeling about this. We're headed for big trouble with this guy. I'm tellin' you, Roddy. It'd be a whole lot easier if we just come clean."

"Stay calm, Danny. Just stay calm. Listen."

"But, Roddy, I don't want—"

"Listen up, Dan. I just got back from the city. I spoke with Omar and Crystal."

Danny inhales deeply. He fights off a hollow feeling and says, "You get anything?"

"Not really. Omar doesn't know a thing. He's working at another steakhouse now."

"And Crystal?"

"She's moved up in the world."

"How so?"

"She's living in a condo on the Upper East Side, renting from the owner. The place is on 79th and 2nd. It's called Continental Towers."

"Sounds familiar."

"Why? Have you been there?"

"Yeah, a while back," says Dan. "Some Christmas party a few years ago. It's a huge building, a kind of yellowish brown thing, right?"

"You got it. It's more than forty stories high."

"Yeah, I was there . . . at an apartment. It was a huge bash for lots of big shots. It was quite a while ago, before we got involved with Kenny and McLaughlin's."

Danny's thoughts leap back to two years ago. "I remember Angela and I drove into the city," he says. "The building had an underground parking garage. The apartment was a three-bedroom place—it was huge and had incredible nighttime views facing south. The place was owned by some megabucks hedge fund manager with offices in Manhattan. He wanted to sell it. People swarmed in and out all evening. They served champagne and caviar, and some high-priced catering company was running the food end of things. Yeah, it was at Continental Towers. We were invited because I'd structured some deals for a realty company in White Plains."

"Crystal's place is two bedrooms, furnished to the nines," says Roddy. "It's on the fortieth floor with a great view. She moved in a few months ago. How much you figure a rental like that goes for in the city?"

"It's gotta go for eight, nine thousand a month, maybe more."

"It's way above her pay grade. She's working as a trainee for a real estate company . . . some place called Regency."

"Never heard of it."

"She wants to become a real estate broker. But there's no way Crystal would be making the kind of money it takes to rent a place like that. Not unless she won the Powerball—or has a very rich boyfriend."

"So who do you think's picking up the tab?" Danny asks.

"Some sugar daddy."

"A woman with her looks would have no trouble getting someone to pay her way. She mention anyone?"

"We never got into that, and besides, what's it got to do with us?"

"She say anything new about Kenny?"

"Nothing we didn't already know."

"Anything about mob connections?"

"Nothing new there, either. But something struck me, and it goes along with what I've been thinking. She said Russians were flooding McLaughlin's. It was a Russian hangout."

"And?"

"The guys I saw in the garage looked Eastern European, maybe Russian. Same with the guy in Yonkers, driving the Navigator. And the guys who were following me when I went to the city . . ."

"So, maybe Kenny owed big bucks to some Russian honchos."

"If Russians are after us, why would they want us dead? Wouldn't they want the money Kenny owed?"

"You're right, Roddy. Because dead men don't write checks."

"True. So just *maybe* something else is going on; maybe it has nothing to do with Kenny owing money."

Danny waits. He can almost hear Roddy's mental gears whirring, as though he's scanning his brain's database.

"None of this makes sense, Dan. If Grange was really named Gargano, why would all these guys be Russian or Eastern European? It's not the way the mafia settles a score. They'd avenge the death of a made man, but there's no way they'd outsource it to the Russians. We know how the mafia operated back in Brooklyn."

"Yeah, back in the good old days," Danny mutters.

"And McLaughlin's was a Russian hangout by the time it closed."

"You sure of that?"

"According to Crystal it was, and she was there until the bitter end. So maybe something else is going on."

"You know, Roddy, I've been going over it all, again and again. I've thought about every single day leading up to when I got shot. I've tried to re-create everything to see if it leads up to that night in my office. Because I've been thinking about what you said, that maybe *I'm* the primary target of whoever's coming for us. I've been racking my brains for some connection to something, to *anything*. But there's nothing, not a thing."

"Keep at it, Dan. Because I have the feeling whoever's gunning for us isn't doing it because of Kenny, or McLaughlin's, or Grange. It could be something else."

"Like what?"

"I don't have a shred of an idea, Danny."

"Russians, Italians, Eastern Europeans, Kenny, not Kenny. I'm gonna go nuts."

Danny feels his cheeks burning.

"And, Dan, don't say a word to anyone—not Morgan, not a priest—nobody."

"We can't keep going like this."

"We gotta do it, Dan. There's no choice."

"There're always choices. *Always.*"

"Not in this. I don't choose to spend the rest of my life in prison."

"I gotta say somethin' to you, Roddy."

"Yeah, what?"

Dan inhales deeply, letting his lungs fill with air. "Time's against us, Roddy. We need to end this real soon."

"Meaning?"

"The clock's ticking."

Chapter 25

It's nearly seven o'clock in the evening, but Roddy's not hungry. He feels exhausted. His trip into Manhattan added nothing new to the mix of questions plaguing him since this nightmare began.

It occurs to Roddy that through the entire time he's been in hiding, he's never told Dan he's holed up at the Marriott in Brooklyn. Does he trust Danny, or has he grown so wary he can't even let his closest friend know where he's staying? And could Danny actually be the primary target?

Danny mentioned having structured deals for some guy in White Plains. Was he helping someone launder money? Has Danny been part of some illegal financial crap? Roddy thinks back to what Crystal said about the Russians taking over McLaughlin's. They're into lots of things, those Russians—much more than just prostitution, gambling, and other rackets. One of their biggest things is money laundering. Maybe Danny was helping them set up some legitimate enterprise in Westchester to cover their money tracks.

But if *that's* at the root of all this, why is Roddy also being targeted? Wouldn't they—whoever *they* are—have only Danny in their sights? What's the connection between Danny, himself, and the Russians? The only possible connection—if it could be called that—was the restaurant. He was involved in that. But like Danny said, "*Dead men don't write checks.*" So who—and why—is someone or some group after both of them?

Roddy slips out of his jeans and lies down on the bed. His thoughts turn to Morgan. The guy tracked Danny down in a heartbeat. And he wants to talk to Roddy. So does the BCI. Could they be onto something about Grange and Kenny? Did Danny say something to Morgan?

Roddy feels like the jaws of a bear trap are ready to clamp down. Sooner or later, he'll be dead or in custody. He'll be lucky if Danny gives him the week he promised before running to the police. It's clear: Dan can't tolerate the cesspool into which they've stumbled. And who's Roddy kidding? He's not on the offensive; he's being hunted like he's a blind animal in the wild.

His disposable rings. It's gotta be Danny again.

Roddy picks it up from the bedside table. The readout says it's a call from a Manhattan number—a 212 area code. His heart kicks like a mule. He sits up straight, at the edge of the bed.

"Hello."

"Roddy, it's Crystal." Her voice quavers and sounds nasal, as though she's crying.

"*Crystal?*" he says as a pang shoots through him. "What is it?" He clutches the cell phone so tightly the plastic creaks.

"Can you come over as soon as possible?"

"What's wrong?"

"I have to talk with you." Her voice is shaky.

"Are you okay?"

"Yes, but I have to . . ." She sniffs. "I have to talk with you."

"I'm listening."

"No . . . in person."

A jolt of adrenaline dumps into Roddy's bloodstream, the way it did before a boxing match or a street fight years ago.

He waits and says nothing. Static streams into his ear.

"Roddy, are you there?"

"I'm here."

"Can you come?"

"Crystal, just say yes or no. Is anyone with you now?"

"No, Roddy. No one's here. I'm alone, and I have to talk with you. It's too important to discuss over the phone."

She didn't answer yes or no. She gave a full answer and didn't sound surreptitious. It seems she's alone. Still, there could be someone listening in on the line, using an extension. For an instant, Roddy wonders how paranoid he's become.

"Crystal, are you alone?"

"Yes, Roddy. I'm alone."

He strains to hear something: anyone breathing into an extension or a voice whispering, coaxing her. He tries to sense if her voice sounds faint, the way it would if someone's on an extension, listening in. Does she sound staged, forced, or does she seem genuine? Is she playing a role—the way she did at McLaughlin's?

"Where are you? How long would it take you to get here?" she asks.

Why would she ask where I am? Or how long it'll take me to get there?

"Yes or no, Crystal. Are you asking for someone else?"

"No."

"We were talking this morning. What do you want to discuss now, only a few hours later?"

"It's important, Roddy."

"You have to tell me or I'm not coming."

She sniffles into the phone. He hears her swallow.

"Crystal?"

He waits and hears static and the sound of his own breath.

"I know who's trying to hurt you and Danny."

Roddy's heart nearly stops. His hands go weak. Thoughts rampage crazily through his head.

Is this really happening? Is this some kind of imaginary

conversation? How does she even know he and Danny are being targeted? And what could she possibly know about it?

He's not sure he can speak, but hears himself say in a small and distant voice, "You know who it is?"

"Yes. I can help you."

Could this be a trap? What if he shows up at her apartment and some guy puts a bullet in his brain, like what happened to Walt McKay? It could happen right there, in a residential building with a thousand tenants. It could mean he sees a flash of light and hears a low-level popping sound the instant the apartment door opens.

Or he could be blown away after he steps off the elevator; they'd know he's coming after the doorman announces him on the intercom. It would be a small-caliber pistol with a silencer on its end. It could happen even if he has his own gun ready; they'll have the element of surprise—whoever *they* are—because they'll be expecting him. They could lie in wait.

A sickening medley of thoughts swarms through his mind. How could Crystal know about people coming after him and Danny? And why is she calling him now? Why didn't she say something this morning—face-to-face in her apartment? What's changed over the last nine or ten hours that makes her say this now?

"I know who's trying to hurt you and Danny."

Is she being forced to call him? Is a gun at her head? And how do they know he'd paid her a visit this morning? How long has she known he and Danny have been running for their lives? And exactly what does she know?

Should he call Danny and let him know what's happening?

Maybe it's best to move on this alone—reconnoiter the situation. Get a bead on things.

"Okay, Crystal. But I can't get to your place any earlier than eleven."

"Why so late?"

"I'm nowhere near you. I'll be there at eleven, no sooner."

"I'll be waiting."

Leaving the hotel shortly after seven gives Roddy a nearly four-hour jump start on whoever might be waiting for him.

He glances at his watch: seven twenty. They won't be expecting him until eleven. With the pistol in his pocket, he walks briskly toward the Court Street subway station. His eyes roam the street. No one is tailing him.

He hustles down the subway stairway and walks to the end of the nearly empty platform. He catches the 4 train heading toward Manhattan. Scanning the subway car, he sees no one suspicious. There's the usual mix of people and a polyglot of voices amid the subway roar and clatter: English, Spanish, Urdu, and Haitian patois. Roddy makes certain to keep his distance from everyone, which is relatively easy to do because the car isn't crowded. If anyone approaches too close, Roddy moves away—discreetly. He leans against the car's middle doors as the train rushes through the tunnel beneath the East River.

Roddy scrutinizes everyone entering the car at each stop. He's never been so primed, so completely wired, in his life. His senses are on high alert. He's reminded of a dog with its nose to the wind, sniffing for the faintest hint of danger. His old street moniker—Mad Dog—comes to mind, and he recalls the days in Brooklyn when his life was a daily trek through a minefield of danger.

Emerging from the subway at 86th Street in Manhattan, he walks east and passes Lexington. He decides to head south on 3rd Avenue. It has a wide sidewalk where it's less likely someone could brush up close to him. And the avenue is packed with bars and restaurants. It's a hotbed of nightlife every night of the week. Maybe it's less likely someone would attack him in such a public place.

He walks toward 79th Street on the east side of 3rd Avenue. His eyes shift left and right as he scans the busy thoroughfare. Nothing out of the ordinary, and no one who looks overtly suspicious. As a precaution, he crosses 3rd Avenue at 81st Street, walking past a Con Edison crew jackhammering a hole in the asphalt. Brilliant Klieg-type lights illuminate the area. Roddy glances about and steps into a Korean-owned grocery on the west side of the street. He circles the salad bar and examines the offerings, using his peripheral vision to see if anyone enters the store. An elderly woman comes in and begins picking through the vegetables. There are no other customers.

A few minutes later, he stops near the cash register and picks through some banana bunches, glancing out the store's plate-glass window. Through the river of traffic on the avenue, he sees a man loitering in front of a pizza stand across the street. Roddy waits, circles the salad bar again, and peers out the front window. The guy is gone. A moment later, Roddy leaves the store and walks quickly to 79th Street.

At 79th and 3rd, he crosses the avenue and heads east toward the intersection of 79th and 2nd Avenue. In the distance—nearly a block away—he sees a swirling medley of red and white lights in the night. As he approaches 2nd Avenue, he notices a crowd. The breath vapor of hundreds of people is backlit by brilliant lights. Something's going on at the intersection's northeast corner—in front of Continental Towers.

Roddy slips through the gathered crowd to the front of the horde. Yellow police tape is strewn from one lamppost to another. Wooden sawhorses are strategically placed, keeping the crowd at bay. Lights swirl and flash continuously.

"They're only letting residents into the building," a woman says.

At the police barrier, Roddy sees EMT guys and two police officers talking. They peer down at a rubberized tarp on the sidewalk. Beneath the covering, Roddy sees the outline of a body.

Car horns blare incessantly. Traffic is at a standstill. A siren pops and then woops. The keening sound comes closer.

"How terrible," a man says.

"What happened?" asks another.

"A woman jumped from a balcony on the fortieth floor."

"Oh my God," cries a woman. "The *fortieth* floor?"

"She must've burst apart like a blood blister," someone says.

"I think I'm going to vomit," the woman mutters and pushes back from the barrier.

The fortieth floor... and at the southwest corner of the building.

Roddy peers closely at the tarp. Bare feet protrude from beneath an end of the covering.

It was only this morning he was here, in apartment 40-A. The A-line balconies are at the southwest corner of the building. He looks upward amid the swirl of lights at the intersection. The A-line apartments—and their balconies—are directly above where the tarp-covered body lies. The corpse lies at least five feet farther from where it would have landed from a direct drop. Meaning Crystal could have been thrown from the balcony. She landed farther from the building than would have resulted from a straight downward fall.

"Was it suicide?" someone asks.

"Looks that way," says a man.

Roddy is certain the dead woman is Crystal. And there's a good chance she was pushed or thrown from the balcony.

"Anyone know her name?" someone asks.

"The police aren't saying," replies a woman to Roddy's left. "But she lived in the building."

Roddy turns to make his way back through the crowd.

He freezes: there's Bluetooth Guy.

He's eight feet away, standing in the crowd, blue and red police lights dancing over him as he stares up at the building. Same grizzled face, those dead eyes, and the Bluetooth device is angled over his right ear.

Has he seen Roddy? Was this the plan? To lure him into Manhattan and ambush him when he got to the apartment? No, it couldn't have been. The place is crawling with cops. If they threw Crystal from the balcony, they must have planned to intercept him on the street—exactly where he is now.

In a few seconds, Roddy dopes out their possible game plan. Soon after Crystal called him, they tossed her from the balcony, thinking he'd arrive by eleven. By then, the body would be gone and the crowd would have dispersed. They'd be waiting for him on the street. He'd be an easy target since they know what he looks like—from that guy in the Navigator. It would be an ambush, right here at the intersection or maybe as he'd approach the building entrance. Or maybe they'd wait for him to arrive at eleven and follow him.

Arriving early saved his life.

Pushing through the crowd, Roddy quells a hot spike of panic that jumps through him. His heart pounds insanely as he slips through the throng and heads west on 79th Street. Dread gnaws at him as his thoughts race in frenzied profusion. Did Bluetooth Guy see him? There's no way to tell. There must be two of them, maybe three or more. They're in contact with each other. Are they tracking him at this very moment?

He turns right on 3rd Avenue and heads uptown, staying on the east side of the street. He passes retail stores, a health club, and a string of restaurants overflowing with patrons. The avenue virtually throbs with nighttime activity. His eyes sweep left and right, behind him and across the street. A parade of people move along the sidewalks on both sides of the avenue; it's impossible to tell if he's being tailed.

Craning his neck, he searches the avenue for a taxi. A stream of cabs moves uptown on 3rd; not a single one has its top light on to signal it's available.

He stops in front of a closed video store and ducks into the recessed entranceway. Huddled there, he peers down the avenue toward 79th Street, watching people stream by. He decides to wait for anyone suspicious-looking who might be coming from 79th Street, heading north. Or, he'll wait to see if someone loiters on the avenue. He would certainly recognize Bluetooth Guy if he passes. Roddy's right hand slips into his pocket to the pistol.

He could ambush whoever might be following—stick the revolver in his back and force him into the alcove. Then what would he do? Put a Ranger move on his larynx? Grab his windpipe and squeeze it like a vise so the guy yields to the pressure and talks, tells him exactly what's going on? *Tell me, motherfucker, or it's your last breath.*

And then what? Snap the edge of his palm into the guy's larynx so the cartilage is crushed? The hyoid bone or the cricoid? It's a simple matter of knowing the anatomy. Or, break his neck with a chopping blow behind his fifth cervical vertebrae? Let him drop slowly to the floor of the alcove and walk away?

And then what does he do?

Roddy waits in a state of primed anticipation.

No one suspicious passes by. There's no sign of Bluetooth Guy.

He steps out from the doorway and rejoins the flow of people. Between 82nd Street and 83rd, he comes to the Gael Pub. The door opens, and two young men amble out amid a burst of noise from the tavern's interior. Roddy steps into the place before the door closes.

The change from the frigid air of outdoors to the pub's interior is an assault on his senses. The alehouse is overheated and jammed with young people—men and women in their twenties and thirties—*millennials*, Roddy thinks they're called. The crowd is so dense, it heightens Roddy's sense of estrangement, his loneliness.

The place is dimly lit, noisy, and redolent of malt, burgers, and fries. It's stacked with humanity—wall-to-wall people—guzzling beer, ale, and wine, talking, shouting, and laughing above the din of rock music. Roddy recognizes "Bohemian Rhapsody" by Queen soaring through the sound system. If anyone's following, this place seems as good as any to get lost in a crowd.

Roddy glances about, trying to find an empty barstool, but there's none. He decides instead to head to the rear of the pub. He could be safe in this tavern, but you never know. In Ranger school they were taught to always know escape routes from any situation.

He threads through the crowd and makes his way to a dimly lit hallway past the kitchen's clatter. The restrooms are on his right: *Women* closer to the main room and *Men* toward the hallway's rear. A metal door with a steel push bar stands at the far end of the corridor—a fire exit. He pushes the bar down, opens the door, and peers out to a poorly lit alleyway. About twenty feet away, it angles off to the right, leading to 82nd Street.

Back in the corridor, he opens the door to the men's room and peers in. It smells of deodorant cake and piss. It has two unoccupied toilet stalls. On the opposite side of the room, two urinals are affixed to a white tiled wall. A small window is at the far end of the room. He enters, goes to the window, and slides it up. It would be a tight squeeze, but with some squirming, he could slip through it onto a covered Dumpster just below. Then he'd be in the alleyway leading to 82nd Street. There are two escape routes—the rear door and the restroom window.

Back in the tavern, there's still no sign of an empty stool. People are bellied up to the bar—three and four deep. Roddy edges into the bar crowd. Soon, a young woman gets off a stool and melts into the throng. Roddy grabs the stool, sits, and takes in his surroundings. It feels like he's back in Brooklyn: pumped and primed—ready to brawl. The music seems louder and pounds in his ears.

He gazes up at the tin ceiling: no wonder the noise level is cacophonous—every sound bounces off the ceiling. All hard surfaces: wood, tile, and tin. Music and voices bore into his brain. The bar is well-worn mahogany. Roddy eyes a line of decorative tap handles, some with leprechauns, others with logos for Killian's Irish Red, Caffrey's Irish Ale, or Guinness. The wall behind the bar is stacked with tiers of every known whiskey brand, all sitting beneath a pale green light radiating from a source recessed in the ceiling. The barroom bluster is boisterous—even deafening—but doesn't seem rowdy. It's the kind of place Roddy might have enjoyed twenty years earlier. He inhales the aroma of sizzling burgers mixed with beery malt and hops.

Catching the bartender's eye, Roddy orders a mug of Guinness stout on draft. He'll kill fifteen or twenty minutes—just to be safe—before getting out of here. *Kill a few minutes . . . kill . . .* and his thoughts spin back to the sight of Crystal's body beneath that tarp on the sidewalk. A knot forms in his chest as he recalls talking with her only a short while ago. Now she's gone; she's nothing but a broken corpse. Jesus, the world's such an ugly, hateful place. He closes his eyes and leans his head in his hand with an elbow perched on the bar.

A frothy mug of beer plops onto the bar. He drops a twenty down next to it and then lifts the mug and sips through the foam to the brew. The taste is smooth, creamy, even chocolaty. The barkeep deposits his change on the bar. Peering about the place, Roddy realizes he's older than everyone in the room. He can't recall the last time he was at a bar alone—without Tracy. Thinking of Tracy and the kids, a wave of sadness floods him.

Sitting amid the tavern's maelstrom, Roddy is again assaulted by an image of Crystal's body lying on the sidewalk. She died because of him. Pushed or thrown to her death because someone knew he visited her this morning. Another poor soul who's dead because of him: Crystal Newcomb along with Walt McKay.

He senses a presence to his right. Roddy turns; a thirty something woman with short blond hair and painted red lips stands beside him. She's virtually pressed against him in the crowd's crush. Somehow, she managed to squeeze through the mob. She shoots Roddy a quick smile. He nods in return and, to his surprise, she leans closer to him, so near that he smells spearmint on her breath. She keeps eyeing him. Her eyes brighten and she smiles again, this time more broadly. She raises her bottle of Murphy's Stout and takes a quick swig, never averting her eyes from him. She wears silver eye shadow.

Roddy senses danger. It bubbles up from inside him. Just who is this woman, and what does she want?

"How ya doin'?" she asks in a husky voice.

Have the Russians sent her as a lure? He hasn't shaved in days—not since before Walt was killed—he looks seedy, especially sitting in a tavern where he's decades older than anyone else. Yet this attractive woman is coming on to him. Or is she?

She's peering directly into his eyes. Feeling self-conscious, it occurs to Roddy he's nearly old enough to be her father.

She seems to be making some assessment of his willingness to engage her. "Ya doin' okay?" she asks.

"Just fine," he replies, as his legs feel like coiled springs.

"Haven't seen you here before, have I?" she asks as her eyes rove over him.

"No. It's my first time here." He wants to move away from her, but the mob presses too closely. His stomach clenches.

"You live in the city?"

"No. Brooklyn."

He wonders what on earth made him say *Brooklyn*. But for the last few days, he hasn't been there in decades. But why care what he says? Who the hell is this woman, and what does she want?

"Brooklyn?" she snorts. "Like everyone lives there now." Her eyes roll upward.

"It's where I'm from," he says as memories of Sheepshead Bay streak through his thoughts.

She takes another swig of beer and then looks into his eyes once again.

He squints and scrutinizes her; he's so close, he can see the blond hairs on her cheeks. She's pretty in a hard kind of way, and there's a rough-hewn edge to her, something that makes Roddy wary. She's obviously trying to engage him, maybe entice him into something—a dalliance. For all he knows, she could be one of *them*. They don't *all* have to be men. And they don't *have* to be Russian or Eastern European. She's slithered next to him in this jam-packed tavern, having just come out of nowhere like an apparition. He can picture the scenario: she comes on to him, and if he were a fool or a horn dog, he'd drink a bit more, get a buzz on, and they'd leave together.

So, they'd get into her car and she'd drive to the Bronx or Queens—she's probably part of the bridge-and-tunnel set. Most likely Queens—it's a short hop over the Queensboro Bridge—where her apartment is supposed to be. They'd pull up in front of a two-story house in Astoria or some other section of Queens—maybe Flushing or Corona—and they'd get out of her car. It's a quiet area—residential, tree-lined, a deserted street with maybe one or two lampposts casting pinkish light—and as they walk toward her place, two guys would come out of nowhere. Russians—menacing thugs—and there'd be a moment of utter clarity as he'd see their pistols with sound suppressors pointing right at him. He'd see the "O" at the end of each piece. Then he'd hear a *pop*, and he'd be clipped. Down and out.

Or it could happen here—in the press of flesh in this noise-filled tavern. People are packed so tightly at the bar that if she shoved a shiv into his gut, he wouldn't even fall to the floor. He'd be held upright by the sardine-packed mob, and he'd drop only when the crowd thins out.

Another thought comes to Roddy—one he hasn't had for twenty-five years, since his days as a Ranger: the femoral artery. She could slice it open in a second. Other than the carotid, it's the most superficial artery in the body—very vulnerable to attack.

Yes, it's the huge artery supplying the leg with blood, not far from the surface—right there in the upper thigh—and could be severed in a second by someone with a knife. A razor-sharp blade doesn't cause pain as it slices through trousers and flesh. The victim barely feels it—just a slight sting, and before he knows what's happening, things look bleached white and his leg is wet and warm. It's death by slashing—up close and personal. For the victim, it's over in ten, twenty seconds. It's a quick, pumping bleed-out as your life's blood spurts everywhere. Your pulse goes thready, you grow light-headed, and within twenty seconds, you're dying amid a spreading lake of your own blood.

He suddenly realizes he's peering down at his beer—paying no attention to the woman at his right. A pang of alarm seizes him and he whirls abruptly toward her.

She's gone.

Does he feel wetness on his leg? Is blood shooting out of him?

He peers down at his lap, feels his thigh, and moves his leg.

The crowd roars in his ears.

There's no cut, no wound. He's not bleeding.

He gasps with relief.

Jesus. You're turning into a paranoid maniac.

He closes his eyes as an image of Crystal again crosses his mind: the tarpaulin-covered body on the sidewalk, her telephone call—no doubt, someone had a gun to her head. Seeing her this morning as she sat at a table across from him, young, vibrant, beautiful, filled with plans for the future, thanks to a connection she made at McLaughlin's. McLaughlin's, even the fleeting thought of the place turns his stomach. Images of Walt McKay dead in the garage and of Crystal's toes protruding from beneath the tarp play in endless loops through his mind.

It's all my doing, even without intending it. The fault lies with me.

Roddy peers out the pub's front window at the tide of humanity streaming by. Is anyone lingering? Anyone looking too casual, like he's just killing time? His eye catches a young man leaning against a parked car, smoking a cigarette. He's so Irish looking, it's as though the map of Ireland is etched on his face. He's soon joined by two friends—guys in their twenties. Beneath the conical light of a streetlamp, they swig beer from amber-colored bottles and smoke cigarettes, enjoying the immortality of youth. They're obviously bar patrons who've stepped outside for a quick smoke. Probably from the outer boroughs, as are most of the patrons of the place. Young, working guys—maybe apprentices to plumbers, electricians, and carpenters—and most likely still living at home with their parents. The needle on Roddy's danger meter hovers near the zero marker.

A guy in his late-thirties approaches them. He's wearing a dark blue coat buttoned up to his neck in the winter air. He could be Eastern European. He has an unlit cigarette between his lips and says something to the others. One guy whips out matches and lights the guy's cigarette. There's a brief exchange of what appear to be friendly words and smiles all around.

The guy turns and eyes the pub in a way that appears far too casual. Cigarette smoke streams from his nostrils and dissipates in the wind. He nods to the other three and moves on. Roddy's danger meter needle quivers in place.

He takes another swig of beer when, suddenly, someone slams into his back. The impact causes beer to slosh over the rim of his mug onto the bar top. Roddy whirls around and faces a young man with short hair and a Vandyke. The guy turns and says, "Sorry, friend."

"No problem."

"Lemme buy you a beer."

"That's okay. I'm just leaving."

It's unlikely the kid had bad intentions: his back was toward Roddy when they made contact. But he begins to feel tingling in the small of his back. It occurs to Roddy it wasn't a good idea to slip into the pub. Yes, it seemed a good place to lose anyone who might be following, but the crowd makes it easy for someone to slink up close and gut-shank him.

Shanked. Your blood dribbles your life away, and you die as blood pools and collects in your innards. Like father, like son. All these years later and he's still reciting the same mantra.

Roddy collects his change from the bar top, leaves a tip, and moves toward the front door. The tavern's sound system blasts "I Gotta Feeling" by The Black Eyed Peas, which Roddy recognizes from Tom tuning in Z100 whenever he's in the car. Tom, struggling with all the early adolescent shit his life can hand him and Sandy, wanting more than anything on earth to be like her father.

And Tracy. Who knows what she's thinking or planning to do? God, how he misses all three of them and how lost and alone he feels in the vastness of Manhattan.

"We're so over" is what she said. His stomach clenches.

Nearing the door, Roddy looks through the tavern's front window. The young men are gone. There's no sign of the guy wearing the blue jacket.

He sees a taxi slow down and pull over to the curb in front of the place. Two young men are perched on the backseat. One guy pays the driver. When the right rear door opens, Roddy darts from the pub and waits beside the taxi's open door for the two men to exit the cab.

He jumps into the taxi.

"Where to?" asks the driver.

"Head over to the FDR. We're going to Brooklyn."

Chapter 26

A t the Marriott, Roddy takes the escalator to the mezzanine level. He can't know if he's been followed, though he kept looking out the rear window of the taxi during the trip back to Brooklyn. He wonders where Crystal's family is and tries to imagine them being notified of her horrific death. There won't be a broker's license; there won't be a future for her.

Waiting for the elevator, Roddy's aware of an urge to keep moving, as though he wants the world to speed up. He looks up at the indicators; the elevators are taking forever to get to the mezzanine. A white-haired elderly woman waits with him. Finally, a soft *ding* sounds as the elevator stops at the mezzanine. The doors slide open. Roddy waits for the woman to enter before he does. She smiles at him and moves into the compartment.

Roddy hears footsteps: someone's running for the elevator. The woman presses the "Open" button, and a man appears at the elevator door. He steps in without thanking the woman.

She presses a button for the eighth floor.

From the corner of his eye, Roddy watches the man—he's in his thirties, wears a black, waterproof anorak, is nearly Roddy's height, clean shaven, and has light brown hair. He stares up at the indicator. On the street, he'd be just another guy, but not now. Wariness seeps through Roddy as he waits; every muscle goes taut. He reaches into his pocket; his hand rests on the pistol.

Roddy casts another sidelong look at the guy. He's not the one who was outside the tavern. That guy wore a blue jacket and had a very different look. This man could be nearly anyone you'd see on the street in wintertime. Roddy wonders if the guy is sizing him up, and his muscles tense as he feels ready to pounce. He leans forward and presses the button for the fifteenth floor, though his room is on the twentieth.

Roddy's pressing the button seems to be a prompt of some kind; the man hits the button for the seventeenth floor.

Why'd he wait until I hit a button before he did? And why the seventeenth floor, two above the one I pressed?

Heat crawls into Roddy's face. When the woman gets off on the eighth floor, will the guy pull out a gun and shoot? Then get off at the seventeenth floor? And press the elevator's button for the twentieth story so it goes to the top of the building with Roddy dead on the elevator floor?

An electric storm forms in Roddy's head as the doors slide shut. The elevator begins a gentle rise. Roddy tries—from the corner of his eye—to determine if there's a bulge in the man's jacket. He can't tell. Roddy's palm rests on the pistol grip and his index finger slides onto the trigger. With the gun inside his pocket, Roddy points it at the guy.

Does the guy look Russian, Italian, or Eastern European—Slavic? It's impossible to know. Ethnic stereotyping can be misleading. The man leans against the elevator's rear wall and looks casual. Maybe too casual. He seems barely aware of the woman or Roddy. Music—some nondescript instrumental—is piped into the car; it blends with the hissing in Roddy's ears. As the elevator ascends, his vision sharpens and the elevator light seems to brighten, as though Roddy's pupils have dilated. He feels adrenaline washing into his bloodstream. His nerve endings fire, and a jangling sensation courses through his chest. Gooseflesh crawls over his arms.

What will happen in the next few seconds? After the woman gets out of the elevator, will the guy pull a pistol? Should Roddy begin sliding the gun from his pocket or maybe angle himself so the pistol is pointing at the guy through his jacket?

It occurs to Roddy that these days, hotels and office building elevators have hidden cameras. Everything in the cubicle is digitally recorded. It would be a poor place for a hit man to strike. And this guy's face is in full view. He wears no hat or sunglasses, and the anorak's hood is down. Roddy looks up, tries to spot a camera, but sees only a laminate of cedar with decorative cornice work.

The elevator stops at the eighth floor. The woman nods at Roddy and gets out. He looks at the indicator and glances at the guy. Roddy's pistol still points at the guy through his jacket pocket.

The doors slide shut. Roddy feels electrified. The guy is a blurred presence to his right. He seems so nonchalant; it makes Roddy think he'd be a perfect hit man. He plays it cool, pulls a pistol, and pops the target. Or maybe he's just another guest in a hotel at night, going to his room. Maybe . . .

The elevator rises steadily. Ninth floor . . . tenth . . . eleventh . . .

Roddy is coiled for action. If the man blinks the wrong way, he's ready to fire. Or maybe he'll leap, shoot a knee into the guy's groin, and pound him to the floor. Put a choke hold on the bastard and force him to talk.

The elevator stops at the fifteenth floor. It sits there for an eternity before the doors slide open. Roddy makes certain not to turn his back; he moves sideways, his hand in his pocket on the pistol grip, his finger on the trigger. Watching from the corner of his eye, Roddy's ready to whirl and fire. He'll blow the guy away before he can get his hand on his weapon, wherever it's hidden.

Roddy darts from the elevator; he moves past the doors and to the right. He waits while the door stays open. His heart hammers as his hand clutches the pistol. His breath is ragged. The elevator doors close.

Roddy struggles to catch his breath. His legs go weak and begin trembling. He's soaked in sweat. It's the depleted sensation after an adrenaline rush. He's safe now, alone in the corridor. His arms feel leaden and hang at his sides. A chill overtakes him. He waits for the feeling to pass and stumbles to the nearest stairwell. On liquid legs, he climbs to the twentieth floor and makes his way to his room.

He fumbles with the keycard; his hands shake violently as he tries slipping it into the slot. On the third attempt, the door lock clicks. He enters the room, closes the door, double locks it, and tumbles onto the bed.

As he lies there, staring at the ceiling, the room spins. He closes his eyes. His mind swarms with a rush of images and thoughts: Crystal's body on the sidewalk, Walt McKay dead in the garage, Danny near death in the hospital, Tracy and the kids in Nutley, Angela and her kids in Riverdale, Gargano, the Russians, Charlie on Arthur Avenue, the pistol, the guy in the Navigator, the men in the garage, Morgan. All of it: an insane series of events in a confusing jumble of time, places, and people. Roddy's lost track of his life. He's uprooted, and everything seems alien and senseless. He wonders if life is supposed to boil down to this: alone in a hotel room, isolated from all meaning, boxed in with nowhere to go. A strange thought comes to him. *No one gets out of this life alive.* While he's always known that, it's never been so clear and so drearily inescapable.

Time passes—it must be minutes, but it seems like hours— and finally, his breathing slows. He feels his mind and body downshift to a lower level of intensity. It's the cooldown period after an adrenaline dump and a system overload.

He removes his jacket, sets the pistol on the end table, picks up the cell, and dials Danny.

"Yeah?"

"Can you talk?"

"I'm alone."

"Crystal's dead."

"*What?*"

"She took a forty-story fall."

"*Jesus.* Was it suicide?"

"I'll bet she was helped out the window or, more likely, off the balcony."

Roddy describes Crystal's telephone call, his trip to Manhattan, and seeing Bluetooth Guy at the scene. "I'll bet a gun was at her head when she called me."

"I don't get the connection to Crystal," Dan says.

"Neither do I. But whoever's after us knows her."

"Knows her *how*?"

"It's gotta be the restaurant."

"Think you were followed to her place this morning?"

"I have no idea."

"Roddy, do you think they followed you back to where you are *now*?"

"Could be. I'm getting out of here."

"Roddy, you realize, of course, you never told me where you're staying."

"In case they pinpoint these cell phones."

"Really? Is *that* why? Because I told you where I am, and the only one who came here was Morgan."

Roddy detects a hint of doubt in Danny's voice.

"Just playing it safe, Dan. But if you really need to know, I'm at the Marriott in Brooklyn."

"Well, get the hell out of there."

"You gonna be okay, Dan?"

"Yeah."

"I mean the asthma."

"It's under control. Just get outta there."

"I will."

"This beats the shit outta me, Roddy. I don't get the Crystal connection."

"It's gotta be the restaurant."

"Maybe, but something's nagging at me," Dan says.

"What's that?"

"I'm not sure. Lemme think about it. And call me when you find a new place."

"Hey, Dan, when something nags at you that can be a good thing."

"Yeah, well, it might be the first good thing that's happened."

In the bathroom, Roddy looks in the mirror. He sports a seedy-looking growth of beard. In the bright light, he notices many hairs are bristly and white. He's never seen them before because, up until last week, he shaved every day. His eyes look glazed; dark, puffy pouches perch beneath them. His forehead is furrowed; deep creases show above his eyes. Worry lines. He never realized they were so prominent. He barely looks like the guy he was the day Danny got shot.

A pulling sensation begins in his lower back—where the guy in the bar crashed into him. Did he do anything to him?

Don't be absurd. It's muscle tension. I'm on edge, and when that happens, you can feel all kinds of sensations.

He undresses and looks at himself in the full-length bathroom mirror. Twisting around, he looks for a mark or a bruise on his lower back but sees nothing.

He turns on the shower and waits until the water heats up. He steps into the stall and lets the stream pour down onto his back. It feels like needles prickling his skin. Steam rises around him as he lathers up. The muscle tension—corded knots—begins loosening beneath the hot torrent.

After dressing, he dials the reception desk. "I'm checking out. Please have my bill ready. And a car service. Ask them to be here in fifteen minutes. I'll be going to Manhattan."

At the closet, he decides to leave behind the dark gray ski jacket and baseball cap he'd worn earlier that day. He'll wear the nondescript black jacket, along with a black cap he bought yesterday on Livingston Street. Even though it's night, he'll wear the wraparound sunglasses he picked up at CVS.

Then it happens: he hears something on the other side of the door—in the hallway.

His body goes rigid. He listens intently. He waits, but hears nothing. Just hissing in his ears again. Nothing more.

Yes, his senses are aroused. He's so primed—in a state of hyperalertness—he can misinterpret the most benign things. As though he hears blood rushing through his brain or senses his arteries pulsing.

He hears whispering again. Just beyond the door. And shoes moving on the carpet.

He moves closer and listens.

Someone is outside his door.

His body stiffens.

He again hears whispering voices.

At the bedside table, he grabs the revolver and gently pulls back the hammer.

He approaches the door again and stands off to the side, pressing his ear against it.

More whispering. Indecipherable. He can't make out what they're saying or tell if it's English.

Two or more men are at the door.

The hissing in his ears intensifies.

He waits, but there's silence.

Have they gone away? Is he mishearing? Was it just two people walking along the corridor?

He sizes up the door: it's thick, sturdy-looking, and double locked. But he won't look through the peephole. He backs away toward the bed, his revolver ready.

A knock on the door—a gentle rap.

Roddy's body jolts in a galvanic spasm. He feels hot-wired and breaks out in a sweat.

Another knock.

"Room service, sir," says a muffled voice.

Is there an accent? Doesn't matter; it's them. He didn't order anything from room service. He was followed. How could that have happened?

He pictures two men outside the door, glancing left and right, just waiting for the door to open. Their hands are buried in their jackets, where they have pistols—most likely .22s with silencers. If he opens the door, he'll see quick flashes of light. He'll hear nothing, just a slamming thwack as lead rips into him. There will be a slug to the head and a couple to the heart.

And it's over.

Or, he could stand off to the side, unlatch the door handle, let them push their way in, and blow them away.

Too risky. Too many complications.

He crouches behind the bed with his pistol aimed at the door.

Another knock. More whispering, barely audible.

He picks up the bedside telephone receiver and dials reception.

"Please send hotel security to room 2017," he whispers. "Someone's at my door claiming to be room service. I didn't order anything. In fact, I'm checking out."

"Right away, sir," says the receptionist. "Do you want me to stay on the line with you?"

"No. Just send them up."

There's the faint sound of footsteps fading down the corridor.

A minute later, he hears a forceful knock on the door.

"Hotel security, sir," calls a voice.

Roddy moves to the side of the door. "Will you please slip some ID under the door?"

A plastic laminated ID card slides beneath the door. Roddy picks it up and examines it. It's the real deal. Opening the door, he sees two burly men in dark suits. They have that security look—buzz cuts, thick necks, jutting jaws, and supplement-enhanced body builds.

"What's the problem, sir?" asks one, a crew-cut guy with a flattened nose.

Roddy explains what happened.

"You did the right thing calling for us. We have two conventions in-house right now. Some of these guys get loaded and play dumb pranks."

"I'm checking out, guys. Will you escort me downstairs and wait until I get into the car I ordered?"

"Of course. And please accept the hotel's apologies, sir."

At the reception desk, Roddy sneaks a few glances around the lobby. Is anyone loitering or watching him? It's ten p.m., and the place is quiet. A few people sit in lounge chairs nursing nightcaps—mostly couples at tables set strategically around the lobby and mezzanine.

He glances at the security guards; one of them casts a knowing glance at the other. They think he's paranoid. They flank him as he makes his way out the front entrance to Adams Street, where a town car waits for him.

"Take the Brooklyn Bridge to the FDR and then go uptown to Grand Central," Roddy tells the driver.

As they head over the bridge, traffic thickens to a sickeningly slow pace. There's a car stalled in the right lane of the Manhattan-bound side of the bridge. Passing the choke point, the car picks up speed. Roddy looks back at the squall of headlights behind him. Is he being followed? No way to know. The town car's tires drub heavily on the roadway. Roddy slips the Metro North train schedule from his canvas bag but can't read it in the car's dark interior. He won't turn on the lamp, fearing he might be seen by anyone tailing him. Besides, Metro North might not be a good idea. Because Roddy's sure those were hit men outside his door, and he has no idea where they are now.

He was being watched as he checked out of the hotel. He's certain of that. Was he followed back to the Marriott from the pub? It could have been that guy who asked the young men outside for a light. He might have been lurking in a nearby doorway, watching when Roddy left the place and hopped into a taxi. Or it could have been the woman who approached him at the bar. It barely matters: he's being tracked.

The town car crosses the bridge and loops onto the FDR Drive heading uptown. "Go to 42nd Street," Roddy tells the driver.

The car exits the FDR at 42nd Street and heads west, toward Grand Central Terminal. "Let me off at the far corner of Lexington," Roddy says. He fishes a fifty from his wallet and hands it to the driver.

Roddy jumps from the car and races into the Lexington Avenue entrance of Grand Central. He walks briskly past the interior entrance to the Graybar Building. At the end of the walkway, he makes a sharp left and turns into the Lexington Passage, as though he's headed toward the Lexington Avenue subway line. At this hour, the stores in the arcade are closed and very few people walk along the passageway. Nearing the stairway leading to the subway, he turns abruptly into the passageway leading to the Grand Hyatt Hotel.

Entering the hotel, he glances around. An escalator leads to a futuristic expanse that reminds Roddy of the movie *2001: A Space Odyssey*. Everything is in grays, blacks, and whites. At one of the many registration desks, he hands the receptionist his credit card and gets a room for the night. He scans the lobby and sees nothing suspicious.

"I'd like to order a town car for nine in the morning," he tells the receptionist.

"Surely, sir. Where will you be going?"

"To Westchester County, near Port Chester. I have the address."

"It will be taken care of, sir."

"And one other thing."

"Yes, sir?"

"Can you send a barber up to my room at seven forty-five in the morning? I'll need a shave and a haircut."

"We can arrange that, sir."

With his hand holding the pistol in his pocket, Roddy heads for the elevator.

Chapter 27

Roddy pays the barber, who has finished wrapping up his equipment.

In the bathroom, he looks at himself in the mirror. It's a strange sight: he's been shorn bald and his face has been shaved clean. The air feels cold on his bare scalp.

When the barber has gone, he telephones the concierge. The town car is waiting on 42nd Street.

In the lobby, Roddy pays his bill and walks out the hotel's main entrance. The winter air feels frigid on his bare scalp. The morning glare is blinding as he heads toward a sleek black town car with blackened windows.

"Rye Brook," he says to the driver. "The Doral Arrowwood Hotel. Take the FDR to the Major Deegan. From there, take the Cross County Parkway to the Hutch."

Roddy gazes out the window at the hotel grounds. He watches an elderly couple cross the parking area, huddled against the February cold.

"I've been thinking, Roddy. This thing with Crystal," Danny says.

"Poor woman. She was more than eye candy. She had a brain and had plenty of soul, too."

"The thing I said was nagging at me . . ."

"Yeah."

"It has to do with Crystal—indirectly, but there could be a connection."

"So, let it fly," Roddy says.

"When you mentioned she was living at Continental Towers, it rang a bell in the back of my mind."

"How so?"

"That party I mentioned, the one Angela and I went to, there was champagne and caviar, the whole nine yards. I remember the building very well. It was an open house thrown by a real estate broker—guy named Art Nager. He was trying to sell the place for this honcho . . . name was Nathanson . . . Barry Nathanson. He ran a hundred-million-dollar hedge fund.

"The gathering was part of a pitch for the sale. Nager must've spent thirty grand of the seller's money on the bash. You know, there's a TV program where they show that kind of thing—*Selling New York*.

"I remember it because the place was like an office building . . . so tall. I felt uncomfortable riding in the elevator. My ears were popping."

"Uh-huh."

"That's where I met John Harris."

"The real estate guy I met visiting you at St. Joe's?"

"Yeah. I met him that night. It was long before we got involved with Kenny and the restaurant."

"I gotta tell you, Dan, I didn't like the guy with his three-thousand-dollar suit. I didn't care for his goddamned Gucci shoes and his smugly superior attitude."

Danny chortles. "Roddy, you've never been good at hiding your feelings. But there's something else." Dan's voice trails off. He strokes his chin with his thumb and index finger.

"What is it, Danny?"

"About two weeks before I got shot, I was working on this file for Harris—some property in Aruba—and there were a few figures that looked a little *off* to me, if you know what I mean."

"Yeah, so?"

"I called John to make an appointment to go over the numbers. It looked like an accounting glitch, but when I got ahold of him, he said he was too busy and didn't have time to see me. I made some kind of stupid joke about it. I don't even remember what I said. But he said he'd get back to me."

"So?"

"I didn't hear from him. I remember thinking it was strange, like he was avoiding me for some reason; and soon after that, I got shot."

"You saying you think *Harris* is behind all this?"

"I don't know. When you mentioned Crystal living at Continental Towers, it came back to me—meeting Harris there a couple of years ago and this thing with the Aruba deal."

"So what's nagging at you?"

"You remember seeing Harris that day at St. Joe's?" Dan asks.

"Yeah, sure."

"I've been to his home plenty of times and I've had dealings with him. I know the guy pretty well. He looked nervous that day at St. Joe's. And the first thing he talked about—after asking how I was feeling—was the Aruba deal. He said it was being put on hold."

"Yeah, I remember hearing that."

"I thought it was weird that he'd kill the deal."

"Okay. So maybe there are some financial shenanigans going on with this Aruba thing. What does that have to do with you getting shot?"

"I don't know."

"And whoever had you shot is also coming after *me*? How does *that* fit?"

"It doesn't."

Dan shakes his head.

"Look, Danny, Harris never even *met* me until that morning at St. Joe's. For him, I barely *existed*. And whoever's coming for us wants us *both* out of the picture. How could Harris be involved in *that*?"

"You're right. It doesn't compute."

"And don't forget, this guy Grange—or Gargano—was a made man. And word on the street is he's missing. People're looking for him. We don't have any idea about who might have known he was trying to extort us."

Danny nods and begins pacing.

"And how did Crystal know someone's after us?" Roddy says. "And why was *she* killed? The only connection between Crystal, you, and me—and Kenny, too—was McLaughlin's. And that place was a mob hangout . . . mostly Russians by the time it closed, according to Crystal. So it's either the mafia or the Russian mob. *That's* where this is coming from."

"I guess so."

"Listen, Dan. In medicine—and in life—you're always best off going where experience and past history point you. It's common sense. If you've seen five hundred patients over the years with right-sided pain in the lower abdomen along with nausea and vomiting and it turned out to be appendicitis, it's a good bet the next patient presenting the same way has appendicitis. You don't make a leap in your thinking and conclude it's the gallbladder."

Danny shrugs his shoulders. "Sounds logical."

"Let's face it, Danny. We don't know any more now than we did ten or eleven days ago."

"Maybe so, but I'm gonna find out more."

"Meaning what?"

"I gotta talk to someone first."

"Who?"

"Guy who does some IT work for me."

"Why? What's going on?"

"It's just a hunch."

"So tell me. But before you do, tell me this: we still on that deadline?"

"I don't know. I don't know a goddamned thing anymore."

Chapter 28

Danny peers out the right rear window of the town car. Looking at the Yonkers streets, he realizes how good it is to get the hell out of the hotel. Just the change of scenery makes it worthwhile. He tells the driver to slow down as he sees the four-story yellow brick building on McLean Avenue. It sits amid the last Irish enclave still existing in Yonkers, adjacent to the Woodlawn section of the North Bronx. *God, how time changes everything . . . and nothing,* Danny thinks.

But one thing's certain: he's gotta get a handle on this situation. It can't go on this way.

Danny gets the bleak feeling he's wasting his time. Roddy's probably right; Danny's barking up the wrong tree. When you look at everything that's happened since they got involved with McLaughlin's, it all points to either Kenny's gambling or Grange's death.

And with Crystal dead, the finger points clearly to the Russians—a ruthless bunch of bastards. They'll kill anyone who gets in their way or who needs to be killed for them to get what they want. *Jesus, they could come for our families,* Danny thinks. It wouldn't take much to find out where Angie and the kids are living. And Roddy's family, too.

Then what happens?

And what's Danny doing? Going to some computer guru for

advice? Absurd.

When he really thinks about all this, Danny realizes it would be a helluva lot easier to tell the driver to head for South Broadway—police headquarters—where he can find Morgan and tell him exactly what's going on. He could end all this today by confessing, and Angie and the kids—and Roddy's family, too—would be safe. It would take only a brief conversation with Morgan, and the game's over. Their families would be out of danger.

And he and Roddy would go to prison.

Confinement can drive you crazy. Hell, he's even going out of his mind at the luxurious Doral. Dan tries to imagine a penitentiary existence. How big is a cell? How much room do you have to move around? Do you ever see the light of day? Are you confined to the four walls of your cell—what can it be, maybe eight-by-ten—and the mess hall? He's seen enough movies to get the sense of how claustrophobic it is, how dangerous prison can be, and how your life is a threadbare shadow of what it once was. And they wouldn't be doing time in some white-collar country club. It would be a hard-core prison for violent offenders: murderers, rapists—the lowest of the low, the rock-bottom dregs of what passes for humanity. The horror of it can make you want to die.

Die? Danny's lucky if he's alive a month from now.

The car stops across the street from Kevin's building. To his right, across the street from Kevin's place, Dan sees Fagan's Ale House, a bar on the ground floor of a two-story building. Above the bar is the Rockin' Robins Bar and Night Club. It's been there as long as Dan can remember, through all the years he's had his office in Yonkers.

Jesus, some things remain constant: bars, booze, and bullshit.

From the rear seat of the town car, Danny gazes at Kevin's walk-up building with its crisscrossing red fire escapes on the front facade. A storefront Nationwide Insurance office is located on the ground floor. The building is next door to O'Rourke's Saloon. An Irish food market flanks the other side of the bar. The place is reminiscent of the old Sheepshead Bay neighborhood back when he and Roddy were kids.

Danny's thoughts turn to those days and to his long-dead mother. Ma worked her fingers to the bone after Da died, busting her ass as a cleaning woman to put food on the table and keep a decent home. If he tries, he can still smell the Clorox on her hands when she came home from work. His throat thickens. He fights off a feeling of nostalgia and holds back tears.

He's about to get out of the car when he thinks again of going to police headquarters instead of visiting Kevin Valentine. It's only five minutes from here.

Five minutes and a few words to Morgan—and all this ends. It would take so little to save his family and end the life he's known. And right now, what's his life worth? Danny hesitates, stays in the town car, and ponders his choices. His thoughts stream back and forth and he finally comes to a conclusion: *What do I have to lose by taking this one chance?*

"Wait for me here," Danny instructs the driver as he opens the right rear door. Stepping onto the sidewalk, Danny feels a bracing wind on his cheeks. It feels so good to be out in the fresh air. He inhales deeply and feels his lungs fill with air. He'd love to walk around after seeing Kevin, but he can't afford to take a chance of being exposed. He could get clipped.

Clipped. Now I'm even thinking like a gangster.

In the building's vestibule, Danny looks at the directory with its call buttons and presses the one next to Kevin Valentine's name. Within seconds, a buzzer sounds and Dan opens the inner door. He makes his way up a musty stairway to the fourth floor. After the climb, he's surprised: he's not wheezing like an air bellows.

Kevin waits at the open door of apartment 4-A. He's a tall,

solidly built man with a well-trimmed Vandyke beard. What little hair he has is shorn close to the scalp. Kevin looks like anything but a computer nerd; in fact, Danny's often thought the guy looks like he belongs in a mixed martial arts cage—all tattooed up and ready to kick, punch, and grapple. He's been Danny's high-tech guru for the last five years. And he's very good at what he does.

"This is a first—you coming here instead of me going to your office," Kevin says. "Come in." They shake hands.

Kevin's apartment overflows with computer towers, monitors, manuals, and electronic components. A tangle of cables snakes across the bare hardwood floor. A pile of boxes is stacked in one corner of the place. The sunlit apartment is bedecked with discs, pamphlets, and technical paraphernalia.

"Jesus, this is like walking into OfficeMax," says Danny, looking about the place.

Kevin laughs. "Welcome to my home office."

"How do you keep track of all this technical stuff?" Dan asks.

"The same way you keep up with the tax codes," Kevin says with a snicker.

On a desk, Danny spots an open bag of Fritos and a huge, half-empty bottle of Pepsi. It's, no doubt, Kevin's idea of a decent lunch. Dan recalls from Kevin's visits to his office: the guy lives on junk food. And technical manuals. "Here. Sit down," Kevin says, pointing to a wheeled typing chair. He sits in a similar one.

"I read about what happened in the paper. How're you doing?"

"Much better. Thanks for asking, Kevin."

"Hey, you gotta be careful working at night."

"Yeah, tell me about it."

"Want some Pepsi?" Kevin asks, reaching for the bottle. He takes a swig and regards Dan with a caffeinated gaze.

"No, thanks, Kevin."

Just what I need: more calories to expand my gut. And a shot of caffeine to pop me into an even higher gear.

"So, Dan, what can I do for you?"

"I need some information and help with a technical matter."

"So tell me." Kevin crosses one leg over the other and swivels in his chair.

"If I want to access someone's computer, how do I do it?"

"Well, it depends on the situation. Is this a personal computer or a corporate situation?"

"Probably personal, though it's used for business, too. It's in a guy's home, not in an office or anything like that."

"Should I ask why you need to access the computer?"

Shit. Kevin's been around this block plenty of times.

"Maybe it's better you don't ask."

Kevin nods.

Dan detects a gleam in his guru's eyes.

"Do you know if it's part of an internal network, like you'd see in a bank or any office setup?"

"It isn't, as far as I know. It's not connected to any in-house network."

"Have you seen the computer setup?"

"Yes, a number of times."

"Does it look like an elaborate arrangement?"

"I don't know if I'd be able to tell. It's a Windows 7, if that's any help."

"Yeah, that puts me in the ballpark. The reason I ask is that most computers, especially those used for business or personal finance, have encrypted files for sensitive information, so you'd need a decryption key to gain access to them."

"Encryption? Decryption? I know shit about that stuff."

"Encryption is the way you encode information on a computer so unauthorized people can't access it. The encryption process uses an algorithm that turns the information into something unreadable. It's called ciphertext. It's done with an encryption key that specifies how the information is encoded. Basically, you'd need a decryption key to access the files."

"Not a chance of that happening, Kevin."

"There's always the option of hacking into a computer, but that's not so easy, especially these days, with firewalls and sophisticated encryption software. And it's illegal."

"I wouldn't ask you to do that, Kevin."

"And I wouldn't feel comfortable doing it."

"Okay," Dan says, "so let's assume this guy's computer's files are encrypted. Or that some files are, and I need the password to get to those. Assuming I'm in the guy's house and near the computer, is there any way I can get into the thing to copy or extract the files?"

"The only way you can do that is if the computer's already been opened and the file's been accessed. In other words, the user's already typed in the password, which is usually a combination of letters and numbers. Most people are pretty stupid about it: they use a favorite pet's name, the year of their birth, or their anniversary date coupled with some other name. It's usually easily accessible, or stuff that can be guessed if you know the person well enough and play with the computer for a while." Kevin pauses and then says, "Look, Dan. We all use encrypted data. Like when you check your account balances at the bank or your brokerage firm, you have to type in your user name and password, right?"

"Yes. So, Kevin, are you telling me I can get the information if the guy's already typed in his user name and password? Then I can access the files?"

"Sure. If the user's already decrypted those files—that is, if he's typed in his user name and password—all you need to do is slip a flash drive into a USB port on the computer and copy the files onto the flash drive. Then you pocket the drive, take it home, and insert it into a port on your computer . . . and you've got whatever it is you want."

"How much space would I need on the flash drive?"

"It depends on the kind of files you're transferring. Would it be mainly text or pictures and videos?"

"I suspect mainly text, with a few pictures."

"I'd say it'd be safe to use a thirty-two-gigabyte flash drive. That'll handle any text and probably allow for the transfer of pictures, too."

Danny waits and then looks out the window at the bright morning light on McLean Avenue.

This could be a pretty complicated operation. But what choices do we have left?

"I assume you'd want to do this without the owner's knowledge," Kevin says.

"Absolutely."

"In that case, you'd want to have the computer open with the files already accessed—meaning the user's already typed in the user name and password—and he wouldn't be there when you insert the flash drive."

"I understand." Dan pauses. "One question, Kevin. How long would it take to transfer the files?"

"That's hard to say. If the files are text only, even if they're extensive, it could take a while. Maybe a few minutes. For instance, a two-hundred-megabyte file—that might be three thousand documents—could be transferred to a flash drive in about ten minutes. If there're pictures, it would take longer. But it's doable. Bottom line—you'd want the computer's owner to be away from the thing for at least ten minutes. Ideally, fifteen minutes or even more, if that's possible."

"Okay. I think I've got the idea. I just need a thirty-two-gigabyte flash drive and a window of time, let's say ten or fifteen minutes—long enough to slip the flash drive into a USB port after the file's been opened, right?"

"Correct. And here," Kevin says, reaching into a desk drawer. "Here's a flash drive . . . thirty-two gigs. It's still in the box, never been used." He hands it to Danny.

Dan slips it into his overcoat pocket.

"Anything else I can tell you?"

"No, that should cover it. Thanks, Kevin. I owe you, big-time." Dan moves toward the door. As he's about to grab the doorknob, he stops and turns. "I almost forgot. There's one other thing, Kevin. If I give you the flash drive—assuming I can get the information I want—would you be able to post it on a public forum, a website or something like that?"

"How about YouTube?"

"That would be perfect. For the whole world to see."

"It's tougher to do these days, but I could post it anonymously."

"You can do that?"

"Sure. I'll get to a computer hooked up to an anonymous proxy. The file gets sent through a series of random nodes, and it's very hard to trace."

Danny nods.

"Sounds like you're out to embarrass someone, big-time."

"You could call it that. One other thing, Kevin. If I give you the flash drive, how long would it take to get the information posted once I give you the go-ahead?"

"A few minutes. I can set everything up ahead of time."

"Dan, lemme ask you. Do I need to know what this is about?" Kevin's head tilts and his eyebrows rise.

Danny hesitates, knowing he's asking Kevin to act illegally. "Believe me, Kevin, you don't want to know. The less you know, the smaller the chance anything can come back to you."

Kevin gets up from his chair.

"You okay with this?"

Kevin nods again. "I am . . . for you, Danny."

"Thanks, Kev. Okay. I think I know what to do. You'll hear from me again."

About to leave, Dan reaches into his pocket, takes out his

wallet, and extracts a hundred-dollar bill.

"That's not necessary, Dan."

"Oh, yes, it is. It's *absolutely* necessary."

He drops the bill on the table, opens the door, and heads down the stairway.

In the town car, Danny leans back in the rear seat. He closes his eyes and inhales. His thoughts swirl, and before another moment passes, he says to the driver, "Take me to 104 South Broadway."

Looking out the right rear window, Danny realizes the Yonkers Police Department building reminds him of every public school he'd ever seen in Brooklyn. An early 1920s edifice, it's a three-story, off-white, brick building with elaborate cornice work. A colonnaded portico surrounds the main entrance. It's a striking contrast from the modern-looking Stein Center across the street, which is part of St. Joe's, where Danny spent time recuperating from bullet wounds.

"Here we are," says the driver. "How long you think you're gonna be?"

"I'm not sure."

Danny reaches for the door handle but hesitates. He wonders if this is the right thing to do. He knows he's betraying Roddy by going to the police. But there's the danger to Angie and the kids. He could be jeopardizing them by letting this go on for even one more day.

Dan closes his eyes and finds himself praying.

Dear Jesus, what should I do? And, Ma, I know you can hear me. Guide me. Tell me what's right, because I'm lost. I've sinned terribly, and I know I'll pay for what I've done. What's the best thing to do to save our families? They're all I care about now.

Time passes. He doesn't know how long he sits there. He feels a stream of tears on his cheeks. A lump forms in his throat, and he keeps praying. Slowly, from deep inside, he feels calmness spread through him.

A thought—actually, an inspiration—comes to him: *Trust your hunch. Give it one last shot before going to the police. Don't betray Roddy now.*

He looks up and says to the driver, "Take me back to Arrowwood."

Chapter 29

Danny points to the syringe and needle lying on the kitchenette counter. His finger looks ludicrous poking from the cast engulfing his right hand. "You think Harris'll go for this?"

"It's worth a try. After all, the guy loves truffles, right?"

"And your friend gave you the needle and syringe?"

"Yeah. I didn't want to risk going back to the office in Bronxville. So I made a trip to the Bronx, to a friend's clinic."

"Your friend—the guy who found out about Grange? Or should I say Gargano?"

"That's the one."

"Anything new about our fat friend?"

"Nothing."

Roddy looks at the bottle of Dulcolax and the package of Ex-lax Ultra. "You sure you wanna do this? I don't see how this leads to anything."

"I gotta check it out," says Dan.

"We're wasting time."

"I just have a feeling."

"And truffles are gonna do it?"

"Every time I've been there, he gobbles at least three of them."

Danny picks up the Dulcolax. "How's this stuff work?"

"It's called bisacodyl. It's a laxative that stimulates the nerves in the colon. At the recommended dose, it works within six to eight hours."

"I'm not gonna have *nearly* that long, Roddy."

"At the hospital, we use an extra-strong preparation to clean patients out before surgery. When I combine this with the Ex-lax, it'll bring on a massive purge."

"Ex-lax," Dan muses. "I remember my father taking it when I was a kid."

"It's been around for centuries. Each Ex-lax has fifteen milligrams of sennosides, which is a laxative that comes from senna leaves—a tropical plant. South American natives used it for centuries. And the combination of sennosides and bisacodyl should do the trick."

Danny picks up the box of Teuscher truffles. "How much this set you back?"

"Twenty-seven bucks, plus the FedEx charge to have it overnighted from the city. You can't buy this crap just anywhere, you know. I had to call the store and use my credit card."

"Twenty-seven dollars? For nine lousy truffles?" Dan says, reading the box.

"Your friend's got fancy taste."

"Jesus. That's three bucks a truffle."

"This should be easy," Roddy says. "These champagne truffles have a semisoft inside."

Danny holds the box up and reads aloud. "Our house specialty, world-famous Champagne Truffle made with a champagne cream center surrounded by dark chocolate ganache, covered with milk chocolate and dusted with confectioner's sugar."

"Okay," says Roddy. "I'm ready. You mixed it up real well?"

"Yeah. This place supplies everything. I could cook full meals in this room if I wanted to."

The Dulcolax was crushed up and dissolved in water; Roddy added a small amount of sugar to mask any lingering chemical taste. The Ex-lax was melted in a small pot. It's all been mixed together.

"Now for the injection."

Roddy sucks the solution into the syringe and injects the liquid into the center of each truffle.

"This remind you of anything?" Danny asks.

"Yeah. Slipping that Mickey Finn to Grange."

"How long you think this'll take before Harris is running for the toilet?"

"Each truffle has at least three times the dose you'd need to bring on a movement. If he downs two or three, it'll take maybe half an hour."

"And I'll be able to get into his computer."

"Dan, what if Harris *is* involved in some money scheme . . . playing a rich man's money game? So what? What could it have to do with us? And what's the connection to *me*?"

"I don't know, Roddy."

"So how was Sheepshead Bay?" Danny asks as they sit in lounge chairs.

"Leo's is gone and so's the Johnny Fell Inn."

"Figures."

"There's a much bigger mix of ethnics now—Latinos, Greeks, Russians, Asians."

"Are our houses still there?"

"Yup. I saw them both. It felt lousy. I have only bad memories of my place."

"You didn't have a home, Roddy."

"*You* did. I always felt at home at your place."

Danny swallows hard. "We were Ma's *best boys*," he says. His eyes grow wet, and he blinks away tears.

"You know where it felt good?" Roddy asks. "I went back to that rock on the esplanade where we took our oath."

"The same one?"

"The very same one. It's still there ... solid. Like our friendship."

Danny's eyes redden. Tears form at the corners. He says nothing.

Roddy feels a lump form in his throat. He lets his thoughts stream back to Tracy and the kids and the life they've had.

"Roddy, we're so over."

He peers at Dan, who sits on a recliner and looks out the window at the bare trees swaying in a winter wind.

A minute later, Roddy says, "We're just wasting time with this Harris thing."

"What can we lose?"

Chapter 30

Roddy glances to his right.

Danny looks ghostly sitting in the passenger's seat as they head north on 684. Though they're on a highway with three lanes going in each direction, there are no overhead lights. The dark landscape on each side of the road reminds Roddy of the night they drove on the Taconic State Parkway with Kenny and Grange in the backseat.

There's something so strange about riding to where they're now going. Roddy once again hears the words of Bravo Company's Sergeant Dawson: *"Once a man's jumped from an airplane, there ain't nothin' in the world can scare him, nothin' at all."*

If Roddy ever believed it, he doesn't anymore. They might be words a young man could live by, words he could place abiding faith in so many years ago, but not now that he's lived forty-six years. There was a time when he could eat snakes and tree bark to survive, but those days are long gone. No mercy and no fear was the mantra back then, but not now. Roddy doesn't believe any of it.

Not when he's close to losing Tracy and the kids, his only reason for living.

Not when this whole mess made him mistrust Danny, his lifelong and closest friend.

Not after killing two men a short distance from where he,

Tracy, Sandy, and Tom spend their summers swimming, fishing, and hiking.

Not after living through the fear of thinking the police would discover the grave and lost cartridge at Snapper Pond. And he and Dan would be tracked down.

Not after he's been running for his life.

Roddy knows one thing is certain in this life: you live with the consequences of your choices.

He recalls when he spoke with Tom after the kid hot-wired a car. "*Tom, there's a little voice inside your head. It tells you what's right or wrong. Without anyone lecturing you—me, Mom, anyone. You've gotta listen to that voice because it'll tell you the truth.*"

And there's a voice inside Roddy's head at this moment. It's crying out to be heard, and Roddy can no longer ignore it. Glancing again at Danny, he says, "Dan . . ."

"Yeah?"

"I have a confession."

"What's that?" Dan peers at him; his lips are twisted and his forehead is furrowed.

"I'm ashamed to say it, but for a while, I didn't trust you. I thought maybe you might've been in on all this. I can't explain why I thought that way. I was confused and scared and saw everything falling apart, and I blamed you." He feels he's choking on his words. "And I'm sorry to say there were times when I wondered if you had a hand in what was going on. I just want you to know that."

"I know it, Roddy."

"More than that, I wanna apologize."

Danny sighs. "Remember that argument we had at St. Joe's that morning, before Morgan popped in?"

"Yeah."

"I blamed you for getting us in this mess. I was wrong, dead wrong. You were right. We had no way out with Grange and

Kenny. I was trying, I guess, to clear myself of any responsibility. I was laying it all on you. I'm sorry I said what I did."

"Forget it."

"I can't, Roddy. And there's another thing. Since that argument, even before that morning, I had the feeling I'd fucked up. No, even more than that. I felt like I'd betrayed you."

"*What?*"

"I felt like . . . I just felt like I'd undone everything in our lives. I was too hot to trot—to get into the restaurant business. I wasn't careful. I let my ego get in the way of common sense. It clouded my thinking. I should have lived by my own financial philosophy—the numbers never lie. I should've looked into Kenny's finances more carefully, and I didn't."

Danny sighs and shakes his head.

"What it really boiled down to was simple and stupid: I let my ambition, some greedy idea that I wanted *more* in my life . . . I let *that* make the decision for me, for both of us. So we ended up in McLaughlin's, in that goddamned snake pit, and here we are. It was *my* fault."

"So, Dan, what can we say? Right or wrong, we made our choices and live with them."

They fall silent. Roddy drives on for a few minutes.

"You used cash for this heap?" Danny asks.

"Yup. Nothing but Ben Franklins."

"Not easy to do these days. Everyone wants credit cards."

"Not this guy in Rye Brook. He's rinky-dink . . . completely off the books. He rents out a few old models. I gave him two hundred for this junk pile. No questions asked. I said I'd have it back tomorrow."

"You have dinner?" Danny asks.

"Yeah."

"In the atrium?"

"You got it."

"People see you there?"

"Uh-huh. And I made sure to charge it to my room."

"And then what?"

"I went back and waited for your call."

"So there's a record," says Danny.

"Right. And you?"

"I ordered a couple of burgers in my room."

More silence. The parkway is dark and lightly traveled.

"It's funny how you called it with Harris," says Roddy.

"He's a greedy fuck. It's his character."

"The scorpion and the frog thing, huh?"

"It's his nature," Danny says.

Roddy veers into the right lane, still driving at a steady fifty-five. Not a chance of getting pulled over for speeding.

"So here we go again," Dan says.

"Yeah, but we're not gonna do murder."

"Jesus, don't put it like that."

"Can't kid ourselves, Dan. We did what we did and we gotta live with it." Roddy pauses and then says, "Funny, isn't it, how the Continental Towers thing tells the story?"

"Yeah, but it all came out because you went to Omar and Crystal."

Roddy shakes his head. "I keep thinking about her. I can't get her out of my mind. She'd still be alive if I hadn't visited her."

Roddy drives on. It isn't far until they reach the exit.

"You confident about the numbers?"

"One hundred percent."

"It looked like hieroglyphics to me. All that debit and credit crap drives me up a wall."

"We all have our areas of expertise. For you, it's the human body. For me, it's bank records and balance sheets."

"You sure he's home?"

"I called on my disposable and he picked up. Then I hung up."

"And he has no idea we're coming?"

"None."

"What if someone else is there?"

"We turn around and come back another night. His wife winters in Palm Beach, so she won't be there. He likes to work alone, especially at night. And the help doesn't work on Wednesdays."

"How do you know all this?"

"He told me when I dropped by—unannounced, of course—to thank him for his kindness when I was in the hospital. And we talked about my getting back to doing some more work for him. That's when he ate the truffles."

"How many times've you been there?"

"Since I've known him, at least four. He likes working at home rather than going to the city. He has an office upstairs in the house."

"Anything else I should know?"

"Just that he thinks I'm gonna invest money in one of his projects. That's what I told him when I showed up with the truffles."

"Greed's an amazing thing, isn't it?"

"Yeah, it's an insatiable appetite," Dan says. "Like you said, it's his nature."

"Reminds me of Grange," Roddy says, picturing the loan shark's protruding lower lip, his hangdog dewlaps, heavy-lidded eyes, rotund belly, and sausage-like fingers. And the huge star sapphire ring he wore, now sitting at the bottom of Snapper Pond, along with three .45 caliber brass casings and the gun.

But there's that one missing shell casing.

"Don't remind me of the fat bastard, Roddy. Or of Kenny, either."

"Greed amazes me, Dan. It drives people to incredible lengths."

"I know. I see it every day with clients. People making tons of money, who'll never have a financial worry, even if they live to be a hundred, and they risk it all trying to cheat the government out of a few bucks."

"Greed's the most powerful force in human nature."

"Even more than sex?"

"It's right up there. For some people, money's an aphrodisiac."

"Greed's a cardinal sin," Dan says. "But we committed murder. The worst of the mortal sins."

"This is no time for religion, Dan. And you gotta forget about our being Peggy Burns's *best boys*."

"Yeah, I know." Dan sighs. "Jesus, this hand aches like hell."

"When's the cast coming off?"

"A few weeks. Then I wear a soft cast."

About a mile from the exit, Roddy says, "I still can't believe what's on that computer."

"It tells the story."

"A sad and ugly story," Roddy says.

"Sad and ugly, that's the world."

Chapter 31

Roddy exits Route 684 and crosses South Bedford Road. At Bedford Corners, he turns onto Baldwin Road, a dark, tree-lined road with grand mansions spaced acres apart. The trees arch over the road, forming a dense canopy. There are no street-lights. A few houselights glow in the surrounding darkness; the homes are set far back from the road. Many are hidden behind high hedges and elaborate stone walls.

"You sure there're no cameras?" Roddy asks.

"As sure as I can be."

"And there's no electric gate? You don't have to announce yourself over an intercom?"

"No. It's a very long driveway and it's isolated."

"No guards or dogs?"

"None."

"What does he do when he travels? He doesn't just lock up and leave, does he?"

"No. The staff lives there when he and his wife are away. Otherwise, he's home alone during the winter."

"Whaddaya think the minimum zoning is here?" Roddy asks.

"Four, maybe five acres for each property . . . pretty substantial. These are country estates. You know, Martha Stewart lives around here."

"You mean there are no attached houses?" Roddy says with a

soft laugh.

"No. It ain't Brooklyn," Dan says with a snort.

"We must be getting close."

"Slow down. It's coming up on the left."

They turn into a driveway between two massive stone pil-lars at the driveway's Belgian-block apron. Rows of high hedges nearly obscure the entrance. A huge iron gate rests in an open position. Roddy drives at least six hundred feet on a slight up-grade toward the house. The Toyota's headlights sweep along hedgerows and elaborate plantings lining both sides of the drive-way. They ascend between two rows of ancient sycamore trees. The trees end about one hundred feet from the home, where the driveway forms a circle in front of a Normandy-style mansion. A stone tower topped by a conical roof projects upward at one side of the house.

The main entrance is set in the middle of the structure. Stone steps lead to the front door. A protruding Juliette-style balcony sits above the entrance. The balcony—fronted by an ornate wrought-iron railing—extends a few feet from French doors on the second floor. The balcony's underside forms a canopy over the main entrance and the steps leading up to it. Two decorative lanterns bathe the area in a soft orange light.

"You sure he's alone?" Roddy asks.

"No cars parked out front. His Benz must be in the garage."

"He does most of his work from here?"

"We live in a virtual world, Roddy. If you're in the financial industry, you can do most of it from home. You can trade all over the world."

They get out of the car. It's a balmy night—quite warm for March. Roddy thinks he smells something reminiscent of spring; maybe it's a fragrance similar to the one he detects in Tracy's gar-dens back in Bronxville. Roddy wears his ski jacket; the pistol is tucked into a side pocket, which is zipped closed. Dan wears a Windbreaker. Roddy walks along the front of the house and peers upward.

"What're you doing?"

"Checking for cameras."

"See anything?"

"No. But you never know."

The balmy night air feels refreshing on Roddy's face. It's a relief from the dry, frigid air of the last few weeks. Dan inhales deeply, looks at Roddy, and they climb the steps. Dan rings the doorbell.

Roddy has that taut, wired feeling that's become too familiar lately. It's the harbinger of menace, of confrontation. But he's certain he can maintain a veneer of calm.

Dan rings the doorbell again.

Roddy feels his heart pumping at a quickened pace. Sounds come from inside the house.

The door opens.

John Harris stands there, looking as aristocratic as when Roddy saw him back at St. Joseph's. He wears dark gray slacks, pleated in front, and a blue shirt open at the collar. A powder-blue cardigan covers the shirt. His silvery hair is stylishly barbered and brushed back. He has a deep Florida tan, pale, ice-blue eyes, prominent cheekbones, and a strong nose. His teeth are toothpaste-ad perfect, gleamingly white, and contrast with his deeply tanned face. Roddy detects a fragrance—some high-end cologne—wafting through the air. The overall look is upper-crust patrician.

"*Danny*," Harris says, nearly drawing back from the doorway. "What are *you* doing here?" Harris's eyes flit to Roddy, back to Dan, and then to Roddy once again. His gaze shifts to Roddy's bald scalp. Harris's mouth drops open as he stands with one hand on the door handle.

"Well, John," says Dan. "As I said the other day, I'm interested in putting money into the Costa Rica deal, so since I was passing by, I figured I'd drop off a check. I hope you don't mind the intrusion at this hour."

"No . . . no, not at all," Harris says, nearly sputtering. "But this is *unprecedented*, to say the least."

"It's one hundred thousand dollars. How's that for a surprise?"

Harris's mouth opens again. His eyebrows arch and his head bobs up and down.

"John, you've met Dr. Roddy Dolan. He'd also like to invest, and I thought we could kill two birds with one stone."

Harris's face brightens. "Oh yes, Dr. Dolan. We met at the hospital, but I didn't recognize you with your hair gone. Of course."

They shake hands. Harris's hand is soft and feels delicate in Roddy's grasp.

"Come in. Come in," Harris says with a forced smile—really more a wince than a genuine smile. "Good to see you, both of you. And what a lovely surprise. So you're *both* interested in the Costa Rica property?"

"You got it," says Danny.

"It's the new playground of the Western world," Harris says as they enter the foyer. "It's so nice to have the pleasure of meeting another investor. You know, it never gets old, this feeling of accomplishment and gratitude when I realize someone has confidence in me. Why don't we go upstairs to the office?"

Harris leads them past a medieval suit of armor. The living room is furnished with ornate French-style furniture. Each piece is intricately carved and adorned with ivory insets. Baroque cupboards and consoles are set against rough stucco walls. Oil paintings of French country scenes hang on the walls. Thick chestnut beams cross the ceiling. Heavy drapery covers the ground-floor windows. The place reminds Roddy of a castle.

At the far end of the living room, they ascend a wide carpeted stairway to the second floor. Roddy estimates the ceilings are fifteen feet high. The stairwell walls are filled with oil paintings depicting eighteenth-century French aristocrats.

"You live here alone?" Roddy asks.

"Just for the time being," Harris says. "I'll be joining the wife in Palm Beach next week. From there, it'll be some time in the Caribbean and then Europe—the Greek islands, in particular. There are some very interesting properties in the Aegean and on Corfu also."

They turn right at the top of the stairway and walk along a hallway with walls displaying impressionist oil paintings. Roddy recognizes them from Tracy's art history books: Pissarro and Sisley, all in gilt frames and lit by angled ceiling spotlights.

They enter a spacious room. Roddy can tell it's at the center of the mansion, above the main entrance. It's Harris's home office. The room feels overheated on this balmy night. To the right of Harris's desk are those high French doors leading to the Juliette balcony directly over the main entrance. The doors are opened outward, and a soft breeze sweeps into the room.

Harris's rococo desk looks like it's been taken from a period piece movie—maybe from some French baron's estate. The desk legs are slender, carved, and curved. The desktop and sides have inlaid mother-of-pearl, ivory, and ebony markings. The chairs are upholstered with bronze-colored fleur-de-lis patterns against a background of red chenille. The rest of the furniture is uphol-stered in richly colored brocades and damasks. In contrast to the antique furniture, two sleek computer monitors sit on the desk. The computer tower stands beneath the desk; the wireless router and modem are off to the side.

"Sit, gentlemen. Sit down and make yourselves comfortable," Harris says, waving at two chairs facing his desk. "Do either of you care for a drink?"

"None for me," says Roddy.

"Thanks, John, but I won't have any either," Dan says.

"At the risk of seeming self-congratulatory, I always enjoy a bit of cognac when new investors come along," Harris says. "This is such a pleasant surprise." He opens a cabinet behind the desk, removes a brandy snifter, and sets it on the desk. He rummages through the cabinet and comes up with a bottle of Martell cognac. "The finest cognac in the world." He nods at the bottle and pours two-fingers of it into the glass and then returns the bottle to the cabinet. He sips the cognac, sets the snifter on the desk, and settles into the high-backed chair behind the desk.

"Let me boot up the computer and we'll talk about the Costa Rica property. You know that Costa Rica means 'rich coast' in Spanish," he says with a quick chortle. A half smirk forms on Harris's lips, one signaling self-satisfaction and, in Roddy's mind, a sense of entitlement.

Roddy stifles the rage he feels simmering inside him.

They wait as the computer comes to life. Harris keeps his eyes on the screen and steeples his fingers. The beginnings of a smile form on his lips. Roddy notices Harris's nails are buffed and sport a coat of clear polish.

When the computer is booted, Harris leans forward and types briefly on the keyboard. Roddy is certain he's keying in his user name and password to decrypt the computer. Roddy feels a sense of voyeuristic pleasure knowing what he does about Harris. It's like understanding a foreign language when others, not realizing it, talk about you in that tongue as you stand there in presumed ignorance, absorbing every word.

"What was it, Dan? You want to invest a hundred thousand?"

Dan remains silent. He stares at Harris, who's engrossed in the monitor's display.

The silence seems to expand. Roddy feels his blood humming.

"And how about you, Roddy? You guys are very good friends; you grew up together. Am I correct in assuming you'd like to invest a hundred thousand also?"

Roddy hears a breeze rustle through the evergreens outside.

Harris looks up from the monitor. His eyes meet Roddy's and then flit away.

"How do you know that?" Roddy asks, feeling his chest muscles tense.

"How do I know what?" Harris asks, turning back to Roddy. His eyebrows arch. A smile is pasted on his face.

"How do you know Dan and I grew up together?"

"Oh, I recall Dan telling me about you two back at the restaurant . . . when we were there for lunch one time."

"That's right, Roddy. I told John we're friends from way back," says Danny.

"You grew up together, what was it, Brooklyn? And you've stayed good friends your entire lives."

There's silence.

"Well, whatever," Harris says and waves his hand. "Am I right, Roddy? You'd like to put in a hundred?"

"I don't think so."

Harris looks up from the screen. He leans back in his chair and peers across the desk at Roddy. His eyes shift to Roddy's bald scalp. His eyebrows arch again, and the half smile fades. "I don't understand, Dan. What's going on?" Harris looks in Danny's direction. "I know you want to get in on the Costa Rica deal, so what's happening?"

"Actually, John, we're not here to invest. We're here for another reason entirely," Dan says, crossing one leg over the other. He stares steadily at Harris.

Roddy glances over at Danny. In all their years together, he's never seen Dan look as intense as he does now. There's something hard in Danny's look—something brittle. Roddy's reminded of the night at Snapper Pond.

Harris shakes his head. His face twists into a look of bewilderment. His lips thin in a grimace as his eyes narrow. "What *are* you talking about?" His voice drops an octave.

"I'm talking about your offshore accounts, John," says Danny.

"My *what*?"

"The offshore accounts and the shell corporations you've created."

"Yes, I have shell corporations in a number of locations. You know that, Dan. You're one of my accountants. What's the problem?"

"Why don't you tell *me*, John?"

Roddy detects menace in Danny's voice. It reminds him of when Kenny was down in the hole with Grange's body.

Shoot him, Roddy.

"Frankly, Dan, I don't like the tone of your voice," Harris says as his posture stiffens. He leans forward with his elbows on the desk. "You're an accountant. You know shell corporations are perfectly legal."

"Yes, John. They're legal in principle. But when they're used to launder money, well, then they're not legal."

"What on earth are you talking about?" Harris's eyes widen into a quizzical stare.

"I'm talking about the multiple companies you've formed and the intricate money transfers you've made over the last few years while the companies have no assets or operations. Your corporations are dummy setups for money laundering. We both know shell corporations can be used to conceal the origin or distribution of money."

Harris's eyes dart back and forth from Danny to Roddy and then back to Dan. His face turns chalky white as the blood drains from it. His mouth droops slightly.

Roddy feels a twitching sensation in his chest. Something triggers itself inside him: it's a neural overload—an electric spasm of energy so intense, he feels a sudden jolt.

"I don't have to be a forensic accountant to know your game,"

Danny says, leaning forward in his chair. "You've been taking money from investors and spreading the funds through transfers and financial transactions to make it nearly impossible to follow. There've been bank-to-bank transfers between and among shell corporations. There've been wire transfers between different accounts in different names, and they've been in various countries and currencies in offshore accounts."

Harris's chin begins trembling. He sets his palms on the desk. His hand shakes as he reaches for the cognac snifter, sips quickly, and sets it down unsteadily.

"Then, John, you use this altered money to purchase high-end items so the cash is converted into tangible assets."

"That's ridiculous, utterly absurd. I've done no such thing."

But Harris's lips go pale as they press together. His eyebrows rise and knots appear at the sides of his face, as though his teeth are clenched. Roddy's certain if he places his fingertips on Harris's wrist—if he feels for the man's radial pulse—it would be galloping at over a hundred beats a minute. In fact, Roddy thinks he can actually see Harris's carotid arteries pulsing in his neck.

"After all, John, with these assets soaking up all that cash, it becomes tangible," Dan says. "We call it real property in the accounting trade. Like the hundred-foot yacht you keep at Santa Monica, the house at Laguna Niguel, or the beachfront mansion in Palm Beach. Oh, I almost forgot: the ski lodge you bought in Aspen and the hundred acres you own in Sun Valley, Idaho. These have all been purchased with laundered money."

Dan turns to Roddy as he uncrosses his legs. "Just so you know, Roddy, that's part of John's scheme. It's a two-fold operation. The last part is called integrating the money. The cash reenters the mainstream economy in legitimate form and looks like it came from legal transactions, like buying a house or a boat. The first part, where the money is moved all over the place, is called layering the money. And it's something John does quite well."

Danny turns back to Harris. "I have to say, John, I'm impressed by your criminal skill."

Harris exhales audibly. "Well, Dan," he warbles, "I had no idea you came here tonight to accuse and insult me. I thought you popped in the other day because you wanted to get back to doing some more work for me and were interested in making an investment in the Caribbean. I never dreamed you were here to malign and accuse me like this."

Harris leans back in his chair and assumes a look of nonchalance.

"But now that I think about it, I shouldn't be surprised. You're such an altar boy, Danny. Always doing what you think is the right thing." He shakes his head, smirks, and leans forward with his elbows again on the desk. "Now, I think it's time for you and your doctor friend to leave my home. And you can rest assured, I'll be calling my lawyers to discuss your accusations."

"We're not leaving," Roddy says. "There's plenty more to discuss."

"I have nothing more to say to either of you," Harris says, scowling. "Now, I'm asking both of you politely to leave. Otherwise, I'll call the police." He leans toward the telephone, but the receiver stays in the cradle on top of the tortoiseshell inlaid desk. Harris's hand remains motionless, about a foot away from the telephone.

"Oh, go ahead, John. Call the police," says Danny. "We'll have no trouble telling them what you've been up to. I'm sure the SEC and the federal government will be interested, too."

"Oh, really?" Harris says thickly. Roddy knows the man's throat is filled with phlegm. "What else do you allege I've been doing that makes you so certain I won't call the police?" He leans back in his chair. His smirk reignites.

Dan stares long and hard at Harris. "I'm a numbers cruncher, John. It's what I do for a living. And the numbers are going to send you to prison."

Harris's face turns ashen. He blinks repeatedly.

"The numbers and much more," says Roddy as that neural impulse shoots through him. "And it's time to tell John exactly what we know."

Chapter 32

Harris remains rigid. He doesn't even blink.

Heat seeps into Roddy's face. He has that exhilarating yet ugly feeling of butterflies looping crazily in his stomach—the adrenaline-pumped prefight jitters of years ago. It presaged the sound of the bell when he plunged into animal mode, where it was kill or be killed. Like the feelings he had on the Army Ranger infiltration course or before his first jump from a C-17 transport plane.

"You've been issuing false annual statements to your investors, John," says Dan. "Or should I call them suckers?"

Harris's jaw is clenched. His pupils look so dilated, his eyes no longer look blue.

"You see, John, I know those statements are doctored," Dan says. "No, they're more than that: they're completely fabricated. What it boils down to is that your investment company is nothing but a Ponzi scheme. You pay off anyone who's leaving with new money, and your clients' fine returns are figments of your imagination. Your annual reports show the clients' accounts growing at a decent clip, but in reality, the money moves between offshore accounts and ends up converted into your personal assets. You're nothing more than a mini-Madoff."

"What leads you to this conclusion?" Harris asks. His semi-smirk remains, but a flicker of doubt appears in his eyes. He blinks repeatedly, and his Florida tan seems bleached. He sits stiffly behind the desk.

"Everything in your computer tells the story, John."

"Everything in my *computer*?"

Harris's head shakes from right to left as though he can't believe his ears.

"Yes, it's all there."

"How did you get into . . . ?" Harris stops midsentence. His eyes widen. His pupils are huge, dark circles obliterating his irises. "You *didn't*."

"Yes, I did."

"You mean the other day when you showed up here?"

"Yes, John. I accessed it when you were temporarily indisposed. I believe it might have been a stomach virus, or maybe it was something you ate. It might have been those truffles . . . those Teuscher truffles. The finest in the world, aren't they? Who knows? Anyway, while you were indisposed, I looked at your computer files, and there it was, all the little details about your Ponzi operation. Funny, isn't it? Technology can be a boon or a curse. And for you, John, it's the latter. Your computer shows it for the whole world to see."

"You hacked my computer?"

"I accessed it, that's all. You'd already opened it and typed in your user name and password."

"That's illegal."

"Not nearly as illegal as what you've been up to."

Harris's face takes on a sickly greenish hue. His eyes bulge in their watery sockets. "This . . . this isn't what it looks like."

"It's exactly what it looks like. It's a Ponzi scheme. You take in loads of money, launder it, and issue false statements to investors, while you convert their money into personal assets. I'm sure you intend to sell them and eventually leave the United States—no doubt, to a country that doesn't have an extradition treaty with the US."

"But . . . but that's all a supposition." Harris's chin quivers.

"Is it, John? Is it something I'm just supposing, or does your computer show you're a conniving con man who'll take anyone's money as long as they can pony up fifty grand or more? You really think I'm speculating about this?"

"You can't prove a thing." Harris shakes his head, but beads of sweat form above his upper lip.

"We'll see about that." Dan says, leaning forward in his chair. "But there's another thing, John."

Harris's chair creaks as he leans back. "What's that?"

Roddy's brain fires charged impulses. He feels the blood rush of aggression and knows he could explode in another second. But he waits for Dan to go on.

"It has to do with the Aruba deal, the one you put on hold," Danny says.

"What about it?"

"This all began after I asked you—really quite innocently—about some of the numbers on that deal back some weeks ago. You remember?"

Harris shakes his head. His eyes flit back and forth between Danny and Roddy. Sweat droplets form on his forehead.

"Sure you do. I asked about the Aruba deal. I said something about the numbers being a little off, maybe a bit strange. There was either some arithmetic error or the money was disappearing in some Caribbean accounts. Actually, I was being a bit facetious and made a joke about it. I sometimes do that with clients, kid them about the IRS when I see something that doesn't look right on their worksheets or in their books. It's just a stupid habit of mine.

"And I didn't realize it at the time, but I've thought long and hard about it recently. I've figured it out—completely. When I made that offhand comment—that stupid little joke—I must have hit a nerve somewhere deep in your nonexistent soul, John. I must have triggered some warning signal in your reptilian brain, because I recall as clear as day that my comment got you very upset. No. You were *more* than upset; you were absolutely beside yourself. You even told me to forget about it, that the Aruba deal was on hold. My God, even when I was at St. Joe's, you popped in and made sure to tell me the deal was off. You remember that, don't you, Roddy, seeing him in my room?"

Roddy nods his head but says nothing.

"So? I visited you in the hospital. So what?" Harris says in a shaky voice. Sweat sheen covers his face.

"Well, when I *really* began thinking about it all, when I went over the chain of events, I realized it was soon after I asked about the Aruba deal when I got *this*."

Dan holds up his casted hand. Harris stares at it. His lower lip trembles.

"It goes to show, Roddy, how some innocent question, or even a dumb joke, can lead to some very bad consequences." Dan waves his casted hand in the air.

Harris is drenched in sweat. "Just what are you saying?" he asks in a voice thick with phlegm.

"I'm saying you wanted me out of the way. You thought I knew more than I actually did." Danny pauses and stares at Harris. "You thought I suspected something about your Aruba scheme and about the other investments you've been making on behalf of the suckers entrusting money to you. Actually, the truth is, John, I had no fucking idea what you were up to. Not until I put things together and thought it was quite coincidental that soon after I asked about the Aruba deal and you got all bent out of shape, someone comes to my office and tries to kill me."

"Don't be *absurd*."

"I'm being 100 percent logical. I'm using what I now know about you to come to very precise conclusions."

Harris rubs his chin with a trembling hand. "You're actually accusing me of attempted *murder*?" His eyes widen again. "This is the most insane thing I've ever heard. I don't know where on earth you got this ridiculous idea. This sounds like a paranoid man's ravings."

"Is it paranoia that someone came into my office and shot me twice?"

Harris's body is trembling. His palms again go to the desktop and press down on it in an attempt to steady himself. His shoulders are hunched.

"Is it paranoid that a doctor got killed in the garage at Lawrence Hospital, a guy who from behind looked just like Roddy Dolan and who left the hospital at about the same time Roddy did? And that murder happened only two days after I was shot? Is that paranoid?"

"What are you *talking* about?" Harris says, shaking his head from side to side. "I had nothing to do with Dolan until this evening. I never even met the man until that time in your hospital room. And you're saying I tried to *kill* him? Danny, you're disturbed."

"Am I?"

"This is insane. It's . . . it's absolutely . . ." Harris sputters and stops speaking. Specks of spittle form on his lips.

"Well, then, John, who's been coming after both of us? Oh yeah, could it be someone who knows we're best friends who go a long way back?"

"I have no idea what you're talking about."

"Oh, yes, you do. I can prove it."

Harris's face is florid. It shines in the room's soft lighting.

Danny turns to Roddy. "Why don't you take over, Roddy? I'm tapped out. And my fucking hand's killing me. It's just killing me."

Chapter 33

Roddy gets to his feet and moves toward Harris. He walks around the desk to where Harris sits and hovers over him. Harris's leather chair creaks again as he leans back.

"You said something interesting before," Roddy says. "Know what it was?"

Harris shakes his head. His hands grip the arms of his chair as he looks up at Roddy. His mouth opens, and the whites of his blue eyes are bloodshot. His sweaty face glistens in the lamplight.

"You said you know Danny and I grew up together . . . in Brooklyn."

"So?" Harris croaks in a strangled voice.

"Danny never told you that."

"I don't recall who I heard it from." Harris leans back so far, the chair seems ready to topple.

"You heard it from Kenny at McLaughlin's."

Harris shakes his head. "Kenny's not the kind of person I particularly cared to talk with." Harris coughs and then swallows hard, keeping his eyes on Roddy.

"Okay, John, you didn't hear it from Kenny. You heard it from Crystal, who probably heard it from Kenny."

"Crystal?" Harris's forehead creases in deep furrows. Sweat dribbles down from his hairline.

"Yes. Crystal. That pretty blond woman Kenny hired as a

hostess. Remember her?"

"Vaguely."

"How vaguely do you remember her, John?"

Roddy's face feels incendiary—as though the blood vessels in his cheeks are about to burst. Doc Schechter's words from Herbie's Gym bolt through his brain.

"Don't be an animal in the ring, Roddy. You gotta execute a strategy."

"What are you talking about?" Harris says in a shaky voice. "She was a hostess at a restaurant where I went occasionally for lunch when I was at the New York office, for the love of God." He shakes his head back and forth.

"So you never spoke with Crystal?"

"Just a 'Hello,'" Harris warbles, leaning as far back as the chair allows.

Roddy can virtually smell the man's fear. He perches himself on the edge of the desk and plants himself there as his hands begin throbbing.

"Tell me, John, where does Crystal live?"

"I have no idea." Harris's tongue slides along his lower lip.

"Is that so?" Roddy says. "We have her living at 301 East 79th Street in apartment 40-A. Does it sound familiar?"

Harris's eyelids flutter like a hummingbird's wings.

"Tell us, John. Do you know that apartment?"

Harris says nothing; he stares vacantly at Roddy.

"Okay, let's cut to the chase, John. You own that apartment. It's a condo, so you can rent it out. True?"

"I own the apartment?"

"Oh, I stand corrected. Your corporation owns it. That's what your computer says."

Harris opens his mouth, but nothing comes out.

Roddy's skin feels like it's blistering.

"And I don't think Crystal could afford the rent a place like apartment 40-A would command. You're a real estate guy. You know what a two-bedroom apartment on the fortieth floor of a concierge building on the Upper East Side goes for, right?"

Harris shakes his head back and forth.

"So, John, you were letting Crystal Newcomb live there rent free."

"In exchange for sexual favors," Danny calls, still seated in his chair.

"Talk to us, John," Roddy says. "Just talk to us."

"I have nothing to say," Harris whispers. He clears his throat once again. His eyes dart back and forth from Roddy toward Danny and then to the door.

"Nothing?" Roddy says.

"My personal life is none of your business," Harris squeaks.

"Let's get something straight," Roddy says. "I don't give a shit about your personal life. But some other things are important. Do you understand?"

Harris says nothing. His chair looks like it will tilt over.

"*Answer* me. Do you understand?"

Harris flinches, turns his head sideways, and nods.

"Certain things are very clear—*crystal* clear, if you know what I mean. Like the fact that you also own apartment 40-B, just across the hall from 40-A. A pretty convenient arrangement, don't you think? You just walk across the hall and Crystal's right there."

Harris's face looks sea green. Spittle forms on his lips and turns frothy.

"Am I right, John?"

"No." Both of Harris's hands rise reflexively, as though he's trying to shield himself.

"Tell me the truth, John. It'll go easier if you do."

Harris shakes his head.

"Stand up."

"Please . . . don't do anything." Harris's lower lip begins trembling.

"Do what the man says," Dan says from the chair. "Stand up, John."

Harris hesitates and then, grasping the armrests of his chair, rises slowly to his feet.

"Now," Roddy says, inching closer. "I'm going to ask you one more time. Did you own both apartments in Continental Towers—40-A and B, right across from where Crystal lived?"

Something volcanic surges through Roddy as though he's about to erupt.

"No . . . no . . ."

Roddy shoots a lightning-fast, stone-heavy fist into Harris's belly.

There's a whooshing sound as Harris's lungs empty. He doubles over, gasps for air, and clutches his abdomen. Still bent at the waist, he retches and then coughs; a sticky thread of mucous-tinged saliva slides from the corner of his mouth. He gulps hungrily for air and looks like he'll sink to the floor. An animal-like grunt comes from deep in his throat. Roddy is certain a rope of vomit will gush from Harris's mouth, but only frothy drool hangs from his lips.

Roddy's hands move in a blur.

He grabs Harris's shirt and sweater and slams him onto the desktop. Harris lands on his back. His head bounces on the surface from the force of the impact. Roddy hauls Harris's hips onto the desk. The man is pinned there, lying on his back.

Roddy feels an urge to pummel Harris with hammering blows; he wants to pound him until the man's face is a wet slab of pulp. This spineless bastard is a shit-ridden con man who's fucked over people's lives. Roddy feels the beast inside him surfacing—the monster he thought he'd buried so long ago—and he knows he could tear Harris apart, shredding him into a million pieces.

But Roddy holds back, knowing more must be done.

"Kill the bastard, Roddy," Dan mutters from his seat across the desk. "Just kill him."

Roddy shakes his head. "I'm not gonna kill you, John," he whispers. "You'll live through this, but the life you know is over."

Harris gasps.

Roddy presses him on the desktop and shakes him violently.

Dan calls from the chair, "You know, John, Roddy was an Army Ranger and learned hand-to-hand combat, how to disable an enemy without killing him. Isn't that right, Roddy?"

"Yes, that's right," Roddy rasps into Harris's ear. He moves his face so close, their eyes are inches apart. Roddy smells cognac on Harris's breath. It's mixed with the ureic odor of sweat dribbling from Harris's fear-filled pores. Adrenaline surges through Roddy. He fights to keep his fists from bashing Harris's face to a macerated paste. He knows he could pulverize the man in a few moments of fury. But he won't do it.

"Kill the bastard, Roddy," calls Dan.

"No. I won't," Roddy growls. "That would be too kind. I'm gonna do worse, much worse."

Chapter 34

Roddy's palms go to the sides of Harris's face. It's a gentle touch, with four fingers over each ear. Harris's face feels sweaty. Roddy's thumbs cover Harris's closed eyes. Harris trembles as Roddy holds him down. Roddy presses so his thumb tips fit into the corners of the eye sockets on each side of Harris's nose.

"Now, John, this is called a gouge move. If I push my thumbs in a little bit deeper and snap them to the sides, your eyes will be plucked out." Roddy's thumbs sink into Harris's eye sockets.

"No," Harris gurgles. "Please don't."

Roddy feels the spongy pressure of Harris's eyes beneath his thumbs. He pushes inward. The eyeballs sink deeply into their sockets. Roddy maintains the pressure.

"Oh, I'll do it," Roddy says with a snarl. "I can show you by taking out only one eye. Which one do you want to lose, the left or the right?"

"Please . . . please . . . don't." Harris's trembling intensifies.

"Choose an eye, John."

"No, *please* no."

Maintaining the pressure, Roddy moves his thumbs laterally, pushing Harris's eyeballs slightly to the sides. He feels them move beneath his thumbs as the muscle attachments in the sockets stretch.

"No . . . no . . ." Harris yelps. "Please don't."

"John, talk to us."

"You wouldn't do it."

"Yes, I will."

"You'll go to prison," Harris cries as his breath whistles through his nostrils.

"I don't care, John. My life's over anyway. You've cost me everything. Nothing matters anymore, least of all whether or not you're a blind man or if you go on with your miserable little life."

Roddy increases the pressure—downward and outward. He feels something tear inside Harris's eye sockets—a stretching of tissues near the ripping point. Just an ounce more pressure and Harris's eyes will pop from their sockets.

"Okay. *Okay*. What . . . what do you want to know?" Harris gasps.

"You killed Crystal, didn't you?"

"No . . . no."

Harris's eyeballs are pressed as far laterally as they can go without severing the attachments.

Dan remains silent.

"Tell me the truth, John."

Tears pour from Harris's eyes; they snake down the sides of his face, which grows slippery and wet. Harris groans and tries to turn his head.

"Don't move, you son of a bitch. Don't even try, or you'll lose both eyes. It'll happen very fast."

"Okay . . . *okay.*" Harris sobs. His body shakes.

"Why'd you kill Crystal?"

"I didn't do it."

"Tell me the truth. I'll rip your eyes out if I even *think* you're lying. It'd be the last lie you ever tell. It takes very little pressure. Understand?"

"Yes. Yes, I understand," Harris whimpers. "Please . . . *please.*"

Roddy keeps pressing.

"Who killed Crystal?"

"Two men."

"Which two men?"

"They came to my apartment."

"40-B?"

"Yes." Harris groans.

"And then?" Roddy maintains the pressure; he feels something stretching in the eye sockets.

"No . . . no," Harris pleads.

"Tell me what happened."

"They went across the hall and made her call you on the number you left."

"So they could get to me?"

"Yes."

"What then?"

"They . . ."

Roddy presses harder. Harris's eyeballs are at the tearing point. The slightest pressure will do it.

"No, please," Harris cries. "Please don't."

"You'll be blind with a flick of my thumbs. You understand?"

"Yes . . . yes."

"What happened then?"

"They threw her off the balcony."

Harris moans.

"Who're those men?"

"People . . . hired . . ."

"I said *who* are they?"

"Russians. I don't know their names."

"How'd you meet them?"

"I didn't. I don't even know them. I met some people at McLaughlin's." Harris wraps his hands feebly around Roddy's wrists.

"Don't fight me, John. You'll lose your eyes."

"Okay . . . okay." Harris's breath comes in short, honking gasps.

"Were they the same guys you had coming after us?"

"Please don't," Harris whimpers.

"Answer me. Were they the same guys who came after us?"

"Yes."

"The same ones who killed Walt McKay?"

"Yes." Harris goes limp.

Roddy's hands tremble as he's flooded by a cocktail of emotions: rage, disgust, disbelief, and sorrow. A sickening, out-of-control part of him could emerge at any second.

"Why're they coming after us?"

"Please. It was all a mistake. Believe me."

"What mistake?"

"When Danny asked about the Aruba deal, I thought he'd figured it out. I didn't want . . . I didn't want an investigation. Please don't . . ."

"I didn't know a thing, John," Dan says from the chair. "I just thought the numbers were a little off, and I didn't understand why."

"I . . . I thought you did. I thought you were onto it, and . . ." Harris's voice trails off.

"And *what*?" Roddy snarls.

"I thought he'd tell you."

"Why would he tell me?"

"Because . . . because Crystal said you two talk about everything, that you've been friends all your lives. You have no secrets from each other." Harris gurgles. His breath whistles through his nostrils. "And . . ."

"And what?"

"And . . . oh God . . . please don't hurt me. *Please.*"

"I will if you don't cough it all up."

"I came to the hospital to check on Danny—before the time you and I met—and when I got to the room and stopped at the door, I . . ."

"What?"

"I saw Danny asleep in the bed and you were sitting in a chair, reading a newspaper. I knew . . . it confirmed you two were very close." Another gurgle, then a cough. "And I thought for sure, since he survived, I was sure he'd tell you. So, I . . ." More coughing.

"You *what*?"

"I had to do something," Harris burbles as tears stream down his face. Roddy's hands are taut and soaked.

"So what'd you do?"

"I contacted the Russians again."

"Who are they?"

"I don't know." Harris whimpers.

"Tell me or you know what'll happen."

"Someone I met at the restaurant. He set it up. I don't know any of their names. Please believe me."

"How much did you pay them?"

"Fifty thousand."

"Up front?"

"Twenty-five each, with another fifty when it was done."

"And extra for Crystal?"

"Yes."

"How much?"

"Oh God."

"How much?"

"Twenty thousand."

"Why Crystal?"

"I didn't want any loose ends."

"Meaning what?"

"She knew too much."

"You bastard."

Roddy flexes his thumbs, increases the pressure.

"Please . . ." Harris screams. "Please. I can make it worthwhile for you. I have money . . . cash . . ."

Rage scorches through Roddy. How tempting it is to press harder, to push deeply inward and snap his thumbs sideways, to enucleate this bastard's eyes. He could rip the globes from their sockets—sever them from the muscles and small arteries inside the orbits. God, how tempting it is to forget he's a doctor—yes, he swore by the Oath of Hippocrates that above all, he would do no harm. *I swear by Apollo Physician and Asclepius.* But that's all a bunch of deluded bullshit for the self-righteous who know nothing of the cruelty and harshness of this life.

Roddy wants to do more to this rotten son of a bitch, this money maggot, this blood-sucking bastard—a poor excuse for a human being who had Danny shot, Walt McKay killed, and Crystal thrown from the balcony of his apartment, all with forethought and without mercy . . . and this bastard wanted him dead, too.

And why? To save his greedy little ass from being exposed as the Ponzi-scheming shit-worm he is. So he could keep ripping people off—without remorse or concern—so he could buy more houses, yachts, condos, cars, and toys.

For what? To have more and then more after that?

Roddy's hands are quivering. He's ready to spill Harris's eyes onto his fancy rug in this well-appointed mansion. Sweat prickles on Roddy's forehead, and he feels his armpits soaking. Tension builds in his arms; they feel like they're about to spasm. God, how he wants to lose control, go into mad dog mode, but even as he wants to blind this man—force him to live in darkness—he feels his arms and hands and shoulders ease the pressure.

"Oh, please . . . please . . ." Harris squeals.

Roddy thinks he hears Danny's voice in the distance. Is it telling him to blind Harris, to kill him or maim him? Is it urging him on the way it did at Snapper Pond when Kenny was in the hole begging for his sniveling little life after admitting he and Grange had been partners in a scheme to bilk them out of a million dollars? Is Danny's voice propelling him to more violence, or is it a voice of calm and reason?

"Ease up, Roddy," he hears Dan say from very far away. "There's no need for more."

Hearing Danny, Roddy realizes it's the voice of reason. He lessens the pressure on Harris's eyes. The man sniffles and moans as he lies across the desk.

It's finally out in the open: the deaths and near deaths are explained. No more need be said. And no more must be done. Roddy can control the beast. He won't go into that default setting of the mad dog. He'll use sound judgment because, as he's told Tom, you live with the consequences of your actions. The heat and rage, the intensity of the feelings, ease into restraint . . . tranquility.

"Okay, John, you'll tell the police everything?"

"I will. I swear, I will."

"You'll tell them about your Ponzi scheme and about Walt McKay and Crystal? And about trying to have us killed?"

"Yes . . . I will. I swear. Please let me go."

"Okay, Danny's gonna call the police. And when they get here, you'll tell them everything, won't you?"

"Yes . . ." Harris groans, trembling.

"Just so you know, John, Danny's recorded everything. We have it all."

"Okay . . . okay . . ."

"You know it's over, don't you?"

"Yes. Please don't hurt me."

"Is there anything else?"

"No."

"And the Russians have been paid fifty thousand?"

"Yes."

"With another fifty to come if they finish the job, if they get rid of Danny and me?"

"Yes." Harris moans. Roddy's hands remain on Harris's face.

Dan stands and nods at Roddy.

Roddy eases up on the pressure and stands back. Tears ribbon down Harris's face as he lies on the desk. He's depleted. He sobs. Mucous has collected around his nostrils. His arms are spread outward and his eyes remain closed.

Roddy stands over him. His pulse has already slowed.

"Now, before you get up, John, let's go over what you're going to say to the police."

In a halting, weak voice, Harris repeats his suspicions concerning Danny, the hits he'd arranged, the killing of Walter McKay, the staged suicide of Crystal Newcomb, and the Ponzi scheme.

"Very good, John," says Roddy. He pats Harris on his cheek.

Harris gasps and turns sideways on the desktop. "Can I stand?" he whispers.

"Yes, slowly."

"I feel so dizzy," Harris says, and then retches.

"Swing your feet down," says Roddy. "Let them hang. Then stand slowly, not fast. Otherwise you'll faint."

Harris moves his feet to the side. They come off the desk and drop to the floor as he twists his body around. He raises his torso and sits at the desk's edge. His head hangs with his chin on his chest. He places his hands over his heart. "I'm going to die," he whispers.

"No, John. You won't die here," says Roddy. "You'll die in prison."

Roddy positions himself next to Harris. "Stand up slowly."

Harris gets to his feet. He wobbles and nearly falls, but Roddy grabs his arms and supports him.

"Nice and slow. Otherwise the blood will rush to your feet and you'll faint."

Harris stands with his head bowed. He holds himself up with his right hand on the desktop. He coughs a few times and keeps his head down. He rubs his eyes with his left thumb and middle finger and inhales deeply. He keeps his eyes closed.

"We're calling the police now," Danny says, reaching for his cell phone. He sets the digital recorder on Harris's desk. "Just so you know, John, we have copies of your computer files and we'll be giving them to the police. It's a done deal. There's no way out. It's over."

Harris nods his head, still looking down. He straightens out a bit, still stooped. He leans back on the desk. He looks like a beaten dog.

Roddy watches Dan raise his cell phone. He sees a blurred movement in his peripheral vision.

Harris's right hand shoots to the desk. The top, right-side drawer slides open, and before Roddy can move, Harris's hand clutches a revolver. The pistol is out of the drawer, but before Harris can slip his finger inside the trigger guard, Roddy lands a fist to his gut.

Harris's breath explodes from his chest. He doubles over, still clutching the gun, then staggers back. The weapon sways unsteadily in his hand as he tries to find the trigger.

Still staggering, Harris raises the revolver; it's nearly chest high and points at Roddy.

Roddy lunges toward Harris and slams into him. Harris stumbles and staggers sideways. Roddy spins him around and lands another blow to his belly.

Harris bends at the waist as air leaves his lungs again. Roddy is about to throw an uppercut when Harris spins away. Gasping for air, he raises the pistol; it points directly at Danny, who reflexively jumps back with his hands raised.

Roddy grabs Harris from behind and wraps his arms around him. Harris's arms are pinned to his sides. He spins with Roddy at his back; Harris stumbles forward, and Dan—using his un-casted hand—tries to wrest the pistol from him. Harris squirms in Roddy's grasp and, gurgling, manages to free both arms. He clutches his right wrist with his left hand and spins away from Roddy. The weapon angles toward Roddy. Harris's finger is on the trigger.

Danny launches a solid kick behind Harris's right knee and slams his casted arm into his head. Harris's knee buckles; he groans but still holds the pistol. He spins toward Danny; the weapon is at eye level, pointing at Danny's face.

Roddy launches himself toward Harris and lands a hammer blow to Harris's right kidney. The punch thumps into the lower back with such force, Harris staggers toward Danny, who jumps aside. The revolver drops to the carpet. Harris is propelled forward a few feet. He cries out in pain and keeps going—caroming forward—and hurtles through the open French doors onto the balcony.

Roddy and Danny watch—frozen in place—as Harris goes over the iron rail at the balcony's edge.

He flips over the railing and plummets to the driveway below.

Chapter 35

Roddy stands at the French doors. His heartbeat pulses into his skull. Danny stands beside him, breathing heavily. Roddy hears bubbling from deep in Dan's chest.

The night air looks purple, and the doorway light below the balcony casts an orange luminescence on the Belgian-block driveway. Roddy can't see Harris, unless he walks onto the balcony and looks straight down.

"You think he's dead?" Dan asks from very far away, even from a distant room.

Roddy's in a daze; rolling banks of fog close around him.

"Roddy?"

Danny's voice sounds closer.

"Roddy, you hear me?"

"Yeah?"

"You think he's dead?"

"Could be . . ."

"Think you oughta go down and check him out?"

"No."

"Did he jump?" Dan asks.

"I don't know."

"Do you care?"

"No. He deserved it," Roddy says. "He deserved worse."

Roddy's hands feel weak; they hang at his sides.

Get ahold of yourself. This is no time for reflection.

The room seems brighter, as though Klieg lights have detonated. Roddy turns and looks at Harris's office: the desk, furnishings, and the pistol on the carpet.

He moves closer and examines it without touching the thing. It's a Smith & Wesson stainless-steel revolver. Looks like a .38-caliber piece.

"I'll call the police," Danny says.

"Call the cops? If we do, we'll have a lot to explain. It'll get very complicated."

"It could go either way," says Danny.

Gotta make a choice, which way to go. Call the cops or get outta here?

A few moments pass. Roddy looks into Dan's widened eyes.

"You're right, Roddy. Let's get outta here."

"Okay, but first, grab one of those towels by the bar."

With a hand towel, Roddy lifts a pen from Harris's desk, slips it through the trigger guard, and carries the revolver back to the desk. He drops it in the drawer, and using the towel, slides the drawer shut.

"What have we touched in here?" Roddy asks.

"The wood on the sides of the chairs," Dan says.

Using the towel, Roddy wipes down the arms of each chair. "Anything else?" he asks.

"My prints might be on the keyboard and mouse from the other day," Dan says.

"I doubt it. Harris has been on the computer. Any of your prints would be smudged by now. And covered over by Harris's prints."

"What do you wanna do with the recording?"

"If Harris is dead, we won't need it."

"What if there's a security camera we didn't see, something on the house or at the front gate?" Dan says. "It could link us to tonight."

"Good thought."

"We need this recording so if it ever comes back to us, we can prove Harris had people murdered and we didn't murder him."

"You're right. Gimme the recorder, Dan. I'll open a new safe-deposit box and store it for safekeeping."

Danny hands Roddy the digital recorder.

"Let's go downstairs," Roddy says. "And leave those French doors open."

Roddy returns the hand towel to the rack.

They make their way downstairs. Using his jacket sleeve, Roddy opens the front door. He adjusts the inner lock so it'll snap into a locked position when the door closes. Again, using his sleeve, he closes the door. It clicks shut.

Harris lies unmoving on the stone driveway. Roddy peers up at the balcony. It looms above them in the night light. It looks like Harris fell to the driveway—a distance of at least fifteen feet below. The decorative lamps on the sides of the door cast an eerie glow over his crumpled form.

The angle of Harris's neck is an instant giveaway: it's broken. The vertebrae have snapped. His spinal cord was severed in the neck region. His skull is smashed inward, completely caved and flattened. Harris is as dead as any cadaver Roddy's ever seen in a morgue. A glistening delta of blood seeps slowly from his head onto the stones. It gleams like purple paste in the lamplight.

"Bastard broke his neck and smashed his brains in," Roddy says.

"Son of a bitch . . . killed himself," says Dan.

"Died the way he had Crystal snuffed."

"Good riddance, you piece of shit," Dan murmurs.

In the car, Roddy rotates the key. The engine turns over.

Roddy peers about. He sees nothing but darkness and the glow of a few lights from inside Harris's house. They make their way along the driveway with only the Toyota's fog lights on. When they reach Baldwin Road, Roddy flicks on the headlights and drives back toward Route 684.

"Make that call, Danny."

Dan's on his disposable cell. "Kevin, post those files online now."

There's a pause as Dan listens.

"Yes, now. Upload everything." He listens again. "Yeah sure. On any other site you know so long as it's anonymous." Another pause. "Thanks, Kevin. I owe you big-time."

"Dan, when we're on the highway, pull that phone apart, including the battery. Then toss it piece by piece. And wipe each piece down."

Roddy drives toward the highway. His hands clutch the steering wheel so tightly that his fingers nearly cramp.

Danny keeps silent.

"How do you feel?" Roddy asks.

"It's strange. Back there in Harris's office, I didn't give a damn. I didn't care if you'd plucked the bastard's eyes out. But now I feel sick."

"It'll pass. You need time."

"Did you mean for him to go over the railing?"

"No. He was trying to kill us, so I punched him."

"You think he committed suicide?"

"We'll never really know, will we, Dan?"

Danny shakes his head.

"He was alone in his house and he saw that stuff posted on the Internet," Roddy says. "His Ponzi scheme was exposed, and his whole life crumbled right there. He couldn't take it, so he jumped. That's what it's gonna look like."

"You think the cops'll buy that?"

"What else can they conclude? We were never there."

"Any signs of a struggle?" Dan asks.

"I don't think so. His body's broken. I don't think he has any bruises from what went on in the office. He just jumped—couldn't take the disgrace."

There's silence as Roddy gets to the on-ramp of 684.

"You did good detective work, Dan, getting into his computer and seeing all the crap there."

"Yeah, but it was your idea to visit Omar and Crystal. That's what got me thinking about Continental Towers, Harris, and every single thing that happened before I was shot."

Roddy drives on; he makes certain to stay in the middle lane and keeps the car at a steady fifty-five miles an hour.

"Your guru's posting that stuff on the Internet?"

"As we speak."

A few moments later, Roddy veers into the right lane and says, "Begin tossing that cell."

Danny takes the phone apart, wipes each piece clean with a handkerchief, lowers the passenger window, and tosses the pieces, including the battery.

He closes the window on his side and turns to Roddy. "Lemme run something by you."

"Yeah?"

"We have a recording of everything that happened back there. Why not contact Morgan and give it over to the police?"

"No, Dan. Not the way to go."

"Why not? It would clear up everything. We have Harris confessing to everything—my getting shot, Walt McKay's shooting, and Crystal's death. And, Roddy, it'd be the right thing to do."

"Listen, Dan. It'd clear things up for the cops—close a few cases for them—but it'd open a Pandora's box for *us*. Especially for me. I tortured Harris, and they'd hear a struggle on the recording. And then Harris goes out the window, and there'd be a million questions about . . . who knows what? And before we know it, we'd be getting more questions about Kenny and the whole McLaughlin's thing. Forget it."

"But Morgan's gonna keep sniffing around about Kenny and about me getting shot."

"Let him sniff. What's he gonna find?"

"Jesus, I dunno. But this way, we gotta keep a lid on all this. We'll be living a life of lies."

"We live the lives we live, Dan. Let's just do the smart thing . . . even if it's not the *right* thing."

Danny shakes his head and sighs. After a brief silence, he says, "We gonna take the car back now?"

"No. I don't want any connection between our having a car and what happened to Harris. Let's take it to the Doral and I'll return it tomorrow, like I told the guy. From there, I'll take the train back to Bronxville."

"You checkin' out?"

"Yup. I gotta get back to the hospital and take care of things."

"Won't it look suspicious? Harris dies and we're back at work."

"Gotta get back at some point. So we take a chance."

"Think we're safe now?"

"From the Russians? Yeah. Once word of Harris's death hits the news, we're fine. He paid those guys plenty. Up front. And when they hear he's dead, why bother finishing the job? They won't get paid another nickel. We're safe."

"I hope so."

"I keep thinking of Walt McKay and Crystal Newcomb," Roddy says. "Such tragic deaths and so needless."

"Forgive me, Roddy, but I keep thinking of what happened to *me*."

"You're one lucky Irishman."

There's silence as Roddy drives.

"I gotta apologize to you, Roddy. I just do. If I'd been more careful when Kenny first came to me, none of this would've happened."

Roddy shakes his head. "Still beating up on yourself, Dan? I owe you an apology for not trusting you, for thinking somehow you could've been in on the whole scheme."

Jesus, how feeble is my sense of trust? Suspecting Danny? Shame on me.

"So what happens to you now?"

"First, I try to set things right with Tracy. Then I talk to Ivan and the hospital. I'm on thin ice everywhere. Then I don't know." Roddy pauses. "How about you?"

"I'll talk to Angela. I think we'll get our lives back on track."

More silence as they ride on.

"You think things'll ever be the same?" Dan asks.

"Probably not."

"How about between you and me?"

"I hope they will, Danny. I really hope so."

"Me, too."

Dan shakes his head.

"What?"

"Nothing."

"C'mon, what is it?"

"Roddy, I just have this terrible feeling."

"About what just happened?"

Danny pauses. "I don't know. I just feel like . . ."

"Like what?"

"Like this isn't over yet."

"It's over, Dan. Believe me, it's over."

"I don't think so."

Chapter 36

Roddy sits at a table in the Doral's atrium. He feels calm—he's luxuriating in a sense of tranquility. It's the first time in weeks his insides aren't thrumming. It's as though the dread has leached out of his body. He feels almost like his old, normal self. *And just what is normal, anyway?* he wonders.

He's polished off a big breakfast—orange juice, scrambled eggs, buttered toast, a croissant, and coffee. It's the first time in weeks he's had a hearty appetite. A warm morning glow fills the atrium's expanse. It's going to be a lovely day. There's a slight breeze outside—he can tell by the movement of the rhododendron leaves swaying languorously in the morning light. It's rare in early March for the weather to be this mild, but Roddy senses the weather reflects his mood: calm, clearing, with a good chance of things brightening.

Roddy asks himself if his feelings this morning even begin approximating the apprehension he felt the day after he'd killed Grange and Kenny. *My God. How long ago did that happen? It was nearly a year ago, but it seems a lifetime away.* In contrast to that dark morning, Roddy has a vague yet discernible sense of satisfaction, a freedom of spirit he never expected. Maybe it's because Harris had arranged for innocent people to be killed. Walt McKay's wife is a widow and his kids are fatherless. Crystal Newcomb's brief life was cut short, and somewhere, a family is mourning her.

He asks himself if his lack of remorse over Harris's death is because he and Dan hadn't planned on killing Harris—they'd simply intended to expose him and call the police.

He wonders if he'd punched Harris so hard he was propelled out the window and over the balcony railing, or if the man just ran and launched himself to his death.

And Roddy wonders if Harris deserved to die. The answer seems obvious.

It's strange how you can rationalize anything.

Roddy finishes breakfast and heads back to his room. He turns on the television to *Good Day New York* with Rosanna Scotto and Greg Kelly. It's the lead story at nine a.m.

Real estate developer John Harris was found dead early this morning in front of his home in Bedford Corners, New York. According to Bedford Police detective Peter Hastings, Harris was discovered when staff members arrived at six a.m.

Harris's body was on the driveway, in front of his mansion. Initial evidence indicates he jumped in an apparent suicide from a second-story window. In a related development, Internet postings were released overnight that claim to have information hacked from Harris's own computer. The source of the postings, which involved information about international money laundering, is unknown, and their authenticity is not verified at this time.

Bedford police theorize Harris may have leapt to his death upon learning of the postings. Formal cause of death is awaiting an autopsy report from the county's medical examiner.

Standing at the window, Roddy thinks about last night in Harris's office. It's been only a few hours, yet it seems forever ago, just as it does with Kenny and Grange. Time will blur the rawness of it all, not only for him, but for Danny, too. Danny was a different man last night than the one he'd been at Snapper Pond. He'd come to terms with the need to squeeze Harris and do whatever was necessary to save themselves and their families.

Roddy luxuriates in knowing no one is looking for him and he can return to the hospital and try to resume his family life at the lovely Tudor-style home in Bronxville.

There's only one big question left: will Tracy be in it?

Chapter 37

Roddy pulls into the driveway of the white clapboard house on Beech Street. *Nutley is a pretty little town*, he thinks. Bare sycamore and maple trees line the street. It's only a matter of a few weeks before the small swellings of buds form a lacy green canopy over the street. Getting out of the car, he inhales deeply. He can smell spring in the air—a good omen. It's just past noon, and the sun shines brilliantly in a cloudless blue sky.

He climbs the front stairs, certain Colleen won't be home. She's very likely running errands, so he and Tracy can have some privacy.

Even as he rings the bell, Roddy's heart pounds heavily. His legs feel like water. When the door opens, his heart tumbles inside his chest. He's stunned by the reality of Tracy standing there. Her hair looks golden in the noon light. It's pulled back in the simple ponytail he's always loved. While he could never forget her skin, he's suddenly struck by how pale, creamy, and inviting it looks. It reminds him of seeing her that first time in the library all those years ago. Her green eyes look into his; he detects a hint of sadness in them. Searching her face, he tries to determine if she's softened since they last talked. When was that? He's unsure if it was three or four days ago—maybe longer.

"Come in," she says.

Roddy searches for an intonation in her voice. Is there some meaning in the way she tilts her head? Does she open the door widely or not? Does she look directly in his eyes, and what do those lovely eyes say? But inference and intonation won't be enough. He needs more than subtle hints about the direction their lives will take. He knows he must try to make things right.

He enters the house. He's been here many times, usually for family events, but this is very different. It's not a birthday, anniversary, or a celebration about a promotion.

"Can I get you anything? Coffee?"

"No thanks, Trace."

Everything feels tentative, conditional, unsettled as they sit at the dining room table. Despite the fact that Tracy's his wife—even though they've been married all these years and have two children—Roddy feels like an intruder. It's as though these past few weeks have been a lifetime and have altered everything. He gazes at Tracy's face, knowing he could stare at her forever—at the deep green of her clear eyes, at those incredible golden eyelashes, the sculpted shape of her nose, the plump underbelly of her chin, the curve of her bowed lips, and the texture of her skin. He could never tire of looking at her.

She's a work of art. Everything about her is so beautiful. I never want to lose her.

"God, how I've missed you," he says in a shaky voice as his throat closes and his heart thrashes. He's on the verge of tears, and for a moment, he feels like throwing himself onto his knees and burying his face in her lap.

She remains silent, but her eyes look wet. Her lips move slightly, as though she's about to smile, but she doesn't. Her eyes close for a moment.

"I owe you an explanation," he says.

"I'm listening." She sets her elbows on the table and rests her chin in her hand.

Yes, she's willing to listen. She'll hear him out. He knows in a very real way, he and their marriage are on trial.

"I never meant to lie to you. Trace, I didn't even realize I was lying until you pointed it out. I understand mine were lies of omission, and I'm so very sorry." He looks into her eyes, searching for some sign of acceptance.

She nods her head, blinks, but remains silent.

"I want to tell you exactly what happened. I hope you'll understand."

"I'm listening."

He relates the story he and Dan rehearsed—from the restaurant closing, Kenny owing money to the mob, Danny's being shot ten months later, and finally, Walt McKay's death two days after that.

As he's talking, Roddy searches her face, but there's no hint of how she's reacting.

Tracy simply nods as he talks and looks into his eyes. Occasionally, her eyebrows arch and he can't tell if it's a sign of acceptance or disbelief. She looks steadily into his eyes, never wavering.

Roddy pauses and thinks about what he'll say next. He knows he's offering up a mix of lies and half-truths.

"After Walt was killed, Detective Morgan was convinced we were all in danger. So I insisted you come here, and I went into hiding. I had to keep you and the kids safe, and I didn't know what else to do."

Tears shiver in Tracy's eyes. Her lips tighten and begin trembling.

"I just can't stop thinking about Walt's family," Tracy says in a half whisper, shaking her head. "Have the police linked his death to what happened to Danny?"

"No. And I don't think it's related. There've been plenty of robberies at gunpoint recently, especially in garages. Remember the ones in December at the White Plains Mall? Nobody was killed, but it was bound to happen."

"But the police said nothing was taken from Walt. He was just shot and they took off."

"There's been a lot of gang activity, too. Some of these gangs have initiation rites where they go to another town and just shoot someone for no reason. Walt may just have been an unlucky victim. No one really knows."

A spike of shame pierces Roddy. How easy it is to weave this web of deception. He senses the tide is turning: the farther he pulls Tracy away from the truth, the more willing she may be to forgive him. He's constructing lie upon lie, one after another, but how can he allow her to learn what really happened at Snapper Pond? There's no turning back, and he's forced to live the life he's now living.

"What about Danny getting shot? Why did that happen?"

"It looks like it was a robbery that got out of control. You know that section of McLean Avenue is a rough neighborhood, especially at night."

Tracy exhales. Her hand drops to the table and rests there. His hand moves toward hers and their hands clasp.

"Tracy, I miss you so much," he says, his voice softening to a near whisper. "I want to come home."

"I don't know."

"What don't you know?"

"I've missed you, too, Roddy. But I don't know."

"What . . . what is it?"

"I'm not sure I . . ." She closes her eyes as tears slide down her face. "I'm not sure I really know you, Roddy." She brushes away the tears with her index finger. "I can't understand how you kept things from me. Kenny, his gambling and mob ties, what happened with Sandy, and how you lied . . ."

"Tracy, I did the best I could. I didn't want to frighten you. I thought everything would just go away. I know I was wrong.

Please forgive me."

"It's not a matter of forgiveness, Roddy. It's trust. I have this terrible feeling that deep down you don't really trust me, that you've never trusted me. Not really. It's so disturbing and I just . . . I can't make that go away."

"Let me prove to you that I *do* trust you. Please give me a chance."

"Roddy, there's something missing in our marriage. I didn't realize it until this happened. I feel like there's always been part of you that you've kept secret from me." She blinks and looks searchingly into his eyes.

He knows she's right. Secrets and lies are what his life's been since that night at Snapper Pond, but before then? Yes, trusting people has never been easy, and what happened with Kenny and Grange picked at the scabs of his younger years, exposing the rawness of his childhood and youth. Tracy sees him as secretive, even unknowable.

"Can you give it a chance? Can you give *us* a chance?" he asks, feeling an ache so deep, he feels hollowed out.

She breathes in deeply and closes her eyes. When she opens them, they brim with tears. She says, "Roddy, it's the strangest thing. I've been feeling you never trusted me, not really, even after all these years. And now?" She brushes away more tears. "Now I don't know that I can trust *you*." She swallows hard as tears dribble down her cheeks.

He brushes them away with his finger.

"And now, Roddy, I don't know if I can get it back, the feeling of trusting you."

She sobs, pulls her hand away, and buries her face in both hands.

His heart speeds to a gallop.

"I'm so sorry, Trace," he whispers as he sets his hand gently on her hair. "I don't know how I can get you to trust me again.

But I'll do everything I can to make that happen. I swear I will." He trembles. "I just want to come home and be with you and the kids. I miss you all so much. I can't even put it into words." Tears brim on his eyes.

She shakes her head and says, "The kids want to be with you, Roddy."

"And you?"

A pause as she inhales deeply. "We can try." She closes her eyes, opens them, and says, "But only under one condition."

"Anything, Tracy."

"You've got to promise you'll never hold anything back from me ever again."

"Tracy, I promise. No, I *swear* I'll never hide anything from you. Ever."

God, he's missed her. How he's yearned for her these past few weeks. There's been a sickening void—a dark hole—in his existence without her. It occurs to Roddy that in some strange way, he feels better for missing her as he has. He truly needs Tracy and the kids in order to feel human, because without them, he's a beast in the wilderness.

"And, Roddy, the police have ruled out any connection between Danny getting shot and the mob? And you're sure the kids will be safe at home?"

"Yes. There's no connection. We'll all be perfectly safe."

"And you've told me everything? You've told me the entire truth about the restaurant, about Kenny Egan, you, and Danny?"

"Tracy, I've told you everything—every single thing," he says as his heart pummels his ribs.

They embrace again and kiss deeply.

Roddy is overcome by the feel and scent of Tracy. She fits so perfectly into his arms, and their bodies seem to melt into each other. His hand goes to her neck and then her hair. He strokes its golden softness. He nuzzles her, burying his face in her neck.

Inhaling, he's nearly overcome by the incredible fragrance of her—the scent of Tracy, like no other woman he's ever known. He inhales again. It smells like home.

And now he's back in the library at New York Hospital the day they met—when she jumped from the rolling ladder and landed next to him—how startled they were, suddenly thrust into kinetic awareness of each other. At that moment, looking into her green eyes as a nimbus of light surrounded her face, he realized he'd never been so powerfully seized by a woman as he was at that moment. There was something elemental about her, something combustive in her look and mien, and he felt heat as though they were both on fire. In that electrifying second, he could never have imagined over the course of years they'd build a life together—how they'd marry, have Tom and then Sandy, move to Bronxville, construct their own little world away from everything he'd known in his past; nor could he have envisioned how all the days of his life would narrow down to this apprehensive moment of yearning at his sister-in-law's house on a mild March day on a quiet side street in Nutley, New Jersey.

Her head rests on his shoulder. The heat of her breath on his neck excites him.

They pull away and stare into each other's eyes.

"I can't imagine trying to live without you," Roddy whispers.

A smile forms on her lips. It conveys sadness along with other feelings—perhaps regret, but love and caring, too. He waits for her to say something else, but she doesn't.

"Let's go home," he whispers.

She nods, squeezing her lips together.

He thinks she looks resigned.

He senses what's going through Tracy's mind—uncertainty, worry, perhaps even acquiescence. He can't be sure. But at least he has the luxury of time now—time to try setting things right. He knows that for as long as he lives, he never wants to spend another day of his life thinking he might lose Tracy.

And Roddy can never make good on his promise to tell her everything.

Chapter 38

Danny sits at his desk poring over Lynda Ling's worksheet. She owns a Chinese restaurant on Central Avenue, and her return is always complicated. It's his third day back at the office, and Natalie kept things running smoothly while he was away. He'll clear up a few minor glitches and be out of the office by six this evening. Angela and the kids are back in Tuckahoe, and life's getting back to normal.

The intercom sounds: a soft buzz. Dan picks it up.

"Danny," says Natalie, "Detective Morgan is here to see you."

Dan's scalp dampens and begins tingling; the sensation spreads to his shoulders and neck. "Tell him I'll be out in a minute, Natalie."

Morgan . . . this guy's a recurring nightmare. He's like an asthmatic attack, always lying in wait. Okay, so Yonkers is his turf, but what does he want now? There's no news about who shot me. It's all old. Just take a cue from Roddy. Say nothing. Less can be more.

Morgan is sitting in the reception area, leafing through a magazine. Seeing Danny, the detective looks up and stands to his full height. "How're you doing, Mr. Burns?"

"Much better, thanks. What can I do for you, Detective?"

Dan feels his heart kicking and thinks he hears a high-pitched squeak in his chest, but he maintains a calm exterior. He can tell from Morgan's poker face the detective thinks he has something up his sleeve.

I should've known it. He's not gonna stop probing and snooping.

"Could we talk for a few minutes?" Morgan says. He gestures to a nearby conference room.

"About what, Detective?" Danny feels his lips tingling.

I gotta keep from hyperventilating.

"Just sorting out a few details on your case, Mr. Burns."

"Okay, but let's make it quick, Detective. I've been out of the office for a while and now I'm swamped."

Danny leads Morgan to the conference room and closes the door. Morgan sits at the head of the rectangular table.

A bullshit power tactic . . . the guy sits at the head of the table in my own office.

"I see you're back at work. How come?"

"Whaddaya mean, 'How come?' I work for a living."

"Understood, Mr. Burns. But there're a couple of things I'd like to talk to you about."

"What things?"

"Well, I've been looking into the whole business of you getting shot, and you know what I discovered?"

"What's that, Detective?"

"You do know, of course, that all hospital visitors have to check in at the front desk and get passes to go upstairs, right?"

"Uh-huh."

"Funny thing is, when I checked the visitor log at St. Joe's, it turns out that one John Harris visited you."

"Yeah?"

"In fact, he came to see you twice. And both times were days Dr. Dolan also visited you."

Danny keeps his look neutral. He's exquisitely aware his facial muscles tend to go tight when he's tense; and he knows that by concentrating—by incredible force of will—he can look relaxed, even though his insides are churning. Nope . . . he won't show a scintilla of emotion. And he'll say absolutely nothing.

"Well, Detective, the fact is, I did some part-time work for Mr. Harris."

"Yeah, I know. I checked with a connection of mine at the Bedford PD and got to examine Harris's computer files. Your name pops up here and there . . . on a deal in Aruba and a couple in Westchester County."

"That's right."

"What do you know about Harris?"

"Whaddaya mean?"

"About his whole Ponzi scheme."

"I didn't know a thing about it." Danny's stomach clenches.

"But you worked for him, right?"

"I just did some work on a few properties here in Westchester."

"What kind of work?"

"What is this, Detective? Another interrogation?"

"I'm just wondering how it is that Harris is dead, and a few days later, you're back at work. It's pretty strange. After Dr. McKay got shot with the *same* gun used to shoot you, Dolan and you lie low like two sewer rats. And then, right after John Harris dies, you come out of your holes. And, of course, Harris's computer records show you were working for him."

"That's right. I was working on a property in Rye he was converting into a golf course. And there's another in Larchmont he was thinking of turning into an assisted-living facility. But I didn't think he had the capital for it."

Shit, I'm already talking too much. Shut the fuck up, Danny Boy.

"Did you know about his properties in the Caribbean?" Morgan says, tilting his head.

"He mentioned something about a deal in Aruba and asked if

I was interested in making an investment."

"Did you?"

"No. I've had enough trouble with unusual investments, if you know what I mean."

Morgan nods. "Did you do any accounting work on his Caribbean properties?" The detective's eyebrows arch.

"Nope."

"You know who did?"

"No, I don't. So far as I know, he had an entire cadre of accountants. But I don't know who the others are . . . or were."

Morgan's elbows rest on the table; he steeples his fingers.

"I understand your friend Dolan's back at Lawrence Hospital. How come?"

"You'll have to ask him, Detective." Danny stands and moves toward the door. "If you don't mind, I have lots of work to do."

"I just find it strange that both you and Dolan get back to work right after Harris dies."

"And just what are you implying?"

"Why don't you tell me?"

"I have nothing to tell you."

"When was the last time you saw Mr. Harris?"

"I think it was two or three days before he died. I went to his house to discuss getting back to doing some part-time work on the Westchester properties."

"Why part-time?"

"Because I have other clients I have to take care of. Any work I did for Harris was a small part of my practice."

"Did Harris want you to work for him full-time?"

"He never asked, and I wouldn't have done so if he had."

"Why not?"

"I'd never put all my eggs in one basket by having only one client."

"You know, Harris's home was searched thoroughly by the

Bedford police and by New York State's CID."

"So?" Danny's heart shoots into overdrive. It's slamming like a racehorse storming out of the gate. But he's sure his face reveals nothing.

"His computer showed all the schemes, just like what was on the Internet."

"Yeah, so?"

"It's very strange. Harris apparently jumped from the balcony and killed himself because it was all exposed online."

"Yeah?"

"But when his computer's Internet browsing history was accessed, there was no evidence he'd visited the sites where his files were posted."

"So?"

"So . . . how'd he know his scheme was exposed if he hadn't seen those sites before he jumped?"

"I have no idea, Detective." The racehorse inside Danny's chest pounds its way around the track's first turn.

"Where were you the night Harris died?"

"Which night was that?"

"Four nights ago."

"I'd have been at the Doral Arrowwood."

"Can anyone confirm you were there that night?"

"I have no idea, Detective. I'd have had dinner in my room."

"Why in your room?"

"Because I was eating too much in the dining room. It's a buffet; and in my room, I could control what I ate. Now, if you'll excuse me, I have a ton of work to do."

"Was anyone with you? Your wife, for instance?"

"No, she was in Riverdale staying at her brother's place."

Dan opens the door.

"Mr. Burns?"

Danny stops and turns. "What, Detective?"

"You sure there's nothing else you wanna tell me? Like why you're back at the office now . . . and Dolan, too. Or about your work with John Harris?"

"Detective, I don't want to talk to you anymore. You insinuate all kinds of crap and you're harassing me. My office manager will show you out."

"All right, Mr. Burns. If that's the way you want it, I'll—"

"That's *exactly* the way I want it." Danny stands in the open doorway and calls, "Natalie, will you show Detective Morgan to the door?"

"Mr. Burns?"

"Oh, and, Detective, on your way out, please make sure the door is closed. We've had a new lock installed, and sometimes the door doesn't close properly. I can't get the landlord to call a locksmith. At least he's put security cameras in the lobby and stairwell . . . just so you know. That's why I feel safer now."

"That's very wise. But, Mr. B—"

"Oh, and if you ever find out who shot me, I'd like to know who the bastard is, okay?" Danny waits a beat. "Now, you have yourself a good day, Detective."

Danny turns and leaves the conference room.

He can only assume Morgan's concern about his relationship to Harris is no more than mere speculation.

At least that's what Danny hopes it was.

Chapter 39

Roddy and Danny sit in forest-green Adirondack chairs beneath a cover of shade provided by a large sugar maple. Holding bottles of Bud, they look out over a grassy meadow to a stand of majestic spruce trees in the distance. Beyond that, the gentle hills of the Berkshires rise against a plate of deep blue sky. It's a brilliant June day; the temperature is in the midseventies, and the mountain air is clear and crisp. A cool breeze plays at the back of Roddy's neck. The fragrance of field flowers is in the air. A house wren burbles while finches and black-capped chickadees peck at seeds in the bird feeder Tracy has hung from a low bough of the maple. The kids are playing volleyball.

"Roddy, are you going to get the grill ready?" Tracy calls.

"As soon as Ivan and Sylvia get here."

"Where are they?"

"They just called. They'll be here soon. They took the wrong exit on the Taconic."

"How're things going with Ivan and your new partner? Is it David?" asks Danny.

"Dave's working out fine. We really needed another team member."

"So maybe something good came out of what happened back in February."

"It's all worked out. Things are back on track, better than ever.

And Tracy might become executive director of the library. They realized her value during the two weeks she was gone."

"So here we are at Lake Rhoda," says Dan. "I never thought of coming up here with Angie and the kids. Maybe we'll buy a place. You should think about that, too, Roddy. If you sink a few bucks into a place, you'd have equity."

"That depends on what the homeowners association says."

"What do they have to do with it?"

"There's a meeting this evening. Wanna go?"

"You don't own this place."

"We rent from Ann Johnson. She wants to sell, and we're thinking of buying the place."

Dan leans close to Roddy. "You know," he murmurs, "whenever I'm with a client and the word 'equity' comes up, I think of McLaughlin's." He sighs and shakes his head.

"I try not thinking about it . . . ever."

"Roddy, it'll be with us for the rest of our lives."

"Yes, it will." Roddy takes a pull on the beer. "We all live with secrets. It's part of being alive."

"You think there was a better way we could've handled Harris?"

"I try not to second-guess it. I guess we could've called the police as soon as we saw what was on the computer, but we'd never've known for sure who was after us or why. I'd hate to go on thinking some mob goons were coming for us because of Kenny . . . or Grange."

"You know Morgan called me last week. I hadn't seen him since that last time he came to my office a few days after we got back to work."

"Yeah? What'd he want?"

"He just asked how I was doing."

"And you said?" Roddy's heart jumps.

"That I'm fine. But he started to ask a few questions about

John Harris."

"Yeah? What'd you say?"

"Absolutely nothing. I was tempted to tell him off, but I didn't say a word."

"Keep it that way. The less said the better."

"I know. Sometimes I talk too much."

"Silence is golden, Danny."

"You know, we were really lucky with Harris."

"What do you mean?"

"There were no security cameras. It's hard to understand. A guy with all that money and no cameras."

"I guess he thought he couldn't be touched."

"More of the scorpion and the frog thing, huh?"

"I guess so."

Dan gazes at the hills on the far side of Lake Rhoda. He turns to Roddy and says, "I sometimes think . . . in his office, after he confessed, I should've called the police right then. I shouldn't have waited."

"C'mon, Dan."

"He'd never have gone for the gun."

Roddy leans close to Danny. "Listen, Dan. You gotta stop beating yourself up. That *best boy* inside your head is gonna get you. You gotta control that. We all make mistakes, and we live with them. End of story. Show me a single person alive who hasn't made mistakes or who doesn't have regrets. Show me *one* person who has no regrets. You can't because there's nobody like that."

"I know . . . I know . . ."

"I have plenty of regrets," Roddy says softly. "That the whole thing with Kenny ever happened, that I sent him to you when I should've gone thumbs down on the proposition about McLaughlin's. But most of all, I regret what this did to me and Tracy." Roddy feels his throat close.

"What do you mean?"

"It's different between us, and I don't know if it'll ever go back to how it was. There's a certain distance, almost a coldness. I don't know if she'll ever feel really close to me again."

"Why's that?"

"She feels I don't trust her enough because I hid things from her. And you know what, Dan? She's right. I have trouble with it, with *really* trusting someone." Roddy feels like he's choking.

Danny sighs and closes his eyes.

"It's the way I grew up. It's just hard to trust."

"Roddy, you're the ultimate pragmatist."

"Maybe I am. But it's probably better to be like you, to feel things so deeply and have such a strict conscience. You're better off that way."

"I don't know, Roddy. I get too worked up, and I feel guilt so easily."

"Lighten up and look around, Dan. Here we are: it's a gorgeous day; the sun's shining; we're sitting near this pristine lake high in the mountains. Pine trees and spruce are everywhere. I know it sounds corny, but birds are singing, the air is clean, our wives and kids are having a great time, and we're here right now—together. And we're free, absolutely free to enjoy the beauty, the peace, and the pleasure of it all. What else can I say?"

"That's pragmatism. And you're right, Roddy."

"How else can I put it? We can't undo a thing. It's over and done. We gotta make the best of what we have. And you know what? That's what I'm gonna do. I'm gonna take it as it comes and be grateful for what I have. And I'm thankful we got past our mistakes. And we've made mistakes . . . plenty of them. They're part of being alive. And now we have to live our lives the best way we know how."

Danny looks out into the distance. "You think you'll ever tell Tracy about Kenny and Grange and Harris?"

"Not a chance."

"You think she knows you haven't told her everything?"

"She knows. In her way, she knows. And it's changed things between us."

"Think she'll ever let it go?"

"I don't know."

Dan leans close to Roddy. "I gotta confess to you. Sometimes I'm tempted to tell Angie."

A swell of alarm washes over Roddy. He looks at Dan. His head is bowed. Roddy's hand goes to the back of Danny's neck and he shakes it gently. "What the *fuck* are you saying, Danny?"

"It's stupid, I know. Sometimes I just feel that way."

"*Jesus.* Don't do it. Don't *ever* tell her. If you do, it'll put a very heavy burden on Angie."

"But she's an incredibly strong person. She can handle anything. And I trust her completely."

"Dan, if you tell her, if you even *hint* at it to her, you'll ruin everything in your life. One thing's for sure. You'll ruin your marriage."

"How do you mean?"

"If you tell Angie, you make her an accessory after the fact."

Dan's breath sucks inward. "*Jesus.* I never thought of that."

"So, Danny, just hold your tongue . . . for the rest of your life."

Dan closes his eyes.

Roddy leans closer to him and says, "Danny, we all live with *some* secrets. That's just the way it is."

Roddy, Tracy, Danny, and Angela sit in the last row of folding chairs. They're in a recently built empty lakefront house. The chirring of crickets can be heard outside. Though it's five o'clock, bright sunshine filters through the windows. The interior smells of cedar and pine. Nearly fifty people are present, mostly owners of cabins near the lake, along with a few renters.

Joyce Fama, president of the homeowners association, stands at a lectern and explains that Braddock Development Corporation has gotten permission from the county to build condominiums around Lake Rhoda. She describes the proposed plan and introduces Charles Braddock, president of the development company.

He's a tall, thin man who describes the plan for the condominium complex. Some members of the audience ask questions. "Let me assure you," Braddock says. "Those of you who sell will be paid generously for your existing properties. But the really good news is: when the condominiums are built, each of you, whether a homeowner or renter, will be able to buy in at an insider's price. That will be 15 percent below market value paid by buyers from the outside." He explains the buyout option in detail.

"Are there any other plans for this development?" asks a woman in the front row.

"Oh yes. We've purchased land in the surrounding area." Braddock describes an eighteen-hole golf course to be built, along with other facilities, all to be detailed in the prospectus, which will be ready in two weeks.

"Where will you build the golf course?" someone asks.

"Most of the surrounding area is unused," Braddock says. "There's one area called Snapper Pond, which will become part of the golf course."

"What will you do with that swamp?" someone asks.

"It's a mosquito-infested blight, and we'll be dredging the pond."

Roddy's thoughts blitz through his head in a frenzy.

Dredging the pond? That's where I threw the .45 and the three shell casings, along with Grange's finger and ring. It's physical evidence of what went down.

"After dredging," Braddock says, "which will include a wide swath of land surrounding the pond, we'll fill it in, and we'll clear the surrounding forest for fairways," Braddock says.

They'll dig up Grange's and Kenny's remains.

"We expect to have the dredging and filling done by the end of the summer," Braddock says.

Roddy peers over at Dan.

Danny's face is drained—chalky white. Their eyes lock. Roddy feels he can actually read his blood brother's thoughts.

And Roddy is certain Danny knows exactly what's going through his mind, too, because without uttering a single word—it's all there, written on their faces—they convey the same thing to each other.

What's done is done and there's no going back.

Acknowledgments

I owe a great deal to many people.

Kristen Weber, my fabulous editor, always believed in me. As usual, she added her wisdom and incredible skills to my efforts to tell a story. She's made an incalculable difference in my writing life.

Other writers with whom I've spoken have been sources of inspiration. I've learned more from them than they could ever know. Just speaking with them, sharing author panels, or interviewing them has taught me more about the craft of writing than I can describe. They include Steve Berry, Barry Eisler, Elissa Grodin, Andrew Gross, Rosemary Harris, Dorothy Hayes, John Land, David Mamet, Judith Marks-White, Joe Meyers, David Morrell, Scott Pratt, M. J. Rose, Larry Sabato, E. J. Simon, Jessica Speart, Cathi Stoler, Simon Toyne, Karen Vaughan, and Jane Velez-Mitchell.

I owe a special debt of gratitude to Barry Nathanson and Susan Nathanson for having read an early version of the manuscript and providing valuable feedback. David Copen also read the manuscript early on and assuaged my concern that readers who hadn't read *Mad Dog House* might have difficulty understanding elements of this sequel to the first novel. He assured me the chain of events was comprehensible to someone who had not read the first novel.

Other people have had an enormous impact on my career as a psychiatrist and writer. In psychiatry and for helping me understand human development and character, I owe an enormous debt to Bill Console, Dick Simons, and Warren Tanenbaum.

Others who have helped my writing life are Melissa Danaczko, Jerriann Geller, Sharon Goldinger, Veronica Grossman, Sarah Hausman, Kristen Havens, Martin Isler, Natalie Isler, Helen Kaufman, Phil Kaufman, Arthur Kotch, Jill Kotch, Sam Kuo, Lynda Ling, Penina Lopez, Pam Miller, Tracy Minsky, McKenzie Morrell, Meryl Moss, Kevin Vallerie, Skye Wentworth, Lester Zabronsky, and Judy Zuklie.

My wife, Linda, is my editor-in-chief, my sage adviser, and an indefatigable activist on my behalf and has blessed me with her enduring patience, guidance, and love.

About the Author

After graduating from NYU with a degree in business administration, Mark Rubinstein served in the US Army as a field medic tending to paratroopers of the 82nd Airborne Division. After discharge from the army, he gained admission to medical school. He became a physician and then took a psychiatric residency, becoming involved in forensic psychiatry and testifying in trials as an expert witness.

He became an attending psychiatrist at New York Presbyterian Hospital and a clinical assistant professor of psychiatry at Cornell University Medical School, teaching psychiatric residents, psychologists, and social workers while practicing psychiatry.

Before turning to fiction, he coauthored five nonfiction, self-help books for the general public. His first two novels, *Mad Dog House* and *Love Gone Mad,* and *The Foot Soldier* (a novella) were published by Thunder Lake Press. He blogs for the *Huffington Post* and is a contributor to *Psychology Today.* He is working on his next novel.

You can visit Mark at www.markrubinstein-author.com. Or, chat with him via Twitter using @mrubinsteinCT. Mark's e-mail address is author.mark.rubinstein@gmail.com.

Preview of *Assassin's Lullaby*

One

I should have known everything would change the moment I saw her. But I could never have known the life I knew and loved would come to a disastrous end.

It began fifteen years ago at a West Village party when John Coltrane's saxophone stopped crooning "You Don't Know What Love Is" on the sound system.

The sudden silence was odd for this maxed-out throng gathered in a brownstone apartment. It seemed strange because this crowd—artists, actors, musicians, and writers—was always clamorous. Plenty of booze, coke, and weed made for stratospherically high spirits.

But when Coltrane's saxophone stopped—leaving a wake of silence—the lights began dimming.

That's when my life changed.

Because that's when I saw Nora.

I didn't know her name. I simply saw a raven-haired, olive-skinned woman take the dance floor. Her hair was drawn back in a bun, accentuating her strikingly high cheekbones. She had dark eyes, a sloping nose with flared nostrils, and luscious lips. Her crimson-red pencil skirt was slit high on one side and was so very Latin-looking—so sensuous.

The crowd edged to the periphery. A low-level voltage pervaded the room. This incredible-looking woman—Nora, I later learned—stood theatrically poised, as some svelte Latin-looking guy slipped an arm around her.

She gazed into this conquistador's eyes hungrily, yet there was distance, too. I felt my pulse throb as my heart drubbed wildly. My legs felt like rubber. She reminded me of Carmen in Bizet's opera and a trampoline sensation filled my chest.

Suddenly, voluptuous tango music swelled through the sound system.

The dance began. Nora moved with intense feline grace. I was riveted by the arch of her back, by its muscularity, by her toned arms and the sheen of her bronzed skin. As they tangoed, Nora's head snaps were violent. They were at one with the music, turning, swirling, gliding, dipping.

It was a dialogue of passion, a promise of something to come—the prologue of a love story.

Heat rose in my face, and my scalp prickled deliciously. I ached with desire. Watching Nora, I felt I could have been at a *habanera* at a lantern-lit café in Buenos Aires. My writer's imagination was working overtime.

Applause rocked the room as the lighting returned. Nora disappeared into the crowd. Standing in a state of stunned silence, I was certain she was unattainable.

"Unbelievable, isn't she?"

A woman about my age—midthirties—looked up at me. She, too, had that Latin look—sensuous, pulsing with life. Yet she looked partly Eastern European, maybe Polish or Russian; it was hard to make out. Her features were more Slavic than the dancer's. But there was that black hair and dark, laughing eyes.

"What do you think?" she asked.

"She's the most beautiful woman I've ever seen. And . . . expressive . . ."

"She's my sister, Nora."

"Yes, now I see. There's a resemblance."

"That's the best compliment I've received in years."

"These things run in families."

"I'm Lee. Lee Walsh," she said, extending her hand.

"Bill Shaw."

"Would you like to meet her?"

Was I hallucinating?

"Of course. But I . . ."

"The only 'but' is that she'll eat you alive."

"I'll take my chances," I said, wondering if this was truly happening. Yes, I'd had luck with women, but this was more than I could hope for.

"I'll be right back."

It occurred to me that, despite all the women I'd known, I suddenly felt like a callow high school kid—even nervous. I belted down the rest of my scotch, feeling its warmth spread through my cheeks.

When they approached, I was actually quivering with nerves. In her stiletto heels, Nora was my height. Close up, her eyes were large, dark, and liquid. They roamed over me. I felt I could lose myself in the depth of her gaze.

"Nora Reyes, this is Bill Shaw," Lee said.

I grasped her hand as tingling coursed through me. I'd never felt such a sensation simply touching a woman. Her hair glistened in the overhead light. Her nose swept down to those flaring nostrils. And her chin was full, with a plump underbelly—soft and inviting. Her olive skin appeared moist. I could smell its oil; it wasn't lotion or perfume. It was her.

Her eyes moved brazenly over me. I felt exposed, vulnerable. Yes, Lee was right: I was being devoured by this gorgeous woman.

"I'll leave you two alone," Lee said, and melted into the crowd.

Coltrane's sax sang "All or Nothing at All." I felt a deep

yearning seep through me, and somehow I knew I'd always remember this night.

"Tell me, Bill Shaw," she said, "Have I made a mistake all these years avoiding these West Village get-togethers?"

"You've done the right thing."

"And tonight? Coming here?"

"The right thing again."

She laughed. "I suspect so . . ."

"Hopefully, your suspicions will be realized."

She laughed with an open mouth. Her teeth were perfect. Her lips were sensuous, bow shaped, pliant, and moist looking. I felt an insane urge to press my lips to hers, to taste the wetness of her tongue. It was a craving so intense, I thought for a moment I would clutch her in my arms, press her to me, feel her heat, explore inside her mouth.

"That was a beautiful tango. Argentinean, right?" I said.

"Yes. Most people don't know the different types," she said, her finger brushing my cheek. My face burned. Her touch left my skin tingling.

"I could teach the tango to you."

"I would like that," I said as my body thrummed. "Are you a professional dancer?"

"No. I'm an actor."

"Have I seen you in anything?"

"Not unless you watch soap operas. I'm in *The Burning World*. But tell me what *you* do, Bill."

"I'm a writer," I said, hoping I didn't sound like every fool at this gathering.

"Really? You look like a . . . a cop."

I laughed self-consciously. I'd been told this so often I sometimes felt I should have an honorary badge.

"Yes. You're tall and well built. You have a strong face. And those eyes. Such a deep blue. You look very . . . rugged. I *like* that in a man. And a writer . . . brains *and* brawn," she said, canting her head.

My face felt flushed.

"Have I read anything you've written?"

"Only if you read crime fiction." My God. Did I sound vainglorious? "There was *Fire and Ice.*"

"*Fire and Ice?* Isn't that a *movie* about a serial killer?"

"It's a standard detective cliché," I said, feeling awkward. "It was adapted from the novel."

"Now I'll have to read the book. I'm an avid reader. You wouldn't be looking for a freelance editor, would you?"

"That could be arranged."

"Bill, we can arrange anything we want," she whispered, moving closer.

"How about we arrange to go to dinner?" *God, where had that come from?* It simply slipped out. My legs were turning to liquid.

"Where will we go?"

"There's a lovely Spanish restaurant on Charles Street . . . El Charro," I said, afraid she might think I was patronizing her.

"And then what?"

"Then . . ." I said, suddenly at a loss for words.

"I'll bet you live near the restaurant," she said with laughing eyes.

"I *live* on Charles Street . . . a garden apartment in a brownstone."

"That would be wonderful," she said, grabbing my arm.

That night—fifteen years ago—was the beginning of the end of everything.